OBLIGATIONS OF
THE BONE

Also by Dick Cluster:

Return to Sender
Repulse Monkey

OBLIGATIONS OF THE BONE

DICK CLUSTER

St. Martin's Press
New York

Design by DAWN NILES

Library of Congress Cataloging-in-Publication Data

Cluster, Dick.
    Obligations of the bone / Dick Cluster.
        p. cm.
    ISBN 0-312-08274-6
    I. Title.
    PS3553.L88024   1992
813'.54—dc20   92-1650
                                                                CIP

First Edition: September 1992

10 9 8 7 6 4 3 2 1

For Bruce Millies

ACKNOWLEDGMENTS

For answering my questions about medicine and the medical world, I am grateful to Janet Belanger, Liz Dreesen, Joanne Geake, Joan Goldberg, Holcomb Grier, Eugenia Holbrooke, Peggy Lynch, and Sandy Shea. These helpful informants are in no way responsible for any of my interpretations or inventions, nor should the medical institutions in this book be seen as portrayals of the places in which any of them may have received or provided care. I would also like to thank my companions in a wonderful writers' group (Lucy Marx, BarbaraNeely, Kate White), my agent Gina Maccoby and editor Keith Kahla, and fellow writers Jane Langton and Judith Van Gieson for their comments and support.

DAY MINUS
ONE

ONE
Engine Block

The night before he met Jay Harrison, Alex Glauberman sat at home listening to all ten and a half minutes of "Sad-Eyed Lady of the Lowlands" again. For all its streetcar visions and holy medallions, he was thinking, this was a love song really. It was a particular type of love song, a wooing song. Like, if I keep telling you how great you are, maybe you'll let me come see you sometime. He was also noticing for the umpteenth time how the words to this song were engraved on his brain—even if he never would know what the hell Dylan had meant by "matchbook songs" or "curfew plugs."

Words that stuck with you that way were the kind of thing poets described as being in your marrow, Alex thought. Not only words, of course, but all kinds of triumphs and tragedies and trivia: the things you grew up on, whether those were pop music or classical drama or the Dodgers or the horses or protest marches or patriotic wars. Your marrow was the place you stored the stuff that made you who you were. What made this Dr.

Harrison a big deal was that he arranged for people to live, temporarily, without it.

Alex felt queasy about the idea of living without any marrow. The scientific terminology, in the medical journal article his own doctor had given him, centered on the processes involved. The authors—and H. J. Harrison of Boston's Dennison Center for Cancer Treatment and Research was among them—wrote in a dry and technical fashion about harvesting, cryopreserving, reinfusing. They didn't take much note of the patient, the one who was waiting, doing nothing, doing without.

When the song ended Alex let the turntable click off. He turned out the light, went into the bedroom, and lay down next to Meredith, who was asleep. He felt an impulse to say something flattering and persuasive to her. He wasn't sure what, so he didn't wake her up, only hugged her tight.

The next morning she wished him good luck with Harrison before they each went off.

Alone in his shop, Blond Beasts, Alex started installing new oversize pistons in a rebored engine block. The shop, located in Union Square, Somerville, was called Blond Beasts because Alex specialized in Nordic, Northern European cars. When he looked at the reamed-out Volvo cylinders he started seeing bones and marrow again. Inside your bones were cavities, spaces, and inside those spaces was where the marrow dwelled. Removing it and then replacing it would be sort of like rebuilding an engine: you broke the machine down to its basics, and then you put it all back together again.

I could try that image out on Harrison, Alex thought. With doctors, it helped if you could make them feel you already knew what they were talking about. Otherwise they thought you couldn't understand—or rather, to be fair, they thought you couldn't understand in the time they had available for you.

After he fit the rings and bearings and piston rods, Alex sealed it all up underneath the cylinder head. He checked the tightness of each bolt with his torque wrench to be sure the pressure was even, nothing was out of equilibrium, nothing overtaxed. He stuck the card representing this particular customer into the antique Bendix time clock that he'd found in a Maine junk shop and finally managed to repair.

4

This particular customer, whose name was Lisa, happened to be a nurse. She'd called first thing in the morning to ask how the rebuild job was coming, and, fishing for background, Alex had asked her some questions about the reputation of the Dennison Center. One thing she'd told him was the nickname of the place in Boston medical circles. "We say, 'We're sending Mrs. So-and-So over to the Death Star today.' "

Not a cheerful nickname, Alex thought. Nor was it, at first glance anyway, a cheerful place. Like a hotel lobby, the big room on the ground floor was sectioned off into small areas where you could sit and wait in well-stuffed chairs. It was different from a hotel lobby in that the ceiling was low and the lighting flat, fluorescent. Everybody was there for a common purpose, and they all knew it too. Near where Alex stood, a man in a wheelchair talked with bent head and slurred voice to what Alex took to be his wife and grown-up kids. "Didn't I tell ya?" the son said, like a coach trying to pump up a Little Leaguer who had successfully drawn a walk.

Another father walked by with a kid slung on his hip. The man turned left out of sight under a hanging sign, black letters on clear Lucite. Alex turned his head slightly sideways and squinted the double image away. PEDIATRIC. Probably leukemia, Alex thought. For some of these people, he knew, medical intervention would save their lives. Then they could put their illnesses behind them and move on. For others it wouldn't, and they might not leave this place at all.

Death Star, Life Star. From his own experience with cancer and medicine Alex had concluded that survival depended on a combination of technology and will, and mostly, he was convinced, luck. For the first, you probably couldn't do better than this place here. The Dennison was a high-magnitude star in a galaxy fairly bursting with the newest and best medical toys. Its sleek glass tower stood smack in the middle of the Longwood Medical Area, a triangle of Boston health-care powerhouses framed by the Fenway, Huntington Avenue, and the border of suburban Brookline where so many of the doctors lived. The Medical Area included at least a half dozen affiliated hospitals plus the Harvard Medical School. In a geography text, Alex

5

thought, its products ought to be listed as doctors and discoveries and cadavers and cures.

ALL PATIENTS MUST CHECK IN HERE BEFORE APPOINTMENTS, the sign at the front desk said, but Alex wasn't a patient here, not yet anyway. When it was time for his appointment he went directly to the elevator and rode up to the fourth floor, looking for room 486. The numbering system was complex, with arrows pointing in many directions, the scheme complicated by diverging hallways that seemed to lead to separate units or suites. A bit intimidated in spite of himself, Alex stood next to a cart full of rubber-banded bundles of mail. After a minute the kid in charge of the cart stepped out of an office. He was wearing headphones and bobbing his head energetically, but he took off the phones and politely directed Alex to take a left and then a right.

Room 486 was locked. Next door in a cubicle labeled 485, Alex found a woman sitting at a desk, talking on the phone. She wasn't a kid, she was closer to Alex's age, with a square, pleasant face and short black hair beginning to be streaked with threads of gray. She was wearing a sweatshirt that had a picture of some sculptures and hieroglyphics and said CLEOPATRA AND THE ART OF ANCIENT EGYPT. If she was Harrison's secretary, Harrison wasn't a stickler about formality in office attire. Carol Wagner, Alex's doctor, had said she thought he might like Harrison. She'd said, "He isn't a run-of-the-mill Dennison Center type."

"I'll call you later, honey," the woman said, holding up a finger to let Alex know she'd only be a minute more. "My daughter is home from school today," she told him after she hung up. "More tired than sick, though, I think. Are you looking for Dr. Harrison or who?"

"Dr. Harrison," Alex told the secretary. "I'm Alex Glauberman. I have an appointment with him at two."

"Oh, right, Mr. Glauberman," she said. She looked at her watch. "He's still at rounds, he's giving a talk today." She looked Alex up and down. She said, "You're not quite what I expected. I mean, you don't look like Humphrey Bogart or Magnum P.I."

"No," Alex said. He sometimes ran into this problem himself. Growing up in the fifties, his image of detectives had been formed by watching Perry Mason on TV. Mason himself had been a lawyer, but for his legwork he'd depended on a hired hand named Paul Drake, played by William Hopper, Hedda Hopper's

6

son. A detective, Alex had therefore thought, was a big blond hunk with a business suit and a Hollywood face. Even Sam Spade, in the book if not the movie, was supposed to look like a "blond Satan," whatever exactly that was. Alex on the other hand was tall but thin—some said cadaverous—with black curly hair and a black beard. He smiled his slightly cockeyed, thin-lipped smile, the one his oldest friend had once told him made him look like a friendly, furry shark. Friendly and furry had sounded wrong, like a teddy bear. The shark had kind of appealed to him.

"No," he repeated. "But at best I'm a part-time detective. Mostly what I do is fix cars." He handed her one of his business cards, which featured a drawing of a horned creature, half car and half beast. Kim had contributed the drawing, the same friend who'd made the comment about his smile.

"Oh." The secretary frowned, knitting her penciled brows together till they almost touched. "I didn't mean anything critical, I was just looking for something to say. My name is Deborah McCarthy. Jay should be back any minute. He had to give a presentation. Today is attending rounds. All the attendings take turns giving lectures."

"Alex," Alex reciprocated. He shook hands with Deborah. "What are attendings?" He'd needed to teach himself some medical jargon over the past few years, but still he generally felt everybody in hospitals was talking in code.

"Huh? Oh, attending physicians. The attendings take turns supervising the fellows, who supervise the residents, more or less. Jay's the attending on the transplant unit this month. If I can help you understand how things work around here, while you're waiting. . . . Sit down, anyway. I guess he'll want you next door in his office, not the examining room there." She jerked her head toward a doorway that led out of her cubicle.

"Thanks," Alex said. Since she seemed sufficiently garrulous, he asked, "Do you know what he wants me to look into, by the way?"

"I do, but I better let him tell you that himself. You know about him getting his picture in *People,* right?"

"No," Alex said. "Actually, I have to confess I don't."

"Oh. Well, why should you, unless you're an addict? To the magazine, I mean. He treated this baseball player. A catcher for

7

the, uh, the St. Louis Cardinals, I think that's the team. Larry Mitchell, a nice guy. So they did a feature on it, they called it, 'A Big-League Catcher Fights to Nail Cancer at the Plate.'" She repeated the headline with an amalgam of sarcasm and respect.

"Uh-huh," Alex said. He had spotted this story in the local sports pages, if not the glossy weekly. The ballplayer had only been a second-string catcher, but that plus the lymph cancer plus the high-tech medicine had made him a celebrity of sorts. Anyway, the words *lymph cancer* always jumped out Alex, however buried on the page.

"But Dr. Wagner seems to feel you're somebody to boast about too," Deborah added as if he might need placating. "Doctors like to brag about their patients, just like mothers do about their kids."

"Uh-huh," Alex said again. Wagner had been pleased, definitely, when Harrison had called her last week to ask for the name and number of her patient who did investigations. "I don't have any idea what Jay would want," Wagner had said when she called Alex to alert him, "but if I were you I'd look into it. You don't *need* any special connections to be accepted as a patient in his study, if you were to be a candidate for that treatment someday. Still, I wouldn't look a gift horse in the mouth."

"No," Alex had said, determinedly meeting her cliché with one of his own. "And clients for my investigation business don't grow on trees."

TWO
Closers

Harrison might run an informal office, but he seemed to be in some kind of uniform himself: he returned from attending rounds in scuffed black dress shoes, gray flannel slacks, a dress shirt and knit tie, and a doctor's white coat with name tag attached. He wasn't fat, exactly, just an average, rounded middle-aged American male. His face was clean-shaven and pinkish, topped by brown hair in a dry, expensive cut.

None of this impressed Alex one way or the other. He did, though, like the way the doctor bounced on his toes for a minute between catching up on messages with Deborah and focusing in on him. The bounce testified to high energy. It also seemed like a kind of discipline, a fast-track meditation, a way of separating one thing from the next. Harrison stuck his hand out to be shaken. The fingers were short and squared off. Not surgeon's fingers, blunt ones.

"Next door's my burrow," he said. "Let's go in there."

Walking into Jay Harrison's burrow, Alex could see more of what Carol Wagner had meant. The small room had been done in some special wallpaper with very delicate Japanese nature scenes on a creamy background tinged with blue. No diplomas hung there, just some framed photographs that Alex guessed were superenlarged images of cells. And on the back wall on either side of the single window were blown-up photos of baseball players in uniform. Dennis Eckersley peered from the mound, sharp-eyed yet bemused. Big Lee Smith glowered impersonally.

Both former Red Sox, Alex noted. The Dennison Center was the favorite charity of the Red Sox and of many sports-world figures besides, and treating that catcher Mitchell would only have tightened Harrison's links. But something more particular about Harrison's choice of posters occurred to him.

"Those are both ace relievers." He found it a bit odd they were two right-handers. A matched pair, righty and lefty, would have been more scientific, more of a representative sample, he thought. Unless maybe this *was* a representative sample: one white ballplayer and one black. Most people didn't bother about such racial niceties these days. He added, "Your marrow transplant operation is a kind of relief pitching, if I understand it right."

Jay Harrison looked Alex over with blue eyes that seemed a little lost inside the padding the cheeks and forehead had acquired over the years. He gestured toward a chair at right angles to his own. This was the patient's chair, the one that allowed the doctor to swivel ninety degrees and face the patient with no desk in between. They'd come in here from the examining room—Alex noted a connecting door—and sit here and discuss the good or bad news.

"You do understand it," the doctor said. "In baseball terms, the question is whether our protocol, our treatment, can be a closer. We don't just want to stave off the opposition for another inning or two, we want to get the game won. We hope to produce a significant number of permanent cures instead of temporary remissions. Carol said she treated you about two or three years ago. Nodular lymphoma, isn't that right? And you're doing very well?"

"Yes," Alex said. He'd been diagnosed with this particular cancer when Meredith, on their third night together, felt a funny lump in his neck. There had been similar lumps—tumorous lymph nodes—in his neck and groin and armpit. When the swellings had started getting in the way of organs and vessels, Alex had spent five months taking a mountain of very unpleasant pills for one week out of every three. Since then his own immune system had kept in check whatever small population of malignant cells had survived. As malignancies went, nodular lymphomas were relatively lazy and also relatively responsive to drugs. But they tended, sooner or later, to come back. That was where bone marrow transplants came in.

"If I understand it right," Alex continued, "we're talking about something like reboring and rebuilding an engine. You clean the body out, then put the essential parts back in. When I do it, I go buy new pistons from a shop. You have to reuse the old ones, though."

Harrison smiled. It was a smile of approval, but a mischievous quality crinkled the corners of his eyes. Alex felt accepted into a secret society. If this was really a job interview, it seemed to be going okay.

"Well put," the doctor said. "You need bone marrow, can't run without the stuff. The cells in bone marrow are the ones that replenish all the crucial kinds of cells in the lymph and the blood—lymphocytes, leukocytes, red cells, platelets, all of that. The problem is that the treatments we use to clean out cancers, chemotherapy and radiation, kill bone marrow cells for the same reason they kill cancer cells: they interfere with cell reproduction, so they zap any cells in the body that are reproducing very fast. So what we do is take out a quart of marrow from your hipbones, clean it up in a test tube, and cryopreserve it in liquid nitrogen. Then we zap you with much higher doses than we'd otherwise dare. Then we thaw your frozen marrow, put it back in you, and let it regenerate itself and your blood supply. We keep you in the shop for about a month while that's happening. Then we let you go home, we cross our fingers, and we wait. Sometimes a relative's or even a stranger's marrow can be transplanted, as you may have heard, but your own marrow is safest and best."

"Yes," Alex said. He'd heard most of this before. But Harrison obviously liked to talk medicine, and Alex wasn't one to turn down free information.

"I say 'you,'" Harrison added, "but I don't mean you personally, necessarily. If you should have a recurrence, the treatment would depend on the exact type of cell deformity, the size of the tumors, and other factors, as I'm sure Dr. Wagner has explained. The transplant procedure is still classified as experimental in most cases, and it does entail risks. Until your marrow regrows, you've shut down the factories that produce the components that make your immune system work. Killing off the marrow is like giving yourself AIDS, or putting yourself through Chernobyl, except that it's only temporary, until you get your previously harvested marrow reinfused. During that period while you're myelosuppressed—while your counts of all these blood cells are down—you could get any kind of bug and not be able to fight it off. It's a risk, though we have enough experience in the use of sterile environment and antibiotics to keep that risk small."

Harrison leaned back, letting his eyes take a quick tour of his pictures and his wallpaper while those sobering words started to sink in. Then he watched Alex without trying to hide his observation. Alex was warming to Jay Harrison. Not too much bullshit here.

"So," the doctor said after a while. "That's my research. Carol says you sometimes take on research too."

"Yes," Alex said. "It's a sideline. People come to me by accident or through word-of-mouth, and I'm strictly self-taught. But I do have a lot of experience taking things apart and seeing how they work. I started doing that with other people's problems during chemotherapy, when my psychological and pharmacological situation pushed me to, um, be myself, only more so. To do things I'd only imagined doing, if you see what I mean."

11

This much was a variation on the set speech that Alex delivered often enough, if always with some distaste. He didn't like having to justify himself. Besides, in the few years he'd had this sideline, he'd drawn some conclusions about the type of clients who came to him. They came to him because they had stories that were either too screwy, too illegal, too countercultural, or too damn obviously a pack of lies to lay in front of a shingle-on-the-door private detective or a cop.

Jay Harrison tapped his fingers on his desktop. "I see what you mean," he said. Then he opened a desk drawer and took out a triple-folded sheet of paper, which he handed across. It was a photocopy of a short typewritten letter. The letter asked Harrison to send ten thousand dollars to a certain post office box. The writer called the money a loan but didn't say anything about terms or interest or paying the money back. Alex drew the obvious conclusion.

"Blackmail?"

Harrison scratched his head and then shook it. "Somebody *thinks* it's blackmail. But as far as I can figure out, they haven't got anything to blackmail me *with.*"

THREE
A Beautiful Person Stops

Alex read the note again:

> It's been a pretty long time but I guess you still remember me, Jay. It's hard times for me now and I could do with a loan of maybe ten thousand or so. I hope you can see your way to this, because if you can't then I have to tell some people some of the things I know. My name is Foster. We met on the Baltimore Beltway on a hot sunny afternoon when I stopped to pick you up, me and my girl. About the loan, you can send it all in cash in a package to this address. I give you two weeks, that's all.

There was no signature, just the single paragraph and a return address, a post office box in Baltimore, Maryland, zip code 21218.

"Oh yeah." Harrison nodded, and Alex watched the corners of his eyes get that amused, approving look again. "It's been a long time, but he's right, I still remember him. He picked me up hitchhiking, May of 1971. I haven't seen him since. But apparently he saw my picture in the magazine when he was standing in line to buy groceries or whatever. The letter came addressed to me here at the hospital. Regular white business envelope, Baltimore postmark. Almost three weeks ago."

"Three weeks," Alex said. The sender had given a deadline of two. Had he made good on his threat, whatever the implied threat had been? "Why am I sitting here now?"

"To be honest, you weren't my first resort. The first thing I did was call the cops."

"And showed them the letter?"

"I showed them *a* letter. I mean, I had Deborah type a substitute that was more or less the same. Only the name was Arnie Johnson, a name I pulled out of the air. The place was the New York Thruway, and Deborah said as long as I was doing that why not make the weather cold. I told the cops I didn't know any Johnson and I didn't know what incident this could be about. Do you see why?"

"Sure," Alex said. "It's a chain letter. You send the black-mail note to ten friends and soon you get a hundred thousand dollars tax free." He watched the doctor's forehead come down like a knight's visor. Harrison didn't need to put diplomas on his walls, but he liked to demonstrate that Doctor knows most, and he didn't seem to like being challenged about that. Or maybe it was simply a habit, the way Alex too often let sarcastic comments get away from him—his father's philosophic patience, as he sometimes put it, but his mother's smart mouth. "Sorry," Alex added. "But I'm not one of your medical students. You don't have to quiz me about why you're feeling inside the pa-tient's armpit. Just tell me what you want me to know."

Harrison's frown slowly dissipated. "Okay," he said finally. "You're not a student, an intern, or even a resident. We're fellow professionals, that's what you want me to see?" He laughed, a surprisingly infectious laugh. He said, "Let me get at it another

13

way. You ever hitchhike, before you were up to your ears in cars?"

"Yeah, some."

"Some," Harrison repeated. "Then you'll know what I mean if I tell you it was hot, maybe eighty, the way it can get suddenly hot in the Middle Atlantic states around the beginning of May. I was standing on the shoulder. It was a bad place to hitch, a place nobody had any reason to slow down. Everybody's roaring past at sixty-five, seventy, and I'm feeling like an ant that might get stepped on or reverberated to death by this herd of elephants roaring by. I'm also starting to give the finger to the rear ends of cars, even though I know it's a spoiled and stupid thing to do. Then all of a sudden the world is a beautiful place because a beautiful person stops for me, a person who understands the importance and kindliness of picking a stuck hitchhiker up. I'm inside a delivery van made over into a camper. The van's picking up speed, while I'm lying on a nice soft bunk listening to Coltrane blow his sax."

All those words came out in an even cadence. This wasn't a spurt of unexamined memories tumbling from a suddenly loosened faucet, it was something to which the doctor had given some thought before he spoke. Still, Alex thought he caught a glimpse of a younger Jay Harrison, less confident but brasher—a kid who might just speed-rap, letting rivers of unconsidered thoughts pour out.

"That's one of the things I liked about hitchhiking," Jay Harrison went on. "Besides that it was a cheap and interesting way to meet people. I liked the sudden interchange of ups and downs. Anyway, the point is, there *was* a Foster. That's who was driving the van, and he didn't just take me a few miles, he took me all the way to California. I thought I was headed for Boston, but I couldn't turn California down. So I do owe him a favor, if not a ten-thousand-dollar one. I didn't want to get him in any trouble, unless I was sure I had to, so I took the liberty of showing an amended letter to the police. I told them it was Greek to me but still I was concerned, I didn't want the reputation of the Center damaged by some crazy unfounded accusations against myself, I just wondered could they maybe get the PO box checked out."

Sure enough, Alex thought, Jay Harrison was not exactly

run-of-the-mill. He'd come up with a scheme that might get him some information while protecting this Foster's identity. When the cops came to call, Foster would see that his old friend Jay was protecting him, but Foster would also see that the old friend wasn't taking any shit.

"The police did their job. This is a prestigious institution, after all. They found out that the post office box belongs to a travel agency, a real operation, nothing suspicious about it at all. They showed me a list of all the employees, and even the family members of the employees who handle the mail. None of them was Johnson, of course, but none of them was Foster either. The closest thing to a connection would be that all the owners and employees, like Mr. Foster, are black. No connection at all, really. Two weeks went by, and nothing happened. I said thanks, just some nut I guess."

"But you're not sure?"

"*Somebody* sent me that letter, whether it was Foster himself or maybe somebody he might have told about me. Possibly I scared him off, them off, or possibly it was all somebody's idea of a practical joke. But I find myself still waiting for the other shoe to drop. I want you to find Foster for me. Maybe he really needs help and I can help him. Or maybe he's gone paranoid schizo, and I'm his idée fixe, and someday in a year or two, he'll walk in here with a sawed-off shotgun and open up. Besides, I've got a responsibility to protect the work I'm involved in, and to protect my patients. So I want to know about Foster, what the story is. You sound like you could find out in a delicate way. Are you interested?"

"I'm interested. And curious. You say he hasn't got anything to blackmail you with. I'd need to know what you were into, besides hitchhiking, around May of 1971. You didn't seem to have any trouble coming up with that date."

"I know where I was coming from, I was coming from the Mayday antiwar demonstrations in D.C. Ten thousand people got busted in two days, if I remember the numbers right. It was just after the Vietnam Veterans Against the War camped on the Mall and threw their medals back up the Capitol steps. I got out of jail after a night and got my act together and started hitching up this way."

"And ended up going to California. With Foster and his

15

girlfriend, the letter says. So, it's safe to say you weren't just hitting the books and getting ready to be a doctor in those days?"

"Nope. I'm a little less boring than that. But it's a long way from what I was into then, to anything that qualifies as a ten-thousand-dollar secret. On my résumé, it's just three years missing between college and medical school. There ought to be a couple of misdemeanors in my police record or my FBI file, and a couple subversive collectives I belonged to. Since I got the letter I've been over all this ground myself, and I've come up with zero every time. We're talking the medical, scientific, grant-getting world here. There's lots of internal politics to it, and it's very old-boy, but nobody gives much of a damn about your opinions or private life. Nobody cares what the hell your political activities might have been twenty years ago. All they care about is that I went to the right schools and impressed the right people, for better or for worse."

Harrison ran his hands through his hair and then tried to pat it back into place. Alex had to admit that he looked truly confused. "Not even in George Bush's Washington?" Alex pressed. "Not even in the AMA?"

"We're talking medicine," Harrison answered. "We're not talking arts funding or what's allowed or not allowed in the schools. The medical world is conservative on doctors' salaries, on taxes, on national health service, and they like to keep the pharmaceutical companies happy too. But beyond that, most of them don't even know what laypeople fight about, then or now. The worst thing I did—from a right-winger's viewpoint, I mean—is that I helped active-duty GIs get to Canada. Out in California I worked on a kind of underground railway thing. Number one, the line today is that we've put those divisions behind us, right? Number two, I can't believe Foster would be holding that over me, because he was AWOL himself. That's what got me into aiding antiwar soldiers, meeting him. . . . So look, before we get any further into this, do you want this job?"

"I want the job," Alex said.

"Good." Harrison stood up and reached out to shake hands again. "Please call me Jay," he said. "Titles don't gratify my ego, you'll find."

"Alex," Alex said. "So how I am going to start looking for him? If that travel agency's a dead end, I mean."

"I've got other things you could go on. I know a little about his background. In prying data out of record keepers you'll have use of the sanctified Dennison Center name. But I need to be up on the unit in fifteen minutes, so we'll get into that later. If you want a tour, though, you can come up with me. We'd just have time for a look at the cryopreservation facilities on the way. If you want to, I mean. I just thought that, considering . . ."

"Sure," Alex said. He wanted to understand about marrow transplants. He wanted to see what it would be like to go through this, to see what the journal articles left out. And besides, showing off the process he was pioneering did gratify Jay Harrison's ego, if Alex understood him right.

FOUR
Balancing Act

Somewhere in his subconscious Alex had formed an image of what a quart of bone marrow would be. He'd pictured a narrow-neck opaque white plastic jar, heavy with unseen contents. If you shook it, you'd hear a slushy primeval ooze rocking around. You wouldn't shake it, though, you'd just place it in a deep-freeze cabinet as solid as a vault.

What Alex held in his hands in a back room of the Dennison Center's blood bank wasn't anything like that. He held a pouch of thin, transparent plastic, maybe four inches by seven. This one was empty, but it wouldn't be more than half an inch thick even when filled. The pouch had no neck, no mouth, no screw cap, only a pair of built-in flexible plastic tubes. To Alex it looked and felt like the seventy-nine-cent pencil cases his daughter Maria bought to slip into her three-ring loose-leaf binder each fall. Alex didn't like the idea of his or anyone else's bone marrow being stored in such a container. Even if it might be strong, space-age plastic, it still left the marrow so—well, indecently exposed.

Nor was the blood bank anything like the kind of bank with armed guards and vaults. The rooms through which he'd come

17

had been a confusing clutter of machines, computer terminals, beakers and test tubes, file cabinets, and rows of silvery re-frigerated cabinets that seemed to belong in the hospital's kitchen more than anyplace else. All this hodgepodge had been tended by a bevy of white women in white coats.

"What color would the stuff be?" Alex asked as he turned the plastic pouch over and looked at it some more. Purified, he assumed, marrow would be a kind of ghostly white. He hoped his voice sounded steadier than it felt.

"Oh, reddish. It looks like pale blood. Most of what we're freezing is blood serum, just a little of it is really the marrow itself. From the marrow, we separate out just the nucleated—well, pretty much just the cells I was talking about, the ones that can multiply and differentiate into blood components. We sepa-rate and concentrate those, using a cell washer, one of those dozen machines we went by on the way in. Then what we've got is, oh, say a half cup of the primo, high-grade stuff, but that half cup contains billions of cells. We wipe out any cancerous ones with monoclonal antibodies—I can explain that later if you want—and then we stir the good stuff into a mixture that's derived from the patient's blood plus a preservative chemical we use. That's what we put in the pouch. Then we freeze it down to nearly two hundred below. When we've finished treating the patient, we thaw the mixture in lukewarm water and then rein-fuse it through a vein. The DMSO—that's the preservative—has a kind of garlicky odor. Patients say they can smell the garlic from inside."

"Uh-huh," Alex said. He was remembering a science teacher's demonstration of how cold liquefied gases were. The teacher had poured liquid air, mostly nitrogen, into a Styrofoam bowl and dropped a rubber ball in. He'd fished the ball out with a pair of tongs and dropped it on the floor. The superfrozen ball had shattered like glass. Alex concentrated on that problem, if only to avoid the notion of smelling garlic from inside.

"What happens if somebody drops the bag of marrow, say?" he asked.

"Well, we do our best to protect it," Jay said with a short laugh. "When the sample comes out of the programmable freez-ing unit here, the pouch goes inside one of these aluminum cases, and that case fits into a rack in the storage freezer over there."

The case looked like a metallic VCR cartridge, only thinner. The freezing unit looked like a cross between a photocopier and a microwave oven. The storage unit was just a wide top-loading barrel, joined by a thick flexible metal hose to a tall gleaming tank.

The barrel reminded Alex of an immense thermos, and the tank brought back faint images of the equipment at a dairy he'd visited as a kid. He felt flushed and weak-kneed, like a child that needed to get out of an overwhelming place into the fresh air. The feeling didn't improve as he watched the doctor slide his hands into a pair of heavy gloves and raise the hinged top of the barrel. A swirl of what looked like smoke emerged, the kind that usually precedes the genie out of the bottle. Jay reached into the smoke with a long pair of tongs, lifting up a rack with slots for those metallic VCR cases. Most of the slots were empty, but not all. Now Alex felt a wave of cold whiteness go through him, felt his blood drain right out of his face.

"That was the specimen rack," Jay said once he'd closed the top of the storage unit. "That mist is water vapor condensing from the cold. The bottom third of the thing is full of liquid N-two, liquid nitrogen, and that's where the specimens sit. An automatic sensor monitors the N-two level, and an automatic draw device keeps adding more from that Dewar, that shiny supply tank on the other end of the hose. The only time the specimens are out of the cases is when it's time to thaw them. During the thawing the pouch sits in an outer plastic bag, and we keep changing that outer bag about once a minute just to be sure it's intact. I don't know of anybody spilling a specimen, ever, but we always extract enough marrow so we can keep an extra sample frozen, just in case. . . . You're looking pretty pale—why don't we get the hell out of here, okay? I guess I sound pretty matter-of-fact about all this."

"Well," Alex said weakly. "Usually I'm pretty good about seeing the body as a mechanism, but . . ." He didn't elaborate, just followed Harrison out a back door into the corridor of the basement level, where the blood bank had been installed. He felt ridiculous, like the patient he'd always prided himself on not being. That quivering mass of fear and doubt.

"Did you ever do any acid?" Jay Harrison asked suddenly.

He asked about LSD the same way he'd asked about hitchhiking earlier. A little wistful, and a little defiant of convention, too.

"Well, yeah." Alex took some deep breaths and let his muscles get themselves together. He told himself what his t'ai chi teacher said: whatever you're doing, remember to breathe. He stood up straighter and felt the cold sweat evaporating off his skin.

"Then maybe you've had the experience where the parts of everything solid dissolve into atoms, and you're conscious that it's all a balancing act, that everything is suspended in so much empty space? That same thing happens when people see their blood, or the insides of bodies—when they really see all the components that make them up. We like to think of ourselves as solid, unitary, no matter how much we intellectually understand that we're not. Come on, let's get you some caffeine or fat or sugar or whatever your poison is. Then we'll get up to the unit. There's only whole people up there."

Jay put a fatherly hand on Alex's shoulder, the way Alex might with Maria after telling her something she wasn't allowed to do even though she was almost twelve. Go to boy-girl get-togethers without a parent present, for instance, or ride the subway without a friend. Wait'll she wants to smoke dope and hitch across the country and drop acid if there is any, he told himself sternly, if only to distract himself from the out-of-body bone marrow again.

There had been a time when Alex had told himself not to count on living through Maria's teenage years, but now those years were beginning and Alex found himself feeling very much alive. Not that he didn't get danger signals—there was the tinge of double vision that had been bothering him for the past few weeks. It was just that looking forward, he tended to see at least as many dangers for Maria as for himself. She was going to be coming of age in an era that Alex, perhaps like all parents, saw as more dangerous than his own. Wrenching as the sixties had been, that era had been fueled by hope as well as fear and anger, because it had seemed there might be a new world to gain.

He let Jay steer him toward the cafeteria. Jay was saying, "Only whole bodies, I promise, though some of them may be hooked up to a lot of tubes."

*   *   *

20

"Rounds on the unit," seemed to mean something different than the "attending rounds" Deborah had spoken of before. Alex had expected Jay to make some kind of presentation, but in fact he was going from patient to patient, looking at charts and talking with medical staff. He'd let Alex follow him into the "anteroom," as this long lobby or buffer zone was called, introduced him to one of the nurses, and told her to show him around.

Inside the anteroom everybody else was in scrubs, hospital green pajama things like surgeons on TV shows wore. Alex didn't have to wash or change clothes, the nurse Yvonne Price told him, but he had to be careful not to touch anything, and of course he couldn't be allowed into any of the patients' rooms.

The guts of the transplant unit consisted of ten patient rooms arranged off two buffer zones, the one he was in and another identical one off the main corridor farther down. Not that Alex was comfortable calling the patients' quarters "rooms." To him a room was a place you could shut yourself up in when you chose, and leave when you chose, too. Here you had neither of those privileges. Alex tried to understand what it would be like to live here. He was standing in front of a temporarily empty room that belonged to Yvonne's patient.

The wall closest to Alex was clear plastic. It looked like a heavy shower curtain except it had arm-length gloves built in so that objects could be manipulated from outside if the need arose, and at one end was a three-foot gap where the "wall" was nothing but a current of air. For a month, the patient didn't walk out through that doorway, because out here, even in the buffer zone, lay a world of bugs and bacteria in which the patient couldn't yet survive.

Were there such things as jails without cruelty, Alex wondered—institutions that rehabilitated you to the point where you really could make it with your newfound strengths and skills? If so, that's the way he'd have to describe this place. A place where you were always watched, and which you couldn't leave. It gave him the creeps. Yet his heart went out right away to the invisible occupant of this room. "She's down getting TBI," Yvonne had said. Alex managed to translate that to total body irradiation. The patient was a woman, just now getting the treatment that would kill off her cancer, everyone hoped, and would kill off her remaining bone marrow too.

21

"Remember not to touch the wall," the nurse said again. Alex stopped a good foot away from the plastic curtain but leaned forward to peer through. He noted the room's right-hand wall, which was all air vents, and the phone and TV and VCR that provided contact with the world outside. He noted the pillar adorned with tubes and probes and gadgets, sort of like a glorified dentist's rig, and also, taking up about a quarter of the space, one of those pretend-you're-climbing kind of exercise machines.

"The air in the room is as sterile as we can get it," Yvonne explained, "and it changes over at a rate of sixty times a minute. Filtered air comes in through all those vents, and the old air flows out into the anteroom here. Nobody goes in without a surgical scrub first thing in the morning, and another wash each time. You don't notice the air flow except in the doorway, where there's kind of a breeze. The blower makes a lot of noise, but it's constant and after a while the mind tunes that out. Like a lot of worse things," she said, smiling, "that your mind has to tune out too."

"I guess so," Alex replied, guessing at all the things a person with her job might mean by that. Yvonne Price looked as if she smiled easily and often. She had that kind of face that seemed to be mostly cheeks, cheeks that worked hard at pulling genuine smiles out of her eyes and mouth. Alex had never been able to imagine what it would be like to have that kind of face, though he'd learned after some years of suspicion to be grateful for many of the people who did. Yvonne's face was a pale brown that suggested she breathed a lot of filtered air but not much fresh. She was probably about twenty-five, but she lacked the healthy outdoor glow a young African-American in a soda or cigarette ad would have. Of course, it was still only the end of April. Maybe she'd get out more once Boston's always tentative spring got more of a grip.

"Somebody else can show you the kitchen and stuff if you want, but you'll have to get out of my way now, because my patient is coming back up," she said by way of dismissal. This time she didn't smile, possibly because she was saving that reassuring energy for her patient. "Just tell them at the desk that I was showing you around for Dr. Harrison, and ask them whatever else you want to know."

Alex left the anteroom and turned right. He stood for a

minute near the central desk looking for Jay Harrison, but he didn't see him. They had a new appointment for "around three," back down in Jay's office. Alex noticed a man with a stethoscope dangling from his pocket, who was giving him a curious glance. The man wore green scrubs under a long yellow thing, partly open in back, that Yvonne had referred to as a "gown." For patients especially at risk, she'd said, the medical staff had to go into the room gloved and capped and gowned.

"Excuse me," the man said. "I'm Dr. Kramer, the senior resident. You look a little lost." Kramer also had on a round paper cap, a flimsy thing that covered his hair and ears. The whole getup reminded Alex of the habits nuns used to wear. He remembered how they'd seemed like mannequins, not real people, when he passed them in the street.

"Oh," Alex said. "No, I'm not lost. Yvonne was showing me around, for Dr. Harrison. But her patient is coming up from radiology now."

The resident nodded and went on his way. Apparently dropping Jay's name was enough to prove that you belonged. Alex looked back toward the anteroom just as Yvonne reappeared. She turned the corner into the main corridor and went to wait by the double doors of the transplant unit. The doors bulged and then opened, admitting a long cart covered with plastic, pushed by a black man in white jacket and pants.

Alex noticed tanks on the bottom of the cart, and hoses from the tanks feeding into the plastic. The shape of the person lying inside the plastic was vague. Yvonne Price accompanied the orderly, the cart, and the patient into the anteroom. The cart was a midget, mobile isolation room. Somehow Alex didn't want to wait around to see the empty cart reappear. Nor did he need to see the kitchen and find out more about what the inmates could and couldn't be permitted to eat. No salads, Yvonne had told him. Raw vegetables were too hard to disinfect. He looked around for Jay once more and noticed that Kramer, too, was watching the anteroom door through which the cart had disappeared. Somehow Alex suspected this was Yvonne's patient's last day of TBI, that the woman had reentered the sterile area for the duration, with her cell counts now down to zip. Did the medical staff ever feel like zookeepers, he wondered. Ministering

23

to the needs of creatures just slightly less human than themselves?

You'd better get out of here, Alex told himself. He walked down the corridor and through the double doors, which on the other side had big red stop signs reading AUTHORIZED PERSONNEL ONLY—INTENSIVE CARE. When he was alone in the elevator he let out a deep breath and said, "I'd die before I spent a month like that." He knew, however, that the opposite was true. Like anybody else, he'd spend a month or two or three in there if he was convinced it could help him stay alive.

FIVE
The Other Shoe

"You're back." Deborah looked up from the keyboard, then ignored him while she finished entering whatever she was entering, then finally looked up again.

"I'm back," Alex agreed. "I visited the unit and took a walk outside—dirty air, but fresh. Has our boss come back?"

"He said to tell you he's a little hung up, he'll be free again about four. You can start the meter ticking, or whatever you do. I'm supposed to get clear with you about the charges and all."

"Thirty an hour plus expenses, the same thing I'm losing by not being in my shop. Only this is tax free, because I don't report it, because I don't actually have a license for this kind of work."

"Yeah, everybody moonlights these days. My husband's a pilot, he sometimes gives flying lessons to friends and acquaintances on the side. Strictly illegal. I hope to God none of them ever crash. You can sit here or in the examining room if you want to wait around."

She didn't offer him the boss's office, Alex noticed. Did she think he'd go rifling through the files? He would, probably. He wasn't convinced his new client was planning to tell him everything he needed to know.

"This letter he showed me," Alex said. "Did you open it, when it came?"

"Uh-huh, I did. It was addressed to Dr. H. J. Harrison, personal, but he gets a lot like that—patients, or people that want to be patients, especially since that article. Not really personal at all, they just hope that will get them past somebody like me. But letters addressed 'Jay Harrison, personal,' I don't open, I just give them to him. Why?"

"I want to know how he reacted, whether he seemed scared, shocked, surprised, what?"

"You don't trust him?"

"Say I'm professionally skeptical."

"And born suspicious, too, I bet. Like I'm a born blabbermouth. That's what you're counting on, right? Well, he told me I could tell you anything you wanted to know." She looked at her watch and then at a daily calendar on her cluttered desk. "As long as I'm getting paid to be a blabbermouth, can we go out for coffee?"

"Sure," Alex said. "Downstairs?"

"No. Their coffee's a lot better across the street. Let me just call home and check on Jennifer. I think she's about as sick as me, to tell you the truth. She just needed a day off. Don't we all?"

Across the street meant a pseudo-French fast-food eatery on Brookline Avenue. To get there Deborah McCarthy led him through a maze of corridors and a connecting building and out a service door. They got coffee and pastries and then, over a rickety round table on the roofed outdoor patio, Alex learned a few things. Deborah's daughter was going on twelve, the same age as Maria, but Deborah was still married, and so unlike Maria the daughter lived with both parents full time. Alex explained about being a parent one week on, one week off. Deborah also had a boy two years younger than Jennifer, and another boy two years younger than that.

Catholic but careful, one way or another, Alex thought. Her husband was a private pilot, not airline. Sometimes Jay talked about taking lessons from Richard, but it hadn't happened yet. Jay was interested in Richard, they all socialized occasionally, but Jay couldn't ever really keep the kids and their ages straight. No, Jay wasn't married. Jay didn't have any kids.

"When I gave him the letter?" she repeated when Alex pressed her about it again. She'd just taken another bite of her chocolate croissant, so the first part of what she said came out garbled, the words getting caught in the pastry. "I opened it, the way I said, and got kind of a shock. Jay came in and asked about the mail, so I just handed it to him. I didn't know what to say. He kind of just stood there like his mind was a long way off. He has an expression, it's kind of like, ironic, I guess."

She tried to imitate the crinkling Alex had noticed at the corners of the doctor's eyes. All that did was show off her eyebrows. She had dark, interesting brows, the curvature accentuated with pencil. They knitted together like sketches of birds' wings, or waves.

"He didn't try to hide his reaction, if that's what you're asking. I was curious, I admit it, and he let me read what passed over his face. Then he went into his office for about five minutes. No lights went on on my phone, so he didn't make any calls. I *told* you I was curious. I wondered if he'd call somebody, and who. He came back and explained what he wanted the new letter to say, the one he showed the police. He told me a little about this Foster, that hitchhiking adventure and all."

"Why do you think he involved you in writing the substitute letter, instead of doing it himself?"

"You don't have a secretary. Guys with secretaries, this gets to be a habit, especially doctors. Women doctors too. Jay can type, but not accurately, even though he once ran some kind of printing press, or so he says."

"Do you think he wanted your advice? Or did he want an accomplice?" Alex didn't know where he was going. He was just trying to understand his client. The way to understand any mechanism was take it apart.

"Well, he knows me, and I already read the real letter, so . . ." Deborah took a big bite of her croissant and waved her free hand in a circle, whatever that meant.

"Do you think he could have made this up, this letter, and sent it to himself? People have been known to want other people found and to make up the reason why."

"Oh, is that what you're getting at," Deborah said with her mouth still half full. She finished chewing. "Sure. That's possible." She started to say something else, then raised her arm straight up and waved the remaining end of the croissant. "Here he comes, you can ask him that yourself. Looks in a hurry, dammit. He must want something done. I *can't* stay late today.

26

Richard's away on a job, and I promised Jen I'd be home on time."

A new look passed over her face, not an expression really but a pallor, as if she'd seen something she didn't like. Alex turned to see Jay Harrison standing a few feet behind him, heaving deep breaths. Jay was sagging visibly at the chin and shoulders and knees. He looked as if somebody had sucker-punched him on his way in. Unless he was having a heart attack. But he kept catching his breath. Just ran too far too fast, Alex decided, but why?

The other shoe dropped. The doctor sank into a chair. Deborah's color had come back. Her dark brows were drawn together now as one.

"I don't believe this," Jay rasped, then stopped to catch his breath again. "We're missing a marrow sample from the tank."

"Jesus," Deborah said, already on her feet. "Let me get on it. Who did the surgery? Nobody can keep track of anything anymore. I bet it was sent over to the Brigham by mistake."

Alex felt his spine, which had gone rigid at Jay's words, grow supple again. Right, he thought, a mistake. The Brigham and Women's was a major teaching and research hospital somewhere back on the other side of the Dennison toward Huntington Ave. They must also do marrow transplants. Overlapping staffs must make for confusion sometimes.

"No." Jay looked bewildered. "Why can't I get this out?" He banged a fist on the table, which rocked onto two of its legs and then bounced back. "Somebody took it, that's what I mean. For ransom. They want money." Once he'd gotten that much out, Jay seemed to get himself in hand. He used a napkin to dam up the spilled coffee rolling off the table onto his knee. "They called me with a message: no cops, no questions, just the money, tomorrow morning, left exactly where they say. I'll have to go through some channels to get the money. Dan, for a start, and he'll have to go to whoever can authorize Joe Topakian. But she's my patient. I'm just going to keep saying this is a medical decision and I make the call."

He'd gone from disbelief to command very quickly, Alex thought, impressed. Alex himself was still watching a gloved hand pull a thin metal box out of the swirling mist. *Don't fucking spill it,* Alex was saying to the hand.

Jay said, "Deborah, I'm going to need you to run around with whatever paperwork, if you can possibly—"

"Richard's off on a job but I'll call somebody to go stay with Jen."

"And Alex, I need you to help with the ransom. They said one person, alone, and they said the person shouldn't be me."

"Sure," Alex said, without hesitation. "How much ransom?" What he meant was, did these kidnappers seem rational and businesslike in their demands? He didn't consider why he thought of them as kidnappers. If you held somebody's life for ransom, that's what you were.

"Three hundred thousand."

To Alex the hand seemed to hold the box more firmly, more carefully. Somehow this price seemed within reason. A marrow transplant cost the patient or insurer about a hundred thousand, Jay had said on the way up to the unit. Three hundred thousand didn't sound completely out of line.

"Who's the patient?" Deborah asked.

"Linda Dumars."

"Oh, Lord." Deborah grew two pink spots with white centers on her tightened cheeks. "I mean, it would be horrible whoever it was, but . . . She's the one with the two little kids, right? The husband's a doctor, he left them in my office while he was in with you."

"Uh-huh. She—"

"Who's her nurse?" Alex interrupted suddenly.

"Her nurse? Yvonne Price. Why?"

"No, no. I just meant . . ." He meant this Linda Dumars would be the one he'd seen inert, muffled, wrapped in plastic like some freeze-dried food packet waiting for the hot water that would restore her real appearance, texture, motion, life. "This patient's already well into her treatment, is that right?"

"She's just been on three days of chemotherapy and then two days of radiotherapy, yes. Tomorrow is day zero, and effectively zero is what all her counts are going to be. Tomorrow morning is when she's supposed to get the marrow reinfused."

Deborah said, "You're sure it's true?"

"I got the call. I took down the information. I didn't believe it either, so I ran downstairs to check. I didn't tell Edie—the cryopreservation specialist—I just said I wanted to check something in the back. I can't believe that none of us ever thought about security, special keys, a combination lock. Look, let's get going. The fewer bankers Joe needs to pull away from the dinner table, the better off we'll be. He can tell them any goddamn thing he wants except the truth. Alex, we need to leave at three A.M. Dress warm. If you don't mind, I won't tell you where we're going until we go. The fewer people who know, the fewer people to fuck it up."

"Do you think it's Foster?" Alex asked.

"Let's make the trade and get Linda back on schedule. Then we can worry about who took it, okay?"

SIX
Double Vision, Long Drive

At 2:30 A.M. Alex and Meredith sat waiting on the front steps of the house in North Cambridge which they had bought together a year before. Actually they had bought only the second floor and attic, whereas Alex and his daughter had lived as tenants in the first floor apartment for six years before that. That was long before Meredith Phillips came from England and Kim fixed her up with Alex under the guise of finding a mechanic for an ailing car.

"Are you warm enough?" Meredith asked.

"Warm enough," Alex said. The temperature was in the mid-forties and he was quite comfortable in wool socks, blue jeans, a T-shirt, a sweatshirt, and a new wool jacket, a souvenir of the trip the two of them had recently taken to Hudson Bay. He was comfortable except for an icy feeling deep in his bones.

Meredith said, "I was just talking. I'm glad it's a cold place, wherever you're going. The colder it is, the more likely the kidnappers can take good care of what they've got."

"Once it's been frozen the right way, Jay claimed, all you need is a decently insulated container so the liquid nitrogen doesn't heat up and try to expand back into a gas. He said if they

29

were shipping a frozen sample they'd usually use a special double-walled steel tank, a glorified thermos bottle. But in a pinch you could probably use a picnic cooler as long you handled it gently enough."

"I wouldn't want mine in either one. I've been thinking about her a lot. Trying to imagine how she must feel. If I were in her place, I'd feel robbed, defenseless, like a sort of jellyfish with my organs all exposed." Meredith shuddered. She shook her wide shoulders and lowered her eyes. They were direct, thoughtful eyes set in a long, oval face. Meredith always stood straight, enjoyed her height, liked to walk, to ski, to play racquetball at the university where she taught. Even her fingers on her computer keyboard, when Alex sat watching her work, seemed vigorous rather than subtle, determined rather than playful. When she played she played hard.

Alex thought sometimes she loved him for his vagaries, his meanderings, his preference for messing around in his head or with his hands rather than getting straight to the point all the time. Sometimes you loved what reflected you, sometimes you loved what you lacked. What scared Alex when he thought about Linda Dumars living precariously without her bone marrow was the loss of essence, of identity. What scared Meredith was the loss of strength, of physical structure. What scared them both was that, metaphors aside, if those frozen cells were to thaw and die, the patient would die too.

"What about Harrison?" she said. "Does he have enough power to get the money and hand it over without surveillance, without the police?" She sniffed, or maybe sniffled. "I suppose it depends on how many grants he's pulled in."

"I don't know," Alex said. *Come hell or high water I'm not trusting my patient's life to some damn SWAT team,* was what the doctor had said. Alex watched a Toyota Celica, a few years old, turn the corner. Sporty, but kind of low-end-of-the-scale for a doctor. Apparently cars weren't what Jay Harrison liked to spend his money on. "This must be him."

"He," Meredith said, sliding her arm around his waist for an instant. She'd confessed only recently to a longstanding temptation to correct his grammar, a desire she claimed had arisen at about the same time as the temptation to take him by the beard and see what he would feel like to kiss. She'd indulged the second, not the first. Both had to do with her casting him as some kind of American frontier type, Alex suspected. Books about adventurers and explorers had always fascinated her, she said, when she was growing up.

This was one reason why during Meredith's vacation week in mid-March, they'd ridden the single-track Canadian railroad from Winnipeg to Churchill on Hudson Bay. To Alex growing up, Henry Hudson had primarily been the name of a highway leading out of New York City, but now neither he nor Meredith would ever forget the treeless plain alongside the shore, or the vast ice-strewn expanse of bay. As they stood there hand in hand Meredith had explained that Hudson had been one of those explorers who ventured too far, until his crew mutinied and put him ashore to die somewhere not far away. In Alex's past investigations, Meredith had cautioned him about venturing too far, about taking chances just to prove he wasn't any more vulnerable than anyone else. Tonight she hadn't. It seemed that by mutual consent they'd avoided discussing the danger involved in what Alex was about to do.

Now the Celica stopped and Jay Harrison leaned across to open the passenger door. He seemed in a hurry. "Let's go," he said. Meredith stayed the porch steps, watching Alex get into the car. As Jay pulled away from the curb, Alex opened his window to wave good-bye. Meredith nodded back, then rose and went inside.

On Jay's back seat, Alex saw, rested a miniature version of the storage unit he'd seen in the blood bank: a small nitrogen tank linked by a hose to an insulated cooler. Next to it was a canvas mailbag, stuffed full. "Did you get any sleep?" Jay said. Alex felt like another piece of equipment. Jay was checking him for readiness. Thorough, the way you'd want your doctor to be.

Alex shook his head. "That's the money, in the mailbag?"

"As specified. It's full of twenties and fifties. I weighed it; it weighs about thirty pounds. You're going to be carrying it on a beach, I don't know how far. That's another argument for the kidnappers' rationality. They knew how much that many twenties and fifties were going to weigh."

Jay circled the block and drove onto Alewife Brook Parkway, toward the Charles River. Everything was quiet. The night was clear. A lot more stars were out than cars.

"What happens," Alex said, "if we don't get her marrow back?"

"If we don't get it back, we have to try for an allogeneic transplant instead of an autologous—that means we try to find somebody whose marrow is a close enough match, instead of using her own. Sometimes a brother or sister will work, or sometimes you find a match through the national computer data base. But there are a lot of buts. Linda Dumars doesn't have any siblings, I already checked that out. We'll try the donor data bank, but the process takes six weeks, when you're lucky enough to find somebody at all. And after transplant there are still a lot of risks from GVH—graft-versus-host disease. In the meantime . . . well, let's just say a whole lot of things could go wrong. So let's get her marrow back, that's tonight's project. This morning's actually. We're supposed to make the trade at dawn."

"Dawn on a beach," Alex said, "and we're leaving now." Jay had just told him that this exchange was crucial. Where would it happen? Maine? Someplace far out on the Cape? "Will it take us that long, or are we getting there early to set up some kind of trap?"

"No trap. The caller said you're supposed to start walking up the beach from a certain parking lot at sunrise, with the bag over your shoulder. An unknown spot on an empty beach is a tough place to set a trap. We're taking the kidnapper at his word. Or her word, whatever." He'd explained earlier that the caller had used a computer-generated voice, had sat at a keyboard somewhere and typed in the message. You could get the necessary hardware and software for any personal computer, Jay had said.

"I'm supposed to start walking," Alex said. "Is that because the person collecting the money thinks you would recognize them?"

"Or because they want me to think so? All I know is they said it shouldn't be me. Otherwise I wouldn't trust it to anybody else. No heroics, no theatrics, just make the trade. I know the beach, so I can tell you about the terrain anyway. It's in Truro, if you know the area at all."

Truro. Near the end of Cape Cod, the last place before Provincetown. Alex was pleased to have figured the possibilities right. He rolled down his window and looked up at the night sky.

The stars seemed extra twinkly. That was his damn double vision again. He'd had it for three weeks now. When he did highway driving, sometimes he found it more comfortable to shut one eye.

A particular malfunctioning nerve, the neuro-ophthalmologist had explained, caused a particular muscle to fail to align the right eye quite correctly with the left. It could be a virus; that sometimes happened. Considering Alex's history, though, Wagner and the neuro-op had gone for a brain scan and a spinal tap right away. Only a remote possibility, Carol Wagner had assured him. A very remote possibility of metastasis of the lymphoma to the spinal fluid or the brain. The tests had been negative. This wasn't completely conclusive, but it made the remote possibility even more remote. Now there was nothing to do but wait and see whether the double vision went away. Alex supposed he could run this all by Jay for a free third opinion, if conversation flagged and they needed to talk to stay awake.

Jay turned onto Storrow Drive, heading downtown. He'd pick up the Mass Pike in Allston, then the Expressway, then Route 3 following the coast south. He was driving fast. An hour, maybe less to the bridge over the canal. Another hour out the bent arm of the Cape. "What time is sunrise?" Alex asked.

"Five twenty-eight, according to the meteorologists. So we'll be early. It doesn't take a weatherman to know which way the wind blows."

"You weren't a Weatherman or anything? That couldn't be what the blackmail note was about?" The blackmail note might not be connected to the theft, Alex knew, any more than the double vision had to be connected to his disease. But the note was something to hold on to when everything seemed to be just so much guesswork, empty space. If Jay had been hiding something before, maybe he'd come clean about it now.

"No, I wasn't. I told you—no bombs, no kidnappings, nothing like that. Maybe on that trip out West we fantasized about snatching Henry Kissinger, you know, but fantasies are legal the last I heard. Maybe we did a few illegal substances, but I'm not running for office, and even if I was I could say that I'm very, very sorry and anyway those substances never did anything for me. I'm not even running for medical director, for Christ's sake. I'm just a scientist and a doctor, or a doctor and a scientist. I admit to being confused about which order, okay?"

33

"Okay," Alex said. "Sorry." Jay had a right to be touchy tonight. They drove in silence past the left-field wall of Fenway Park, under the Prudential Center, downtown along the old New York Central right-of-way. Foster remained shadowy, as vague as the hand that had pulled Linda Dumars's marrow out of the swirling vapor. Linda Dumars, a shape under plastic, was shadowy too—except for the fact she had two little kids and was married to a doctor, and that Alex could be her, she could be him.

"What do you know about how it got taken?" Alex asked. "Did you find out who's been in and out of the blood bank, or are you keeping completely quiet till we get it back?" He adopted Jay's assumption that this trade was going to happen as planned.

"Nobody keeps track of who goes in and out of there. You saw how we just waltzed in ourselves. We had to go by Edie—she was in the room just outside the cryo room—but she's not always there, she goes out for meetings, lunch, she's got stuff to do in other parts of the blood bank. But yeah, we questioned. So now we've got a long list of names, probably incomplete, of people who did or might or might not've stepped into the back room. Including all the blood bank staff. And the woman that cleans there, who was a substitute, not the regular one today. And the delivery guy from the gas supplier, who came this morning. Not to mention you and me. I argued we could hold off questioning people till we make the trade, but I couldn't get Dan or Sandy to back me on that."

"Who are they?"

"Dan Weinstein is medical director of the transplant unit. Dan and I go back together, I was a fellow under him. Sandy Sorenson's medical director of blood bank. Everything has a medical director who sits in an office; the medical director's always an M.D. Dan's insisting to the high gods that I get to handle this my way, so far."

"So this isn't exactly being kept quiet, but so far no police."

"Not as quiet as I might have hoped. I hope it's quiet enough that we don't piss the kidnapper off. Nobody knows the ransom arrangements; I drew the line there. Fire me later, I said."

Jay let those words hang while he maneuvered in front of a trucker and around the sharp curve that got them up onto the elevated Fitzgerald Expressway, a mass of poorly patched pot-holes over half-exposed steel. On this road there was always lots of traffic, even now. It was scheduled to be torn down before the end of the century, though nobody knew for sure whether the money existed to rebuild the thing underground.

"Doctors think a lot of themselves," Jay said once they were up and doing sixty-five over the ruts. "We think a lot of ourselves because of all the secret shit we know about how the body works, and then we think a lot of ourselves when we forget all that scientific certainty and talk about certain decisions coming down to a hunch. I'm playing a hunch about the kidnapper. Not who they are, but how they think. I'm also playing a hunch that you're the right person to send with the money. Because I can trust you to identify with the patient above anything and any-body else."

You know it and I know it, Alex thought. And maybe too you trust me more than some SWAT team because we seem to share things out of a common past in which helmeted cops and federal agents were definitely not on the same side as us. To the left, out on a point jutting into Dorchester Bay, was UMass, where Meredith taught. The dark buildings, brick on stilts, looked lumpy in the night. Rumor had it, Meredith said, that the fortress design was supposed to discourage student demonstra-tions and building takeovers. The campus had been designed at the cusp of the sixties and seventies. So had the decoration on the next point south, the big gas tank painted with an abstract design by Corita Kent. It remained a matter of debate whether the left edge of the blue stripe was a profile of Ho Chi Minh.

"So," Alex said. "It's a long drive. You never got time to tell me about Foster this afternoon."

SEVEN
Just Because You're Paranoid

"He was driving that van, the way I told you, and he was AWOL, technically a deserter since he'd been gone for a lot more than ninety days. He'd walked off an army base in Germany a few years before, spent most of the time in France, and now he was coming back to test the waters. He was kind of scary-looking at first. I mean, here's this big husky black guy, head shaved, full beard. I had a moment of doubt when he first stopped. Who he is today, what he could be into, I don't have a clue. He could need money to get his kid out of the inner city while the kid's alive and not addicted. There's just too many possibilities and not enough information. In my gut I don't think Foster is the kidnapper. Yet I don't have a shred of data to back that up."

"So just tell me some about that trip," Alex said.

Jay didn't say anything for a while, just drove, as the highway came back down to ground level and veered away from the coast. He kept his thoughts to himself until past Braintree, and then he said, "That trip. You ask me to tell you about riding with Foster and Dee, and all of sudden I start to feel lonely. I start to remember this business about being a mascot again."

"A mascot?"

"No, not really a mascot. I had a job, a function, but . . . See, Dee and Foster picked me up when I was at personal and political loose ends. I'd been working in this printing collective. We printed movement leaflets and posters, newspapers, stuff for antiwar groups and community organizers, the Black Panther Party chapter—were you in Boston then?"

"Not yet," Alex said. "In May of 'seventy-one, I guess I was traveling up and down the west coast. I'd been busted in D.C. a year earlier—after Kent State, Jackson State—if that's a credential. I got thrown out of college, too." He put a sarcastic twist on the words. He was still half-expecting Jay to pull some skeleton out of the closet if he could pass some additional test.

"Oh. Well, I didn't, but after college I worked in this collective, and we worked pretty hard. Half of our customers didn't have any money, we were always looking for quasi-commercial jobs to keep the thing afloat. By the time I'm talking about, though, the operation was on its last legs. I had said I was leaving. Then Dee and Foster said, want to go to California? So I went. It turned out they had a job for me to do."

Workaholic, Alex was concluding. Always some kind of project: printshop, underground railroad. Didn't quite have it in you to be a hippie, Dr. Jay.

"So what was it they wanted?" Alex asked as casually as he could.

"Protective coloration. Like a lizard that can change the color of its skin. Old van, rebuilt as a camper, big black man, white woman with this long blond hair? Cops were pulling over freaks for the hell of it, you know, plus the chance they'd find an ounce or two and chalk up an arrest. Plus here it was this race and sex thing. Foster wasn't hot, I mean nobody was after him, and he had a phony passport that looked good. Still, if he got busted a fingerprint check would show he wasn't really who the passport said.

"So there I was on the shoulder, a kid with long hair and a backpack and a thumb. Dee was driving, and Foster must've said something like, 'Why don't we pick up that hippie so we blend a little better with the landscape, babe?' Whenever Foster got to feeling paranoid—no, that's not fair. Just because you're paranoid doesn't mean they're not out to get you. Whenever he got nervous, he'd ride in the back of the van, on one of the bunks. Dee and I would ride in front, and one of us would drive. So that was one thing. Also I think they each wanted a kind of buffer, 'cause it turned out they'd jumped into this cross-country trip as soon as they met. They both wanted the journey to work and not to come flying apart too soon."

"And when you think about it, you get lonesome. . . ." Alex heard himself sounding like a shrink on automatic pilot, just reflecting back whatever the client said. There were similarities about shrinks and detectives, he'd thought more than once.

"I remember how I felt. Like at night, when they'd get in the van and I'd sleep outside. You can imagine, I was jealous. Not of Foster because Dee was, after all, what, she must have been thirty, which seemed awful old to me then. I was jealous of their situation, though."

"So what else happened on this trip?"

"Oh, we had a good time. We picked up some other hitch-hikers, teenage runaways, so they were around for a while. We got across the country and we didn't get busted after all. We hit the Pacific someplace up in Mendocino County, sneaked across somebody's property and spent a last night there on the beach, toasting the waves, the ocean—though I remember being conscious, too, that Vietnam was what was on the other side."

Alex tried to picture these people, this crew, but so far they were only stick figures Jay was doodling, and Jay's mind didn't seem to be on them anymore. He was doing seventy-five now, as if getting to the beach early would do any good. For the first time, Alex thought to wonder what effect this theft was going to have on Jay's career, his reputation. Up till then he'd focused only on the patient, but that wouldn't be true for the man next to him. When Jay started talking again, he was explaining about his career, but from the other end.

"I stayed out in the Bay Area. I worked on a project for military resisters—I think I said that before. I knew a lot of chemistry from college. I was going to be a research chemist until, you know, Dow, napalm, soured me on that. Anyway, in San Francisco, I worked nights in a medical lab to pay the rent. Eventually I got seduced by the idea of medicine. It seemed very clean and well-intentioned and precise. I got into med school at Cal, and then it was like traveling through a long tunnel where nobody even knows there's a world above, below, or on either side. Once people get into that tunnel, once they invest the time and money and everything, there's not usually any more detours even when they come out on the regular road again. Maybe that's why there's a lot of doctors that are no good with patients. Once you find out, it's too late to go be a disc jockey or a travel agent or stockbroker or whatever it is. Anyway, that's how I got where I am."

"Uh-huh," Alex said. "And does it still seem . . . ?"

"Clean and well-intentioned and precise?" Jay might have been defensive about his choices in that long speech, but now he seemed happy Alex had brought him back to his point. "Not exactly, no. We work miracles, sometimes. Yet a half mile away, in Roxbury, you've got infant mortality rates that rival the Third World. Death Zones, as the medical statisticians say. Poverty, crack, lack of access to prenatal care. In adults you've got treatable cancers and heart conditions that don't get diagnosed until it's way too late. I like what I do. I don't think it's saving the world, unlike colleagues I could name."

"Does that attitude make you unpopular?"

"Yeah, sometimes. But, I get the Center's name in the paper and I bring in grants. Look, I think we better talk about what you're going to do when we get to that beach."

"How well do you know it?" Alex asked. "I don't know Truro much."

"First camping place of the Pilgrims," Jay said, "speaking of the underside of the American Dream. They stole a cache of Indian seed corn, cooked it, and ate it. Didn't know it was the beginning of a trend. But the ocean beaches are wonderful. I've never seen beaches like those anyplace else for the combination of surf and fine sand and big high dunes behind. I own a house, a summer place, there. If the kidnapper did any research he might know that—he, she, they, it. Maybe they know and they're trying to taunt me. Not enough data, again."

"What can you tell me about the layout?" Alex asked.

"Every few miles there's a road access, where there's a hollow, usually, a break in the dune. You're supposed to start where they said, at sunrise, and walk north. The next road is maybe a mile, mile and a half up the beach. Somebody could come ashore from a boat in a dinghy or a kayak, I guess, though the surf is apt to be rough, and it's not usually done. Somebody could come along in a four-wheel-drive, along the beach. They could hike along the beach on foot, or they could climb down from the dune. You'll be all by yourself. From the dune, with a rifle, maybe a good shot could take you out. I don't see why they would, but it's a possibility I thought I ought to raise."

Yeah, now, Alex thought. When it's too late to get anybody else. But it didn't matter. He was going, of course. He thought that Linda Dumars, whoever she was, would do the same for him. "Do I just hand over the money? Or do I demand the merchandise? Do I inspect it? How do I know it's real?"

Jay let out a long sigh, indicating he'd been over Alex's questions in his mind quite a few times.

"You just hand it over. Whatever they give you, don't open it until you get it back to me and this tank. If they don't give you anything, I still don't see how we have any choice. Maybe the idea is we get another call that says the stuff is under a crate of toilet paper in some storeroom in the basement. For the moment, all we do is act in good faith. We do unto others as we'd have them do unto us."

"Listen, Jay," Alex said. "Suppose we don't get it, and you're looking for that matching marrow, and either you take a long time to find it or you don't find it at all. What happens? How long can she live without producing blood components, all of that?"

"Do you remember the Bubble Boy? Well, that was different, he had aplastic anemia, but he lived inside a sterile environment for eleven or twelve years. Somebody in Linda Dumars's situation, debilitated from the side effects of her treatments . . . you know from experience, for instance, what chemotherapy does to the gut. All kinds of opportunistic infections find an easy toehold. Without bad luck, a few weeks shouldn't be a problem. With good luck, a few months, maybe more.

"But if you had to bet . . . ?"

"I already told you, didn't I? I'd put everything I had to wager on what we're doing right now."

EIGHT
A Million Sand Fleas Waking Up

They turned off the highway and followed a narrow, twisting blacktop lane to where it dead-ended in a small parking lot occupied by one pickup truck, its windows covered with dew. Nobody emerged from the truck to greet them, so they zipped their coats and stepped out into the damp salty air. When they got over the top of the dune, the wind came pouring off the Atlantic, cold through Alex's cotton jeans, cold even through the woolen jacket from Hudson Bay. They followed a path that

40

angled down the sandy cliff. The sky was still dark enough to show a few stars overhead.

To the east over the water, the stars were gone. The wind piled the edge of the ocean into wild breakers that darted forward and upward in the leaden waves. This was shipwreck country, or it had been, not long ago. The ocean at night always made Alex feel that here was nature reminding humanity who was boss. Today he didn't need any reminders. There was something foolishly arrogant, if also daring and hopeful, about thinking you could take out somebody's marrow and know you'd be able to put it back.

They sat on the beach and waited for sunrise. Alex didn't find any second thoughts. He sat and watched the breakers settle down as the wind subsided and the sky went from black to dark blue, developing pinkish streamers in the east and turning very pale, ethereal, overhead. The wispy clouds became tinged with red, suggesting coral reefs, outriggers of the continent, first signs of land. The sun rose a red-gold ball, rose very quickly. Alex stood up and hefted the mailbag full of cash.

"Do anything you can think of to put them at ease," Jay advised. "This isn't a trap, and we want them to know it. For your safety, and Linda's, we don't want anybody to overreact."

Alex shouldered the mailbag like Santa Claus. The tide was low now, but high tide must have come all the way to the base of the dune, because the whole beach was wet. Alex kept his shoes on, though earlier he'd imagined himself trekking without them. He'd formed a picture of his trail of barefoot prints, marching north till it met up with a similar trail coming south, sort of like the Union Pacific meeting the Central Pacific at Promontory Point.

He looked at his watch. Just past five thirty. Jay's meteorologists had been right. "See you later," he said.

Jay said, "I'll be right here." Alex started walking, bent over to put the bag's weight on his back, but Jay said, "Wait." Alex turned to see a figure coming down the dune from the lot with a big surf-casting pole. He waited a minute. The man got to the bottom and waved but headed the other way, south, and then stopped and got to work casting his lure out into the water.

"Now I'm late," Alex said. "I better get going."

Bent forward under the bag, it was hard to look ahead.

Periodically he stopped and straightened and shielded his eyes. All he could see was the waves on one side and the dune on the other and the long slowly curving stretch of sand, empty except for gulls, in between. The dune had a red-gold cast to it, the same as the sun but much fainter. The sun made a shimmering gold path on the sea, which everywhere else was a surprisingly light blue. Alex couldn't help but take all this as a good omen—a beautiful start to what would have to be a successful day. As he trudged on, getting warmer, he watched a million sand fleas waking up. At every step their translucent bodies hopped about his shoes. He stuck to the middle of the beach, halfway between the breakers and the dunes. Away from the hollow that held the road, the dunes now towered more than a hundred feet high.

When he'd been walking for ten minutes by his watch, he was sweating. He stopped, lowered the mailbag to the sand, stripped off his wool jacket, and stuffed it in the bag. He thought about the kidnapper, or the kidnapper's contact, watching him reach into the bag to retrieve the jacket before handing the bag over or placing it as directed on the sand. He might appear to be reaching for a weapon. He took the jacket out again, tossing it toward the dunes to collect on his way back.

As the sun rose higher, the clouds were losing their color, turning to white. The concave fronts of the breakers were starting to darken in their own shadows. They looked almost black, like immense hollow logs, dissolving as they broke into bright white foam. Alex wanted Linda Dumars to be able to come here, to see this. Up on the dune he began to notice green, wispy grass, and gray-green leafy plants like desert sage. The sun's path on the water had widened and grown yellower. The sky was a richer blue. It was really day now, not dawn.

"Here I am," Alex yelled. "It's time." Only as his words were drowned did he notice the sound of the surf, which up till then he must have tuned out because it was so constant, like the white noise of the blowers in the transplant unit rooms. He picked up the bag and kept walking, watching the jumping bugs or crustaceans or whatever sand fleas really were. He watched his shoes sink into the damp, clinging sand. Every now and then he looked ahead. As the Cape curved back toward the mainland, the beach curved to the left behind the line of dunes.

In the sharper light, he could see a double image of the cliff formed by his misaligned eyes. *Damn,* he thought, because each day he really expected this problem to disappear, as the neuro-op said it might if it was viral in origin. If the goddamn eyes were car wheels, Alex could adjust camber, castor, toe-in just by adding or subtracting shims until the angle was just right. He wouldn't have to wait or get CAT scans or depend on anybody else.

Suddenly he saw a fishing boat ahead offshore, with a faint light blinking. Way ahead on the beach, he made out what might be two tall poles. No—he looked sidewise and squinted—it was only one. He heard an engine behind him. He turned around, walking backward, watching the vehicle approach. This was an enclosed four-wheel-drive rig, like a Cherokee or a Land Cruiser. Two tall fishing rods extended upward like whip antennae. They threw long shadows up the base of the dune. The vehicle came toward him, the long lancelike shadows traveling beside it.

The car got closer, its growl sending the gulls wheeling and squawking. Jeep Cherokee. It came alongside him, swerving to pass above him, slowing but not stopping. Two guys in caps and nylon jackets, one bearded and one not. The bearded guy, the driver, waved. Alex stopped and hefted the mailbag. The Jeep kept going, though the passenger turned around to stare at Alex and his bag. *I'm in training to be a peddler,* Alex wanted to say. Or *I'm out here collecting seashells and I'm going home to glue them into the largest shell sculpture ever devised by human hand.* He willed the driver to make rapid tracks up the beach so as not to scare off the contact. Or else to decide that all was well, the coast was clear, and swing back around to come to a stop in front of him and complete the deal.

The Jeep kept going. Alex stopped, thinking he might be near the right spot but the vehicle might have thrown the timing off. Had the kidnapper carefully plotted time and distance, like a NASA engineer plotting where and when a space probe ought to meet its target? Or, at the other extreme, was this all a wild-goose chase, a test, a tease? Alex put down the bag. He planted his feet and swung his hips and arms. He stretched and, deliberately but faster than usual, moved through the opening positions of the t'ai chi form. He wasn't a beach lover—that was, he didn't like lying still and baking in the sun—but he did like the beach off-season, and he did like being alone on a beach were he could do his stuff without an audience. The t'ai chi, like his investiga-tive sideline, was something he'd gotten into after his diagnosis—something he'd come to value both for its own qualities and because it seemed to help keep him alive.

When he got to White Swan Spreads Wings, he was facing the cliff, which here was fringed with long grass at the top. One well-aimed shot was all it would take, and the contact could collect the money, no trade and no questions asked. But the operating assumption was that the kidnapper wanted to limit the crime to extortion, or whatever the hell this was in a legal sense. Alex held the position, balancing on his right foot, his left toe just touching the sand, one hand up and the other down, until the intrusive vehicle was nearly out of sight.

The boat was closer, clearly a fishing boat, not trailing any dinghy to bring anybody ashore. His watch said twenty minutes past sunrise. He stopped after White Swan, swung his arms a little while, and then picked up the bag and walked again. He plodded, switching shoulders with the sack, bending over and keeping his head down. He passed an old wooden staircase, half collapsed, that led up to the top of the dune. Jay had said there were houses up there, and some ruined shacks. This was national seashore, federal land, had been since the fifties. But some pri-vate property remained, grandfathered as part of the deal when the park was created.

By Jay's estimate of how long it would take, Alex thought, he must be almost halfway to the next beach access now. He looked ahead and saw the pole he'd seen before. It wasn't so tall, not as tall as himself, but it was stuck into a sort of ridge, a place in front of which the waves had worn away the beach. The ridge ran out to a sandbar sticking into the sea. Opposite this, on the dune, a second bleached, half-ruined stairway came down. Some-body was standing on the steps, about fifty feet up, waving. He waved back. The figure stopped waving and then flung some-thing in an arc down onto the beach. Alex trudged toward it, angling up the sand. It was a bottle, a green bottle. It had landed about ten feet from the base of the steps—from what had once been the base of the steps, now just the tops of two posts rising out of the sand.

It was a green wine bottle, corked. Alex put down his bag of money and picked up the bottle. Somebody had a sense of humor. There was a rolled message inside. And somebody was careful. They'd found a way to communicate without getting too close. He looked up at the figure on the steps. It was a woman, in a black wetsuit with red stripes down the side. She looked like a resort advertisement, a good figure, long blond hair, shades over her eyes. They were reflective shades, flashing yellow in the sun. Twisting the cork out of the bottle, Alex shook out the note, neatly rolled and secured with a rubber band.

Leave the bag at the bottom of the steps, it said, *and walk away, down to the water. Don't try to come close. When I get back up where I am now, come back where you are.* The note had been typed by a dot-matrix printer, anonymous as could be. Alex did what it said. He walked down to the edge of the ocean. As an added touch, he rolled up his pants and took off his shoes and socks and stood where breakers would wash over his feet.

The cold brought shock and instant pain. Late April, no time to be in the water. Why was she wearing a wetsuit? Could she have swum ashore from the boat? She was leaping down the dune over the buried steps. The legs of the suit came to her ankles. Her feet were bare. She moved easily, but Alex couldn't guess her age. She had to work to drag the mailbag back up to her perch, where the stairs were not yet buried in the sand.

Alex approached the bottom of the steps. She seemed to be checking the money. Then she reached down in the sand beside the steps, came up with another bottle, threw it. She was left-handed. Alex walked over to where the bottle landed. The woman in the wetsuit picked up the bag and started climbing.

This cork was in tighter. Jay hadn't thought to issue him a corkscrew. The contact method seemed amateurish but sensible. Finally Alex worked the cork loose. The message read, *Dig under the pole.* Alex took off his sweater, realizing he was drenched again with sweat. He tried to pull the pole out. It was smooth, not driftwood but a milled piece, with some remaining flakes of red and white paint. It had to be buried deep, because it wouldn't budge. Had the woman buried it, early this morning, or just made use of the fact that it was here? More important, did it mark where the treasure was? Digging in a circle around the pole with his hands, he uncovered a blue nylon strap. By the time he unearthed the cooler itself, the woman in the wetsuit had disappeared over the top of the dune. In her absence he noticed the crashing sound of the waves again.

NINE
More Genie Smoke

Alex found the going a lot easier with the little cooler riding on his hip than it had been with the big mailbag on his back. The cooler was of a size to hold a six-pack and a few sandwiches. Alex fingered the hard plastic exterior, dark blue, which ought to cover a rigid core of insulating polystyrene foam. The plastic was cool but not freezing to the touch. A thin white line of frost had formed where the top of the container met its body. So far so good, he hoped. He jogged down the beach with the cooler hanging from its strap on his left shoulder and his hand bracing it against his right hip. He jogged not pell-mell but steadily, as if his friends were waiting at the picnic and he was bringing the beer. He stopped only to tie his sweatshirt tighter around his waist.

When he got to where he'd left his jacket, he paused to pick it up and catch his breath. Only then did he notice how different everything was. The bits of cloud looked pure white now, the dune yellow, minus its gold cast. The sun on the water was an ordinary yellow too. A lone long-necked goose flew overhead, and a few crows pecked at something near the bottom of the cliff. Far ahead a beachcomber came toward Alex, then stopped to examine something swirling in the low tide. Alex jogged some more, slowed to a walk, waved at the beachcomber, and finally broke into a run when he saw Jay. By the time he reached the doctor, he was panting hard.

"I haven't messed with it," was all he said. "It seems full enough and cold enough to me."

"No trouble?" Jay asked, taking the cooler and giving it a

very slight experimental shake. Should I have handled it like glass, Alex wondered. If so, he'd still be halfway back along the beach with the day continuing to warm up. Jay held the cooler in both hands as he climbed the path up the sand to the parking lot. Three more cars had joined his, and the pickup was gone. Alex watched him unlock the front door, reach to open the back one, and then fiddle with a knob on the nitrogen supply tank. From the car floor Jay pulled up a pair of heavy gloves and a pair of metal tongs like the ones in the blood bank.

"Okay," he said. "Let's see." He put on the gloves and snapped open the latches that held the top of the beach cooler. A wisp of steam appeared along the rim. Not steam, Alex corrected himself. What had Jay called it? Vapor. Alex leaned over Jay's shoulder and felt the cold. "Get back," Jay said. "This stuff can burn your skin if it splashes or boils up fast."

Worse could've happened, Alex thought, but he pulled his head out of the way. Jay lifted off the top in a swirl of that genie smoke and reached in with the tongs. Alex craned his head over Jay's shoulder again.

"Get back, damn it," Jay said again. Then he said, "What?" and groaned. He turned and pushed Alex out of the way and poured the hissing liquid onto the asphalt, where it didn't stay liquid very long.

With the tongs, Jay was holding a plastic bag about the right size, but he wasn't rushing to get it safely into the freezer in the back seat. When the vapor cleared Alex saw the bag was empty. No, it wasn't empty. It contained something white, a note. Another fucking note, again typewritten. Alex groaned too. He felt kicked in the gut. He felt teased, foolish, duped, and drained.

"What's it say?"

"Wait," Jay said, but Alex couldn't wait. He grabbed for the bag, only realizing at the last minute that the plastic was all cracked, shredded, from being handled while frozen. Jay pulled it away. "Jesus," he said, "let the damn thing thaw."

Alex dropped his hand, sat down on the pavement where the puddle of liquid nitrogen had just been. Back here, in the hollow behind the top of the dune, the sun was just peeking over the wispy grass that grew out of the sand. Sunrise all over again, this time heralding a more frightening and difficult day. "Sorry," he said. "Read it to me, okay?"

"Yeah. It's, um, it's a poem I guess. Rhymes and verses. Promises delivery in two days. But it doesn't sound too . . . clearheaded." Jay's brow came down in that visor again.

"Read it, okay?"

"Yeah. Sorry. It goes like this." Jay read in a singsong rhythm, and shakily:

> "A bone that has no
>   marrow
> what ultimate for that?
> It is not fit for table,
> for beggar or for cat.
>
> A bone has obligations,
> a being has the same.
> A marrowless assembly
> is culpabler than shame.
>
> You've met your
>   obligations,
> you've handed me the sack.
> Two more days from now,
> You'll get the marrow back.
>
> But no police, no dragnet,
> Nothing that isn't pretty.
> If you err, I swear,
> I'll feed it to my kitty."

Alex swallowed, a dry swallow. No, it didn't sound clearheaded. The first part made no sense that he could follow. The second part felt very dangerously flip. "That's all?"

"There's a little sketch. In pencil." Jay held the letter out to Alex with the tongs. "Don't touch," he said.

The sketch was of a stick figure. Alex knew he'd been thinking about stick figures recently but couldn't remember when. The stick figure had a horizontal line for the body, four legs, a round head with pointed ears. Below the head was a bowl, a flat oval with a semicircle below. In the bottom of the bowl was a splash of brown, either a good imitation of dried blood or else the real thing. Next to that, in block letters, the single word MEOW.

DAY ZERO

TEN
The Snowman With a Club

Linda Dumars knew it meant trouble when Yvonne looked at Dr. Harrison that way. It was the look you used when the sauce doesn't thicken, when the car doesn't start. The look that says come on, hurry up, don't poop out on me now. She couldn't understand why Yvonne should look at Harrison that way. Unless there was something wrong—something important that he needed to hurry up and do. It turned out there was nothing he could do, it was just something she wanted him to hurry up and say.

Before she knew that, Linda pushed the button that raised the upper section of her bed. This made her feel like a quadriplegic, controlling her movement with motors, but that was how a fancy hospital bed worked. She was benefiting from a marvelous technology and shouldn't complain about small things that might be overdone. Temporary, temporary, she told herself sternly. It's all temporary. I get to walk out of here. Thirty days, forty days, I start to be my own woman again.

The doctor looked pouchy. He looked as if he'd been up all night. He really looked like that, it wasn't just his face being filtered through her own heavy-lidded eyes. She thought, I don't care. I'm too tired and I hurt too much to care about why you were up all night.

Today was her day, Day Zero, the day her charts would all bottom out but also the day all the variables should start to climb back up. Predictably, like a sine curve. She'd been dosed and zapped beyond what the body was designed to take. She'd felt as nauseous as the drunkest and most seasick she'd ever been, and as weak as the most flu-sick and hung over. Right now she had tubes giving her blood products, tubes giving her antinausea medicine, catheters sewed into her chest and another coming out of her bladder. Besides everything else, posttreatment they needed to give her insides a good hosing out. Fine. All fine. Because today she'd start being herself again. She wouldn't feel any better, but that wasn't the point. She'd get five long fat syringes each filled with what would look like colored water injected into her central venous line. She pictured how it had looked on the video. So, she thought, let's get on with it, Doctor. I don't care about your problems today. I don't care that you're hung over. As long as your thumb can still push that plunger, those five successive plungers, that's all you need to do.

The doctor still hesitated, so she picked up the plastic sponge lollipop thing and ran it around the inside of her mouth, so dry and sore, in case she was going to have to talk. Let's get going, she thought. Let's get counting. Kevin, next door, was already on day eleven. Kevin already had his counts coming up. Not that she'd ever met Kevin in the flesh. She'd never touched him, barely seen him in fact. All the staff on the unit had seen them both, touched them both, could usually see them both at the same time. But the two of them pushed buttons and talked on the telephone. Kevin was a godsend. Only she wanted to catch up with Kevin, not to be always a week and a half behind.

"Linda," the doctor said. His voice was taut. "We've got a problem that's going to delay the reinfusion—*delay,* not prevent. I'm going to tell you the truth. . . . We don't have your marrow right now. Someone took the specimens and is holding them for ransom. We've paid the ransom. They've responded and promised your specimens will be returned unharmed. I don't know

52

what else to say. This is—it's something that just never occurred to us. It will never happen again."

For a minute Linda Dumars simply went someplace else. An exact place, a place she had once actually been. She'd already picked this spot, days ago, as the place to visualize when she was in trouble, when she needed to be somewhere in time before now, somewhere far outside this machine-laden cocoon.

She went to a high pass in the Cascade Mountains. She knew it although she couldn't remember its name. The clouds blew through this pass, so that sometimes she stood in nothing but murk and fog. She couldn't see anything. Her feet rested in a snowbank left over from the past winter, that was all she really knew. But sometimes the clouds were gone and she could see that she was standing in a saddle with deep lush valleys below and rocky peaks on each side.

It had been a long time since she'd actually stood there, at that pass in the Cascades. She'd stood there, holding hands with a man—not Tom her husband, a different man, before Tom, before the kids were born. That had felt symbolic, earlier this week, noticing she'd picked a place with a different man.

She felt a hand on hers now, Yvonne's. She shrank from it, and she squeezed it. Nobody was supposed to hold hands with her, not here, touching was supposed to be kept to a minimum, only what was absolutely necessary, even by medical personnel. She tried to stay on top of the pass. She'd told Yvonne about this pass, and Yvonne had nodded and said it sounded nice, she wished she could see it sometime. She hadn't meant it that way, but it made Linda understand that Yvonne had never been any-place like that, perhaps had never had the chance. Now Yvonne's hand tightened on hers because someone had *taken her marrow?* Some abominable snowman, some Bigfoot had come up behind her out of the fog and clobbered her with a massive club.

"What?" she said. Not because she hadn't heard. "What?" She heard her voice sound not like her own voice, but like a scared mouse's squeak. She saw her children. It was morning. Tom would be getting them in the car and taking them to school. She couldn't see them clearly because she didn't know the weather, what they'd have on. She felt Claire stamp her foot, and heard her say, "What do you *mean* Mom has to stay in the hospital forever?" She saw Nicky look away, close his eyes.

"Somebody went to the tank and removed the frozen marrow in its case." Once he'd gotten started the doctor didn't hesitate anymore. Really she wished he'd slow down, because she still wasn't quite here and she certainly wasn't up to her ability. But now he was rattling things off, like a text that didn't give you a chance to assimilate each point, each conclusion, before going on to derive the next. "They called me yesterday, after your last treatment, and informed me it was gone. They asked for money, and the money was delivered this morning. What they've done so far convinces me they understand what they've got and how to take care of it. They say they'll return it within two days."

Linda said, "They say."

"I suspect they feel they need that time to get away, or to process the money somehow so it can't be traced. Then they'll return your marrow. In the meantime, we'll take a few extra precautions."

Precautions. Yesterday the room had been sterilized while she was down getting radiation. Then Yvonne had given her a sterile bath and fed her bowel prep. Bowel prep was oral antibiotic, foul-tasting fluid that had her throwing up into one bed pan while she was shitting into another like a newborn not yet able to produce a solid stool. This morning she'd woken up to the drone of the blower, like a machine breathing for her, an iron lung. For a month nobody was supposed to dare to kiss her, touch her face, bring her flowers even, because in flowers there were too many things alive. What more precautions? Fuck precautions. What mattered was somebody getting her goddamn marrow back.

She knew Dr. Harrison was waiting for her to say something he could gauge her reaction by. Her stomach heaved, but there was nothing left in it to come up. Stop it, she told herself. There was the image of the snowman, coming out of the fog to club her from behind. She concentrated on the feel of Yvonne's hand. She liked Yvonne, she trusted her, but the reassurance was automatic, part of the job. She needed to talk to Kevin, to Kevin who had been through a war. You lost my goddamn *marrow,* Doctor, she wanted to scream at this man standing over her now. She wanted to shout and shake him. He searched her with his pale blue eyes and tried to reassure her with a poor attempt at a smile.

That moved her, for some reason. Actually it was a good attempt at a smile, it just didn't succeed was all.

"Do you have any idea who took it?" Linda asked in practically her real voice. She marveled at how cool she sounded. Had she had this nightmare, imagined this possibility? She knew she'd had one in which the line came loose from her vein, and the marrow dribbled incontinently to the floor. "Was it just for money, is that what you really think? Or is somebody mad at the hospital? Somebody whose—who somebody they loved, you didn't save?"

People did that, that was a story that showed up in the paper, men stormed into hospital lobbies with rifles after their father, their son died. But this was more sophisticated. A hand reaching into a tank. The snowman's hairy hand, shoving the marrow into its hungry mouth. No. A human hand, calculating. Calculating money, or calculating hurt?

Linda Dumars was a mathematician. She worked for an insurance company, she developed models for calculating injury and survival rates. Even now, some part of her was able to weigh the possibilities, coolly, while another part tried to fight off the snowman and reach for her children and reach for Tom but also fight him off at the same time.

"I don't know," the doctor said. "We're trying to figure that out. All I can say is so far they act as if they don't mean you any harm."

"Yes," she said. All he could say was nothing, so he might as well get lost. "Thank you for telling me. I'll be okay. I think I want you to leave me alone."

"I'm leaving you my home number," he said, "you can call me anytime, here or there, or through my beeper. I'm sorry this happened, but it's going to be all right." He watched her for a minute, then turned and went through the portal. She called it the portal. The looking glass that didn't reflect but like Alice's was a way into a different world.

"Bowel prep in a few minutes," Yvonne said, businesslike. She waited for Linda to relax the grip on her hand, then turned to go too, pausing to check the drips, the stack of bedpans, and whatever else she checked among the array of instruments and implements and tubes. "I'll be right back."

Linda let the nurse go. She got herself ready to swish and

swallow the foul preparation that cleaned out her mouth, her throat, her stomach, intestines. She needed to get herself together, to figure out all the possibilities about why this could be happening. No matter what, she told herself, it's temporary. No matter what, you're going to walk out of here your own woman again.

She'd already come up with the possibility that it was someone with a grudge against the hospital. In that case she was a random victim. The other extreme: it could be somebody who wanted to hurt her, personally, even to kill her. Someone who wouldn't mind making some money at the same time. Enough money, say, to buy him pleasures that would make him forget what he'd done. Enough money to buy Claire and Nicky substitute mothers galore. This was the only person she could think of who might want to kill her, who at times certainly did want to kill her. Tom.

This isn't happening, Linda Dumars thought. I'll wake up.

It didn't work. She tried a more limited denial. *Nobody can kill me,* she told herself. Not easily. Not without a fight.

When Yvonne came back she swished and swallowed the bowel prep without protest, managing to keep most of it down. Die, you organisms, she commanded. Get you before you get me.

ELEVEN
Dee

Alex sat in Meredith's office and pushed buttons on her phone. The new phone system had cost upwards of a hundred thousand dollars, Meredith said, at a time when budget cuts were driving tuition higher and students and faculty away. After a few tries, Alex figured out he needed to push the send-additional-digits button before he entered his credit card number. Probably there was a way to make the phone's memory store this number so he wouldn't have to enter it for each call, but he couldn't find a user's manual in a quick search of Meredith's desk. He didn't want to search further because, among other things, he didn't want to read the job application letters that would be someplace around. Given the fiscal crisis, there wasn't likely to be a tenured position for her here in either English or Women's Studies. So she'd started sending her résumé all over the country, and back to England too.

"Apply now, pay later," Meredith had said. "It's insurance, really. Maybe I'll get a job someplace else in Boston. Maybe I'll drive a taxi and write my novel. We'll see." The domestic implications of a job elsewhere were clear, and there wasn't much new to say about that. It would be hard for Alex to move because he split custody of Maria with Laura, his ex-wife. If Alex really wasn't interested in having another child, it might be hard for Meredith to stay. She was past thirty-five now and needed to make up her mind.

For all these reasons Alex would have preferred to be sitting in the converted VW Bug bucket seat mounted on a hinged swivel base in his own shop. There he could lean back and put his feet on his own cluttered desk, snooping into the lives of strangers and for the moment leaving Meredith to live her own. But he'd wanted to catch her after her first class and tell her what had happened on the beach. And he'd wanted to know what she made of the poem, if that's what the note was.

He'd told her what worried him about the note: not the two-day delay, so much, but the style in which it was conveyed. It had a craziness, something in the odd juxtapositions and the singsong rhymes, the sudden veering from the abstract to the concrete. He felt that the person who wrote that note might, if thwarted or frustrated, make good on a promise to serve up the tasty, bloody substance as a treat for a hungry pet.

"Say them again," Meredith had said. "The words on the note." She'd brushed the red hair back over her right shoulder and looked out the window at nothing, listening. Alex had known she was trying to find something she could get hold of in this frightening tale. That was a trait they had in common—wanting to find the piece of a situation, a text, or a car that they knew what to do with. If you found a part you knew what to do with, you could start from there. "I don't think it shows the kidnapper's state of mind entirely," Meredith had concluded. "I

57

think at least part of it shows Emily Dickinson's state of mind. I'll check as soon as I get out of my ten o'clock class."

Alex punched the last digit and put his mental picture of Meredith aside as a woman somewhere in Baltimore, Maryland, answered the phone.

"My name is Alex Glauberman," he said into the handset for the second time, "and I'm a research assistant to Dr. Harrison of the Dennison Center for Cancer Research here in Boston. We're doing a longitudinal retrospective study of the incidence of certain cancers among certain populations. I'm trying to track down a member of one of our sample groups who was enrolled at your college. Paul Foster is his name. The community relations office referred me to you."

"I see. Now, what class was he enrolled in, please?"

"I don't have that information exactly, for some reason. The notes I was given just say he first enrolled in the early or middle sixties, I'm afraid."

"Just a moment," she said. She worked in the alumni records office at Morgan State University, an institution whose name was vaguely familiar to Alex, possibly because some pro football or basketball player had come from there. Morgan State had been upgraded from college to university some years ago, community relations had told him. By whatever name, the place was where Jay Harrison recalled that Foster had at least temporarily been enrolled. Foster had gone to school there, or somewhere like that, until a brush with the police had landed him in front of a judge who'd made him choose between the army and jail.

When the woman came back on the line she said, "Now, tell me again whom you said you're working for?" Her voice was soft, southern, and African-American, Alex thought.

"Dr. H. J. Harrison. He's an associate professor at Harvard Medical School and an attending physician at the Dennison Center for Cancer Treatment and Research. I can give you his direct line, if you'd like to call him or his secretary to confirm this. If you could just give us an address, so we can send Mr. Foster a questionnaire. It will be entirely his option whether or not to reply."

"Just a minute," she said again. Alex sighed, but he knew that a mixture of patience and pressure was the key here. That

58

combination came easily to him, because it was a good mechanic's stock-in-trade. Especially when you dealt, as Alex increasingly did, with older cars on which the threads of every bolt grew more and more rusted in. Owners didn't want to hear that he'd busted a bleeder valve or brake adjuster in a vain effort to get it loose. Many such parts could be hard to find, or had to be ordered from a distributor who might be backed up for weeks. Whether he broke the part or the part wore out on its own, the customers wanted to hear that he could rebuild it for them, and soon. More and more he'd been having to handcraft things, to work wonders with his little bench lathe, to change the shape of a wiper motor brush with layers of epoxy, to concoct a new window lifter out of wood when the old one rusted out.

He was putting pressure to bear now, as patiently as he could. As for tools, Jay was probably right that nothing could match a title, an unimpeachable purpose, and a dash of medical jargon delivered in a confident, entitled way. The alumni records staffer came back and said, "I don't have any record of a Paul Foster graduating in those years. I have a Paul J. Foster in 1955 and Paul O. Foster in 1970. And a Pauline Foster, in 'eighty-three."

"No," Alex said. "I don't think any of those are right. It's possible he didn't graduate, or came back and graduated later, in the seventies . . ."

"I told you the only graduates I've got, sir. I don't have any information on students that didn't get their degrees. If you want to try the registrar . . ."

"Please."

She tried to transfer him but ended up cutting him off, so he had to enter all those digits again. The voice at the registrar's office sounded older and more suspicious and gave no sign of being impressed by Dr. Harrison's affiliation. It insisted that only transcripts were available, that copies could be sent only by mail, that no information could be given over the phone. Also any requests had to be signed by the student. "So I don't see how you expect me to find somebody for you. I don't know who told you to talk to me."

"Alumni records. Could you please transfer me back?"

This time at least the call went through. He repeated his story to alumni records, got put on hold again, got his same informant back, and settled for the address of Paul O. Foster, class of '70, now residing in Pikesville, Maryland, which was a suburb of Baltimore, she said. "Is your man Paul O.?" she asked him.

"All I've got is Paul, no initial," Alex complained. "I don't know who puts these samples together in the first place, they don't seem to do much of a complete job. We'll just try sending Paul O. the questionnaire, I guess."

"And the questionnaire, what will it want to know?"

"Whether he's come down with any kind of cancer."

"So it makes his day, right, if he gets to say no?"

"Yes," Alex said, "It makes his day. Thanks a lot, really." But he knew that Paul O. was not his man, because according to Jay the right Paul Foster had been AWOL in France that year. He pressed disconnect and then tried directory assistance in the Baltimore area code. Eventually, Jay Harrison would get billed for all this, as he would for all the time Alex was devoting to this business instead of the shop.

"I say go for it," had been Jay's reaction when Alex asked whether to pursue what he'd originally been hired for or to wait. "No cops, nothing like that, but if it really was Foster, then he tipped me off himself, and he shouldn't panic at a gentle, negotiating-type approach."

Once he'd gotten over his initial shock, Jay had again been determinedly upbeat. "I'd do the same thing if I were the kidnapper," he'd said between bites in the coffee shop where they stopped to refuel. He'd gestured with the bitten-off arc of his doughnut as he made his point. "I'd buy a little time to launder the money or get out of the country or whatever I had to do. To buy time, you have to seem like a credible threat. The note sounds kind of unbalanced, but the procedure was careful as all hell. The contact stayed too far away for you to grab her, and I doubt that she's the kidnapper, I doubt she knows where the stuff is hidden at all. Too easy for you to disable and capture her, if you were an undercover cop with a gun. Plus the site was well chosen. Up there is scrubby woods and beach plum thicket, honeycombed with old sand roads. By now the money's either buried or taken to a house or riding in somebody's trunk miles ahead of us. My hunch is still to take them at their word, but I

60

don't like doing nothing any more than you do. It never hurts to hedge your hunches, in a careful way."

Directory assistance provided numbers for five Paul Fosters—one of them Paul O.—and three P. Fosters, too. This time the longitudinal study was going to involve a sample of students exclusively from Morgan State.

"Morgan State?" the first man to answer said. "What are you, kidding me? Huh?"

"Excuse me?" Alex said.

"Morgan State? You not only got the wrong guy, you got the wrong color too. You're calling from Boston to ask me did I go to college at Morgan State? Geez, you're wasting somebody's money. And why was that again?"

"We're following a particular group to see how many might've developed different kinds of cancer over the next twenty years."

"Well, if I was the one you want, I'd be telling you, 'Yo, mind y'own mu-fuckin' business, bro.' " The man's laugh faded slowly. "No offense," he added. "I'm seeing you as a white man, but no offense if you're not."

Alex said, "Thank you for your time, sir," and hung up.

Two other numbers gave him reactions that were equally baffled, though different in tone. If nothing else, by this time Alex had learned it was uncommon for white people to attend Morgan State. Two more respondents gave him simple nos, one hung up on him, and three didn't answer. He tried Paul O. in Pikesville for the hell of it and got an answering machine. He decided to put Foster aside and see whether he could get anywhere with Dee. Maybe Dee had stayed in touch with Foster. Maybe they were on each other's Christmas card lists. Abandoning Foster, he felt both disappointed and relieved. If he'd reached the man, then Linda Dumars's life might again have depended on Alex's finesse.

No Dee Sturdevant, however, was listed on the shores of San Francisco Bay. Her name wasn't really Dee; originally, Dee was short for Double, according to Jay. Her first and middle names started with the same letter, though Jay couldn't remember what. Alex went through his Dennison Center spiel and asked the operator to look for anything like Carol C. Sturdevant or Penelope P. The operator was willing but came up empty.

Alex tried the San Francisco school department and eventually ended up with the municipal employees' pension fund. Yes, the clerk at the pension fund said, they had current addresses of anyone that had any rights, if the employee or ex-employee kept them informed. But they couldn't divulge it. Why didn't Dr. Whoever send them the questionnaire, and they'd pass it on?

"Well, he told me he wants addresses," Alex said. "It's something about the statistics, the sampling procedure. He needs to know exactly how many get sent out for sure, and whether they reach the person or get returned by the post office. I know you have rules, other agencies have said the same as you. I could have the boss call your supervisor, if that would help . . ."

"Look, wait a minute, why don't I see if we've got her at all. Before we get into any federal cases, okay?"

"Okay," Alex said. "That's Sturdevant, Dee."

"What department?"

"Um, she was a teacher, the last we know, though that's about twenty years ago."

"Board of ed. Hold on, let me put that in. Okay, nope, no Dee, D-e-e."

"That could be a nickname, maybe Delores . . . ?" Once she'd gotten involved in the search, Alex hoped, she'd be willing to scan the records for alliterations too.

"Sure, Delores, Deanna, Desiree—where'd you get this name in the first place, out of somebody's address book?"

"Worse. It's a sample of kids from a particular neighborhood. You know, where there's apparently an unusual incidence of certain kinds of tumors, maybe from the water supply. We're relying on the memories of people who used to live there, what they last heard. It could be important, though, in terms of people being able to get their medical bills paid, if it turns out there were toxic wastes involved." The story was false, but that didn't bother Alex much. The story could very well be true.

"Oh, I got you. Well, don't tell anybody I gave this out, but let me see what I can do. Nope, I got a Jacob Sturdevant, down in San Diego now, and Agnes Amelia Sturdevant, still up here. That's the only ones from board of ed. If I was Agnes, though, I might call myself anything when I was a kid."

"Can I beg you for her telephone number? Agnes Amelia?

Just to check whether she's the right one. If she's not I'll have to keep searching for the right one, that's the thing."

"You got it. If she is the right one, I hope she turns out to be okay."

"Me too," Alex said. "It gets depressing, tracking down sick people."

"Yeah. I can imagine." She gave him both the phone number and the address and wished him luck. Alabama Street, San Francisco. Alex tried but failed to remember where that was—if he'd ever known. His own San Francisco memories were mostly vague and suffused with nostalgia, though they circulated like the current in an electromagnet, creating a field that always made him want to go back. He called directory assistance yet again and worked his way up to somebody who was willing to punch in the number and see what name came up, though not without calling Dr. Harrison's office to double-check. The number for Dee was listed to a Roger Giddings, but at the correct address.

Alex called the number, almost giving up on the tenth ring. The voice that suddenly answered was female and annoyed. If Dee had been thirty then, she'd be fifty now. The exasperated "Hello?" didn't sound fifty.

"Hi," Alex tried without too much hope. "Could I please speak to Dee?"

"Mom's at work. Can I take a message?"

Okay, Alex thought, let's hear it for Mom. "Is there any way I can reach her? This is important."

There was a hesitation, followed by, "Who's this?"

"My name is Alex Glauberman. She wouldn't know my name, but Jay Harrison referred me to her. He's a doctor. It's about a patient of his. It's kind of urgent. We need to locate a man named Paul Foster, and we thought she might know where he is. If she doesn't, we need to try some other way."

"A doctor? A patient? You sure you're looking for the right person? Who did you ask for?"

"Dee Sturdevant. If that's your mother, could *you* call her at work and ask her to please call me. I'm in Boston. She can call me collect."

"Okay," Dee Sturdevant's daughter said, sounding more friendly if only because she now had a way out of this conversation and back to whatever it had pulled her away from. *"Sí, como no?* What's your number?" Alex gave it to her. "Bye."

A half hour later, Dee Sturdevant called back. She said she remembered these names he'd dangled in front of her daughter. She wanted to know what the hell this was all about.

"I'm working for Jay Harrison," Alex said, "I'm sorry to disturb your daughter and to disturb you at work. I'm hoping you might be able to help me reach Paul Foster for him."

"Pardon my up-front-ness," Dee said, "but you sound like a telephone solicitor reading off his crib sheet. I don't need a Sears charge card, and I'm not looking for a new long-distance phone company, no. If you were a phone solicitor, by the way, I would have hung up on you now. But I haven't. In fact, I called you. So, once more, whoever you are, what's this about?"

Alex gambled. He couldn't use the longitudinal study ploy, nor did he want to tell her the real story over the phone. Telling the real story amounted to accusing her ex-boyfriend of a life-threatening extortion, making this accusation over a tenuous wire connection she could easily break. "If you know how to contact him, I'll fly out today and tell you in person, how about that?"

"You'll *fly out today?* From Boston?"

"Uh-huh."

"Then this must be important, no matter how bogus it sounds."

"It is, I promise." He calculated the flying time to California and corrected for the time change. "I could get there this evening, tonight. You *do* think you could find him if you decided to? Or you could at least give me a lead I could follow up?"

"Are you telling me what I think, or asking me? Oh, all right, yes. I wouldn't put you through this if I didn't think I have an address for him as of a few years ago. But my product doesn't come with any guarantees."

Meaning, Alex thought, that if his reasons weren't good enough, even if he had some way of pressuring her, that address would turn out to be a dead end. If she liked his reasons, at the other extreme, maybe she could take him right to Foster, even tonight, if he lived out there.

"Of course," he agreed. "Should I, uh, come to your house?"

"Do that. Twelve-thirty-one Alabama, in the Mission, just below Twenty-fourth."

TWELVE
My Marrow Burning

It was only a minor triumph, finding Dee, but Alex figured Jay would be cheered by any kind of triumph—and so might Linda Dumars, depending on what Jay was letting her know. However, when Alex called, Deborah McCarthy told him Jay couldn't be reached, beepers or no beepers, because he was in conference with the high gods. She assured him, though, that she'd call Jay's travel agent right away to authorize a round trip to San Francisco on Jay's account. "Save your taxi receipts and so on," she added. "And good luck." When Alex got off the phone with the travel agent, Meredith came in, fist pumping in front of her chest. That meant she'd had a minor triumph too.

"Emily Dickinson," she said. "The first half is Dickinson. All that up through the 'culpabler than shame' is the first two stanzas of one of her poems. She didn't title her poems, so 'The Bone That Has No Marrow' is more or less its name. After the first two stanzas the kidnapper seems to have gone off on his or her own. How did you do in your research? Did you find your man?"

Alex told her about not finding Foster, about finding Dee, and about his plane.

"I'll drive you then. Let's go."

The airport sat on a peninsula directly across the harbor, but the drive involved fighting the traffic back into town and then through the Callahan tunnel. Halfway through the tunnel, in the section with the drips and missing ceiling tiles, Meredith said, "This is the first of your investigations I've ever envied you." She said this abruptly, without introduction, which wasn't unusual for her. Anyway, the background was clear. Meredith had always tolerated rather than approved of Alex's sideline before.

"Because it's straightforward and heroic, for once?"

"No, I don't mean about the missing lifeblood. That's— envy is hardly appropriate, I just hope she comes through. And I hope whoever would toy with her for profit gets what they deserve. No, I meant what you're doing for Harrison right now, what he originally wanted. It's such a universal temptation, to want to find out whatever happened to all the people one wonders about—and one wonders whether they wonder about one. Ugh. I mean, and I wonder whether they wonder about me."

"They wonder," Alex told her. Maybe this was how to say something flattering and persuasive, the way he hadn't been able when he'd wanted to try and match "Sad-Eyed Lady" two nights before. " 'That Phillips,' they say, 'the one who always sounded so sure of herself, who had the great red hair that made her stand out, and those level green eyes that never missed a thing.' I bet they have a hard time imagining you older. In my imagination, going backward, I think you always must have seemed already grown up. They worry that while they've been screwing around, you've been knowing and doing just what you want."

That was how he thought of her, garbled as it might have come out. She was tenacious about what she wanted, though she provided much of it for herself. Sometimes he thought she'd spent the first two years of their relationship wanting him not to be dying. When it turned out he wasn't, for now anyway, it was hard for both of them to know how to follow that act.

"Sure they do," she told him. "They say, 'Oh, yes, I recall Phillips, the snippy bitch. Gone to America, I heard. Never satisfied, Phillips. Next it'll be Australia, like as not.' "

"If that's what they say, they're envying you." Alex took Meredith's hand off the stick shift and kissed it. A few minutes later, when they said good-bye at the airport curbside, they kissed for a long time. Alex wished they were someplace less public, more horizontal. Meredith pressed hard against him, breasts and belly and pelvis, and then suddenly laughed through their joined lips.

"What?" Alex said, smiling.

"What Shakespeare would say. Did say." She lowered her arms to his waist and leaned back. She took one hand away, used it to brush the hair out of her face. When they made love, Alex sometimes caught her watching him, not with anything like detachment, but with a kind of merriment of observation. Her straight red hair, parted in the middle, sometimes seemed a kind of silky armor that kept the world apart from her head. She put her hand into her jacket pocket and pulled out a torn-off sheet of notebook paper. She read:

"To the wars, my boy, to the wars!
He wears his honour in a box, unseen
That hugs his kicky-wicky here at home
Spending his manly marrow in her arms.
Therefore to the war!

"All's Well That Ends Well, Act Two, Scene Three. That's what a man's marrow was for, according to the Bard. You can use it up fucking or fighting, but you've got to choose which. It was different for the little kicky-wicky, of course. Don't look at me like that." She held up the scrap of paper and read again:

"My eyes are grey and bright and quick in turning
My beauty as the spring doth yearly grow
My flesh is soft and plump
My marrow burning!

That's marrow from the woman's point of view."

"You just happened to be carrying these around with you, Professor?" Alex said.

"Not just. I found the Dickinson poem in a concordance. I wanted to know what the kidnapper had to choose from, if he or she gathered the material that way. That was the only marrow in Emily's concordance, but Shakespeare's, for instance, had quite a lot. And the dictionaries of quotations also offered a large variety, of male authors anyway. Why did the kidnapper choose that particular poem? That's what I've been trying to figure out."

"And?"

"I don't have a good idea yet, or I would have told you. He or she seems fixated on guilt and obligation, but whose we don't know, do we? To the wars, my boy. See what Foster's former kicky-wicky can tell you."

"You're a nutcake," Alex said.

"Takes one to know one. Most people think I'm over-whelmingly sane."

Alex kissed Meredith once more and then hurried to pick up the tickets the travel agent had reserved. There were matches you didn't mess around with. His and Meredith's had, somewhat to his surprise, turned out to be one of these. His daughter had stated this with a certainty Alex had found touching, if naive. Maria had seen women come and go in his life when she was younger, and apropos of some recent conversation about job applications, she'd said, "To tell you the truth, I really can't see you and Meredith breaking up."

Slumped in a chair by the gate area, Alex thought of sending Meredith a postcard from San Francisco, even though it wouldn't get to her until after he was back. Someplace he'd like to be with her, like Golden Gate Park or the Francis Drake Hotel. His message would be, *My marrow burning, too.*

But marrow burning reminded him of marrow melting, and the reality of this journey and his investigation returned. Linda Dumars's reality came crashing down on his and Meredith's small triumphs and pleasures and problems like a wave engulfing the moats and spires of sand castles at the beach.

THIRTEEN
Dolores Park

A lot of cities, Alex thought, could pretend that's all they had ever been. You joined in the pretense. You went around seeing pavement and buildings, construction, human design. In San Francisco, though, you knew all the time that the streets and buildings were only a skin. Really you were living on a peninsula full of little mountains and deep valleys, where the daily drama wasn't rush hour but the sun's struggle to fight through the moisture coming off the ocean. And once in a while, just to remind you what was what, the whole place shook. Sooner or later the continent would slough both the peninsula and its skin into the sea.

The DC-10 banked right to spiral in toward the airport, giving Alex a view of lights and a darkened ridge of hills bordering blue-black sky. He changed his watch to say nine P.M. instead

68

of midnight. He'd slept about a half hour on the flight to O'Hare and a good two hours on this second leg. Now he was ready to revisit this city, ready to pry secrets out of Agnes Amelia Sturdevant if he could. When the plane disgorged its cargo, he hurried through the airport till he emerged into a clear chilly night with stars coming out overhead. The ridge to the west was dark, but he could picture the brown and folded contours of the mountains between the bayside suburbs and the Pacific. He stood in line until he got a cab driven by a small man who according to the ID on the visor was named Samboun Doungmany.

"Alabama Street, in the Mission," Alex said. He felt his tongue savor the geography and history encoded in those words. The Mission District lay in one of the valleys. It was where Spanish missionaries had founded the city, before the gold seekers came. It was where he'd lived for six months, one of six people crammed into a small apartment, all of them coming or going somewhere. Not for the first time, he asked himself, If I'd stayed here, what?

He dozed without meaning to while the cab took him past Daly City and South San Francisco, past the Cow Palace and Candlestick, and then off the expressway at Army Street. He woke to find the driver waiting politely for a pedestrian before hanging a right.

Dee Sturdevant's block, on the eastern outskirts of the Mission, turned out to be a quiet one with narrow houses packed tightly together. Alex paid the driver and stood outside the house that mattered. It was wooden, clapboard, a typical San Francisco working-class house of the sort you saw a lot in the Mission or the Sunset. In the streetlight's illumination, the white paint and green trim seemed to have needed new coats for quite a while. Instead of a basement, under the house the builder had put a one-car garage. This too was common, familiar. In the garage under that apartment on Eighteenth Street there had been a guy who spent weeks trying to get an old Plymouth starter motor to work. He would take it off and take it apart and put it together and put it back on, and it would work for a few days. When it failed someplace, he'd enlist everybody in the building to help him push-start the car. When he got the car home he'd try again.

Alex, knowing next to nothing about cars then, had been impressed by the guy's doggedness. When he'd landed in Nebraska a few years later, hitchhiking like Jay Harrison, he'd apprenticed himself to a factory-trained Volkswagen mechanic named Hans Heidenfelter who had come to the States to avoid the *Bundeswehr* draft, even though Germany wasn't at war and the U.S. was. I might've become a mechanic here too, he told himself. A Muni mechanic, keeping those ancient cable cars alive.

Above the garage door this particular builder had added some decorative trim, a rising sun with rays radiating out. A gray Honda Accord was parked on the street in front. Upstairs a lit window showed a big plant, an avocado, or maybe a small tree. Alex climbed the steep steps, found a BELL NOT WORKING sign, and banged hard on the wooden door. He banged, yawned deeply, and banged again.

From the name, Dutch, and her age, which would be over fifty, Alex had developed a picture of Dee Sturdevant as somebody sharp-eyed probably, but knobby and round. He wasn't prepared for the lanky woman in faded blue jeans who opened the door. Her hair was cut short, a pale blond like straw, going toward white. She had a lot of crow's feet around pale blue eyes.

"I'm Alex," he said, raising his shoulder under his carry-on bag, as if to prove he'd just crossed the country for real.

"Dee," she said. "Welcome. I'll be back down in a minute. We're going out."

"Sure." He hoped she might have changed her mind and decided to take him to Foster. More likely she was leading him away from something, probably just away from her life, her space. She left him at the door and then reappeared with a long woolen poncho on. It was old like the jeans, its geometric pattern faded. Relic of some trip to Mexico, he guessed. He felt out of place in his jacket from Hudson Bay.

"Do you know San Francisco?" she asked. "Now that you're here, is there someplace particular you want to go and make your explanations, tell me what this is all about?"

"I once lived here, but I don't know what places are like anymore." Alex followed her back down the steps to the Honda. He realized he didn't want to face her across the table of some ritzified coffee shop. He wanted some place that wouldn't have changed—that wouldn't have changed for him, and that might put her in mind of old days too. That might melt some of her

70

suspicions. "I used to live on Eighteenth Street near Guerrero. If it's safe, I don't know . . . what about Dolores Park?"

"We won't be alone. It's safe in that respect." She opened the passenger door for him. "Okay," she said. "Dolores Park."

Dee Sturdevant drove north on Alabama to Twenty-fourth, and west on Twenty-fourth to Mission. She asked him about his flight, delays, coast-to-coast fares. She said she was thinking of visiting friends in Boston sometime. She had a kind of unslurred Midwestern pronunciation that made her words sound less trivial, crisper than they'd otherwise be. He asked where she was from and she said North Dakota. He told her about Hans, about working with Hans until he was ready to keep moving east, about getting a ride east with Laura, which turned into a marriage, a daughter, a divorce. He told her about his sideline, explained that Jay had hired him, that's why he was here.

Outside, at night, the Mission didn't seem so changed. Still the little shops, bakeries, hardware stores, jewelry stores, taco places, pool halls, a few crummy hotels. A fair number of Asian stores had crept into the Mexican and Central American mix. Dee turned west off Mission onto Twentieth, climbing up out of the valley. She crossed the street called Dolores and squeezed into a tiny parking space at the upper end of the park. Getting out of the car, Alex admired the downtown lights spread out along Market and up Nob Hill. *Dolores* meant sorrows, Alex knew. The Spanish priests had called their settlement the Mission of Sorrows, though he didn't know why.

"Nobody much goes into the park at night except to make drug deals," Dee Studevant said. "So why don't we be sensible and circumnavigate it instead?" She set a fast and silent pace. Keeping up with her, Alex realized how truly tall she was, a good five-eleven, just about an inch shorter than he. She broke her stride halfway down Dolores, where a lighted pathway bisected the park. Figures huddled together around the picnic tables near this pathway, the dealers and their customers, Alex guessed. He thought she'd say something, ask something, but she seemed to be waiting for him.

"I once saw the Mime Troupe perform here," Alex said.

"Yeah?" she asked him. "Which show?"

"I think it was something about the Chicago conspiracy

71

trial. I think I remember somebody in a Judge Julius Hoffman mask."

"Could be," Dee said. She pointed toward the statue at the far end of the pathway, just before the fringe of trees where, Alex remembered suddenly, the J-Church streetcar ran. The statue represented Padre Miguel Hidalgo, the Patrick Henry of Mexico, holding a Bible in his hand. "Speaking of performances, I made a speech up there once. They had a rope ladder hung down it, and the kids took turns climbing onto Father Miguel's shoulders to do their thing. I went bombing up the ladder, ready to take my turn with the bullhorn, and then remembered I was in teacher drag. There was no way I could wrap my legs around his neck in a skirt. I just kind of slung my arm around his neck, as if we were partners. I held onto him all the way through my talk, hoping I wasn't going to fall and break my neck."

"What kids? What was going on?" Alex tried to imagine her up there, on top of the life-size statue on its big pedestal. If she was now giving him some of her own history in return for what he'd confided in the car, that seemed like a good sign.

"Mission High School student strike." She started walking again, farther down Dolores toward the Spanish-style, ginger-bread-ornamented school across Eighteenth from the park. "The various races were all cooperating, for once. The kids were striking for a lot of surprising and educationally sensible demands. If they'd won more of them, and gotten to keep them, and kept that brief sense of power and expectation . . . You didn't come out here to have me tell you what's wrong with American education, but let's just say that granting those demands couldn't have made things worse than they are now. It would have made them a lot better, I bet."

Was she testing him now, Alex wondered. Or was she just making small talk? He said, "Did you get away with that? A teacher, addressing a rally of kids on strike?"

"No, I got fired. But the experience was an eye-opener. You're the ambassador from Jay Harrison. That's what puts me in mind of those days. Tell me about him."

There was a tone of command in that sentence. It was like, *Now you tell me about Jay Harrison, young man.*

"He's a doctor, cancer researcher. Um, he's not married, no

72

kids. He had his picture in *People,* sort of by accident. He seems to remember his old days fondly, as far as I can tell."

"People!" she said. "Is he a celebrity?"

"Not a celebrity, I wouldn't say that. He had a baseball player for a patient. The point is, somebody who saw the article wrote him a letter. Somebody named Foster, or so they claimed."

He stopped at the corner, reached into his back pocket, and gave her the copy of the letter he'd brought. Unlike Jay, she had surgeon's fingers, long ones. She didn't wear any bracelets, any rings. Alex thought about how those fingers had, a long time ago, caressed the man that might have written this note. She moved under a streetlight to read, and Alex saw how the veins stood out on her fingers, how the joints were more swollen than they would have been then. These things happened, he was starting to notice among his contemporaries, to women who stayed thin.

He tried to picture her with Foster, whatever Foster had looked like, but he had trouble because she seemed too ascetic, too self-contained. It helped that while she read the letter she licked and then sucked on the tip of her right index finger. The gesture was playful, even though it looked like something she might do if she were getting ready to leaf through a book. People grew more self-contained as they got older, Alex thought. It was good, but you could carry it too far. He'd noticed this in himself.

"Jay wants to understand what's going on," he said. "Without getting Foster in trouble, if that's possible. Or anybody else, as long as this situation gets resolved." He was letting the "situation" unfold in front of her the way it had unfolded in front of him. Letter first, marrow second. They might be connected. They might not.

"And Jay is too busy with his celebrities to track Foster down himself? That's why he hired you and flew you out here? My image of Jay is pretty faint, but I didn't think he'd get as far as hiring other people to handle his personal life."

"Right now he has a patient in a lot of danger. Not anybody famous, just a woman with good health insurance and two kids."

Alex explained at last about bone marrow transplants, and about what had gone wrong this time. Hearing himself tell it erased the separation the long day and the air travel had imposed. He shivered with the hollow, angry fear he'd felt in the beach parking lot when there hadn't been any frozen marrow, only the kidnapper's note.

Dee Sturdevant searched his face with those pale eyes. She seemed to draw herself up to her full height, her eyes nearly level with his.

"One of the few leads we have is this letter," Alex pressed. "If Foster by any chance did this, or has any idea who did, we need to be in communication with him. All we care about—all I care about, anyway—is getting the specimen back in good condition. If you were to pull the thing out of your closet I'd forget where I got it and say thank you very much. I'd do the same thing if Foster were to pull it out of his."

Dee said, "I'm not sure that would be very responsible. Shouldn't the person who did this be punished, once the patient is safe?"

"Spare me the values clarification, Ms. Sturdevant," Alex snapped. He heard the anger flaring in his voice and felt the heat rising to his face. She had asked him for the true story, and what he was saying was the truth. He didn't like her hiding behind her teacher drag, as she put it, now.

"I'm sorry," Dee said. "It doesn't matter anyway, what you tell me you would do. It's been a while since I dealt with fugitives or people living any kind of clandestine life. But I remember the procedures. I'll try to get your message to Foster. Then if he wants to contact you, he will."

"You're saying he's underground, clandestine?" Procedures. The word rankled. It sounded dry and bureaucratic. There might not be time for that.

"No. I'm saying you don't seem to know where he is, so it's not my place to tell you, that's all. His decision, not mine."

Logical. Or loyal. But not helpful. Alex said, "When you dealt with fugitives in the past, did it have anything to do with Jay?"

"With Jay Harrison? No. During the strike I mentioned, a cop discharged his gun into the air right next to my ear. Up there, near Twentieth Street. The cop was arresting a kid named Eddie Suarez, one of the better thinkers and orators, and I made the mistake of pulling on the cop's arm. I was pissed off, and I'd just come charging out of the school in my teacher outfit and full of my teacher authority, so I thought I could interfere with this cop.

Little did I know. Blam! Before that I always thought it was just a slogan, political power comes out of the barrel of a gun. A few months later that same cop got killed. In a shoot-out, or that's what the police claimed, with a bunch of Latino kids. One of those kids was Eddie's girlfriend's brother. There was a warrant for him for the murder of that cop. That was my introduction to hiding fugitives, because it would've been the police shooting first and questioning later, that much I knew. When the case finally came to trial, when things had cooled down, the jury decided there hadn't been any shoot-out, only pushing and shoving, and the officer was most likely shot by his partner, by mistake. All of that was before I met Jay Harrison, though."

"Uh-huh," Alex said. As she talked he remembered echoes of this case. There was no mistaking her sincerity, but she hadn't necessarily answered what he'd asked. "I mean later, after you knew him and Foster. Jay had something to do with an underground railroad for soldiers that had turned against the war."

"I know he stayed around a while. I used to run into him here and there. But I never worked with him on anything political, no."

"Oh." Alex accepted defeat on that one. He began walking along Eighteenth, with the park on the left and the school on the right. Now she matched his pace. He nodded his head toward the school. "Did you keep teaching, or what?"

"I still teach, believe it or not. I didn't for a while, after I got fired, and for a long time I couldn't get a job in the City and County of San Francisco, as they say. But now I teach here again, in a high school for 'newcomers,' which is this year's polite word for immigrants. Why?"

"Curious."

"No, you want to work your way back around to Foster. I don't blame you." She stopped at the next streetlight and ran her fingers along the rough silvered surface as if trying to feel something out, to come to some decision. "It's not that I don't want to help this woman. What you described, this situation she's in scares the hell out of me. It scares you, too, I can see that. It must scare Jay, whoever he grew up to be. But giving Foster your message, *trying* to give your message is all I can think of to do. If he knows anything useful, if he wants to talk to you, he'll get in touch. Or else you'll have to find him some other way. I could have told you all that on the phone, if you'd leveled with me then."

"Well, would it be worth it for me to hang around the Bay Area and wait for a response?"

"No, I don't think so. He's not out here, as far as I know. And let me remind you, my information about where he is might turn out to be wrong, if anyone puts a badge in my face. I wish I could do something else, but I don't know what else I can do. It wasn't only Foster on that trip, of course. Does Jay have you chasing our other companions, too?"

"Your other . . . oh, you mean the teenage runaways?"

" 'Oh,' " she mimicked. "A remote possibility crossed my mind, that Jay made up this whole letter, that he's not really trying to find Foster but to find Barbarella. But if you can really vouch for the missing marrow, that can't be it, can it? Too bad."

This time Alex didn't try to hide his ignorance. The only Barbarella he knew about had been a comic-book sex kitten played by Jane Fonda in the movie version. "Barbarella?" he said.

"Jay didn't mention the woman-child who formed a part of this adventure?" Dee let a smile grow into a laugh. She had a whoop of a laugh, Alex thought. This was only a piece of it. What he'd been seeing had to be Dee Sturdevant under wraps.

"How much did he tell you about that journey, anyway?" she asked.

"Less than I thought, apparently. You're saying Jay wasn't lonely the whole time? He and one of those runaways . . ."

"Oh yes. Not that getting it on with Barbarella is something he could be blackmailed about decades later. That doesn't make sense to me."

"Maybe we could go somewhere for coffee or a drink after all," Alex said. "And you could tell me more about those travels. It wouldn't hurt me to know Jay better. My clients don't always tell me the whole truth about themselves." And as Hans Heiden-felter would say, the only way to understand how anything worked was to take it apart and lay all the parts out in order, one by one. Hans had meant starter motors or clutches or master cylinders, but the same thing applied to tangled histories and lives.

"Who does?" Dee put her fingers back to work on the

streetlight pole again. "I can tell you this about Foster. When we got here to the city, he stayed with me for a while, not long. During that time he talked to a civilian lawyer here who did a lot of military work. The lawyer said he had some procedural, due-process grounds in his favor but he'd have to turn himself in, at whatever base he walked off of, and have a lawyer there, and hope for the best. Foster and I parted ways, but I did get a postcard from Germany, eventually. It said, 'Dishonorable, but free at last.' That's Foster. As far as I know Jay didn't have anything to do with him, or vice versa, except during that short time we all spent driving out. I think you're on a wild-goose chase here, I really do."

"Since I'm here, though, would you mind telling me what you can remember about Jay, or Jay and Foster, during that short time? At least the flavor of it."

"The flavor, the odd detail, even if there's none of the dangerous secrets promised in that note?"

"Please," Alex said. "It might help. You never know."

"Well, in that case you don't need me in person, and you don't need to take me out for a drink. If we can find a copy shop open at this hour, I'm willing to lend you my true confessions from that time."

Dee Sturdevant looked once at Alex, sideways, then turned and started marching back the way the two of them had come. When Alex caught up he said, "You kept a diary, you mean?"

"Religiously. As if somebody were going to write my biography some day, or publish my journals. You know, like Anaïs Nin's. I suppose everybody hopes their journals might be considered a masterpiece in another era. I confess I had that on my mind."

"Really?" Alex said. Meredith had once said that many women tended their journals as devotedly as if they were striving for masterpieces. It was the *as if* that interested Meredith. "Did you ever try?"

"What? To get them published? No. I do accuse my boyfriend of stealing from them, for his stories. He says material is where you find it. Listen, I hope Jay appreciates this. No, I don't care whether he appreciates it or not. I hope *you're* convinced I'm doing anything for this woman that I can."

FOURTEEN
Love and Rain

The plant in the window turned out to be a small tree, a miniature complete with branches and bark. Dee Sturdevant departed
waving a spiral notebook, the five-by-eight kind, tan cardboard
cover faded almost to white. She left Alex with her boyfriend,
Roger, who was white, bearish, gray-bearded and gray-haired.
Roger's eyes swam through thick lenses while the rest of his face
smiled in a hearty way. He poured Alex a glass of red wine from
a local vineyard he liked, which Alex sipped while he called
airlines in search of a seat on a red-eye flight. Then they chatted
about auto engines and auto bodies, the strengths of Japanese
production methods and the weaknesses of Japanese recycled
steel. "Have you read all these diaries?" Alex asked finally. If he
stole from them, he ought to be able to see them with a critic's
eye.

"A lot of them. They're kind of helter-skelter, like cooking
and housecleaning and yoga and a lot of things Dee can get into
for short bursts and then forget about till the next time they
strike her a certain way. She's steady about her work, and she's
steady about Sierra—that's her daughter. She's delightfully erratic about a lot of other things. Delightful to me, anyway. I cook
and clean regularly, and I always drink coffee out of the same cup
and put it on the same corner of my desk."

An hour later Alex sat in a crowded, littered departure gate
area, one of the day's last cohort of passengers, with a sheaf of
photocopied pages in his lap. At the last minute Dee had also laid
a photograph on him, a glossy black-and-white snapshot. Taken,
she said, "by somebody or other with Barbarella's camera, because Barbarella brought a camera when she ran away from
home." The shot was not quite in focus, or maybe the photographer hadn't managed to hold the camera still. The quartet was
posed: female, male, female, male from left to right, arms around
one another's shoulders or waists. Alex recognized the two in the
middle. Jay and Dee, the ones with the one-syllable names.

Jay Harrison regarded the camera with a glare, though Alex had the feeling the glare was mostly to keep Jay from cracking up. His hair hung to his shoulders, straight without much body, secured by a headband, of course. The hair seemed lighter, closer to a dirty blond than today. The build was much thinner, almost delicate. He wore a blue-jean jacket, tattered, open in the front. What did his pose add up to? Youth, insouciance, determination, a certain air of persecution and paranoia too. From his own back pages Alex remembered all of that very well.

Next to him, Dee squinted more than smiled. Her pale hair hung down behind her shoulders, and she wore a denim vest that looked to be cut from a jacket, without any emblems but otherwise like the vests bikers used to wear. Alex imagined her expression meant she didn't like posed pictures, didn't particularly want to be frozen this way. She seemed supple and willowy, more given to movement than the woman who'd lent him this photo and these pages out of her past.

Foster was the same height as Dee and twice as wide. He had on a black motorcycle jacket. His head was shaved and his beard bushy. On his round face he wore a broad smile that might have come naturally from how solid he seemed. Or it might have meant something in that moment, happiness or confidence. Or it might have been designed to conceal something else. He was the second most photogenic of the bunch.

First prize went to the one on the other end, with Jay's arm around her shoulders, somebody who might have called herself Barbarella after all. She wore cut-off jeans that hugged her hips, and a work shirt, tied above her waist beneath the curves of breasts that were full and unconfined. Her smile was young and broad, expectant. Her dark hair, which fell to just above her shoulders, seemed thick and shiny and full of energy. Underneath the photo somebody, presumably she, had written in rounded blue ballpoint script *For Dee, elder sister, trip and a half, with a ton of thanks, love to F.—B.*

Alex turned the photo over, as if it could tell him something more. The back was blank. He riffled through the diary pages, muddy black photocopies on overly white paper, scratchy script, two-page spreads with the wire spiral showing dark and blurry in between. This was what Dee had given him. She hadn't said whether or not it was all she'd written during that particular journey, and he hadn't asked. When he was sandwiched in the center section of the jumbo jet, he began to read.

May 5

I'm sitting at kitchen table in a house in a neighborhood whose name I don't know. Across the table a woman named Ginny is feeding her baby in the high chair. She's Foster's sister-in-law, younger than me. She said no, she wouldn't be offended if I sat here and wrote privately to myself. She's very polite, but not friendly. I'm trying not to take it personally, or even racially. Fact is, I don't think she's been too happy with Foster, I think him living here has been weirding her out somehow. But she's not too sure about seeing him leave with me. I am. I hope I'm not wrong. Let me back up a day.

Yesterday just past sunset I was leaning against the fence of the Washington Redskins' spare practice field a few blocks from here. I was thinking how astounding that name is. As if the Nazis, having taken everything from the Jews, decided to call their capital city's soccer team the Berlin Kikes. The Washington Redskins, Nixon's team. The farthest thing from my mind, I would have said, was looking for a man.

It was drizzling, getting dark, wet, and cold. I had my back against the chain-link fence, trying to tuck my head into my sweater like a duck, sniffing tear gas and wet wool. I was feeling old—admit it, feeling thirty, as in "Don't trust anybody past." Too old to look forward to spending the night in there, even with a thousand others, all stashed in this holding pen because the regular jails were full.

They had posted National Guard around the fence with rifles and bayonets, but with a lot of space in between. The ones I talked to had been friendly, or at least neutral enough. People who lived in the neighborhood—it's all black—had been tossing food in to us over the fence. So there in the dusk, something landed in front of me, splat in the mud. I thought it was a can of like spaghetti or peaches, and I could find somebody with some kind of opener and we could share

80

them around. But no. Wire cutters. Somebody had tossed a pair of wire cutters over the fence.

I picked up the cutters, held them in my hand. I told myself even if these weekend soldiers spotted me they wouldn't shoot a blond thirty-year-old ex-schoolteacher for blocking traffic and then sneaking away from a football field. I knew I might be wrong, but when it got good and dark, I cut a hole to wriggle through and then slithered about fifteen feet along the ground, my heart hammering like a demented drum solo inside my chest. I waited for somebody to call out, in I didn't know what language, "Halt!" When they didn't, I walked up the rest of the hill like a citizen, my head high. My knees shook, I was shivering. I got ready to circle the field and head over toward the highway they brought us in on. Then I heard a low voice, quiet, with a hint of gravel. I dropped into a crouch like a hunted animal, suddenly smarter than I was brave. The voice said, "I thought somebody could get some use out of my brother's old pair of shears."

We ended up spending the night on a mattress in their basement, Ginny and J.T.'s basement, where Foster's been sleeping, J.T. is his brother, younger brother it turns out. I was high off escape and daring, and Ginny and J.T.'s whiskey. Foster is a talker, funny and serious, with an accepting manner and nice hands. Is that really all I know about him? How many teenage girls have I told this to: Sex is a trip, but don't travel without a map. Otherwise you're pregnant too soon, and he's drafted or in the joint or on the street without a job. None of this applies to us grown-ups. Do as I say, not as I do.

Facts about Foster, grown-uplike: He's just back in this country after a few years in France. He worked in auto-body shops, says he met his first Africans there. He also played flute in the Paris Metro and drew sidewalk portraits above ground. Like I said, good with his hands. He's been rebuilding J.T.'s old delivery van—J.T. has a printing business—to sell as a camper, score some bucks. Really he'd like to use it, not sell it. I need to get back to California. I said, "I've got travel money, once I reconnect with my friends. You've got wheels."

In a bar, past midnight, Philadelphia. I'd be hassled here, unmercifully, except I've got a pretend date. His name is Jay. Foster and I have a traveling companion now.

Out of the frying pan into the fire. Forty-five minutes from Nation's Capital, it was Pig City once again. Maryland state troopers this time. All our shit spread on the highway shoulder. I felt naked, cop pawing through my purse. Leers at my pills, then looks at me like wherever Foster's been he has a God-given right to go too. I hated that I had to stand and take it the way I knew I had to do.

I had to do it because when the siren sounded Foster said, "Listen baby I got to tell you something. My name is Pierre Landreau, I'm French, I don't speak much English, I know you can make up the rest." So I did. I did the talking, I made up what I had to make up. He really does have a French passport, complete with photo, that helped. The police let us go with a "warning," as if we'd committed some crime. "Tell him to get his piece of trash out of here," the shorter one said—meaning the van, meaning me.

Then Foster drove but wouldn't talk. He moped, leaving me to guess what he hadn't told me, what was coming next. Damn it, I thought. No more humiliating for you than for me, making like a turtle ain't gonna help. Between the secrets and the self-pity, I rode along with serious second thoughts. Nice while it lasted, nobody with whom I ought to fall in love. Let me out at the next bus station, you go your way and I go mine. But you don't cross these lines without work, I argued with myself. Dee, you ought to know that by now.

All of sudden he said, "Hey, Dee, how about we pick up that hippie?" I didn't know what hippie, because the guy was already behind us. I still don't know how Foster saw him out of his averted eyes.

We took the next exit and we discussed and agreed. We didn't talk about what happened, but Foster explained why the false papers. He apologized for not warning me. He's a deserter, that's all. I said that made him a patriot in my book. Not to wage this war is patriotism, is an attempt to salvage this country's soul. But I asked were we carrying anything I should know about, like any guns or dope. Just a few grams of nice Turkish hash, he said, for personal consumption, buried deep inside his flute. We picked up the so-called hippie, who turns out to be rather overeducated, Harvard no less. Now we're in Philadelphia, where Foster is off looking for an army buddy, then we'll head west. I'm willing to give it another try. I do like him, what can I say?

May 8—Indiana—morning—drove all night

We're making miles, but not so happily. In Philadelphia, Foster came back very bummed. He couldn't find the buddy because the buddy got shipped to the war and died. It really threw him. In my experience, too much experience, it always does. Foster goes very fast from opening up to closing down, from high to low. Not like me and those Sturdevants I'm always trying to get away from. We go marching on like the postman, neither snow nor sleet. I tried to talk to him but he didn't want me around. He drove, Jay sat up there next to him. I went to sleep.

I woke crossing the Alleghenies someplace, fog in the road. Foster was asking Jay what about him and the army, how did Jay deal? 1-Y, Jay said, unfit for service except in time of national emergency. At his physical he kept asking what was the reason for the war. He pissed on the guy taking urine samples, had "Fuck the Army" written in lipstick on his back. Plus all this was backed up by a letter from some shrink. Since then he's been working against the war, "so nobody will have to go." He went into some detail about all of this. Also a patriot, to me, if not especially brave.

"You answered my question," Foster finally said, "so shut the fuck up."

After a while, Foster started talking. Told how he agitated, too, in Germany, after he was in. With his buddy from Philadelphia, the buddy's name was Turk. Why should the black man participate in the white man's war against the yellow, he handed out leaflets like that, off base at the soldier bars. So the brass cut them both orders to Vietnam. They discussed what to do. Foster walked. Turk didn't, because he felt that would only dig him deeper in the shit.

Jay said he was sorry, or something like that. Asked did Foster feel responsible for what happened to his friend. Foster told Jay to shut up again. He wants to put miles between us and that ghost in Philadelphia now.

I learned how Foster got in the army, too, though he didn't tell that to Jay. Spray-painting. Like "Alice's Restaurant," getting out by a littering rap, only not funny, the other way around. He got busted one night for spray-painting black power slogans, and the judge in Baltimore took a dislike to him. Gave him a choice between jail for malicious destruction, or joining up. Foster says in the end it came down to his father. Your country is still your country, his father said, and no son that had taken music lessons was going to be a jailbird, and you got enough going against you without a record, so serve your time in uniform and then finish school. Foster suspects the old man probably changed his mind later. He died while Foster was still in France.

May 11—The Black Hills

I'm cold, the cold woke me up, it's six A.M. This close to North Dakota I start to feel winter, no matter what season it is. So I'm going to write about the day before yesterday when it was sunny and warm. When I knew things were good again for sure—for now.

We were on I-80 where it follows the old wagon route along the Platte. Foster and Jay both wanted to put their feet in the river, I think it was all out of Wild West movies to them. They do have some things in common. They both know about printing, for instance, and false ID. That gives them something to talk shop about.

We bushwhacked through brush and dry channels, Foster swinging his flute like a machete in its case. We got to the river, running fast but shallow, sun-dappled, air hot and still. We broke out the hash and then we took off our clothes and floated downstream in the sun. I felt like the current was washing me free of bad choices, or no choices. I hoped it was doing that for Foster, too. We came to an island and I grabbed his hand and we kicked ourselves to the shore. Now I write this down in the cold morning and get goose bumps— part from remembered pleasure, part from shock about how dangerous that scene could have been. Do we think we carry some special charm that says we can get naked and screw wherever we want, on anybody's turf? But so far we're charmed. Foster, will this end? I know it will end, that's what makes it work. When, though? When we run out of road?

We walked back up the river hand in hand. Jay's stuff was gone when we got to the place we'd left our clothes. I had my T-shirt over my head when I heard rustling. When I could see again, Foster was doing up his belt grimly like a cowboy cinching down a saddle before going out to do some disagreeable chore. Nobody was in sight. Then these two bedraggled white teenagers stood up out of the bushes. The girl said Jay told them maybe they could have a ride.

"Yeah," the boy said. "I'm Henry and this is Barbar— Ellen. The girl gave him a look that could kill and said "I'm *Ellen.*" She proclaimed her identity, even if it was false, the way only a pretty teenager who thinks she just invented womanhood can.

"Barbarellen?" Foster said. He was finished with his belt and just kind of patting his tummy, as if the disagreeable chore had taken care of itself. "You mean Barbarella, I guess." What's funny about him is he has a way of being patronizing that makes you feel he's looking down at least as sarcastically on himself as he is on you. Anyway that's what it does for me. Gives me perspective without making me feel small or dumb, the way so many men need to do. Right then the sun was beaming off his shiny head in a way that made me want to forget these waifs and drag him back to that island again.

"Henri et Barbarella," Foster declared. Since then those have been their names. Young Barbarella, unfortunately, gives young Jay an excuse to show off. Last night around the fire he was telling hitchhike stories. He told about getting picked up by a car full of black partygoers driving the New Jersey Turnpike in the middle of the night. The driver kept drinking out of a bottle in a bag, doing ninety, and one of the

women kept saying to him, "Slow down Jesse, slow down."
Jay said he was scared shitless but also real grateful to this
Jesse for picking him up. So he just figured he'd live if Jesse
lived, and he'd die if Jesse died.

It wasn't a bad story, but Foster wasn't about to let it
pass uncalled. He said, "Jaybo, did you ever in all this thumb
travel see a black man waiting on the road for a ride? You
owe this brother your life, for his skill with the wheel that
night. Do you think *he* could stand out there on the turnpike
at three A.M. and expect any drunken white folks to baby-sit
him?"

Or a woman, I pointed out—white, black, brown, or red.

Leaving the Tetons

There's four of us now, Fab Four says Barbarella, because
yesterday we put Henri—Ernie it turns out—on a bus in
Jackson Hole. Barbarella was Coast or bust, but Henri
found out he wanted to be back in time to take his SATs.
Yours truly mediated, savior of the futures of the suburban
middle class. I even called his mother and told her to expect
him. His mother said, "And what about that Binder girl,
Barbara, he was dating? Didn't they run away together,
that's what everybody says!" I lied that I didn't know anything about that. I did make Barbarella promise to call home
as soon as we cross the Golden Gate.

The remaining four of us hiked up to a lake, still covered
with ice, snow melting all around it, pristine. We stood there
and let the cooling sweat give us the shivers while we watched
winter turning into spring. That was a good feeling, a hopeful one. Then we hiked down to our homestead in the camp-
ground among the tent-trailers and Airstreams and
Winnebagos and such. Foster played the flute, and Barbarella turned out to be damn good on harmonica. This
morning two park rangers in Smokey the Bear hats woke us
up. They came on like cops, not protectors of our flora and
fauna and all. They said some of our neighbors had complained we had a rowdy party last night. They said there were
families around us, families that cared what their kids had to

look at, see. Ranger #2, who didn't talk so much, spread his pudgy hand to take in the two sleeping bags out in the open, plus Foster and me having emerged together from the van. We were back on that Maryland highway, our belongings spread along the shoulder on display.

"Sir, we don't make any loud party," Foster said. He had on his best broken English, French accent. I knew he got off on getting over that way, he needed to stand up to them this much, but I wished he wouldn't take chances he didn't need to. For what? Yeah, and why did I pick up those cutters and slice through the chain link fence? Then I remembered something small but important. We hadn't quite finished off the last of the hash last night. What was left, Barbarella had put in her film can where every cop, even a misguided park ranger, knows everybody holds their stash. Ranger #2 saw the can on the picnic table and took a step that way. We were going to get hauled in for possession, and Foster's number was going to come up.

I coughed in Jay's direction, he was closest. He looked up at me and followed my eyes. He screwed off the cap and dumped the contents into the milk and granola he was eating out of one of those fifty-cent plastic camp-out cups. He swallowed that spoonful fast and rinsed the can with milk while the ranger stared. "Sugar," Jay told him. "Just get out," the other ranger said. Under their watchful eyes we tossed our stuff in the van and left the Airstreams and Winnebagos behind.

Up the road a ways we parked the van and hiked a half mile up to a low meadow full of early wildflowers, nobody there but us. Foster sat and read, in his silent mode again. I tried to go back to sleep, my head in his lap. Jay announced that he couldn't stay still because everything around him wasn't, he felt the field rolling up like a carpet and carrying him away. Less poetically, he'd ingested quite a hunk of hashish and it was threatening to blow a hole in the top of his head. Barbarella volunteered to help him walk it off. About six hours later they came back, bathed in the light of young love.

I don't know where our friend Jay will land once he finally finds his right mind, but apparently he speed-rapped all the way up a two-thousand-foot ridge, lots of it still in snow. On top he clung to Barbarella, each in their own way stunned by the view. Then he asked her to to tell the story of her life, which he absorbed and explored obsessively all the way down. And apparently a romance with a mature and knowledgeable and hip and radical guy is what will make Barbarella's flight from suburban St. Louis complete—especially since she got to take care of such a guy in his hour of drug-induced need.

I know all this because Barbara quickly dragged me off for a mother confessor heart-to-heart. I issued one of my map-and-plan warnings, suggesting he might be a little older, a little more jaded, might not be taking this as seriously as she. She said, "So, you didn't know Foster, right, any better than I know Jay?" She tossed that at me with an adorable defiant look. "Anyway, right now it's just an interlude, dig it? I'm not even telling the dude my whole name."

So now I'm sisters-in-interlude with this precocious teenybopper. Meanwhile Foster chuckles and puts his arm around Jay and slaps him on the ass and like that. I sit here and smell the wildflowers and write down one more fortunate escape on this exceedingly charmed trip. In the distance there's thunder, both literal and figurative, but I try not to let that in. It's a two-line struggle, as the Maoists like to say. Everybody's making love or else expecting rain.

Alex tapped the edges of the pages on the plastic meal tray attached to the seat in front of him, lining the pages up straight. All around him passengers were sleeping or reading or fidgeting, because there was no movie or dinner on the red-eye flight. He drained the residue of bourbon and melted ice from his plastic glass. All in all—maybe it was just the effect of Dee's rendition—he'd rather be crossing the country more slowly, and seeing it, and tasting compressed resins of hemp rather than distilled fermented corn. But had he learned anything from Agnes Amelia Sturdevant that made it worth having crossed the country at all?

She would deliver his message to Foster if she could, Alex did believe that. If Foster was involved in the theft of Linda Dumars's bone marrow, however, the message wouldn't tell the man anything he didn't know, beyond the name and phone and address of Jay's hired hand. Foster himself wasn't quite so shad-owy anymore. He had a shape, a history, a personality, and so did this Barbarella, somewhat, and so did Dee. Alex tried to see Jay Harrison through their eyes, then and now. Did any of them know a secret he wouldn't want known? Did any of them have a reason to want to see him hurt, humbled, or to want to make him pay through the nose?

Foster might resent the ease with which Jay had stepped back onto his career track, certainly. Jay said he'd worked nights in a lab to pay the rent while he supported military resisters, but once the war ended and he decided to go to medical school, he'd no doubt been able to call up Dad for help with the fees. Foster on the other hand would have come back with a bad-paper discharge, no B.A., no vets benefits, no family money, no Dad. Yet Dee's selections had ended a note of comradeship, and all debts paid. If Dee had chosen to point anywhere, she was point-ing toward Barbarella or that quickly eclipsed boyfriend, Henri. More likely she just wanted to convince him he was on a wild-goose chase.

Alex thought he ought to run the diary by Meredith, see whether her eye might pick up something his had missed. But he suspected another message from the kidnapper, however cryptic, would probably be worth a whole lot more than these pages that he was straightening once more against the tray.

FIFTEEN
Bobby

The man who was calling himself Bobby Lynch slid his spine slowly up against the padded backboard of the bed. He tried not to disturb the woman sleeping next to him because he didn't want to explain where he was going now. It was one thing that they'd been drunk and rich together, and that they'd come back together to the room where they were registered as Mr. and Mrs. Lynch. Despite a lot of careful planning, he hadn't planned one way or the other about her. Bringing her along on the spur of the moment had seemed like something Bobby might do. Guys named Bobby were like that—kind of vacant, impulsive and nonchalant. He hadn't realized how much fun, what a relief it would turn out, this business of being somebody else. In advance, he'd only thought about the practical value of having another identity to use. As it turned out, though, he'd been playing with eating different things, drinking differently, and more.

They'd come back up here from their tour of the casinos, collapsed on the bed, and then he'd sunk the pickle, as somebody he had known somewhere used to say. As Bobby might say. And that had been fine for all concerned as near as he could tell. All along, she'd been a good sport if a gullible one, and that was one more reason he didn't want to wake her up now. He didn't want to have to concoct some new lie about where he was going and why, some new elaboration on exactly what they had sold for three hundred thousand dollars in cash.

He slid out from under the covers and smoothed the sheet over her white shoulders. It would be easier to just stay here, but he had an obligation to get up and drive to L.A. Or almost to L.A., since maybe he could use Riverside or San Bernardino, places he knew only from the map. It could be anyplace big and busy where people sent things out by Federal Express and where nobody's memory would register any trace of him even as Bobby Lynch. He'd be one among a string of customers dropping their goods and their contracts and whatnot on the counter, anxious to speed these things on their way.

Once his package was shipped and delivered, his obligation would be over. One other wrinkle would remain to smooth out if possible, and then he'd have more freedom than he'd had in years. Soon he could go where wanted and do what he wanted— what he decided he wanted—and that would surely be a change. He was giving serious thought to Mexico. Bobby didn't seem like a good name for Mexico, but by then he could be leaving Bobby behind. Nice being you, man, and thanks for the loan.

He left a note, just saying he'd be back sometime in the afternoon. He might need to grab a nap, actually, before he could drive all the way back. He went quietly to the bathroom, not turning on the noisy shower but washing up and then putting

on clothes that were clean and anonymous: a short-sleeved ox-
ford cloth shirt, a pair of flannel slacks. He rode down in the
elevator and went out into the casino, where it might as well have
still been day.

Leaving here was harder. Here it wasn't one sleeping
woman, but a twenty-four-hour party that was still in full swing.
He bought a drink and put some dollars in the dollar slots. God,
how many different casinos they'd been in since they got here:
turning cash into chips, winning or losing a few, and then turning
the chips back into cash, but not the same cash, and then the new
cash into bank checks and traveler's checks. This was Las Vegas,
and under the legal limits nobody looked twice at transactions
like that. Probably none of this laundering was necessary, probably he was overestimating how easily the feds could locate specific serial numbers—if they were trying, if they'd been notified
at all. But it was one more way that this trip to Las Vegas made
up, ten times over, for having to skip it that other time.

He laughed when, in confirmation of this thought, one of his
dollars brought him back ten. The whole thing had been a colos-
sal gamble. No matter how well planned, it had been a gamble.
He had told himself it wasn't, it was a sure thing, but now that
it had paid off he could admit what a gamble it had been. The
payoff had been more than money, and more than turning defeat
into victory. He was just starting to feel how big the payoff really
was. The payoff was freedom, nothing more and nothing less. He
bought one more drink and told himself that was the last one and
now he'd just play those ten new dollars, no more. He kept his
promise. He strolled through the casino, watching but not playing anymore, and then took the elevator downstairs to the garage.

You're a little bit drunk, he told himself. You're tired, even
if you feel your nerves zinging like tight piano wires up at the
high end of the keys. Driving the streets, he concentrated on red
lights, on using his turn signals, because right now he didn't need
a ticket or a fender bender. The gamble had paid off, the theft
had been as easy—if heart-stopping—as he'd thought it would
be. There had been one glitch, one unforeseen screwup, but that
degree of error could hardly be avoided, after all. Accidents did
happen, that was why they froze the stuff in two batches. But it
meant that he had to take good care of the cooler holding the

frozen marrow, which rested in the trunk of this rented car. In a few hours it would be on its way home to Mama and then everything ought to be okay. *You've made that mistake before,* a voice told him, *the mistake of relaxing too soon.* Just leave me alone, he told the voice. I'm not making it now.

In a few minutes he was on the highway, out of the traffic and the neon gallery, alone, just him piloting the fast car through the night. It felt great. It wasn't for nothing that in this country the man in the driver's seat was the symbol of success. Even if you could stack up the arguments against the automobile from here back to Boston, there was no denying the way it felt to do seventy-five through the desert this way. So many other kinds of success—and failure—involved doing what somebody *else* thought you ought to do. He pulled over into the breakdown lane, to get out and savor this night. The air was dry and comfortable. Overhead was an intense and powerful panorama of stars. He sat on the hood of the car, lay back against the windshield, looking up. . . .

With a start he pulled himself out of his doze. He'd have to get some coffee. People must drive this road at all hours, there had to be a lot of places you could get coffee, even now. Probably if you knew the right codes you could get more than coffee; benzedrine, whatever you needed. But at the first exit he passed, the gas station with the big tall Chevron sign was closed. He turned on the radio, and his nerves began zinging again. He thought of the marrow transplant unit, where people lived like zombies. They never got out, never felt any thrill of motion. Nothing changed for them except the numbers that came out of microscopes and machines.

The response of the car under his hands and his foot grew more exhilarating, the speed an extension of himself. He drummed in time to the music, an oldies station, a Rolling Stones tune, "You Can't Always Get What You Want." Not always, but sometimes. Right now everything felt right. It even amused him to be Bobby Lynch, Robert Michael Lynch, according to his driver's license. That name appeared next to the photo that was obviously of him.

Sometimes the name, which had popped up by accident, did scare him, yes. But he hadn't wanted the clerk to particularly remember anything, so he hadn't prolonged the occasion by fishing through the lists longer than necessary. The next day he'd gone down to the records department at the statehouse with all the necessary information. His blood had raced as fast as when, later, he'd walked out with the marrow. Would this method still work, he'd wondered? It had. He'd come away with a birth certificate that said he was Robert M. Lynch.

From then on he'd tried to laugh at the prophecy that he'd finish strung up from a tree. He'd tried to settle into the name the same way you could settle in behind the wheel of a rental car like this Buick Skylark here. You put the car through its paces, but mostly you took it for granted. This was temporary, not a permanent relationship, nobody whose long-term quirks and strengths and weaknesses you had to get to know. Acquiring his papers had been a milestone, the first mile down the road that had brought him here now.

Now there were opportunities to stop for coffee, two of them in fact, but the man registered in Las Vegas under the name of Bobby Lynch passed them up. Then, an hour out of Vegas, there was nothing. The names on the infrequent signs weren't even real names, just labels. Maybe that was prophetic. In any case, whatever had allowed him to operate beyond his capacity ran out midway between a place called Mountain Pass and another one called Valley Wells.

He nodded off again. The Skylark veered into the median strip, not flying, just bouncing. If he'd been more alert he might have been able to understand what was happening and bounce his way back up unto the pavement without mishap. But *alert* did not accurately describe his condition anymore.

He woke to bouncing springs and bumpy noises and the wheel going nuts under his hands. In a flash he concluded he must have driven off the right shoulder into the desert. He hit the brakes and threw the wheel to the left. That sent him swerving onto the other strip of concrete, the lanes headed back toward Vegas, the lanes for gamblers who hadn't yet won or lost. Seeing headlights coming from his right and a guardrail ahead, he threw the wheel further and hit the gas this time. Now he didn't have any idea where he was. He just knew he needed to outrun the lights bearing down on him. The car rolled in protest against the turning radius and the speed. It flipped over the rail and crashed down into the hard-baked desert.

The rear end hit first, crumpling like a can. Shards of steel that used to be the trunk split the cardboard shipping box and the insulated container inside. Smoke and cold rushed out. There was nothing left to keep the temperature of Linda Dumars's frozen stem cells below that of the comfortable desert air.

DAY ONE

SIXTEEN
Rhymes With Tinder

Alex followed the receptionist's directions to a door with a frosted-glass panel such as an old-fashioned dentist's office might have had. Now it was part of a suite of offices belonging to an "audio-visual production services" firm. He knocked once and got no response, knocked louder and knocked louder again.

"Come in," a voice yelled in answer to the third knock. "The door's open." The mix of annoyance and openness made Alex think of Dee's daughter, Sierra, blurting out that her mom wasn't home.

Barbara Binder stood over a videocassette deck with a lightweight headset furrowing her black hair, brushed and shiny and parted on one side. She was, if anything, more attractive than the teenage girl in the photo. Her figure was nearly as good as ever, the sultriness not all gone but softened, the air of expectation replaced by a comfort with herself as she stood there and worked. She wore a gold-colored chain with a blue stone that crossed a vein on her neck. Her face was worn enough not to be mistaken for seventeen. If she was conscious of Alex's inspection, she ignored it. She pushed a last button on the deck and another on an audiocassette player, then nodded and took the headphones off.

"Are you here to get the TBC?" she said with a smile. "After I called, the Amiga went out on me too." Alex knew that smile. He didn't know TBCs or Amigas, but he knew she wanted some piece of equipment fixed. Some customers radiated nervousness, afraid you were going to cheat them. Others took your competence for granted but wanted speed, which they tried to purchase with goodwill.

"No, sorry. If you're Barbara Binder, I'm here to talk to you. My name is Alex Glauberman. If you have a few minutes . . ."

"Binder," she said, the smile vanishing. She corrected Alex's pronunciation, as the receptionist had not bothered to do. "It rhymes with 'tinder' or 'cinder,' not with 'blinder' or 'kinder.' I thought you were from the repair shop. The time-base corrector. . . . How can I help you, then?"

"I was referred to you by Paul Foster, sort of."

"Paul Foster? I'm sorry. Is that somebody I did some work for? I don't remember . . ."

"Foster," Alex said. "Everybody just used to call him Foster. When I say he referred me, I mean I was trying to find him. Somebody I talked to, a woman named Dee Sturdevant, suggested that I talk to you."

That was true, literally, and also it kept Jay's name out of the conversation awhile. Alex had called Jay from the airport to report in, and Jay had reported back that there was no new word from the kidnapper, and that Linda was running a fever of a hundred and four. Jay had been rushed, or sounded rushed. He had thanked Alex for flying to the Coast and back. They'd made an appointment for two o'clock; after the noon conference, Jay said.

Alex's report had been succinct and had not included Dee's diary. After hanging up he had opened the phone book, not because he expected to find Barbara Binder but because he couldn't think what else to do for the woman with the fever of one-oh-four. Now he was here in this nondescript professional building sandwiched up against the Turnpike where the Back Bay met the South End. He was more interested than ever in the question Dee had posed to him about Jay's omission. One thing Alex had learned the hard way was the importance of being suspicious of clients whom he liked.

"You mean . . ." Barbara Binder kept her face neutral, cool, businesslike, but her fingers trembled. She didn't do anything about them. "*That* Foster? That Dee?"

"You all met traveling across the country in a converted delivery van. I think at the time you were running away from home."

She smiled a wide, fond, surprised sort of smile, very different than the one she'd greeted him with. She came around the editing table to lean against the edge closest to Alex. She folded her arms in front of her, crossed them in front of her breasts.

"Yes," she said. "I remember them. But who are you and why are you trying to find Foster? And why did Dee, whom I haven't seen since I was an adventurous teenager, refer you to me?"

"I'm an auto mechanic, your guess wasn't far wrong. I'm also—have also been a cancer patient, and that's how I got to know a doctor named Jay Harrison. One of Harrison's patients, a woman named Linda Dumars, is in a lot of danger right now, life-threatening, because something disappeared from the hospital where she is. There's some reason to think Foster could be connected with that disappearance. I went to Dee to try and find him. She didn't think you could help with that. She just noticed that Jay hadn't seemed to want to tell me about you."

"No, he seems to want to hush me up, sweep me back under the rug. Probably there could be mountains of reasons why." She stood up straight and put her hands in the pockets of her pleated slacks. "But I still don't see what you—"

"I don't blame you. I'm not the police, or hospital security, I'm just somebody Jay asked to help him look into this. When push comes to shove, it's Ms. Dumars whose interests are my interests, not Jay's. I think you can see why. If you want to check on my story, you can call either the doctor or the patient at the Dennison Cancer Center. Although neither one of them knows I'm here. Or I can tell you the whole story from the beginning, if you have time."

"Well, I—frankly, I don't know what to say. I'm supposed to show a rough cut to a client in half an hour." She took her hands out of her pockets and put her fingertips on either side of her mouth, a strangely old-fashioned gesture but one that kept her fingers still. She struck a lot of poses, Barbara Binder. That was her way of dealing with something—men who couldn't see past her body, perhaps. Alex remembered the woman in the wetsuit who'd collected the ransom. She'd struck poses too.

"This is really embarrassing to me," Barbara said after a minute's thought. "I don't know anything about whatever is wrong at any hospital, but I did try to get in touch with Jay, recently. I got brushed off in a way I found . . . I don't know. Surprising. No, insulting. He didn't tell you anything about that?"

"He didn't," Alex said. "He didn't mention you at all."

"If you'll come back in an hour, when I'm done with my client, I'll make the time to talk."

Just in case, Alex spent the hour outside, lounging against the railing that overlooked the Pike, breathing exhaust and leafing through the diary again. When he went back up to Barbara Binder's office, she was sitting behind her workbench, waiting, and she had a question for him. If she'd called Linda Dumars, the patient had most likely been in no condition to talk; if she'd called Jay, she didn't say so. If Jay had said Alex was overstepping his mission, she kept that to herself too.

"How the hell did you find me?" Barbara Binder wanted to know.

"You're in the phone book. It didn't have to be you, but it's not that common a name. When I called the number, I got—"

"Francie, out front. I used to be on my own, but now I'm in this sort of group practice, I guess a medical person would say. We're each listed under our own names. But that's not what I meant. When you were here before, I forgot that none of those people knew my last name. I had a, well, a traveling name. I was into a whole concealment trip, as we used to say."

"I know. You called yourself Ellen, but Foster made it Barbarella because Henri screwed it up. Dee lent me her diary, so I'm sort of an expert historian of all that by now." He hoped *historian* had the proper dispassionate, neutral sound. "Let me tell the history of this current problem, okay?"

Alex told her about Foster's letter and the kidnapper's messages and the beach and the visit to San Francisco, from which he had just returned. She sat with her hands folded on the workbench, her expression neutral, except when he showed her the photocopied pages, showed her the page that had Dee's conversation with the boyfriend's mother when they sent the boyfriend home. Then she put her hands to her cheeks again, but only briefly, and said, "You don't understand how embarrassing this is. Only it isn't anything compared to what you're telling me about this woman's life possibly depending on what you find out—which I have to believe is true. Do you want to sit down? Let me figure out how to start."

There was a swivel chair without arms at another bench full of equipment. Alex turned it around and sat down. Barbara Binder, once briefly Barbarella, started to pace back and forth. Every now and then she'd stop to pick up something—a screwdriver, a microphone, some stapled sheets of paper she could roll into a cylinder and point with when she chose. She didn't move like the woman in the wetsuit, Alex decided. That one had waved and swung her arm in a fashion calculated to draw attention. Barbara seemed both more and less genuine than that.

"I had no idea he was here in Boston until I saw that article. I looked at the name and the picture, and I said, 'Uh-huh, that's him.' So I wrote him a letter. I told him some of my memories, and suggested we could get together and talk about old times. I didn't know what would come of it—you know, old lovers getting together, you never know whether it's a good idea or not."

"Yeah," Alex said in a way meant to be encouraging. "Uh-huh."

"Not that this would really be old lovers, it was more like . . . I don't know what to call it. That was part of why I wanted to see him. I wanted to get the various views, camera angles on what happened, so I could straighten that memory out. I'm talking about how I contacted somebody that had once been genuinely nice to me but also had taken advantage of me at the same time. When I was very young. Well, young anyway."

"How young were you?" Alex asked.

"Well, I mean, people get married at that age, and pregnant a lot younger, but I know *I* was young. Just turned seventeen. So when I thought about being in touch with him again, seeing him, I was all flutter-flutter-flutter. Like a teenager. Even though I told myself I've been tempered by good and bad experiences. Even though I told myself he's sure to be old and dull and over the hill. I thought he might not answer, of course. It just never occurred to me he'd have his secretary brush me off."

"His secretary?"

"She sent me a note. I'd written him on my new stationery, trying to show I was grown up and professional too, I guess. For a few days after I wrote him I pawed through my mail here—bills, junk mail, catalogs—looking for his letter. I pawed through message slips, expecting one to be from him. I told myself it was too soon, what was I getting so anxious about? But in just a few days, there was an envelope on Dennison Center stationery. I felt so relieved. And pleased. At least I hadn't made a complete fool of myself. I opened it up and got a very nasty slap in the face."

"Do you have the letter? What did it say?"

She stopped pacing and gave him a quizzical look. "You really don't know, do you? It said, 'Dear Ms. Binder: Dr. Harrison has received your communication but wishes me to tell you he does not wish to accept your invitation at this time.' Or words to that effect. It was a form letter, I mean, that she called up off her disk. If that happened to you, what would you do?"

"Probably," Alex said, "I'd send a nastier note back."

"Would you really? Probably you would, but then you're a man. I told *my*self the sensible thing would be to forget it. Why waste any energy on somebody that acts that way?"

"I don't know," Alex said. "I don't think it's sensible to just sit and take it. You didn't accept your own advice, did you?"

"No. I looked him up in the book, the way you did to me, and went to his house. I let my finger hover over the bell, but I didn't ring it. Instead I walked away and sat in my car, just watching, thinking maybe he'd come in or out, maybe I'd learn something, or he'd recognize me, or he wouldn't. But nothing happened. I still couldn't let it rest. One time I called him at home, just to see who would answer. Nobody, only his machine. I even went and got a look at his secretary, like that would help me figure out whether she brushed me off by her own initiative. She could be getting it on with him on the side and hoping to marry him like a romance magazine. Believe me, *I* was like somebody in a romance magazine."

"You do sound kind of obsessed," Alex agreed. He added,

"His secretary, Deborah McCarthy, is already married, by the way."

"I know. I saw her ring. And yes, that was the name signed to the note, McCarthy, if that's what you're trying to find out. But vanity knows no bounds. I thought, well, so what, they could still be having an affair."

"They could. Did you save her letter? In case we wanted to confront her with it?"

"Hey, wait a minute," Barbara Binder said. She pointed a warning finger at Alex, a finger that shook just a little bit. She was a woman both self-possessed and nervous. "I'm telling you all this because of the patient that's in trouble. I'm rapping it all down like you're a tape recorder or a biographer, a dispassionate observer, okay? I'm not asking for any help, thank you. Anyway, I don't have much doubt about the affair part."

"That you made it up, you mean?"

"No, uh-uh. Obsessed, you said? I called it a mania, but I think obsessed is good too. It was just, maybe I went celebrity crazy, seeing him in *People.* Maybe I wanted to know how come I'm not famous, how come it's him? Or else maybe he's always been lurking in the back of my mind as a . . . well, a future I expected to catch up with, but never quite did. It's hard to explain, unless you already know what I mean. Anyway, I went back to his house one more time, to spy on him. I don't know what else to call it. And I turned out to have guessed right about the secretary, after all."

"You did?" Alex said.

"I did," Barbara Binder said decidedly. "I watched her leave his apartment on a Sunday morning, when she ought to have been with her husband or at church." The words were supposed to be humorous, but she shook her head sadly, as if still in the process of letting it all go. "I thought of marching up and introducing myself, saying, you remember my letter, right? But that would be childish. She was having a hard enough time. I once made the mistake of falling for a boss."

"You saw her, but not him?" Alex asked. He meant maybe Deborah McCarthy had just stopped by to feed her boss's cat or something like that.

"Just her, but I saw the way she looked all around to see who might be watching her leave. Guiltily. Like she didn't want

103

to be so obvious, but she couldn't stop herself. Believe me, I know that way of leaving somebody's bed, somebody's house. And I thought, Ms. Barbarella, you've been sitting out here in your car for an hour on a Sunday morning spying on a man you haven't seen for twenty years. Now you know he's like any other middle-aged executive. Isn't it time for you to go on back to your own life?" She shook her head again, more grimly than sadly this time. "After that, I just packed it away."

"Uh-huh," Alex said. "I appreciate you telling me all this, I really do." He waited. "That's all?"

"Don't look so disappointed," she said, laughing suddenly. "I mean, I know this situation is very serious, but you can't be pinning all your hopes on me. I'm afraid I'm just giving you a sideshow. It's like when you pick up a rock, and whatever you're looking for, you find all these other interesting creatures living their crawly lives underneath." She started to walk again, dusting here and there, picking things up and putting them down. "Look, I hope this doesn't make me sound lonely or desperate or like I'm haunting the personals ads, because that's not really the case. Are you, um, going to be reporting all this to him?"

"I don't know yet," Alex said. "If I find out anything about which one brushed you off, Jay or Deborah, and why, do you want me to call you?"

"I want to say don't bother, but yes, I still would like to know. Or if you need to line us all up and find out who's not telling the truth . . ."

"Thanks."

"Sure," she said. "Listen, if I can help, I will. And, when you can, would you give my regards to Dee? Tell her she was really more of a formative influence than Jay, even if I wouldn't go all flutter-flutter-flutter at the thought of having lunch with her." She shrugged. "You know how these things are."

"I do," Alex said. This wasn't about influences. It was about whatever made you feel somebody else was inside your skin, and vice versa. Fucking them, making love with them, talking your hearts out—you needed that merge to get your balance back, paradoxical as it might sound. That was what had gone on with her and Jay twenty years ago. From her side, at least, it wasn't settled yet. "So," he said, "I'll let you get back to work. Unless there's anything else."

"Not that I know of. I bet there are things about Jay and all of them I've completely forgotten, just like there's other things that burned their way indelibly into my seventeen-year-old brain. I'll tell you something I think about, sometimes, which happened the night before we met up, when it was just me and poor old Ernie on the road. It doesn't really have anything to do with what you want to know . . ."

"That's okay," Alex said. He told himself the truth must be that he enjoyed the role of cut-rate shrink. He liked picking up the rock and seeing what wriggled around underneath.

"Oh, we got a ride, a long ride, in a big open flatbed truck. You know what I mean? Not a semitrailer, but big, and without any sides?"

"A straight job, truckers call it."

"A straight job? Well, this one was full of hitchhikers, not particularly straight, in the old-fashioned 1960s meaning of the term. It was cold, really cold, everybody was huddled up against the back of the cab to cut down on the wind. Ernie and I were last on, so our spot was close to the edge. I was on the outside, because I was tough, you know, I wasn't going to have him protecting me. All night I rode along the edge there, hanging on to a handle that was attached to the back of the cab. I can still feel that handle. It was rusty and had flaking paint. I was terrified I was going to fall asleep and let go of it. I could have had a very short life."

Alex gulped inside, picturing Maria's onrushing adolescence again. Today was Wednesday. On Friday she'd be back with him for a week, and he'd see what new enthusiasms or sullen silences she brought this time. Week by week it seemed to change, especially as the school year dwindled down.

"I'm glad you didn't," he said. "Well, I'll be in touch." He left Barbara Binder laying hands on her equipment. He didn't see why his client should be afraid of her. His client's secretary might be another matter, except this wasn't his take on Deborah McCarthy at all. He would have figured her for somebody who knew better than to mix sex with the power to hire and fire, who knew how to keep them separate before anybody got inside anybody else's skin or bed.

He'd have to confront Jay about all this, sooner or later. But first he needed Jay to vouch for him with Linda Dumars's nurse.

105

SEVENTEEN
Blind Dates

Boston boasts a few hills of its own, but no valleys in between. Boston's hills tend to slope off into flatlands, many of them former marshes landfilled with old riverbed mud. Alex rode an Arborway streetcar underneath such a flatland, emerging onto the surface of Huntington Avenue in time to pass between the Museum of Fine Arts on one side and Northeastern University on the other. He got off at the corner of Longwood Avenue, near the foot of Mission Hill. From here on, Huntington formed a boundary not only between the hill and the flat but between residential, poor, and working-class Boston on one side and the institutional, well-endowed Medical Area on the other. Along Huntington some of the city's entrepreneurs were known to peddle cocaine to the daytime-only residents, doctors among them, heading home toward Brookline or Newton or suburbs farther west.

This particular corner, Longwood and Huntington, had a special place in Boston's recent social history. Here, a few years back, a black man intent on robbery had allegedly hopped into the car of an unwary white suburban couple on their way from childbirth class. Robbery had turned to savage, senseless execution, the bereaved and wounded husband had told police. "A family's shining life destroyed," the city's prestigious daily had rhapsodized, filling page after page with the random viciousness of the crime and with the couple's previous personal and professional bliss. A month later, the husband had jumped off the Tobin Bridge when his perfect murder came awry. It had nearly worked, purely and simply because he'd invented a demon in whom he knew the police and the DA and the press and most white and worried citizens would believe.

Alex walked up Longwood without incident and then twisted his way to the Dennison through old narrow streets that served the hospital towers now. He watched a truck full of gas cylinders back out of a loading dock. NEW ENGLAND CRYOGENICS,

106

the logo on the truck's rear gate said. GASES. FREEZING AND WELDING SUPPLIES. Some tanks were fat and silvery and equipped with gauges, like the liquid nitrogen tank Alex had seen in the blood bank. Others were narrow and rusty with flaking paint, familiar to Alex as the compressed oxygen tanks that welders used. Rusty with flaking paint was how Barbara Binder had described the handle on the back of the big flatbed she'd nearly fallen off of. He wasn't at all sure why she'd told him that story. He wasn't at all sure how much of the rest of her story to believe. Maybe she'd written a letter and Deborah had swiped it. Maybe Jay had gotten the letter and wanted to keep his distance. Or maybe Alex was being led around by the nose and Barbara hadn't written any letter at all.

Though the Dennison's lobby didn't seem any different than two days before, up on the seventh floor a security guard stood by the double doors with red stop signs that led to the transplant ICU. The guard accompanied Alex to the unit desk, then went back to his post. The woman running the desk said Yvonne was inside the sterile area. Alex would have to talk to her on the phone. Alex turned his back and spoke softly into the receiver.

"You showed me around for Dr. Harrison on Monday?" he prompted. "He told you I was a potential patient, if I remember right. Actually I'm an investigator. I'm trying to help about Ms. Dumars's marrow. You can check with Dr. Harrison or his secretary. I'm wondering whether I can talk to you for a few minutes, maybe if you have your lunch break soon?"

"Surely," Yvonne Price told him. If she was surprised she didn't show it. "I can meet you in the cafeteria. I'll be down there about noontime. In the back room."

The cafeteria had been empty when Jay had steered him there after the blood bank tour. Now it was crowded with medical personnel and service staff and patients' families. Alex got in a line for soup and salad, joined another line for a cup of coffee, and managed to grab an empty table in the back room. As in the front room, the walls and tabletops were a deep green, deeper than traditional hospital green, with blond wood trim. The only difference was that more of the service staff seemed to be grouped here in the back. At least, there were fewer ties and fewer stethoscopes. The white men in blue uniforms, with keys on their belts, were probably maintenance or mechanics. The black men and women in white pants would be housekeeping and orderlies. It occurred again to Alex how easy it was for almost anyone to move unnoticed around a hospital, regardless of age or race or class, as long as they had the requisite uniform, and knowledge, and nerve. But to come up with a plan like kidnapping bone marrow? That was what he wanted to talk to Linda's nurse about.

Yvonne came in carrying a tray and slowly looked the place over, nodding here and there. Another woman stood with her, looking around too. She was younger than Yvonne, early twenties, with deep brown skin. She had high cheekbones, a long jaw, and a face altogether as sharp as Yvonne's was round. Yvonne saw Alex and pointed. The other woman squinted one eye at him and shifted her chin to the side in an expression that was lively, almost funny, but that clearly said she was checking him out. Either Yvonne had brought along some protection, or else this other woman had something to tell.

"This is my girlfriend Wallia," Yvonne introduced her. The accent was on the second syllable, the *li*. "She's a nurse here too. Anything you would say to me to you can say to her."

"Thanks for agreeing to see me," Alex said as the two nurses sat. "How is Ms. Dumars? Is she doing okay?"

"She's doing her best. She's already got a fungal infection, inside. We're trying different antibiotics to see if we can find the one that will keep it in check. She's running a high fever and she can't keep anything down."

"Uh-huh," Alex said. He'd been wanting to meet Linda, to give her a chance to call some shots. He wasn't sure when it had happened, but sometime on that flight from California he'd started thinking of her as his client, even if Jay was paying the bill. Apparently he'd have to call the shots for her, for now. "Well, I'm sure you don't have much time, so I ought to get to the point. Jay hired me to look into some anonymous mail he was getting. Now he's got me looking into this mess, quietly. You checked with him?"

Yvonne did not smile now. "With Dr. Harrison's secretary, yes." She didn't emphasize the *doctor,* but she'd made her point. Alex was curious whose rule this was, whether it had to do with nurses and doctors or with black and white.

"He told me to call him Jay. It's not that way with the nursing staff?"

"Hospitals are set up like ladders. It's all what rung you're on. It isn't any different no matter what I call him, you know."

Wallia nodded vigorously. "A hospital is like an army. From the generals down to the privates. The privates wash the sheets and clean up the shit."

"Anyway I'm stubborn," Yvonne said. "The man you're working for is all right, not bad, but he doesn't always notice who's inside the body doing what he wants done." She picked up a fork and looked in a deadpan way at her lunch, ravioli in an orangy-colored sauce. "Now what did you want to ask me about?"

"What nobody's said out loud," Alex pointed out reasonably, "is that it takes somebody with a fair amount of knowledge to plan something like this. They need to know the procedure, the timing, how to handle the specimen. A lot of things like that. If there wasn't anything else to go on, I'd suspect a doctor. Wouldn't you?"

Wallia laughed and stuck her chin out. She looked as if she'd blow a long plume of smoke if cigarettes were allowed. She said, "That's the kind of questions this attending upstairs hired you to ask?"

"He hired me," Alex said. "I ask what I think will get me somewhere." He hoped that was convincing. Would it be more convincing if he looked like William Hopper or Tom Selleck? Not to these two women, he didn't think. Nothing about his appearance would be convincing, because it wouldn't change the fact that he was a white man working for a white man who was their boss. It might matter, though, that what he'd just said was true.

Wallia gave Yvonne a look he couldn't read. Yvonne finished chewing and put down her fork before answering.

"You're asking me do I know how far Dr. Harrison or any other one might stoop if they need a lot of money fast?" she said. "There's not a doctor in this place I know well enough to answer that about. I don't think Harrison would—it's hard to credit— but *somebody* stooped low enough. Either that, or either somebody really messed up."

Wallia nodded agreement. Alex said, "What do you mean?"

"I mean—and anybody who works in any hospital will tell you this—enough things go wrong in the normal way. Sometimes it's things go wrong, and somebody that made the mistake doesn't want to take the blame. So they point at somebody else, or they point without using their finger, if they can find a way."

" 'I *told* the nurse to call for that medication,' " Wallia put in. " 'It wasn't re*port*ed Mrs. X was al*ler*gic.' 'That *damn* Susie Q. didn't have me paged when the family came in.' "

Alex nodded. If a handbrake cable or a brake line went within a month after a car had been in his shop, the customer would be as likely as not to say, "I was wondering whether there's a possibility it could have been damaged while you were repacking the bearings." They said that even if they didn't know whether you packed bearings in a suitcase or surrounded them with foam peanuts or what. These nurses were talking about something different, more devious, but it involved the same human tendency to want to blame somebody, anybody, and definitely not yourself.

"What kind of a mistake could they be covering up, in this case? In confidence, of course."

Yvonne lifted her head just a fraction of an inch, and she gave a tired fraction of her empathetic smile. She knew what Alex's promise to keep his sources confidential would be worth if something like this were really going on.

"Supposing something went wrong about the marrow specimen between the OR and that tank," she said. "I'm just saying it could've been that Dr. Harrison messed up, handling the specimen, or it could've been somebody else on the transplant team, or the cryo tech in the blood bank too. *If* something like that happened, and all I'm saying is *if,* one way to cover that up is to make the marrow disappear by some kidnapper you pull out of the air. If it never comes back, nobody ever knows there was anything wrong."

That wouldn't account for the advance warning in the Foster letter, but there was always the possibility of coincidence. Or it could be that the person knew about the Foster letter, and that knowledge prompted them to choose this extreme way of covering up. Did Yvonne know about the letter?

"Is that what you believe happened?" Alex asked.

"No. I don't know what to believe. I don't know what to

believe, so I just go in there and tell her don't worry, we paid the money to the one that took it, now everything is gonna be all right." She looked at her friend as though this didn't quite cover it.

"Yeah," Wallia said, "tell him. You got to tell somebody. He's the first one that asked."

Whatever it was, Yvonne delayed. "I don't know what to believe," she repeated. Then, "Well, I just told you what I tell her. I didn't say what she tells me."

Alex waited. Yvonne looked at her watch and forked up another ravioli. She put it down uneaten. "Understand, I'm talking about a woman that's shot full of medications, that's sore and sick and run-down. She can't even get out of her bed 'cause of the number of tubes we got her hooked to. Patients like that say a lot they don't mean. Usually it all just blows over like a cloudy day."

Wallia said, "What you said about how it looks to be a doctor. It doesn't have to be one of the doctors here. The patient told Yvonne she thinks maybe it's her husband. Her husband's a doctor, some kind."

"Pediatric." Yvonne said. "Some specialty, g.i. tract or something. The first day she said to me, 'Yvonne, it's Tom, Tom's trying to kill me. He paid somebody to take that box out of that tank. Now he's got the money, he's gonna let me die and run off with somebody else.' A lot of the time the women patients worry about their husbands and boyfriends. They're expecting they're going to run around with some woman that's not locked up—somebody healthy, somebody pretty, somebody that's got their own breasts, if that's what it is they're in for. Or somebody that's got their own hair. I told her about that, it's a common thing we see, but she said, 'No, no, I mean it. He's ashamed to divorce me, but he wants me out of his way. He's always been a sneaky bastard.' " Yvonne emphasized *sneaky,* not *always* or *bastard.* Probably this was what Linda had done. "That's what she said. Then she stopped, and the sedative took too. Later he came in to see her. I asked her, you know, how did the visit go? She just said it was fine."

"Do you know anything about him?"

"As far as I know he's got two arms and two legs and no horns or tail. He came with her when she got admitted and stayed till she got out of surgery, from harvesting the marrow, you know, and then he mostly turned her over to us. He's not over our shoulder all the time like some doctor husbands, doctor wives. He's got his practice up in Boxford or Topsfield or some place, and he's supposed to be at home there too, looking after those two kids, even though they got a woman from Central America to do that work. The kids came in when she first came on the unit and looked at her room and all the equipment with big round eyes, and Mommy told 'em to be good and mind Daddy and Juanita, and they could come back when she'd be feeling better and in between they were supposed to write."

Yvonne looked at her watch once more and said, "I got to finish eating now and go back up. If you want to keep digging on this, you could talk to Kevin Royce, next door. She probably said a lot more to him. Wallia can tell you about what she calls the blind dates. Wallia used to be up on the unit. She works down in outpatient now." With that Yvonne turned her attention to the rest of the meal. She chewed and swallowed methodically, without appearing to taste what she ate. Alex thought she was letting him know she'd given as much as she was going to give.

"The patients can't see each other, right?" Wallia picked up. She preferred talking to listening, Alex thought, though she could listen all right too. "All the staff, visitors, can see all of them, but they can't see each other, like in some kind of riddle or quiz show almost. But the patients know what each other are going through, and they get real close over the telephone sometimes. Sometimes there'll be an organizer kind of thing, just like in any group. Somebody likes to be the busybody, the boss. That one calls around to everybody, they find out who's having a good day, a bad day, what all their counts are and all. So that's kind of a group thing. But sometimes it'll be people will pair off, and get real close that way, even though they can't see each other. That's what I call the blind date. Then one of 'em will get done, and go visit the other during contamination, that means the last couple days when the one that's done can start getting exposed outside the airflow and sterile care. Sometime's they're not what they pictured, and it gets kind of embarrassing. Other times it's different. What happens to them afterward, I'd like to run a study on that. I'd try and get a grant, if I had the letters after my name."

"Pairs?" Alex said. "These tend to be opposite-sex pairs?"

"A lot," Wallia said. "I can see you thinking about nine-hundred numbers." Alex hadn't been, until she suggested it. For a month nobody else could touch you. When you were up to it, you might spent a lot of time touching yourself. Another study, Incidence of Phone Sex Among Patients in Isolation Rooms. By categories: male-female, female-female, male-male. Or maybe, Development of Flirtation Techniques in the Absence of Visual Cues. Each one had experienced or was about to experience what the other one was going through. Talk about getting inside each other's skins.

"And Linda Dumars might be confiding in this Kevin Royce, you think?"

Yvonne said, "They're on the phone together a lot. You can visit him if you get Dr. Harrison's permission." She took one more mouthful, looking with distaste at the rest of what was on her plate.

"One more question, please," Alex said. "Do you have any idea, one way or the other, whether there might be anything romantic between Dr. Harrison and his secretary? Someone has suggested to me that there is."

Yvonne shook her head. "I don't think I can help you about that."

Alex looked at Wallia, who seemed to him to be suppressing a grin. But all she said was, "Rumors like that are cheap in a place like this. Sometimes there might be something to them. Sometimes it's just a way to make the place a little more alive. You know, you don't look much like a detective. I don't really see you sneaking up to people's bedrooms, taking pictures through the window and shit."

EIGHTEEN
Tom Dumars, in the Doghouse, With an Ax

This time the security guard said hello to Yvonne and waved the two of them past. Alex looked around for Jay but didn't see him. He asked Yvonne who else could give him permission to visit Kevin Royce. She said it could be Dr. Jennings, the fellow, or else Dr. Kramer, the senior resident, but Kramer was out of town and Jennings was probably busy in the lab. Jennings was always in the lab working on Harrison's research projects. She said the best thing would be to call Dr. Harrison's secretary and get her to beep him. In a few minutes Jay called back with permission. Yvonne showed Alex to the scrub room and told him what to do.

Alex changed into the faded green outfit, feeling like he was getting into somebody else's old, often-washed pajamas, and as he did so he realized all of sudden how tired he was. He'd stayed up all of one night and slept on airplanes the next. It had been fifty-some hours, he calculated, since he last got any solid comfortable sleep. This was what it must be like to be a resident on duty, from what he had heard. Doctors put their successors through an initiation rite so the successors could thereafter feel they'd earned their privileges and their fees. Did that system contribute to mistakes being made?

Once he'd changed into the scrub suit, Alex opened the sterile washup packet Yvonne had given him. Inside was a kind of bristly sponge impregnated with soap, a sort of Brillo pad for human skin. Alex washed his hands carefully and then his arms up beyond his elbows as he'd been told to do. Then he took the wrapping off the sterile yellow gown and booties and cap. He felt disguised, playing dress-up doctor. Yvonne, waiting at the anteroom door, laughed.

"He's expecting you," she said. "Don't touch your mouth, your hair, your beard. If you can remember, don't touch anything in the room with your hands. Kevin's doing fine, but his polys are just around two hundred still."

Alex remembered polys: polymorphonuclear cells—a type of white blood cells—key to fighting off infection. Even during his own milder, ambulatory chemotherapy, he had gotten his polys counted all the time. With a count below 200, you would guard your isolation as your life.

Once they were in the anteroom Yvonne pointed toward the proper doorway, but Alex stopped in front of the curtain he'd looked through the previous time. Through the forest of IV stands and tubes and machinery, Linda Dumars was barely more real than she had been in the sterile stretcher cart. He could see a shape under a blanket, a shoulder clad in a hospital johnny, and a head like a baby's, sallow and bald.

Experimentally, he put his arms into the long plastic glove things built into the curtain. They were like robot hands for manipulating radioactive materials, only here the danger ran the other way. "Hey!" Yvonne said behind him, suddenly alarmed, but Alex didn't try to touch anything or anybody. He just raised his right hand and gave Linda Dumars a wave. Then he took his hands back out and headed for the room next door, where he belonged. The whole process made him remember looking at Maria through the nursery window, Maria sleeping not long after she'd first been born. He remembered his awkwardness trying to hold her the first time.

Kevin Royce did not seem newborn. He had wide shoulders, muscled forearms, and a head like a wooden block, nearly that rectangular, with piercing blue eyes. Instead of a johnny he was wearing a regular shirt and pants. He was entirely bald, his arms and cheeks and chin as well as the top of his head. One IV line emerged from the V neck of his shirt, carrying a liquid that was nearly clear. He slid off the bed and stepped toward Alex. The IV tube was long enough to let him reach most parts of the room, Alex realized. It made the patient seem like an astronaut maneuvering on the shell of his craft.

"Kevin Royce," he said, in a shaking-hands tone of voice, although he didn't extend his hand. "What was your name?"

"Alex. Alex Glauberman." Alex said loudly enough to be heard over the blower sound. He hoped he wasn't shouting. He stood awkwardly, with his hands in the pockets of the yellow gown. He saw that Kevin had a typewriter on a table, and a desk chair, and also some dumbbells and ankle weights in a shiny metal tray on the floor. The tray looked like something for sterilizing instruments or dissecting livers in. "You seem good. What day are you on, here?"

"I'm day twelve, knock on wood." He sounded confident, the confidence of a man who knew for sure the marrow was regrowing inside his bones. "The nurse said you're working on Linda's marrow. You making any progress, or what?"

"I don't know," Alex said. "Is it okay to sit in the chair?"

"Sure. Long as you don't drool on it." Kevin sat himself on the side of the bed facing the big window. The window looked out on another hospital tower across the street. Alex sat and turned his back to the view. On the typing table was a studio-type portrait of a boy, ten or eleven. Kevin sounded energetic, and he did look good, but compared to the ruddy-cheeked boy he looked pale and tired still. The picture was sealed in plastic, like a drivers' license, and taped to the table, instead of standing upright in a frame. It had been removed from its old frame and sealed up here in the hospital, inside some sterile field, no doubt.

"We're hoping it shows up tomorrow," Alex went on, as if discussing a lost dog. "I'm following up some leads as insurance. Just in case."

"Insurance," Kevin repeated. "For when the ransom turns out to be a con job. This place runs on insurance. That's Linda's job, did you find that out? She works for a goddamn insurance company, figuring their odds. I wish to hell there was something I could do for her, besides listen. I'd give her the rest of my marrow that's still frozen, if it would do her any good." As he talked his eyes shifted from Alex to another sealed photo, a small snapshot taped to the pedestal that held most of the equipment, near the head of his bed.

When he saw Alex noticing, he plucked the photo off the post and held it out. "Don't touch," he said. A woman was standing in front of a tree. She was spreading her arms as if in celebration—of an occasion, the weather, it was hard to say. She wore shorts and a sleeveless shirt. "That's Linda, last summer. How did they know whose marrow to take, that's what I want to know. How did they know she was day zero coming up? Either they knew because they knew her, or they had a way to get at

116

hospital records. I don't see any other way it could be. Do you?

"Don't worry," he added as he saw Alex hesitate. "She's already told me all about it. As much as they've told her, which probably isn't the whole thing. If they knew her, it's as likely they'd be trying to kill her as just going for the money, right?"

He said this without flinching, but with the quiet ferocity of somebody used to saying things that nobody seemed to be listening to. Drunks often sounded like that, and so did very clear thinkers. The speech could be followed either by shutting up or by acting out, verbally and physically throwing things around.

"There must be a lot easier and less detectable ways to kill somebody," Alex said.

"I know that," Kevin snapped. "If he's trying to kill her, he wants her to know it. She says her husband has had to watch kids die. It could unhinge you. He could blame her. You know how guys blame their wives for their own mistakes?"

There wasn't any wife picture in here. Alex guessed Kevin Royce was speaking from experience, gained somewhat too late.

"My mistake was probably who I married," Alex said mildly. Agreeing for the sake of agreement wasn't going to get him anywhere. Kevin obviously had grabbed onto Linda's charge against her husband. Alex needed to know whether Linda had given him more grounds for doing so than she'd given Yvonne. "But I've done my share of blaming like that, wife, girlfriend, yeah."

Did he blame Laura, his ex-wife, for the fact that he couldn't just pack up himself and Maria and move to Missoula or Albany or Seattle if Meredith got a job offer in a place like that? Did he blame Meredith for trying to find a job? Just insurance, Meredith said.

"Is that your kid over there?" Alex asked.

"Kevin Junior. He's marking off my days on the calendar. I promised him a trip to Canobie Lake to ride the roller coaster when I get out."

"Linda's husband," Alex said. "Is there any reason to think he had access to the blood bank, where the marrow was?"

"He's a doctor. He could put on an ID and waltz in like he owned the place. I don't know. I've never even seen the blood bank. Have you?"

"Yeah. Not exactly Fort Knox." Kevin was sticking the

117

snapshot back onto the post. "Were you, did you and Linda know each other before you ended up—I mean, both found yourselves in here?"

"Nope. I'm Malden, she's Topsfield. She wrestles with numbers on a computer, I weld cars and other broken things together. Probably what I do is more likely to give you cancer, though that's not how I got mine. Anyway, I asked her for a picture. She told him, Tom, to bring some in. 'For the others in the unit,' she said. He doesn't tell her about who he runs around with, anymore. She didn't tell him about me."

"How *did* you get your cancer?" Alex asked. He asked partly because he didn't have any clear or fixed idea how he'd gotten his own. Lymphomas tended to be classified as "environmental" rather than "life-style" cancers, which was only to say you didn't acquire them, as far as statistical correlations went, by smoking or eating or not eating any identifiable thing. You didn't get them, they got you. The marrow transplant unit here specialized in lymphomas and leukemias, but Yvonne had referred to breast cancers, and Alex's doctor had said the treatment was increasingly being used in such "solid-tumor" cases too.

"I've got a lymph cancer, same as Linda," Kevin said. "The rate for men my age is fifty percent higher if they served in Vietnam. It's from Agent Orange, and it's about the only Agent Orange damage the VA will admit. They're paying for me, at least. I'm lucky, compared to guys that have to deal with the sterility and the birth defects the government won't cop to at all." He explained this in that same quietly angry way Alex had noticed before. This time he apparently had exhaustive and damning data to back him up. "They're the POWs the country's turning its back on, as much as those guys who might or might not be out in the jungle somewhere."

"Jay Harrison once worked with some kind of underground railroad for Vietnam-era deserters," Alex said. "It crossed my mind that somebody, the ones not ready to admit the war's over, might be taking that out on him now. That he undermined the war effort. Sold out the ones doing the fighting." He didn't need to keep finding ways of saying it. Obviously Kevin would know what he meant.

"Crazy Vietnam vet sucks marrow from woman's bones?" Kevin shot back. "That ain't the right style. It's too sneaky. The guy you're talking about would bust down Harrison's door with an M-16 and say hey, Doc, kiss your ass good-bye."

"Uh-huh. So you think it was the husband. Convince me. Tell me why."

"Huh? Look, you're gonna tell me I never even met the lady, and I'm a guy lying here scared of dying, grabbing at reeds. That's what my brother said yesterday. I didn't tell him about her marrow getting ripped off. He asked why I seemed so down, and I just said I was worried about the woman next door. He said, 'She married?' and I said sort of, and he said 'You see, I know my brother. As long as she's married, he thinks he's in love.' What do you mean, convince you? You're supposed to be the investigator, according to the nurse there. All I can do is tell you what Linda told me."

"Okay," Alex said. "Sorry. That's what I meant. If you can give me anything to go on, I'll try to follow it up. If the marrow doesn't come back, I'll give anything I find out to the police as soon as Harrison or whoever decides to call them in." He hesitated. He knew that everybody knew the last person to trust was the one who rushed to explain how close they came to standing in your shoes. Nevertheless he said, "If it matters, I got treated for lymphoma two and half years ago. If it matters, I wasn't in Vietnam."

Kevin watched him for a minute, expressionless, then put up his hand for Alex to high five. Alex forgot about not touching, but Kevin took his own hand away before their palms actually met. Kevin said, "Did you graduate from alcohol, or did you slip past that one, too?"

"Slipped past," Alex told him.

"Well, batting three-thirty-three ain't too bad. I'm six years sober now, and trying to stay alive. You see that machine over there?" He nodded at the typewriter. "I thought I was getting to the point where I'm going to try and write some of this shit down for my kid. Only it's not my story, it's Linda's story busting out of my veins right now. Now, you want to hear it or not?"

"I want to hear it."

"Uh-huh. She put him through medical school, okay, while she typed and filed and her company paid for her to build up her credits in math? Then she did the diapers and the dishes, and finally her degree, and once they started coming into the cash, she

119

found out he was spending his time and energy and motel and traveling money on some babe. They were going to get divorced and then, bang, she felt these bumps in her armpit and all. They patched it back together while she got better. Lately she knew it was falling apart again between them, only a matter of time. Bang, relapse." He pointed at the wall full of air vents. On the other side of the ducts was a solid wall, on the other side of that was her room. "Now here she is."

"Does she blame her husband for the disease?" Alex asked. If she did, he was ready to toss the husband-kidnapper-murderer hypothesis right out, and Kevin's infatuation along with it too. It made sense to blame your disease on a government that dropped carcinogenic chemicals on a populated countryside and then dropped you in there to inhale and ingest them alongside the natives you were supposed to round up. It didn't make sense to blame your disease on an individual that didn't love and honor you the way he should. That smacked too much of self-pity to suit Alex. He didn't like to jump at reasons and causes that weren't really there.

"No, that's me talking if it's anybody. Not her. She only blames him if he decided to take God's will into his own hands. Like he thinks, oh shit, here she's done it to me again, if I don't fight back I'm going to be saddled with this little sickie that's going to wear out my life too."

Kevin Royce cocked his head sideways at Alex and shut his mouth. Like Yvonne Price, he'd said what he had to say and now he wanted to see what Alex was going to do.

Alex nodded, and then they talked some shop about welding and keeping half-antique cars on the road. Kevin's own marriage interested Alex, because that last bit had sounded a lot like the voice of sad experience again. Still, Kevin's theory might be plausible, and if it was really Linda's theory, then Alex felt morally bound to follow it up.

"Her nurse says Linda told her some of those suspicions, just once," he said after a while. "Then she acted as if she never said it. Was it the same with you?"

"No. But she did say, let's wait awhile and not tell anybody. Maybe the dog'll come back like he's supposed to, wagging his tail. Then we'll be sorry we said Tom took him out in the woods

120

with an axe. Once you make that kind of accusation, then you can't ever take it back."

"Those were her words, about the dog?"

"Those were her words. She had some kind of dream, about Tom killing the family dog because she, uh, looked at another guy. She called me and told me the dream when she woke up." He let Alex have another shot of those piercing eyes. The eyes dared Alex to claim Linda wasn't in love with Kevin the way Kevin was in love with her. Maybe she was, Alex thought. Maybe this was the beginning of a perfect match too.

Inwardly Alex stomped on the pun. If the marrow didn't come back as it was supposed to, a perfect match was what Linda would need, a perfect blood match, and it wouldn't be a matter for jokes. "Linda hasn't got any siblings?" he asked, hoping Jay had been wrong that first night.

Kevin said, "Linda is a loner. An only. Like Kevin Junior." He pointed at his son's picture. Alex could only hope Jay would get lucky and hit the number with some cousin or some random blood donor whose data was close enough to Linda's to warrant further tests. He was due downstairs to talk to Jay now.

Deborah McCarthy looked up from her desk and said, "I'm sorry, Alex, but Jay had to cancel. This was a bad week to start out with, even if none of this had happened, because the senior resident is away now, he's got a job interview. Ms. Dumars's nurse called earlier, by the way, to make sure it was okay to talk to you. And now you must be coming from the next-door-neighbor patient, is that right?"

"Uh-huh," Alex said, wondering what lay behind this chatty efficiency. Was it anything more than the way she did her job? "I'm not hard to keep track of. I have a lot of theories but no data, as the boss would say. When can I see him?"

She looked at the calendar on her desk. At least, she made a show of looking at it. "What about noon tomorrow?"

"Noon tomorrow? I've hiked up and down the beach and been to California and back. Is he avoiding me all of a sudden, or what?"

Alex leaned against the wall and crossed one leg in front of the other. He stared at Deborah, watched her face color, saw a few spots in front of his eyes. That wasn't misalignment, just exhaustion. He sat down in the spare chair as if he might stage a sit-in, though he knew he was really going home to bed.

"I don't think he's avoiding you," Deborah said with a trained flak-catcher smile. "He had to cancel, that's all. He did say he won't get in your way if you want to 'nose around here' like you're doing, but he doesn't want to do that himself, not yet. If you hear from this Foster, or if Jay does, whoever hears should contact the other right away."

"One question, then. Did he ever get a letter from somebody named Barbara Binder? Somebody else he knew from back then, from the Foster days? Another old friend that wrote after seeing his face in the magazine?"

She took a minute to think, and Alex took it to look her over in a new way. He studied the pencil line of her right eyebrow, the right side of her lipstick, the tight pink skin of her cheek, her squared-off jaw. She had nice coloring on a face a little more sharply chiseled than many Boston Irish faces. She was wearing a red V-neck sweater today, no sweatshirt. The neckline revealed a little cleavage, but whether that was display or fashion or comfort Alex couldn't tell. If someone had asked him to describe her, he would have said a perky, reasonably attractive woman who seemed thoughtful and alert. So what? Did that tell him whether Jay Harrison couldn't keep his hands off her, or vice versa? Did those things really have anything to do with looks?

"I don't remember one like that. Of course, if it didn't have any threats or anything, I might not remember it. I'll make a note to ask him as soon as I see him, if it's important. . . ." She sounded just mildly curious, fishing.

"So you didn't answer a letter like that? Or maybe Jay dictated an answer saying sorry, not interested? Or he told you to pull the standard discouraging word off a disk?"

"No," Deborah said. "I don't think so. Is it important?"

"I don't know. This Binder knew Foster. Depending on what she said, her letter could have contained enough information for somebody else, someone besides Foster, to concoct that blackmail note. Or it could be important for another reason: this Binder is somebody Jay had a kind of a fling with once."

"Really?" Deborah looked interested. "Not the one he used to live with, that had the Persian cats?" She laughed. "The trivia we know about these men we work for. But she would have come later. You mean this was somebody who actually knew this Foster guy?"

"Yeah. So ask him for me, will you? Whenever he turns up." Alex stood and headed for the door, but he stopped and leaned against the frame to give his legs a chance to get solid and give Deborah time to find something more to say. "Noon tomorrow, then, but he should call me of course if anything happens, or if he thinks of anything."

"Noon tomorrow. I hope it's all over by then. When you gave them the money, they promised to have it back by tomorrow, according to Jay."

"I saw the note," Alex said. "Two days, they promised. I can testify to that." He wondered about his choice of words. He hadn't meant to imply a threat—or had he? He'd only meant he knew this from his own experience. As opposed to what? He shook his head, trying to shake off the San Francisco fog that seemed to have settled past his brain.

Deborah had said he "gave them the money." Something bothered him about that. He'd seen the note. He hadn't ever seen the money. For all he knew the mailbag could have been full of shredded medical records or leftover supermarket receipts. He shook his head again. That was an occupational hazard of this line of work. You stopped believing anything anybody told you. The old Jefferson Airplane song occurred to him, the one that started "When the truth is found to be lies . . ." He went home hoping he would find somebody to love.

NINETEEN
Still Alive

With a start, Linda Dumars woke to dim light in her room. She thought it must be morning and she ought to be getting up and making lunches and hurrying the kids and going to work. She felt a strangeness but thought it was the accustomed strangeness, the dislocation of sleeping in the former TV and guest room downstairs. Like dogs, people grew accustomed to sleeping in certain spaces. It was hard to adjust to a new space. That was a lot harder than adjusting to sleeping alone.

Only when she reached for the lamp did it all come back. She felt the cold metallic shaft of the pedestal thing, the equipment rack. She knew she wasn't alone, separate, but had these tubes sewed into her, above her breasts, down in her belly. With an effort she made the tubes less awful by remembering the name. They weren't horrid, invasive snakes. They were only Hickman caths.

Now, what about the other dread, the nameless one?

She lay there, on her back in the bed, her extended hand not yet searching for the controls. That was true, it wasn't a dream. Her marrow was missing, stolen. She reached for a bedpan, pushed buttons till she was in a useful position, peed into the bedpan and cried. She tried to concentrate on not making a mess of the sheets. That much she ought to be able to do.

The curtains between her space and the anteroom were closed, but a shaft of light came in through the portal. As always. That was the source of this morning's dim glow. But was it morning? She didn't know whether it was day or night. She put the bedpan on a shelf, wiped herself with sterile tissue, and used another piece of sterile tissue to blow her nose and dry her eyes. Then she fumbled for the button that worked the outer curtain, the picture window one.

The fabric folded itself with a hum, a motor noise, a new noise on top of the blower that never stopped. Outside she could see vestiges of blue and orange sky. Whatever had been happening, which she could barely remember, evidently she was still alive. Otherwise she might have opened the window and found nothing there. To live this way, with no world outside, that would be her own particular hell. She tried to laugh at the idea. It made no sense. She was only here temporarily. Because it was worth the chance. Then she would be her own woman again.

The twilight sky surrounded another building opposite, another hospital, nothing but hospitals here, what was that one called? The Deac. The Deac, Yvonne had said. Deaconess. At the time she'd pictured somebody, some Protestant church official, a woman with long hair and a stern face and a flowing robe. Another time Yvonne had asked what religion she was, because there were chaplains available. Catholic, she'd said, since she and Tom were nominally Catholic, herself from her German ancestors and him from his French ones. Nominally, but when the priest had stopped by to see her, she'd told him with some bravado that she'd neither made confession nor taken communion in too long a time. If she was going to start again, she'd said, she wouldn't want to do so out of weakness. If she were going to return to religion, she'd said, she'd rather do it out of strength. The priest had said something guardedly noncommital, that illness was not the same as weakness, and had promised to stop by again.

Linda opened her eyes. She realized she'd fallen back asleep, but not for long. She took her bearings now, determined to understand what was happening at least: twilight, the Deac, patients over there seeing the other side of the sky, seeing her window, her room. She was hooked up to four drips, it seemed like. She remembered talk of a white-cell transfusion. She remembered what Harrison had told her about white-cell transfusions. That had been in response to a logical, academic question she must have asked in his office, an age ago, before she'd checked in. White-cell transfusions could be done, but the effect didn't last very long. White cells were very important but very short-lived. Also there were side effects: fever, spasms, chills, respiratory distress. Something like that.

Linda looked at the sources of the drips. None of them seemed to be a blood bag. Not like when they'd given her platelets. Platelets and red cells could be transfused. You could live without manufacturing them, as long as you kept coming in for refills, till that drove you crazy. . . .

She started to cry again, at her own helplessness. She didn't know what day it was. She didn't know what was being pumped into her. She pushed the call button. She did not need to go through all this on her own. Too bad it had to be evening, though. The shifts would have changed. It would be Connie on duty now, not Yvonne.

Well, that was one thing she knew correctly, anyway. Connie came in, brusque and businesslike, big and blond with a picture-book turned-up nose. Linda handed her the the bedpan to take away. Connie put it back on the shelf and said, "So I don't have to wake you later, let me take your temp." Unlike the day nurses, the night nurses had several patients each. Linda thought Connie could have told her something, asked her something nonetheless. A thin, sharp chill rose up her spine, a terror of what she wasn't being told. No marrow, and now somehow past the point of no return. The chill turned into a shiver. She let Connie pull the blanket up over her shoulders and stick the electronic thermometer into her mouth.

"A hundred and one," Connie said a minute later. "You're way down, still coming down, that's good."

"But what day is it," Linda tried to ask. It came out a dry whisper, a whisper that hurt. Connie handed her the wet green plastic thing, to rub around the inside of her mouth. "What day?" she whispered not quite so painfully.

"Wednesday," Connie said. "You've been sleeping mostly, and running a high temp, since I came on last night. Now you're coming down."

Wednesday. Wednesday equaled Day Number One, evening. This at least came easily to her, a correspondence between numbers and things. Thirty-six hours late for reinfusion, more or less. "Transfusion?" she asked.

"What? No, don't talk." Connie held out a glass. Lukewarm water. It felt like lead going down. But it must have done something, loosened something up, because Linda could remember more now. She remembered conversations going on around her, herself feeling too tired to follow or participate. Sweating. Tom being there, gowned and masked. Trying to shrink away from him. Trying to spit at him. It was hard to tell what was real, had really happened. Some of it could be delirium, if she'd had a fever for twenty-four hours, if a hundred and one was "way down." She hung on Connie's meager words. She'd had a high fever, a bad sign, but her fever had broken now. She'd survived some kind of crisis, even without her marrow. That was an accomplishment. Linda leaned back against the upright portion of the bed. Physically and mentally she straightened her spine.

Day One, evening, and Harrison had said the kidnappers promised her bone marrow back by Day Two. Promised! Kidnappers who kept promises! She remembered explaining to Nicky about promises, he must have been two or three. When it was a promise, you had to really do it, not just mean to. Thieves' promises! And maybe the tooth fairy would come save her too.

Connie bent down to hear what she was trying to say.

"Transfusion?" she asked again. Drinking had helped her talk; the word came out better this time.

"Huh? Oh, no, antibiotic. Gentamycin. You're coming along great. I'll be back with bowel prep, okay? And then if you want to eat . . . or a bath? I bet a bath would be great." Connie's face lit up with a tired, synthetic smile. Bowel prep and a bath, very efficient. Wash the body, scrub the body, inside and out. "The scrub nurse is gone, but I think I can make time." She means that, Linda thought. Making the time. Everybody does feel bad for me. Everybody does what they can for me, the limited thing they can.

"I feel better," she said. "Wider awake. A bath, good."

The bowel prep wasn't so bad. She kept it down, even if it made her feel for the moment that she never wanted to eat again. Connie's big hands helped her out of the bedclothes. It felt nice to be washed, the warm sponge moving over her. She rolled onto her back and asked Connie to sit her up again. Looking at her naked body, she wasn't surprised anymore by the tubes growing out of it, or by her hairless crotch. But she remembered Kevin saying how he imagined giving her a bath. Did he imagine that part, she wondered? How much she looked like a little girl? She shivered. She had told Kevin so much. She'd told him the dog dream, in detail. Strike that from the record. Tell the jury to disregard it.

Connie said, "Cold?" and finished washing her, dried her, and put a clean johnny on. She maneuvered the garment over all the caths. "Anything else I can do?"

Linda ran the plastic thing around her mouth before answering. "No thanks, Connie. That was great." You were great, darling. "Oh, can you turn me toward the window? I just want to watch the sky get dark, and think."

"Sure I can. Call if you get to feeling hungry. Call me if you want anything at all."

If I *want* anything? When Connie turned her she felt vertigo, but it passed. The nausea would be less from now on, no matter what else. You bet I want something, she thought. I want my kids. I want them here. I want to hold Claire again when *she* throws up, nervous, the way she was about starting first grade.

Six months ago. How nervous she must be now. I want to see Nicky start school, I want to see him grow up, be a man different than his father. I want a chance to make their tedious lunches for ten more years. I want my goddamn marrow, that's what I want!

But she'd made it through one crisis, that much she understood now. She'd been on the edge and come back, and here she was, able to be in control of herself and to feel emotions other than fear. While she was lucid like this, she needed to take some time to try and think.

The orange glow was all gone. Just the darkening blue sky and purplish clouds were left. The sunsets and twilights were actually very pretty here, if you tuned out the buildings. All that pollution did pretty things with light if not with lungs. Linda thought, suddenly and clearly, *I want to live in the city after Tom and I are divorced.* In the city, really? Someplace the kids could grow up not needing to go everyplace by car. Of course, it would depend on how much money she had, what she and Tom worked out. He'd be grateful not to be saddled with her. But how grateful, and who else did he already have commitments to? She hadn't stooped to reading his credit card bills. For all she knew he could have negative balances all over town.

Tom, Tom, the piper's son, stole a princess and away he run. When they'd first met, he'd driven her far out from Spokane over the dry lands of eastern Washington. She liked that sparse country, but he swore they'd both get far away from it. "Drink it in," he'd said. "We're headed for trees and lawns and back-yard barbecue. Oceanside vacations. Symphony orchestras. Major league sports." He'd already applied for residencies the way some people bought lottery tickets, by the tens, and he'd made it seem like by the powers of tens. She'd warned him about the vagaries of probability. "My bright, cautious math major," he'd said. Her stomach lurched at that memory. If there'd been anything in there, it would have come up all over her. Had she really rested in his arms and listened to him say those words? Worse still, had she really lapped them up?

She shied away from that memory, like skin withdrawing from a needle. It wasn't just this one memory of her and Tom, it was that this was the way things happened over time. What seemed touching was fated to seem stupid some day. Like Kevin wanting to be her scrub nurse. Suppose she lived through this, and really took up with Kevin, unlikely as those combined possible outcomes seemed. How would that comment sound in six months, when she started to really know him, whatever he was really like?

He hadn't talked very much about his own marriage, yet. He'd said her name was Carol, and she'd looked like a cheerleader, and it had taken him a long time to get past her looks. Linda hadn't been sure whether that had meant she turned out to be ugly inside—or that Kevin was saying by the time he finally looked inside, it was just too late to get through. But she hadn't asked him to explain, and anyway he'd egged her on to talk about herself.

Kevin had been a good listener, and interested, she had to give him that. Yet going over it again, she saw that what he'd jumped on had been the exploitation, if that's what it was—how she worked and raised babies while Tom developed his skills, and how that wasn't fair. He hadn't had much to say about her own determination, what she'd accomplished lately in spite of that, what she'd accomplished primarily since her first diagnosis, as a matter of fact. That reticence could be because Kevin was intimidated by their differences. She liked to drink, herself, for instance, so she hadn't had much to say about his accomplishments getting sober.

The sky was dark now, almost completely. A lot of lights were visible in the hospital across the street. Here I am going over my phone conversations with the boy next door, she said. I'm dying, dollars to doughnuts, and I'm going over phone conversations with the boy next door. The human soul had a lot of resilience to it. She'd meant to sit here and go over possibilities, try to evaluate them: Tom, again, or an angry relative of some patient who hadn't made it. A disgruntled employee. Instead she was looking for love. And why not dream on, sitting here watching the faint stars come out, not truly faint, truly the stars were bright enough to shine all the way across light years of space and then through the city's murk.

The sky went black, no more stars, which meant clouds must have blown in. She started to call Kevin. Halfway through she hung up. There wasn't anybody to depend on. She pushed buttons to get the bed flat and hugged herself to sleep.

129

TWENTY
Parting Wild Horse's Mane

Alex dreamed. He dreamed he was there in the hospital, the same hospital, not to get treatment but to get put to sleep. That was what they called it, same as you did with the pet cat. The whole thing was very genteel. For some reason he was at peace with being put to sleep, or at least resigned, even though he didn't seem to be sick at all. There were some preparatory procedures to go through first. He was waiting for one that involved removing a vein from the inside of his leg and replacing it on the outside. Maria sat at the foot of his bed, the way he'd so often sat at the foot of hers. She seemed very grown up and calm. Apparently it wasn't time yet to say good-bye.

When he woke up it was dark in the room. He didn't feel he was coming out of a nightmare—no relief, no sweat, no edge of fear to tiptoe up to and then back away. The dream had felt more like a fantasy. It was how he'd heard people describe acupuncture anesthesia. You knew everything that was happening to you but you felt no fear or pain. He sat up, took a breath and blew it out with a sound like *whew*. Maybe he'd simply been too exhausted to manage a nightmare. The clock said 10:30 in red numerals, with another red dot indicating P.M. He'd been asleep since around four.

"Hello?" he tried calling. With an effort he remembered what day it was. Still Wednesday, so Maria wasn't here. She was at Laura's till Friday. But Meredith might be here. "Hello? Meredith? Anybody home?"

Nobody answered, so he got up and trudged into the kitchen. The light bounced harshly off the sturdy wooden table where so much of his life with Maria, his life with Meredith went on. Behind the kitchen was a back stairway, where wooden steps led down and a spiral steel staircase led up to Meredith's study. Alex had put the staircase in when he and Meredith had bought the apartment. The back half of the former attic was now a study for Meredith. In the front half Maria had her bedroom, which

130

she reached by the old stairs from the front of the second floor.

Technically, physically, the arrangement couldn't be beat. Yet if Meredith found a job in England or Iowa, and took it, everybody might need to move again. If not, would they stay here till Maria grew up and moved out? Or could there be another? Alex could not imagine starting over with a new baby. Earlier he'd remembered Maria in the hospital nursery, but now he saw her as a toddler, at the day care center door. He remembered the stoicism she used to display, a contrast to the writhing and wailing or the slow, almost invisible tears of some of the other kids. Though her model behavior had been a relief, he'd worried too about what was going on further inside. He sometimes missed those days—the sense of complete responsibility, of her dependency—but he felt glad they were over, too. Could he do this again now, whether his double images signified a tumor or not?

At the top of the spiral staircase there was light. Suddenly Alex wasn't ready to go up and tell Meredith his dream, or the thoughts he'd had since waking up. He could go up and try to marshall all the unexpected and unconnected facts that radiated out from Jay Harrison and his patient. If he was going to do that, Meredith would appreciate it if he came, as a polite visitor ought to, with a pot of tea. After filling the kettle with water, he left it to heat over a low flame. The low flame would give him some time for t'ai chi.

He went into the living room and he did some slow warm-up exercises to stretch his hamstrings and loosen his arms and work his knees. Settling into a stance with his feet hip-width apart and his weight even and sinking, he paused till he felt some energy coming back up. Then he started at the halfway point of the t'ai chi form, the second Cross Hands.

It didn't take him long to forget everything but the form, and not long after Embrace Tiger, came the movement he was enjoying the most these days. This movement, actually three positions out of the form's total of a hundred fifty, went in English by the name of Parting Wild Horse's Mane.

Parting Wild Horse's Mane was a thrice-repeated sequence of slow-motion chops and blocks. You blocked with one palm facing downward and chopped with the other palm facing up. You alternated between two different opponents by means of deft pivots that let you rock back and forth and swivel from side to side as you advanced. If you visualized anything, Alex's teacher said, it ought to be these opponents, not any horses. Yet the name meant something to Alex, and as Terry, his teacher, said, "Well, if it means something to you . . ."

Three times, once in the middle of each sequence, came a moment when his two hands passed each other, nearly touching in front of his chest. They passed slowly, each radiating and sensing energy, as if they might really be capable of finding a perfect imaginary part in the mane of a lithe, darting wild horse. Once in a while he could feel himself separating the strands of long rough hair and finding some perfect secret within. This was an intense, nearly sexual feeling that he told nobody about.

Alex did Parting Wild Horse's Mane as slowly as he could. He tried to feel the hair on the horse's neck, to make it yield but not too easily, because in t'ai chi your own body is supposed to be less substantial than the surrounding space. He tried to maintain this insubstantiality into Fair Lady at Shuttle, less glamorously known as Old Woman Weaving in some translations of the ancient texts. The kettle whistled shrilly and the phone rang with staccato insistence at the same time. Alex darted into the kitchen, turning off the gas flame and picking up the receiver. The fair lady's loom lay devastated on the living room carpet, but that was the way it went sometimes.

Jay, he thought, and about time.

"Is that Alex Glauberman?" said a deep and somewhat raspy voice that wasn't the doctor after all.

"Yeah."

"My name is Paul Foster. You've been trying to find me, I hear."

"Oh. Uh-huh." Alex reached for some substance behind the voice. Not too hard, he told himself. Reach but don't push. "Did Dee tell you why?"

"Somebody I used to know got a letter. But I didn't write it. I don't have any idea who might be taking my name in vain." Choppy. Decisive. A long way from playing the flute on Metro platforms and collecting francs in a beret?

"Well, I appreciate you getting back to me. Do you, uh, have any ideas at all?" Dumb question, since the man had just said he didn't. "For instance, could there be somebody that

132

wants to make trouble for you? Somebody you might have told about Jay and that trip and everything?"

"It's not a story I tell a lot," Foster said flatly. Meaning what? That he was a man who told stories? That he was the kind who knew how to pick and choose, how to keep people's attention around the campfire, the dinner table, the shop, the bar? Or that he didn't tell stories, that he preferred to be what he was seeming now: a strong and silent type.

"Not a lot," Alex repeated. "You probably have better stories from those days."

"Don't be sweet-talking me, man," Foster said roughly. Alex didn't know whether he was being put on or not.

"This is really Foster, Paul Foster? Just to establish who you are, um, how did you end up in the army instead of in college? I don't mean to be glib or insulting or anything, but I want to be sure. Dee must have told you how serious this is."

The man didn't answer right away. For a minute Alex expected to hear him hang up. "A judge didn't like what I painted on a wall," he said at last. "Actually, that judge didn't like the whole concept of me. All right? Now are you going to listen to what I called to say?"

"All right. Yes. I appreciate it. What did you call to say?"

"What I just told you. That whatever is going on has got nothing to do with me."

Shit, Alex thought. If Foster was really trying to be helpful he had to see that this flat denial wasn't of any use. "No, I heard you," Alex said, pushing, "but then somebody, as you put it, has been taking your name in vain. Maybe somebody, it might've come up if you were telling somebody, not about Harrison, but maybe about Dee?"

"About Dee," Foster echoed, but her name sounded different in his mouth. Why? What burden was the syllable carrying? Anger? Regret? Alex tried to make himself insubstantial, to feel the opponent through his electronically reproduced voice. What was Foster, perhaps unintentionally, letting himself say? "What is it you think I'm telling? Tales of white women I have laid?"

"I didn't mean that," said Alex quickly, though in fact it had been one of the possibilities that had crossed his mind. "I'm just trying to account for your name being signed to that letter.

If you didn't send it, I'd think you'd want to help find out who did."

"And *I'm* saying that there isn't any *if* in this picture. I'm saying I crossed paths with the man once, with Jay, and that was okay. In fact it was fine. But now the paths don't cross anymore. I don't want his troubles, and he doesn't want mine. I'm a blind alley, do you get it? I'm sorry I can't help you out, but there it is." And indeed he sounded sorry. Not conflicted, but sorry. Unfortunately, sorrow didn't do Alex or Linda Dumars any good.

"I get it," Alex said testily, "but I want you to understand. I've been trying to keep you out of his troubles, and so has he. Dee got a visit from a car mechanic, okay, not a California state trooper."

"So far," Foster corrected him. "That's all the visits she got so far. And the reason I called is to try to keep it that way. I don't know anything about this letter." Foster delivered that assurance syllable by syllable this time. "I didn't write it, I didn't have anything to do with it, I can't tell you anything you need to know."

"Can you at least tell me where we can find you, in case we come up with anything, any questions we want to run by you at all?"

"Sorry," Foster said. "Because after you comes that state trooper, and that's the part I'm doing my best to avoid." He said this with a forced calm, as if talking to a child that willfully refused to understand. "If you need to get a message to me, you could try the, uh, channel that you tried before."

"Okay," Alex told him, though unwillingly. "I guess that'll have to do. I realize, um, that it doesn't make any sense. Kidnappers don't sign their ransom notes, and they don't send out warnings in advance. Unless they want to demonstrate their power." Unless you're calling me from Mexico, or from Tangier, and you're sitting happily on those three hundred thousand bucks.

"Yeah," Foster said. "I guess you have a point there. Only, see, I'm not."

"Okay," Alex said. He gave the caller credit for sticking to his story, for being rooted in it, so that it sure sounded like the truth.

Then Foster surprised him, because before hanging up he said, "You can give my regards to Jay." Through that exit line Alex thought he felt a few stray, rough hairs of wistfulness, disappointment, something like that. But maybe he was just projecting his own feelings. If he were in Foster's place, whatever the truth was, he thought he'd want to revisit that old atmosphere, that sparring, sometimes angry camaraderie which came through in Dee's diary. A certain—Alex didn't know what to call it. Something you never quite lost from those unexpected crossings of paths.

Yeah, white boy's romanticism, Alex told himself. Foster might have sealed his soul off from white people since then, or they might have done it for him. Or forget white and black. Foster could just be done and settled with that particular May of 1971 phase of his life. Alex hung up the phone and turned the flame back on. He put tea leaves in the pot, waited for the whistle, and poured. He held on to the handle of the pot with one hand, and two cups with the other, and carried them carefully up the spiral stairs.

It took him quite a while to tell Meredith about the phone call, and about Barbara Binder, and about Yvonne and Wallia, and Kevin and the husband, and everything that had happened since he'd talked to her this morning when he'd gotten off the plane. Finally he got around to telling her about his dream.

"As a cheap shot," she said then, "I'd say that even subconsciously you're riveted to the knowledge that it's really happening to her, not you. That's why you were so coolheaded about whatever was going on. In the dream I mean. I think about her a lot myself."

And Alex knew that neither of them could forget the woman in the isolation room, even later when the two of them were in bed and horizontal at last. Her hands were gathering and squeezing, and his were too, each gathering up the other like snow into a snowman, only warm, but molding the other and melting them that same way. Through the pleasure he felt with a quick stabbing pain that Linda Dumars might never get to make love again. He slid his hands around Meredith's hips, lifting them onto his. He loved her hips, the bones protruding but not sharp. He loved holding her there and easing his way inside her. In the hipbones, the big flat bones, that was where so much marrow congregated. That was where, Jay had explained, you could get it most easily. Linda Dumars's hipbones were where they had "harvested" her marrow from, and now it was missing, gone.

Obligations, Alex thought, obligations of the bone. He tried to forget them, and for a little while he did. When he and Meredith were snuggled together back to front like spoons and Alex was thinking he really couldn't let go of her, he discovered that she too hadn't forgotten for long. She said, "I'm a little older than Linda, not much, right? And we're the same ages as Jay and Barbara, you and I?"

"Uh-huh," he said. He picked up on the comment about Barbara and Jay. "Would you have fallen that way, for a guy that much older, when you were seventeen?"

"I never ran away from home until I ran away from Roger," she said, a finger tracing his own, which lingered on her breast. Roger was her ex-husband, whom she'd married when she was twenty-one and left when she was twenty-three or twenty-four. It was funny he had the same name as Dee's boyfriend. Dee's Roger was bearish. Alex had always pictured Meredith's Roger as a sort of Prince Philip or Prince Charles or one of them—cuter, maybe, but equally stiff. "Roger was four years older, a very proper distance. No, I don't think I had the guts this Barbarella had, not when I was seventeen. Though I don't think I would have stayed enraptured for twenty years of absence, if I had done, you know?"

"Uh-huh. She says she was trying to leap into her future or something. And she never quite caught up with it again."

"Sounds a bit intellectualized. If I'd been more daring, the attraction would have been that he's seen the world and all these women, and look, I'm what really turns him on. I *am* impressed at how she felt—whatever she felt, and at the same time she kept that anchor well dug in."

"Anchor?" Alex said. Sometimes Meredith's metaphors got the better of him.

"How she was adamant it was temporary, a brief adventure, she was just testing her wings, only that and nothing more. She used a trick out of fairy tales, like Rumplestiltskin, where the way to power is not to reveal your name. Like Ulysses and the Cyclops. Like the wizards and dragons in those books Maria loves, the ones by Ursula Le Guin. Well, Barbara, Barbarella understood this. He was older and she was in awe and all that, but also she made the rules. Don't you think he tried to get her to tell? To keep his options open? When I ran away from Roger I didn't let him know where I was for a month, because I was afraid of getting talked into going back. You're asleep, dammit."

"I'm not asleep, Professor," Alex said, though it was true he'd been working hard to pay attention, no doubt about that. She didn't usually talk much about Roger. She consigned him to some distant trappings-of-Empire past. Before falling completely asleep, Alex said, "Tomorrow I'm going to ask you where did you hide."

This time Alex dreamed that Linda woke up in darkness in her isolation room and couldn't remember who she was. He couldn't remember either. But he had to find out and tell her, because every morning they came with plastic-covered stretchers to roll away the patients who'd died from lack of being able to hold on to their names. He ran through corridors ever farther from where the records were kept, practicing the words for how to ask what he needed to know. He couldn't get the words right. He couldn't find the records room because he was seeing all the doorways double and going through every motion twice. The stretcher-bearers were lined up outside the double doors, watching the clock, waiting for the morning bell to ring. *Dumars,* Alex remembered, *Linda Dumars,* but by then he couldn't remember whom he was supposed to tell. Or why.

When he woke up this time he was terrified and drenched in sweat. What he wanted more than anything else was to call up the hospital and be told that Linda Dumars hadn't succumbed to a sudden spiking fever, gone into convulsions, and died.

DAY TWO

TWENTY-ONE
Getting Caught

He was alive, that was the number-one blessing to count. The car had not gone up in flames. He'd walked away holding his torn shirt against his temple to staunch the flow of blood from his only wound. Yet there was a feeling, a familiar feeling, that had settled on him then and never left him since: a heavy weight of failure in his lungs.

That weight had descended immediately, as soon as he'd understood that his newly charmed life had come uncharmed. He wasn't king of the road, he was just a jerk that had totaled his rental car. And then the feeling had threatened to suffocate him completely, when his groping fingers, stained with his own blood, had come upon the cracked, worthless, and bloody plastic pouch. He'd carried this thing far off into the desert where he could be sure—if he could be sure of anything—that nobody would ever recognize it for what it was. Most likely some animal would sniff it out, and for that animal it would only be a tasty meal. As in his bright idea about the cat. *If you're so smart,* as the old refrain went, *then why ain't you rich.*

Well, he was rich. Right here on the plane, under the seat in front of him, he still had most of those bank checks and traveler's checks made out in the name of Robert Lynch. But he couldn't shake the memory of that hour in the desert—staggering out of the car, hiding the evidence, and then waiting for the highway patrol to show up while trying to figure out what the hell to do.

He hadn't been able to concentrate very well. Instead, a million what-ifs had clogged up his mind. What if he hadn't taken that extra drink? What if he'd gotten the coffee? What if he'd let Bobby sleep in the nice bed all night and fuck to his heart's content in the morning and then drive off to work in the daylight, as a sensible citizen would do? What if he were still in bed, therefore, asleep? What if he'd just accepted his lumps and not taken the marrow in the first place? What if he'd perfected the plan in fantasy, even gotten his Bobby Lynch documents for real, but then had the sense to let it lie?

Before he was done with what-ifs he'd been plunged into cops, stitches, and insurance. And then, exhausted, he'd gone and confessed the whole thing to Sandra. And *that* had been truly stupid. The only thing to be said for it was that it had scared her silly. What the hell are we going to do now? she'd asked in a scared-silly squeak. By then, he'd had a chance to think it out. Her fear had made her go along with what he proposed. Besides which, he'd appealed to her greed. If she could pull it off, he'd gladly increase her share. Twenty thousand, he'd said, and he would, happily. Now the two of them sat on the plane flying east, watching the bad movie, each wearing a plastic headset that delivered bad sound.

The movie had car chases, car crashes, make-believe gore. He kept feeling the real stuff on his fingers. That wasn't how he'd meant it to be. If this next gamble didn't pay off, however, he could see the only alternative—to go farther down that bumpy, unlit road. Better more blood than getting caught. Getting caught was a possibility he refused to acknowledge, a possibility he'd simply wiped off the slate when he left the blood bank without a trace. Now he had to acknowledge that it could happen. Getting caught was a disaster he could acknowledge but not contemplate. Lynching would be mild compared to the long and drawn-out inquisition, vilification, persecution that would come.

You're your own worst enemy, his father had said to him more than once. His father had been fond of pet sayings, and ready to trot them out whether they meant anything or not. What you heard repeated over and over had an influence on you. He wasn't his worst enemy, though. Potentially, the woman sitting next to him was, if she lost faith in his ability to pull the fat out of the fire and decided her best chance was to go straight to the police. He patted her hand. He lifted the little plastic cup from her ear, kissed the ear, and whispered, "I'm sure everything is going to be all right."

He realized he'd always hated giving assurances. He'd always hated it whether the assurances were true or false.

TWENTY-TWO
Putting the Kid Back In

At ten thirty in the morning Alex was in his shop, slowly turning the handle of a vise-grip attached to a thread-cutting tap. He knew now that Linda was okay, loosely speaking; he'd called and spoken to Deborah, and she'd been able to tell him this much. So he concentrated on painstakingly cutting threads into the hole he'd drilled inside a small segment of light-alloy steel rod. This cylinder was going to be the new cam for the door lock on an old Volvo 122. After he made the threads on the inside, he'd have to grind off a portion of the outer surface. Then the thing ought to work. It was better, he'd told the customer, than investing the time and money in trying to find a replacement door. When the phone rang, he jumped. The vise-grip sprang loose and landed on his toe.

"Yeah? This is Alex," he growled into the phone. It was probably one of the backed-up customers, wanting to know when they could get rescheduled. Sometimes he shut down for a day or two to pursue an investigation, sometimes he did it because Maria was sick. Customers who couldn't get used to the vagaries of dealing with a one-man shop mostly moved on. The rest stayed, and in return they got personal service like the grinding of this cam. He would have let the answering machine take the call, except it might be important. It might be Foster, calling back with a new thought or a change of heart. It might be Jay, with good news.

"Alex," Deborah's McCarthy's voice said. "You better get right down here."

"What?" Alex said. "Did the stuff, the marrow, did it show?"

"No. Not yet. But somebody tried to steal another sample."

"No," Alex said. He felt as if somebody had rammed something, a rod like the one for the cam, up his gullet from the inside. He felt constricted and raw from his gut up into his mouth. He felt the presence of somebody who purely and simply wanted cancer patients to die.

But Deborah had said *tried to.* If there was a guard at the transplant unit, there must have been a guard at the blood bank too. With a big effort he swallowed and talked. "They got caught?"

"No. I don't know what happened, exactly. Jay's down there now, with the police and all. In the sperm bank."

"The sperm bank?"

"That's where they tried to get specimens out of this time. Um, frozen semen. Jay just called up from there. He wants you to meet him, right away."

"Uh-huh," Alex said. The choking, strangled feeling subsided. The sensation of being in the presence of pure malevolence faded away. Sperm banks were a good idea. Before he'd had chemotherapy, given his new relationship with a younger woman, he'd decided the prudent thing to do was to make use of one himself. Still, they weren't like blood banks. You could live without getting your frozen semen back. You could even be a father. Not biologically, if your treatment happened to leave you permanently sterile, but when it came to fathering, biologically was hardly the most important part. Stealing semen was like stealing diamonds. Antisocial, no doubt, but no big deal. In this case, it might even provide an important lead.

"I'll be right down. Somebody won't be able to lock their car door, that's all."

"Okay," she answered. "It's in the basement, the other side from the blood bank. That's where he wants you to come."

No pun intended, Alex presumed, remembering what went on in the place where he'd banked.

Only as he started his car, his trusty if somewhat battered '75 Saab 99 EMS, did the implications of an attempted sperm-napping hit him like the truck that went barreling past to make the yellow light on Somerville Ave. If this had been done by the same person who took the marrow, it wasn't the act of a kidnap-per or kidnappers about to deliver the goods and close up their own shop. It wasn't what you'd do first thing in the morning before catching a plane for Acapulco and chalking up a job well done.

On the other hand, Alex considered as he forced his way out the driveway into the traffic, how could they expect to get a ransom for some guy's frozen sperm cells if they hadn't made good on Linda Dumars's marrow yet? He didn't like the way none of this added up. Suddenly he felt in the presence not of evil but of madness once again. He didn't know what else to call it but madness. It was the unbalanced, erratic feeling he'd gotten from the note Jay pulled out of the cooler two mornings ago. Unbalanced and erratic, whether the kidnapper composed the rhymes or copied them or both.

Alex drove up Webster Avenue over the old Boston & Maine tracks, then turned right onto Prospect Street into Cam-bridge, across Cambridge to the Charles and across the river into Boston. He drove like any Boston driver, treating yellow lights as hurry-up signals and pedestrians as moving obstacles, passing on the right when there wasn't any room on the left. Inside twenty minutes he was snaking his way up the tight spirals of the Dennison's lot.

He sprinted to the stairway door, where a uniformed Boston policeman stood. The cop looked him over but didn't say any-thing. Somebody was making a show of force. Alex thought about how many specimens of all sorts, more and less essential, were vulnerable to this kind of theft. Once the word spread to potential copycats, every blood bank, sperm bank, lab, and oper-ating room would have to be guarded. Which would never work, because you just couldn't run a hospital that way. The only alternative was a show of force, so the potential copycats would at least have to feel they might get caught.

There weren't any armed guards in the doorway under the sign that said SPERM BANK. That would have been enough to scare the already skittish clientele away. A card on the door said HOURS FOR DEPOSITS, 9–12 A.M. MON., TU., TH. Today was Thursday. In the waiting room, a few customers—patients—sat reading magazines, or flipping through them anyway. If they knew what had happened earlier, they didn't show it. They were waiting for their appointment times and their little jars.

When Alex asked for Dr. Harrison, the woman behind the desk nodded toward a short hallway that ended at a closed door. Through the door was a lab area where six folding chairs had been set up in what space the equipment allowed. The equipment included microscopes and two freezer storage tanks, insulated barrels like the one in the blood bank, the one the marrow had been stolen from. On the chairs sat five people—Jay Harrison, a uniformed security guard, a woman in a white lab coat, another woman in a skirt and sweater, and a man in a dark suit. The woman in the skirt and sweater, short and plump, was talking. Her face was flushed, her tone nervous and excited. She and the security guard were young, in their twenties. Everybody else seemed to be Alex's age. Nobody introduced Alex. He sat in the empty chair.

"So Mary came out and said she didn't remember that one, the one the nurse wanted to know about. She said the nurse told her it was for a follow-up test, not a deposit, we thought maybe that was why we didn't remember. We get familiar with the regular depositors, but the follow-ups, you know . . . So the two of us together were looking at the appointment book. Next to the appointment book just happened to be this memo about tightening lab security, not leaving samples unattended, that came around I guess to lots of labs."

She hadn't been making eye contact as she told her story, just letting her gaze flicker around the circle, but now she focused on each in turn to see whether anybody was going to offer any clues. Nobody did, so she went on, choosing to talk to the security guard this time. He was a short, wide, brown-skinned man in a tan uniform. "So I saw this memo, and I guess that's why I left Mary to dig through Tuesday's slips while I went in back just to check. I went in and like I told you—like I already told him, Ramon—she had the top of one of the long-term tanks up. Whichever doctor she worked for, I didn't see what business she had in there. I said, like, 'Ex*cuse* me.' She whipped around and then scooted for the door." The woman pointed to a door which had to lead from the lab directly to the main corridor outside. "I got a hand on her sleeve, but she jerked it away. I gave Ramon the button that came off."

Ramon produced the button, passing it to Jay Harrison, who passed it to the man in the suit. A shade of doubt crept across this man's high forehead and puckered his plump upper lip. He had a small, turned-up nose and sandy hair, regulation businessman's cut. The cut didn't quite disguise that he was starting to grow bald on top. He didn't seem like a plainclothesman, Alex thought, but he might be from some high-priced private investigative firm. He put the button in his pocket without showing much interest. "That was later," he said. "Let's try to stay in sequence. What happened after she jerked her arm away?"

"She scooted out the door. I couldn't chase her because I was worried about the tank. I yelled for Mary and tried to figure out how to shut it right. It was all steaming—evaporating I mean. Mary came and helped with that. By then it was too late to run after her. Anyway, we had some very nervous guys out front wanting to know what all the yelling was about. Mary called security and that's when Ramon here came. We went and walked around, him and me, up and down the hall, but I couldn't see anybody that looked the same as her. We found the cooler packed with dry ice, right outside in a shopping bag, like I explained before." She shrugged. "I think I would've recognized her, but I can't swear to it. When she first came in, she was just somebody in whites with a name tag. I told you, it's the busiest time. I'm just glad I thought to go back and check."

"You deserve to be glad," the man in the suit told her. "You hit the ground running, I'd say. Try to picture what she did when she first came in."

"Uh-huh. She said, 'Hi, I'm Marcia'—I think it was Marcia. 'From Dr. Weinstein's office.' Or Bernstein maybe. Some kind of 'stein,' anyway. And the patient was named Johnson, wasn't he, Mary? Only she didn't say the patient's name to me, just she wanted some lab values, they weren't in the data base. So I sent her back. Was it Johnson?"

"Ernest Johnson," the woman in the lab coat said. She was thin and curly-redheaded, rather flat-chested, with long legs in white pants, red sneakers on her feet. "She said he hadn't been here to make a deposit, just to get tested, the way Donna said before. Patients that have finished their treatment, we do counts on them. That's another function of the lab."

"Counts," the man in the suit said. "You mean their sperm counts?"

"Spermatazoa quantity, yes," Mary replied. "Semen volume, sperm quantity, morphology, and motility." Why did she feel compelled to one-up the questioner on the jargon, Alex wanted to know.

Jay said, "You could elaborate a little more on that for Special Agent Fridley, Mary."

Aha, Alex thought. Thank you, Dr. Harrison. Only one firm or department of government boasted special agents, and Jay wanted him to know who this man in the suit was. Alex felt all his organs stiffen just a little bit inside him. What some ancestors must have felt when they heard a wolf howl in the forest, not fear so much as an immediate sense of being on guard—that was how Alex felt about the FBI.

Mary said, "Oh. Yes. I meant whether they have deformed heads or deformed tails. How fast they swim, and how straight."

"It's like watching the swimmers in a crowded pool through a high-powered telescope," Jay added helpfully. Special Agent Fridley gave him a baleful look.

"Could you elaborate on what made her request believable?" Fridley said.

"We remember most of the names of the regular depositors." Mary smoothed out her white coat, as if trying to smooth out or brush off any blame. "Usually they've been in for a pre-analysis, and then they come four to six times to make deposits, depending on counts and volumes and how careful they want to be about improving the chances for an eventual insemination to succeed. We recommend twelve to fifteen vials per patient—twelve to fifteen for each child they'd like to be able to conceive. Each deposit tends to yield two to five vials, and they don't always succeed in making a deposit each visit, if you really want to know."

She smoothed her sleeve. "The point I'm making is that regular depositors might come in for up to six or more visits. So this Marcia, or whoever she is, was smart to say her patient was a follow-up. That could be somebody that was never here before, but wants to find out whether his treatment left him sterile. Or it could be somebody who has specimens on deposit and needs to know whether he has to bother to keep paying the rent. Treatment can last for months, and then the patient probably wants to wait for a while more and let his counts come back up, if that's what they're going to do."

Alex knew all this, though there was no reason to think that Special Agent Fridley did. Alex had stopped paying the rent and told them to throw away his deposits, because a test had showed that his counts were fine. The sperm-banking had been a kind of insurance, just as Meredith's résumés circulating around two countries were now. Alex directed his attention back to Mary, the technician.

"So it could be a name we used to know," she concluded, "but by now we've forgotten." She stopped and set her mouth in a line as if challenging anyone to think of any technical information she'd left out.

She was mad somebody had messed with her domain, Alex thought. Fridley was somebody to take that out on now. But maybe not. Maybe she too once got asked a lot of unconstitutional questions about a roommate who visited Cuba to see what was there for themselves, or who sat in at a Congressman's office. Or maybe she didn't think the best way to fight drug abuse was to hire a mayor's ex-girlfriend to talk him into scoring some crack. These days the FBI was refurbishing its image as the pursuer of "America's Most Wanted," but a lot of people remembered that it also functioned as the government's political police.

"Do you have anything to add to Ms. Forziati's description of this Marcia's appearance?" Fridley said in a carefully neutral tone. He was looking at Donna, the receptionist, the one who'd been talking when Alex came in. "Height, weight, age, hair color, jewelry, clothing?"

"Mm, about as tall as me—that's five-seven—blond hair in

149

curls, like a perm. She was kind of young, I think. I don't remember rings or earrings, but she might have had some jewelry, probably did. I didn't really have a chance to look at her, I told you, I was on the computer, and the appointment list. She had a white coat, sort of like Mary's. Some of the nurses wear coats and some don't. It was a long coat. I thought she might be a supervisor or specialty or something. That's another reason I might not've given her a harder time."

"By long, would you mean overcoat length?"

"No, just you know, like that." She pointed at Mary's lab coat, which came partway down her thighs. "On a tech that doesn't mean anything, but on a nurse or a doctor, you know they're somebody higher up."

"We don't always conform to this," Jay put in. He was wearing a sports jacket today, no white coat at all. "But the general rule is the longer the coat, the higher the rank. Attendings and fellows long, interns and residents short, among the medical staff. It may be some throwback to the Middle Ages, scholars' gowns, I don't know."

"And you're in charge of the bone marrow transplant unit?" Fridley said, troubled, looking at his notes or making a show of looking at them, Alex couldn't tell which.

"No, Dan Weinstein is medical director. I'm attending physician for April and May. He does the politics and paperwork, I troubleshoot; that's the distinction between directing and attending. That's why you're dealing with me. If you needed to talk to my superior, or I needed my superior to back me up, then that would be Dan. Then there's the chief of medicine and various other high gods over him."

Fridley lifted his chin as if sensing some condescension from the doctor. Then he turned to Alex. "You're Glauberman?" he asked.

"Alex Glauberman, Jim Fridley," Jay said, performing introductions. "As I explained, Alex is a patient of a colleague, besides being the one who delivered the money. Alex, Jim wanted you down here so he could interview you about the delivery. Jim is a specialist in kidnappings from the regional office of the FBI."

Alex watched a vein pulse in Fridley's neck, just above his collar. He noted this was the first time anybody had said anything about kidnapping or ransom. Fridley turned to Ramon and asked where he'd been stationed or on patrol, how long it had taken him to get down to the sperm bank. Then he said, "You're all confident nothing was stolen?"

"I pulled up the rack and counted the specimens," Mary announced. "The number was right. It'll take me a while to double-check all the labels against our records so I can be sure."

"To hold a patient's sperm for ransom," Fridley asked Jay, "wouldn't the criminal have to get away with all of that particular individual's specimens? Otherwise the patient could hope that even a single vial remaining would be enough to get the desired result. If one individual is fertile and the other is potent, well, that's a lesson many young ladies have learned to their dismay."

"It would depend how nervous the patient was, how much he wanted to conceive a child," Jay said. "But yeah, I think you've got a point. How hard would it be to scoop them all?"

"Oh, we group each patient's vials together, it wouldn't be hard to extract them all, I'm afraid," Mary said. "We don't do inseminations here, so we don't need to handle individual vials once they've been cryopreserved. When a depositor is ready to make use of his deposit, we usually ship all the vials out to the practitioner doing the insemination. The practitioner will keep them in his tank, or hers."

"Did this Marcia have any kind of container with her?"

"She had a purse," Donna said. "A big leather one. Let's see. She had gloves on, to protect her hands. I didn't see her holding anything at all."

"She could have dumped them in her purse or held them in her glove till she got out the door," Jay put in, "and then in the dry ice they'd be okay until she could get them in a proper medium."

"And normally, how often would you check your inventory?" Fridley asked Mary, ignoring the doctor's comment.

"Oh, not often." Mary smoothed her pants leg over her knee. "Well, there's no reason to, not in the inactives, the long-term storage tank. I check the coolant level, of course, but I don't pick up the rack and count. Even if I did, that would only be closing the barn door after the horse is gone. You seem to be suggesting someone had the idea of holding a patient's sperm for ransom? Have you ever run into that sort of thing before?"

"No, but it has commonalities with other cases, and I sometimes doubt there's anything really original left to be developed by the criminal mind. Ransom kidnappings at first were designed to extort the wealth of individuals, and especially of parents willing to pay anything to save a child, as the word implies. A more recent trend is to hit the wealth of institutions: a bank can be expected to shell out to save its vice president. In this case we may be seeing a new step, that's all. In a way, we've traveled full circle, putting the 'kid' back in 'kidnapping,' if you will. That is, an insurance company can be expected to shell out to prevent a whopping big settlement in favor of the patient whose sperm was lost. You can imagine what value a jury might place on inability to have a child."

Fridley looked around to make sure everyone had appreciated this lesson. Or else he'd run that spiel with half his mind while the other was looking for something different, Alex didn't know. Fridley appeared to be the new breed of FBI, more given to Pentagonese than cop talk. Just as the Pentagon now tended to be staffed by M.B.A.s.

"Well, as I said," Fridley wrapped up, "it seems that everybody hit the ground running this morning," He cracked the two women a white-toothed, cold-faced smile. "And the great advantage in this case is that the kidnappers or extortionists don't actually have the victim in their power. She's here, under your care, Dr. Harrison, not off in some basement with a weapon up against her temple all the time. Of course, given the delay in bringing us on board, we'll have to make some adjustments in our normal course of procedure. If I could speak to the blood bank staff as soon as possible, I think that would be the best thing. You know, they've already lost a lot of visual detail in the three days that have gone by."

"Somebody already broke in to the blood bank?" Donna asked, wide-eyed. "That's why they sent that memo around?"

"If somebody had told us that," Mary Forziati said acidly, "we could have been a lot better prepared." This time her disapproval was clearly directed at Jay.

"My sentiments exactly," Special Agent Fridley told her. "In the case of the blood bank, it was a male disguised as a delivery man for the gas supply company. Or that's the conclusion, anyway, that Dr. Harrison and his colleagues have reached."

Jay shrugged. "We had our reasons to try and avoid a panic," he said to the lab tech by way of explaining the secrecy. "I'm not sure yet we were wrong." To Alex he said, "There was a gas delivery Monday. The guy came at lunchtime, when Edie wasn't there. He used the usual procedure, which is to come in the front way and then open the back door, that feeds directly to the hall, like this one here. When we called the supplier, though, they said they didn't have any record of a delivery to us that day." He turned to the FBI man. "I'll tell Sandy Sorenson you want to re-interview his people at the blood bank. Maybe we jumped at the impersonator idea because it lets off all the hospital personnel that went in and out."

"And I'll want to hear the story you promised me from Mr. Glauberman here."

"Sure. I just need him for a few minutes first. We had a prior appointment. Then he's all yours."

Fridley gave Jay Harrison a long and hard stare, but he didn't object out loud.

TWENTY-THREE
To Whom It May Concern

Jay was on the phone talking milligrams of medication when Alex came in. The two ballplayers on the wall, Smith and the Eck, seemed to dwarf him. The wallpaper wasn't calming. The Japanese designs seemed unnecessary, vain. So much seemed to have changed since Alex had first seen this place.

"She's better," Jay said when he hung up. "That's one good thing. We've identified the flora and got the right antibiotic now. But she's weak, so whatever the next damn thing is, we'll be in trouble all over again, and maybe worse." He stopped and scrawled a few quick notes on the pad on his desk. "I'm supposed to be making medical decisions but instead all morning I've been with the fucking FBI. The kidnapper said no cops, and at least tacitly we agreed. We've got twelve hours, more even, before the

153

two-day deadline runs out. Now there's cops all over." He banged his hand flat against his desk in frustration. As he got louder, his face got red.

"So it wasn't your decision to call in police, even after the sperm bank." Alex said. Apparently Jay was pissed not only that a wrong call had been made, in his opinion, but also that it had been made over his head.

"My decision? No. Nobody's even been telling me what's going on. Now they tell me Fridley's been on the case since Monday, when I went to Dan Weinstein, who went to the chief of service, who went to the comptroller to get the money. Joe Topakian, the comptroller, said the insurance company would have a shit fit if they found out the theft wasn't reported to the authorities right away. Because the insurance company would have a shit fit, Joe went to Fridley. He already knew Fridley, if you can believe this, because Fridley conducted a how-not-to-get-kidnapped seminar at some damn executives' club that Joe is in. This is a medical decision, and Joe Topakian wouldn't know a stethoscope from a Foley catheter. All along they've had the FBI on tap, behind the scenes. Today Fridley got his excuse to come in and start making noise. Sperm samples. Who the hell cares?"

Jay banged his desk again, this time with a closed fist. He stood up and bit his raw knuckle, then looked at it as if he couldn't understand why it hurt. Alex would have preferred to give him time to vent some steam, but Fridley had to be suspiciously counting the seconds that went by.

"Well, it's done," Alex said. "You're not going to make things better by antagonizing the guy." Despite all the nonsense about commonalities and kidnapping history, Fridley probably knew how to be organized and businesslike. He might have the time and the staff to check and recheck everyone's movements, everyone's alibis, and something might come out of that.

Jay looked at him with amazement, eyes wide open as if he were being squeezed. "Me antagonize him? Before we went downstairs to interview the tech and the receptionist, he pulled me aside to let me know two things right away."

"What things?" It dawned on Alex that Jay was mad about something more personal than being superseded here.

"Number one, he'd 'developed information' about my connections with 'fugitives' in the past. Translated, he called Washington and asked them to peek into my old file. Number two, he'd seen the 'alleged' blackmail letter I gave to the local police detective, and 'as a matter of course' he'd had it 'professionally correlated' with material generated by Deborah's printer and mine. He'd concluded that I wrote the letter myself."

"You mean he thinks the whole thing is a scam you've been running?" Alex hesitated a second for his emotions to sort themselves out. "To tell you the truth, I wish it were." Which was as close as he'd come to saying, *To tell you the truth, I hope it is.* "Then you'd give the marrow back today as promised, and lawyers could fight about whether you really took it or somebody else did."

"Yeah," Jay said. "Well, under the circumstances, I had to explain about Foster, and why I changed the original letter, and I had to give Mr. Fridley the original, and he had to cross-check my story with Deborah's, and all of that. He still doesn't like me. Only now he's got me and Foster in collusion on his brain. A hell of a lot of good that investigation is going to do."

"Did you tell him about my trip to the Coast, and Dee?" Alex didn't mind the idea of Fridley putting the Dennison Center staff under a microscope. He didn't want FBI men pawing through Dee Sturdevant's diary the way those Maryland state troopers had pawed through her purse. Nor did he want them fingering her as "uncooperative" when her principles got in the way. Alex doubted more and more that finding Paul Foster was important. But if it was, surely the feds had better ways of finding him than that.

"You said it yourself, Alex. What's done is done."

Right, Alex thought. So Jay had told Fridley he'd sent Alex to see Dee in search of Foster. Only he didn't yet know about the diary or about Foster's call. It might not hurt to call Dee and warn her what was coming. In the meantime, Alex wanted to put to Jay the question Dee had raised.

"Jay," he said, "How come you didn't mention you fell in love that time, on the way west?"

Jay looked blank and then chuckled, only the chuckle turned into a cough. He said, "You're as bad as Fridley. Now you're 'developing information' about my sex life while he probes my politics, is that it? You're talking about Barbarella?"

His face colored again, though differently, a soft pink rather than an angry red.

"Uh-huh. You had a lot to say about Dee and Foster and feeling lonesome, after all."

"I don't know. Barbarella. It didn't seem important. Is it?"

"She wrote you a letter."

"She wrote me what letter?"

"An invitation," Alex said, pointedly checking his watch. "Didn't Deborah tell you I asked about a letter? From a Barbara Binder? They're the same person, in case nobody made that clear."

Jay goggled at him. His expression suggested that the space between atoms had yawned open for him to see.

"She asked about a Barbara Binder. I said I didn't remember anyone by that name. She didn't say what was supposed to be in this letter. Are you bullshitting me, or is this some kind of detective methodology? You too, Alex? You've decided it was me and Foster? Or the whole gang of us, Foster and me and Dee and Barbarella, like Ocean's Eleven or the Four Musketeers?"

"Fridley's waiting for me," Alex said. "And right now I don't know what to think. Just tell me whatever you've left out so far, please."

Jay sat down, put his elbows on his desk, and rested his closed eyes on the heels of his hands. He rubbed his scalp with his fingers. Then he slid his fingers down over his forehead, rubbed his eyes with his fingertips, and smiled at Alex in a rueful way. He said, "Okay, the truth, the whole truth, and nothing but. She had a—a kind of round babydoll face, not Kewpie doll, not a Miss America smile, but like a well-made smiling kind of mask. She had a pardon-the-expression Jewish nose that made the face more interesting to me. She looked like a woman, and it was hard to believe all that was new. I told myself it was ridiculous to fall for this teenager, even if she was thirsty for a lot of stuff I carried around in my head and needed to share. And what are we talking about? We're talking about a week or so. We're talking about three or four times we made love together and a lot of hours of long walks and late nights talking, the two of us speed-rapping, as we used to say."

"Three or four?" Alex asked. Whatever was true or false here, there was no way Jay could have heard from Foster, or thought he'd heard from Foster, and not have spent some time in reminiscences about the other members of that crew. The speech he'd just given was proof of it. Alex wanted to goad him into saying more.

"You're serious? Let's see. Four or five, Agent Glauberman. Then a long, long hug in San Francisco International, and then good-bye, out of her life, out of mine. Now you answer me. Who told you she wrote me a letter? I never saw any letter from her."

"She told me," Alex answered. "Yesterday morning, in person, about a mile from here. Look, I have to present myself to the special agent before he kicks in the door. But I want to keep at this, too, in my own way. Remember you said, better you than some damn SWAT team? Now I'm feeling the same. I want a letter from you, to whom it may concern. They should please answer my questions, because I'm undertaking some confidential research for you. The information goes directly to you and will be released by you only if and when you consider it medically necessary."

"Is that true? Or are you going to decide for me what information to release and when and why?"

"I hope it's true," Alex said. "Just write me the letter, okay? We're all trying to get the patient's marrow back."

"The high gods call in the FBI," Jay said as he wrote, "and at the same time they insist that not a word about any of this can get out. So I shouldn't be doing this, from their point of view, but they can only fire me once. You know that if you charge around asking too many questions, and you panic the kidnapper . . . As I told Fridley, you're taking her life, nearly literally, in your hands."

"Uh-huh." Alex read the letter, which seemed to be as good as he was going to get. "Among other things, I'm going to tell Fridley that the patient's marriage has been on the rocks. She thinks, or her neighbor Kevin Royce does, that her doctor husband might just be the one. Can you tell me where Tom Dumars works?"

"He's got a private office up there in the suburbs someplace, Danvers I think. For his real sickies he has admitting privileges at the General."

Alex said, "Thanks." He felt Jay's eyes follow him all the

way to the door. He was almost ready to swear those eyes were honestly and profoundly confused. Alex had done his best to sound tough-minded and confident. He would need to keep sounding that way. It wasn't how he really felt at all.

TWENTY-FOUR
Out of Their Sleeves

Special Agent Fridley had set himself up in the command room of the Center's security unit. There wasn't any sign on the door announcing COMMAND ROOM, but as Alex walked in that was how he saw the place. A bank of video monitors showed the street entrance, the lobby, and several locations that Alex didn't know. A white man in a tan uniform like Ramon's sat where he could view the monitors and a computer screen that had a lot of blue boxes on a pink field. The FBI kidnap specialist was sitting on a desk that must have been swept clean of whatever its usual proprietor kept on top. To his left was a pile of message slips, paper-clipped together. To his right were two empty coffee cups. There were no cigarette butts at all.

Fridley walked Alex through everything Alex could tell him from the first meeting with Jay Harrison on. He especially wanted to know anything Alex could tell him about Foster. What had been his rank in the army? When had he received his discharge, and what kind? What radical groups, if any, had been mentioned by name? Alex answered these questions to the best of his ability, if only because his ability was slight. So far the FBI didn't seem to be having any more success at finding Foster than he'd had himself. Less, even. But Alex kept quiet as planned about Dee's diary and Foster's call. He also kept quiet about his conversation with Barbara Binder. He wanted to pursue that avenue himself first. He told all about Kevin Royce's suspicions. Beyond a few perfunctory questions, Fridley did not display any interest in that.

"Why exactly do you think Dr. Harrison chose you to be his errand boy in all this?" Fridley finally asked.

"I told you. My doctor recommended me, and the idea of a cancer patient helping out tickled Harrison's fancy, I think. When things got serious, he figured who better could he trust? I never met this woman, the patient—I still haven't—but we have a lot in common still."

People asked Alex about the state of his "illness" fairly often, and when he was in a combative mood he sometimes said he didn't think of himself as "ill." When you were sick, you had symptoms, you felt bad. He didn't have any symptoms these days, unless you counted the double vision, and felt no worse than anybody else. What he had was a medical asterisk next to his name. The footnote below the asterisk said, we know what kind of cells are probably lurking in this guy, and we know the statistical chances of these cells succeeding at what they do best, which is to multiply out of control.

Alex got annoyed when people didn't understand this distinction, but he wasn't above using their uncertainty to his advantage when he could. The recovering-cancer-patient designation provided a kind of social protection, because people who didn't have one of those asterisks didn't know how to act around people who did.

Fridley shut his notepad and slipped it into the inside breast pocket of his suit. "All right," he said. "I can understand your motive there. No doubt you're aware that most states have regulations concerning the practice of investigation for any kind of fee."

"Chapter one-forty-nine, Massachusetts General Laws, sections twenty-one and twenty-two." Since his social shield seemed to have failed him, Alex pulled one of his friend Bernie's business cards out of his wallet and handed that to the FBI man. The card bore the name of Bernie's law firm, an immense and expensive one that filled four floors of a former sail factory near the harbor downtown. Not that Alex could afford to hire Bernie, but a certain amount of representation came with friendship, for free. As a warning, Bernie had given Alex a photocopy of the statute regulating private detectives. Alex had framed it and posted it on the wall of his shop. Bernie did admit that no overburdened state official would want to fight in court about the statute's application to some marginal freelancer like Alex—unless Alex pissed some powerful person off.

"This is my lawyer," Alex said. "If you want a police reference on me, you could try Sergeant Robert Trevisone in Cambridge. We've crossed paths a couple of times."

"I did that already. I did that as soon as they told me you were the one to deliver the ransom. Sergeant Trevisone told me he liked you personally, but he didn't see any prima facie reason I should believe anything you said." Fridley paused and smiled that cold smile. "Or words to that effect. I'm done with you for now. Unless you're due for a medical consultation or treatment, I don't want to see you down here again. We're dealing with an individual's life. Her medical care is in the hands of professionals. So is her protection from criminals. Can I make that any clearer for you?"

"No sir," Alex said dutifully.

You could skirt around the truth and you could play thrust-and-parry games, but the one thing you shouldn't do with any brand of cops was directly challenge their authority. Not unless you were prepared to spend a lot of time or money to make your point.

Tom Dumars put his quote-unquote real sickies in the General, Jay had said. Massachusetts General Hospital sprawled downtown on flatlands along the Charles River, a part of Boston's former West End, across Cambridge Street from the back side of Beacon Hill. The General and its associated clinics and hospitals formed a medical area all their own. This was where Alex's nurse customer who had told him about the Death Star worked.

Parking in one of the multifarious MGH lots, Alex hiked to the main lobby and, after several tries, managed to locate his customer, Lisa, on a house phone. She put him in touch with a unit clerk in pediatrics whose name was Patricia Fallon. Alex told the unit clerk that he was working for Dumars's wife, who just wanted to know who Dumars's girlfriend was. Patricia Fallon said that—only because Lisa had vouched for him—he could come up and explain this some more. She gave a series of instructions involving the White Building, the third elevators on the left, and the brown and green zones.

Comparing Mass General to the Dennison Center was like comparing Manhattan to Boston, Alex thought. He worked his way through corridors that were long and busy. Eddies of patients flowed past with the aid of legs, crutches, wheelchairs, and carts, themselves lost in a sea of medical personnel with IDs dangling from coats of various colors and lengths. When Alex got to the right place, Patricia Fallon said she could leave the desk just long enough to walk down to the end of the floor with him and back.

The unit clerk was not long past twenty. She had wavy black hair that cascaded about a round and wide-eyed face. Her large round glasses added to the effect. "Look, um," she said as they walked down a corridor that smelled of antiseptic, with the sound of canned television laughter coming from many half opened doors. "I know Lisa said you were a good guy, but I don't know about this. I wouldn't want anybody gossiping about my love life. Not that I'm involved with anybody married or anything. But it happens. Who's to say what ought to get passed on in any, you know, particular case?"

Looks could be deceiving, but Patricia Fallon did not strike Alex as a sharp-edged, argumentative type. If she didn't have anything to tell, she wouldn't be starting off debating the principles of the thing. He asked, "Is Tom Dumars the kind of guy it happens with?"

"The *kind* of guy? Well, yeah, I mean that's the reputation he has. The kind, he likes to take your hand, rub you on the shoulder, nothing you could prove that he was really up to anything by. I've heard there's girls here that have gone out with him, maybe, from time to time. So you could say he's that *kind* of guy, yeah."

"Would you say there's somebody working here that he might be seeing regularly these days?"

"No," Patricia Fallon said. She sounded relieved, as if she were responsible for the moral purity of the unit—or as if she'd have to deal with the fallout when and if such an affair went wrong. As the person who made the place run, in fact if not in name, she probably would.

Then what, Alex wondered. He thought about Kevin Royce and Linda Dumars, the hothouse relationships that could grow up in places like this. Was Tom Dumars involved with a teenage patient? No, the ward clerk wouldn't consider spilling that to a stranger looking to provide ammunition for the wife's presumed divorce case. If Patricia wanted to blow the whistle on something like that, she'd either go up the chain of command or file an anonymous grievance with the state. What about a patient's mother, though, a single mother in particular, who might develop quite a dependence on him? Alex tried to see a handsome and personable shithead of a doctor strolling down this corridor with his consoling arm around somebody's slender waist. The doctor could nurture in himself a mix of compassion and attraction that he could justify as a part of his job, his burden. . . .

"Dumars's wife is in the hospital, at the Dennison Center," he said, upping the ante a little. "She's really not doing very well."

"Oh," the unit clerk said. "Oh, um, I heard his wife had cancer, yeah. I didn't know she was hospitalized. It must be tough on her, if she thinks he's out having a good time with somebody else." They'd reached the end of the corridor, a picture window with a view of Cambridge and the Museum of Science. Around the corner was a play area, mostly empty now, just a few toddlers building quietly with colored wooden blocks. Patricia Fallon turned to face back the way they had come. "I don't know," she said. "I've got to get back to the desk."

"Suppose it wasn't just a doctor running around and his wife getting suspicious," Alex pressed hurriedly. "Suppose I could show you that a patient's life depended on finding out about this?"

"What are you talking about? Huh? I know the mind and the body, they're so much connected, but you don't sound like you're talking about his wife. You sound like you're talking about malpractice." She uttered the last word in a whisper, as if she were saying *hell* or *goddamn* in a church.

"No, I am talking about his wife, unfortunately. I'm talking about the fact that something went wrong with her procedure, something technical, that didn't go wrong by accident. Some people over there think Tom had something to do with it." He produced Jay's letter and gave her thirty seconds to read it.

"Look," she said. "You're confusing me."

"She's having an autologous bone marrow transplant," Alex said, "and at the crucial time, her marrow disappeared."

Patricia Fallon caught her breath. She looked all around as if she'd lost something herself. Her tongue circled her mouth and then she bit her lower lip, wincing suddenly at the pain. Allogeneic transplants were commonly used for childhood leukemias and immune disorders, Alex knew. The ward clerk must know about marrow transplants firsthand.

"That's terrible," she said. "But Dr. Dumars . . . Look, if it'll help to know who he's been sleeping with, okay, okay. Her name is Claudia Stevens, all right? You'll have to ask Dr. Steinkuhler for details. And don't say I sent you."

"No. No, I won't. This Dr. Steinkuhler, how do I find him?"

"Her," Patricia Fallon corrected him. "Senior resident. I'll page her. But I didn't tell you. You just heard the rumor, so you came and asked to see the senior resident. Okay?"

Dr. Steinkuhler turned out to be a very small woman with very short curly brown hair. She wore a long flowered skirt and a short white coat with a stethoscope in the hip pocket. Alex never did find out her first name. He flourished Jay's letter, unsure whether one doctor's loosely worded request would get another to snitch on a third. She led him around a different corner to a small office and shut the door. The office had a desk and two chairs and a phone and two travel posters, one a mountain and the other a field of flowers. Probably the office was shared by several staff on duty here. "Sit down, please," she said, gesturing toward the desk chair. But she remained standing, as if the conversation wouldn't be going on very long.

"I know of Jay Harrison, of course," she said with a nod and a respectful air. "I also know that Tom's wife is a patient of his. I'll assume there is a medically valid reason for this question, to do either with research or with patient care. Otherwise somebody of Harrison's standing wouldn't ask." Alex thought that statement might be tongue-in-cheek, but Steinkuhler's actual tongue rolled right on. She was in a hurry. She told the story without much prompting, and with a certain flair. Alex leaned back in the chair and listened hard.

"I don't know what Claudia Stevens is really like," she said, "but she is gorgeous to look at and she wears her breeding and culture on her sleeve. Not that she's exactly rich. I don't mean to make Tom out to be a—what's the word?—a gold digger, whatever else he may be. She's a concert violinist, and a widow. Her little boy had a serious and sometimes fatal illness, it doesn't matter what, though now he's going to be okay. When I opened a locked door I thought it was okay to open, I found her and Tom Dumars out of their sleeves and most everything else. You can imagine I was surprised, but I backed out and closed the door, of course. I might never have brought it up—he's quite a bit senior to me—if Tom hadn't approached me the next time he was here on the floor.

"He was all ruffled and tongue-tied and kept saying there really wasn't any impropriety here, no undue influence, consenting adults, and a lot more clichés along that line. I can't say I liked it—you may have read all the recent studies about doctor-patient sexual contact, or you may not. She wasn't a patient, of course, yet in terms of dependence and susceptibility, a lot of the same issues are involved. I told him I thought they ought to cool it until he wasn't treating the child any longer. If she still saw something in him then, and didn't mind that he was married, then as far as I was concerned they could screw all they wanted, it didn't matter to me. He looked at me as if I'd slapped him. Since then he's refused to talk to me, which I can tell you makes things difficult for everyone whenever he admits a patient here."

"Yes. I mean I can see that," Alex said. "When did this happen? Finding them like that?"

"About two months ago. Relations between us have gotten bad enough that I had to explain things confidentially to the nurse manager. Your presence indicates that she felt a need to tell someone else, and so the word has continued to spread. Unless you somehow dug this up on your own?"

Alex didn't answer that. He didn't think she really wanted an answer. "Are they still seeing each other, do you know?"

"No. That will have to be your job, won't it, finding out? She lives on Beacon Hill. It was very convenient, she could walk here to be with her son. He's a sweet kid, I liked him. In fact, I liked her. That may have been why I was so surprised."

"Because you didn't like Tom Dumars, even before."

"No. Since I've spewed all this out I might as well say that too. Too hearty, and I got tired of his hands-on approach with the female staff. I can get you Mrs. Stevens's address, for Jay Harrison's confidential medical purposes, that is. She's somebody people will remember seeing, if you go around asking. Tall and elegant, long blond hair, movie-star type. Who would it be? Faye Dunaway looks. Tom Dumars said I was just a jealous bitch, I was taking it out on him because I'd always dreamed of looking like that."

She stopped and raised her eyebrows. Alex thought a lot of people might call her pretty but nobody would call her gorgeous.

She said, "Well, of course I've dreamed of looking like that. Once or twice. Who wouldn't? Though I bet it gets to be an inconvenience. The way a flashy car impresses the people you want to impress, but it attracts a lot of car thieves too."

"Probably," Alex said. "I assume you know Tom's wife doesn't provide much competition right now. Do you think he could be serious enough about Claudia to . . . wish his wife would hurry up and die?"

"I see," she said, and a trace of a smile flitted across her eyes if not her mouth. Alex found that enjoyment disturbing. Was he supposed to add her to the list of people who *wished* Tom Dumars was a murderer? Kevin Royce might wish it, assuming the murder could be prevented. Alex knew he had a certain investment in Kevin's theory himself. That way the kidnap scheme could involve a doctor, as his gut kept telling him, but the doctor didn't have to be Jay. Except that if Tom Dumars was the kidnapper, and his objective was really murder, then he might already have let the cells thaw and die.

"I did expect you to get around to the missing marrow sooner or later," Dr. Steinkuhler added by way of explanation of the expression that had passed through her eyes. "You didn't really think I would tell you all this just on the basis of Jay Harrison's putative signature on a letter, I hope. You know these things don't stay secret, I'm sure."

So the word had begun to spread on the medical grapevine, just as Jay's bosses had feared. Come grant-getting and fund-raising time, this was sure to have its effect. With an effort Alex pulled himself back from the picture of Linda Dumars's husband casually tossing those two plastic pouches into the trash. If word had spread, he thought it might be useful to know who was doing the spreading.

"It might be useful to know *how* they don't stay secret," he said.

Steinkuhler hesitated over that one, checking her watch and backing off a step as if she really needed to be somewhere else. She said, "People need to talk about things like this. When they get scared. And this news is terrible and scary, as I'm sure that, whoever you are, you understand."

"I mean who as well as how," Alex told her. "I'm an investigator working directly for Jay. You can call him and check, of course."

"Yes," I assumed that. Well, in my case it was Gordon Kramer, we know each other from school. He told me what's been happening there, though he swore me to secrecy, of course. Now that I understand your suspicions about Tom, it occurs to me maybe Jay Harrison *wanted* me alerted for some reason. From what I hear, Gordon is Harrison's current fair-haired boy. He was in an M.D.-Ph.D. program and did his research in Harrison's lab. They say he's going to be his next fellow and all that."

Alex vaguely remembered the doctor in scrubs on the transplant unit that first day, the one who'd asked him, ever so politely, who the hell he was. That would be the same senior resident who was away the rest of this week, the ostensible reason Jay had been too tied up to see him yesterday.

"Look, I'm sure he's not the only one talking," Steinkuhler added quickly. She checked her watch and took another step away. This time she put her hand on the doorknob behind her. "Anyway, I'm just mouthing off now about why people gossip. I do have patients to get to still."

"You didn't answer my question about Tom Dumars," Alex pointed out.

"I know." She sighed, dropping her hand from the knob. She fingered the stethoscope in her pocket, the first time she'd betrayed any nervousness at all. "I have a very hard time believing any doctor did this, including him. Not that a doctor can't be a kidnapper or a murderer, but like this, by taking someone's bone marrow? Anyone who's worked in this area has suffered through patients dying for lack of a match, or because the match came too late. To tell the truth, I hope it's all some mistake—and believe me, that's not impossible by any means. Otherwise, if it's true there's ransom involved, I guess I'd look for somebody in desperate need of money. But that's all out of my department." She reached for the doorknob again, opened the door, and backed out.

TWENTY-FIVE
Deborah's Key

Dr. Steinkuhler, whatever her first name was, made good on her promise to supply Alex with Tom's girlfriend's address. Patricia Fallon handed it to him as he went past the desk. The address was on Joy Street. Alex found his way back to the front entrance of the hospital, turned left on Cambridge Street, and then turned right on Joy. He found the number he wanted halfway up the hill, across from the old African Meeting House, now restored.

Judging by the bells and mailboxes, Claudia Stevens lived on one floor of a narrow old four-story brick building. The small entryway had a scuffed marble floor, painted wooden wainscoting, and plaster walls with cracks showing through the paint. The "back" side of Beacon Hill was by tradition the unfashionable side, the high-class side being the "front," which looked out over the Common and was a short walk from the Public Garden and the Ritz. At various times the back side had housed free Negroes and working-class whites and bohemians, but those times now were gone. Even in an un-rehabbed building like this one, Alex guessed, a two-bedroom apartment must go for at least twelve hundred a month. He realized he hadn't asked whether Claudia Stevens had more than one kid, or the age of the one, or who the statuesque violinist's parents or late husband had been.

He rang the bell but got no answer. His watch said three o'clock. Maybe she was off picking the kid or kids up from school. He had other plans for the coming hours but decided he could afford a few minutes to wait. He loitered against the wall of a Laundromat at the top of her block. He tried focusing on the Holiday Inn sign across Cambridge Street, visible through the brick canyon formed by Joy Street homes. He saw two sets of letters, but just barely, like a TV ghost. When he turned his head the double image vanished, he thought. Still, it was kind of cloudy out. Though the neuro-op doubted this, Alex had observed that the visual misalignment got worse in brighter light.

What I'd like, Alex thought, is to get everybody together in a goddamn room, like an English drawing room, and hear all their answers, all their camera angles, as Barbara Binder said. And then I'd like to show how they don't form an image that holds up. Did Jay owe Foster a favor, or did Foster hold some kind of grudge? The same question went for Jay and Barbara, and for Henri the old boyfriend as a matter of fact. Jay could be the target of the crime, assuming somebody held Linda Dumars's life sufficiently cheap. Or he could be the criminal—but why?—or a confederate, maybe unwilling and maybe even unwitting, though it was hard to see how. Or the target could be Linda, or both Jay and Linda could be random victims, and the money might be all the kidnapper cared about. The kidnapper could be sane and businesslike, ready to return the stuff as soon as all the arrangements were made, or the kidnapper could be nuts, as the sperm bank attempt suggested—unless that was a diversion, a red herring after all. Lots of theories, some hunches, but not enough data, as Jay would say. For a start, Alex wanted to know about that letter Barbara said she'd written. To know about that he needed to know the truth about doctor and secretary.

When Claudia Stevens didn't reappear with a child or children in tow, Alex called Deborah from a pay phone inside the Laundromat. He asked her to meet him for coffee again, after work.

"No, I've got to pick up Richie from his friend's house where he went after Little League," Deborah said. "And my other two are at home with their sitter, and I really have to be there when I said. Monday was an emergency. I know it's still an emergency, but I've got a life to live too. You know what I'm saying, Alex. Richard is away all week. I really just don't have any slack. And I don't know anything that can help. Believe me, I wish I did."

"I know you don't have any slack," Alex said. Starting tomorrow he'd have Maria to think about. He couldn't devote his life entirely to Linda Dumars's cause whether Jay Harrison was paying for it or not.

Suddenly he knew what might be wrong with Barbarella's story. "Listen," he insisted, "how do you get home? Do you drive? Okay, look, just let me ride with you, um, as far as Forest Hills, how about that?"

Deborah told him she didn't go by Forest Hills, she took

Route 1 instead. Alex's knowledge of commuter routes to the southwestern suburbs was foggy, but he did recall the rotary with the sign about Route 1 to Providence where it diverged from the Arborway. He also calculated it would take her only about ten minutes extra to drop him where he'd just said. Deborah agreed, if grudgingly. Alex said he'd meet her on the corner of Longwood and Huntington. He said he didn't want to risk running into Fridley. For that matter, he didn't want to risk running into Jay.

Deborah showed up as promised, in a Ford Tempo. Alex sat in the shotgun seat as they crawled down Huntington toward the Jamaica Way overpass. In his Saab, Alex thought, he'd be shifting back and forth from first to neutral, easing up on the clutch or down on the gas. With the automatic and a high idle, Deborah didn't have to do anything but vary the weight of her foot on the brake. Still she kept her eyes ahead of her, apparently bewitched by the cream-colored Nissan Pulsar in front. On the rear end of the Pulsar was a bumper sticker: IS THAT YOUR HEAD, OR DID YOUR NECK THROW UP?

"This Barbara Binder," Alex said at last. "The one who sent Jay a letter that Jay says he never got. She says she saw you coming out of Jay's house on a Sunday morning. She says you looked both ways when you came out, as if you'd done something that didn't really make you happy. Or it made you happy, but you didn't want your happiness widely known." He realized that sounded snide, which wasn't what he'd meant. What he'd meant was to state exactly what Barbarella said she had observed, without coloring.

Deborah took her eyes off the car in front. Instead she looked at Alex the same way, with her eyes level and her mouth closed. Red circles formed on her cheeks, with white centers inside the red. She directed her attention back to the Pulsar and let her Ford glide forward into the two feet that had opened up. Then she turned back to Alex and said, "So? What's all that supposed to mean?"

"She—that's Jay's long-ago girlfriend—thought it meant you spent that Saturday night, and probably others, tangled up with the boss. Therefore she thinks you might have palmed her letter. You might have sent her a brush-off note on your own initiative, pretending the word came down from Jay."

"That's ridiculous. I told you I never saw this letter. I'm telling you now I don't spend any nights with Jay."

Alex didn't say anything. Somewhere ahead a light had changed. A car-length space opened in front, and Deborah moved quickly to cut off a Jaguar driven by a man in a suit and tie. The Jaguar man had made a dash from a side street but now he hung there, his bumper an inch from the door beside Alex, pretending he hadn't just lost a combat. He tapped a nervous finger on the steering wheel, though.

"Probably a doctor," Alex said. "Accustomed to getting his way. Look, if you and Jay are seeing each other, somebody has to know it. Yvonne Price or one of the other nurses. The unit secretary. Gordon Kramer, maybe. I hear he's Jay's protégé." He didn't know why he'd said that, except out of instinct. What somebody tells you, try it out on somebody else. See whether the images match.

"Was," she said. "Being Jay's protégé is a high-risk thing. Being his lover would be high-risk too." Alex wasn't sure what she meant by this. He thought of the feeling he'd gotten from Jay early on, the sense of a sequence of tests you kept having to pass. "He's the kind of man who goes all starry-eyed romantic and then wonders why it's not like Hollywood anymore. There's nothing between me and Jay Harrison outside of work except a little socializing, like I already said."

She made the yellow light at Tremont Street but got hung up in the intersection when it turned red. A battered old full-size Plymouth coming out of Tremont honked an off-key note as it stopped short. The driver, a young black man in a T-shirt, shook an admonishing finger at her. Alex saw this, but Deborah was avoiding eye contact just as the Jaguar driver had avoided it with her. Instead she searched Alex's face. "Well, do you believe me?" she said.

"About Barbarella's version, I was having trouble figuring out what you did with the kids. It was easy to see your husband being away at work, flying a client somewhere. But unless your mother was in on the thing, not just in on it but enthusiastic enough to cover for you by taking the kids, and it would have to be your mother, not a friend, because the kids would be bound to say, 'Daddy we spent Saturday night at . . .' "

"You don't believe *me,*" Deborah said, "but you've got an eye for those kind of details. Professionally suspicious, uh-huh. My mother wouldn't cover. My mother's of the you-made-your-choice-when-you-got-married school." She laughed, a fond laugh which softened her face. She hit the steering wheel lightly with her right palm. " 'You made your choice, Debbie,' she's always telling me. 'Now learn to live with it.' She's said that about everything from which doll to which job to which boy to which man. But this Barbarella, she has a good eye too. For details, I mean."

When Deborah inched out of the intersection, the Plymouth pulled in behind and gave her rear bumper a nudge. She looked in the mirror but didn't turn around. When she finally made the left onto the Jamaica Way ramp, the driver pulled around her and cut in front. She said, "What's his problem?" as if she didn't know. That didn't make her a liar, it just meant she knew how the game of driving in Boston was played.

"Jay's got a long-distance girlfriend, a doctor down in Washington," she said then. "I don't see much future in that one, either, but that's what you'll find out if you ask around for gossip. Nothing very juicy, believe me. He goes down there sometimes for the weekend, especially if he's got a business excuse. Once in a while he lends me his place."

"Nice kind of boss," Alex said. It did seem in character, though—it made him unconventional, it was a way of sharing the wealth, yet it didn't cost him any status of the kind he cared about. And what extra loyalty, if any, might it buy?

"Yeah, you could say so. That way I can give the kids a weekend in town, and besides I usually cook something to leave behind for him, and I water his garden for him too. He likes his garden, that's the only reason he's got the house instead of an apartment, as near as I can tell. Unless he once expected to, you know, have a family in it and then couldn't find the right person to have it with."

Now she was talking faster, keeping pace with the other drivers as the traffic swirled along the crowded parkway notorious for the frequent fender-benders on its twists and turns. Probably she could do this drive in her sleep and had it clocked to the second, since she'd juggled work schedule and family schedule for the last however-many years. They scooted by Jamaica Pond, which meant she'd better keep talking fast if Alex was going to stick to his bargain about getting off at the T station in Forest Hills.

"The time you mean, though, I bet I know what weekend that was. That weekend I left the kids with my mother, and Richard was away, yeah, and one of my old girlfriends and I had a little time on the town. We had kind of a little party there overnight. I stayed last, to finish tidying up. So maybe I, uh, maybe I did look a little guilty. Like, what were his neighbors going to tell him? Not that he's the kind to care what his neighbors think, or what I do on my own time. If this Barbara really saw what she says, it could be that's when. What was she doing there, though?"

"Spying, fantasizing, I don't know what to call it. Acting like somebody out of *True Romances,* she says. When she saw you come out after this tryst, or so she thought, that helped snap her out of it, she says."

"Tryst? Aren't you polite! Me and Jay, huh? Trysting the night away." She laughed again, relaxing, and passed up the Route 1 turnoff. "This Barbara. She's not married? She *says* she's not married, I mean?"

"No."

"And Jay and her . . ."

"Hadn't been in touch for twenty years, till she saw the article, according to her. And Jay didn't know where she was, according to him. Do you remember a movie called *Ocean's 11?* I don't know, you might not be as old as me. This guy, Danny Ocean, assembles his old army unit, platoon or something, to steal a lot of money from the casinos in Las Vegas. It was Frank Sinatra, Joey Bishop, those guys. Sammy Davis, Jr., played the garbageman, of course. They were supposed to get away with the loot in the garbage truck. It all got incinerated by mistake."

"No," Deborah said. "No, but maybe I am younger than you. Why?"

"Because Jay asked me was I accusing him of something like that? Him and Foster and Barbara and Dee Sturdevant, all the

172

companions from that cross-country trip. What do you think about that? Is he capable of setting up that kind of scam?"

"Suspicious is one thing. You're getting into paranoid, I think."

"Probably. As Jay quoted Foster to me once, just because you're paranoid doesn't mean they're not out to get you. If Jay lets you use his place, does he let you keep a key maybe? Maybe you keep it at the office, in case he locks himself out?"

"What are you getting at?"

"I'd like to borrow it. I won't disturb anything. I want to make a little 'surreptitious entry,' as the FBI would call it. It might help me put my paranoia to rest. Call it practicing conservative detection." Practicing "conservative medicine," Wagner and the neuro-op had sent him for a brain scan and had bored a hole to pull fluid out of his spine. It wasn't any more invasive to take a peek around Jay Harrison's house.

"It's a kind of trust," Deborah McCarthy said, "when somebody gives you their key. Especially when he lends you his place. Especially your boss. A fool and her money are soon parted. Same thing for a fool and her job."

"This party," Alex said. "With your old girlfriend. You said Barbara had good eyes, that she read your body language right. So there must have been somebody else there, somebody besides your old friend. Say, your own version of Barbarella? Some sexual phantom out of your past? Or your present, some unexpected one-night stand?"

"That's none of your business, Alex. And it's got nothing to do with the missing bone marrow, I swear to God."

Alex just shrugged, but he knew he was right. He'd finally understood how the gears meshed in one small part of this mechanism, at least. So when Deborah pulled up at the passenger drop-off for the Forest Hills T station, he sat like a bolt long rusted into place. "I need that key," he said. "And anything you know about his plans for tonight. Tonight would save time, if it's possible. Otherwise I can go tomorrow morning while he's at work."

Deborah drummed her fingers on the wheel. Alex crossed his arms. He wasn't getting out unless she called a cop.

"Oh, okay," she said at last. "You want to ride all the way home with me, I guess you can. I've got a spare key, yeah. In case

173

there's some kind of emergency when he's out of town. You can use it. But I'm doing this for the patient, not because I'm scared of whatever you think you're holding over me."

"Good," Alex said. "Me too."

TWENTY-SIX
You Know You Could Be Wrong

Richie—Richard McCarthy, Jr.—admitted to playing shortstop but otherwise met Alex with a blank yet curious stare. When asked about the Sox chances this year, he only shrugged. Yeah, Alex thought, and how would you feel if you knew I just threatened to rain suspicion and discord down on your happy home? Not that he could picture himself approaching the husband with what Barbara Binder had been sure she'd seen. On the whole, he thought Deborah wanted him to eliminate her boss from the list of suspects, and she'd just needed a little something extra to push her into going along. But what exactly had happened, and why she didn't want it waved in her husband's face, were mysteries he didn't need to probe.

Deborah quizzed the kids about homework responsibilities, put potatoes and a premade tuna casserole in the oven, and said she'd be back as soon as she dropped Alex at the train. On the way to the commuter rail station she said, "There's one other thing that happened, I guess you ought to know. Not that I believe any of this, but you'll hear it sooner or later. Jay's access number showed up on some queries about sperm counts, the way it would if he was trying to find out who was putting deposits in the bank."

"The way it would if he was trying to decide whose to hold for ransom, you mean?"

"In the computer, the patient data system, you can get all kinds of information on who's been admitted, and why, and what tests were ordered and what the results are. If you know what you're doing, you could figure out from this what procedures will be done on them, or what kind of specimens might be stored where. You need an access number to get into the system. Every time somebody queries records on a patient, the access number gets recorded too. You see what I mean?"

"Uh-huh. And Agent Fridley put somebody to work following back these electronic trails?"

"It makes sense Jay would have been asking for blood test values, like on Mrs. Dumars and other patients; it doesn't make sense he'd be asking for sperm counts. But his number doesn't prove he did the asking, because people borrow each others' numbers all the time. Doctors lend them to medical students, because the students haven't got any. Or if your number's being used for one query, you can't use it for another right then, so doctors borrow the numbers of other doctors and nurses and everything too. But it's got that FBI man all up in arms again. I just thought you ought to know about it, that's all."

From Norwood to South Station took Alex half an hour in a mostly empty railroad car. From South Station he took the Red Line subway to Charles and, for fifteen dollars, retrieved his Saab from the MGH lot. He followed Storrow Drive out along the river, cut across Allston into Brookline, and followed Deborah's instructions to Jay's address up on the big hill between Beacon Street and Commonwealth Ave. The sun had long since set. The curving street was lit by pale, clouded moonlight and diffuse circles under the streetlamps. Two days had gone by since Alex had stepped out of a cab on Dee Sturdevant's block in the Mission District. He drove slowly past Jay's house. According to Deborah, Jay wouldn't be home. He'd told her he had an appointment for dinner and then he'd be coming back to the hospital to wait for the kidnapper to meet the self-imposed deadline. Deborah said she kept Jay's business calender but not his personal one, so she didn't know whom the dinner appointment was with.

Jay's place was a two-story brick house with a tiny porch, more of an enclosed stoop really, a brick arch topped by a pointed roof. The stoop was a kind of a miniature of the house, which also had a peaked roof on which the peak ran front to back. *Charming brick one-family,* the ad might say, *with yard.* Assuming there was a yard in back, with garden, as Deborah had claimed. Assuming she hadn't sent him to the wrong place with the wrong key.

No one seemed to be home. No car sat in the driveway, and none of the windows were lit. Alex followed the curve of the street for half a block, parked, and walked back armed with the key plus a flashlight, two screwdrivers, and a pair of pliers from the toolbox in his trunk. He pushed the illuminated white door-bell that Barbara Binder's finger had lingered over, she said. He rang again. When he tried the key, it turned. He eased open the wooden door, pushed it shut behind him.

Just in case, he called out, "Jay?" He left the lights off, in case Jay should show up. He used the flashlight to guide himself up the open, carpeted staircase along the right wall of the living room, just where Deborah said it should be. At the top he'd find Jay's study or office or whatever he might call it. "It's got a couch I sleep on," she'd said. "I put the kids in his room, in sleeping bags. It would just seem weird, you know, sleeping in his bed." The office seemed like a reasonable place to start looking.

Looking for what, Alex knew, was a question with no easy answer, maybe no answer at all. He was here to prove or disprove a negative proposition—that no evidence linked Jay Harrison to any conspiracy to kidnap or appear to kidnap Linda Dumars's marrow. Conservative detection. So he supposed he was looking for a conspiratorial letter from Paul Foster or Barbarella or Dee. Or he was looking for recent deposit slips, traveler's checks, certificates of deposit—or a mailbag still stuffed full of cash or full of something else. He didn't know what he was looking for, except something that gave the lie to anything Jay had told him, or anyone else had said.

He shone his flashlight around the dark study. On the desk was a computer, of course, some kind of MacIntosh. Alex had a passing familiarity with Macs because that was what Meredith had, but a telltale file could be hidden under any cryptic or innocuous name. He gave the computer a pass for now.

Next to the computer was a phone and answering machine, which held only one message, according to the digital display. If he played it the display would go back to zero, but Jay, if he discovered that anomaly, would chalk it up to gremlins or machine error rather than human intervention, no doubt. The message was from somebody named Cathy who said to try her around seven or keep playing message tag if that didn't work. Cathy didn't leave her number and did sound used to this routine. Maybe she was the doctor in D.C.

Also on the desktop were a few piles of mail. Alex checked them, lighting each envelope with the flash, keeping the stacks in order. He found a bank statement, but it showed no big deposits. Harrison J. Harrison had four thousand some dollars in a NOW account.

Alex played his light on the bookshelves, finding a mix of medical books and journals, popular science, novels, travel books, some politics and history; nothing told him what he wanted to know. He let the light linger on a shelf of poetry: Keats, Wordsworth, Whitman, T. S. Eliot, Wallace Stevens, Robert Lowell. Probably left over from a college course that rounded up all the usual suspects, or as Meredith would say, all the boys. Except for the fattish volume lying sideways on top of the others: *Complete Poems of Emily Dickinson.* Alex held that one in his hand. No vibrations, no hair from the wild horse's mane came to his aid. He knelt down and let the book fall open. *My Life had stood—a Loaded Gun,* one poem began. This seemed promising, but neither that poem nor any other on the two-page spread made any reference to marrow or bones. Alex used the index to locate "The Bone that has no Marrow"—Dickinson's punctuation seemed either erratic or profound—but found no bent corners or any pencil marks on the page. He was just putting the book back where he'd found it and getting ready to attack the desk drawers when he heard the front door open and then slam shut.

He switched off the flash and sat down in the dark, trying to remember the room, to recall whether it offered any place to hide. Behind the couch, maybe, if he pushed the couch out from the wall. He heard Jay say ". . . under the circumstances," with a kind of catch in his voice. A quieter voice said something he couldn't decipher. It might not have been a word, maybe just a laugh or a grunt. Then Jay's voice came again but muffled, farther away.

Music came on, music Alex knew, drums and a harmonica drowning out whatever Jay and his guest had to say. The harmonica stopped long enough for the player to take a breath before he started singing: *You say you love me and you're thinking of me, but you know you could be wrong . . .* Alex knew this album by heart, of course. It was *Blonde on Blonde,* the same album he'd been listening to the night before this all started, the night the kidnappers must have been going over all their plans one last time. Now Jay was supposed to be at a restaurant and then back at the hospital. Instead he was home entertaining, grooving on the old familiar tunes.

Alex reached out to shut the door all but an inch and then turned the flash back on. He wanted to know who the guest was, but he couldn't very well expect to creep down the stairs unobserved. He could march downstairs and join the party. Or he could keep doing what he'd come here for and see what happened next. Shining his light around the floor, he spotted a cardboard box in the kneehole under the desk. He pulled this out and started going through it, his ears on the living room and his eyes up here. The box had that musty, moldy basement smell. It turned out to be full of stuff from twenty years ago.

On top Alex found old flyers and leaflets, probably printed by Jay himself. They announced rallies on the Boston Common and boycotts of the producers of napalm and cluster bombs. They said, "A War for Dictatorship, Not for Democracy," and "Run by the Rich, Fought by the Poor." True if trite then, true if trite now, Alex thought. Below the leaflets he found letters addressed to Jay at a Third Avenue, San Francisco address. He took time to skim one letter, from somebody whose name meant nothing, about meeting a wigged-out Czech, dropping acid, and talking rock and politics on some hill outside of Prague. The date was 1970, after the Soviet tanks; without the acid it must have been difficult to see any hope.

Farther down, the pile got less political, mostly stuff from medical school. It dawned on Alex that Jay kept all his old papers in chronological order, just the sort of compulsive thing you might expect a research scientist to do. But he must have hauled this box out to find something in it. Had he found it? Alex felt like an archeologist confronted by a missing layer. Suddenly he realized that the music had stopped. The last song he could consciously remember was "Absolutely Sweet Marie."

He shut off the light again and crawled to the door. He didn't hear anything now. No, he heard breathing. Lying on the hallway carpet, he inched his way forward, easing himself down the open, carpeted stairs. He gripped the lathed posts of the bannister so he wouldn't go sliding into view. Dropping his head just under the ceiling level, he saw the guest hadn't left. Jay and Barbara Binder were stretched out on a big couch with soft-looking cushions. Jay had taken off his shoes and his tie, and somebody had unbuttoned his shirt, which Barbara's arms had disappeared inside. Barbara was wearing blue jeans and a gold-colored necklace like the one she'd worn yesterday. Between jeans and necklace all Alex saw were bare back and one of Jay's hands, the other one being hidden inside the pants. Their mouths were locked. Then they came apart—more breathing—and Jay slid his lips around her chin and started working down her neck. Alex pulled his head back up before it got too red from gravity taking hold of his blood.

Now he knew what Jay considered more important than waiting around the hospital in hopes Linda Dumars's bone marrow might appear. He crawled back into the study and closed the door halfway, the way he'd found it. He remembered Yvonne's friend Wallia commenting about the kind of detective he didn't seem to be. He pushed the box back under the desk and was trying to decide what to do next when he heard low voices and footsteps. The happy couple were on their way upstairs. They were almost whispering, as if they expected somebody to be listening in.

". . . I mean . . . should have . . . didn't bring . . ." he heard Barbara say as she went past. And Jay: ". . . safe sex . . . responsible medical professional," with a slightly hysterical laugh. Then Alex didn't hear any more talking. When he heard murmurs and smacks he thought it would be safe to slip down the stairs and out into the fresh night air.

For a minute, out on the walk, he just stood looking at the house, the charming one-family, and he wished he'd only imagined that scene of Dr. Harrison and Ms. Binder making out on the couch and creeping upstairs to condom and bed. It wasn't that they seemed old or tired or flabby, or whatever made children and teenagers unable to imagine members of the next most senior generation having sex. It was that he'd fixed in his mind an idyllic image of the two of them a generation ago, in a field of Teton wildflowers. Since then, scores or hundreds or thousands of times, each had murmured and cavorted in somebody else's arms. Now what were they trying to prove? He wanted to tuck them back into Jay's box of musty papers. He didn't want to be spying on them. He didn't want to have to ask them what lies they might have been telling him over the past few days.

Alex turned his back on Jay and Barbara and walked up the quiet street to his car. He'd give them a decent interval, as Henry Kissinger might have said. He hoped they'd enjoy themselves. Then, if they didn't emerge, he'd go ring the doorbell and everybody could act all surprised.

TWENTY-SEVEN
Following

Another half an hour would be long enough, Alex decided. At twenty-eight minutes, both Jay Harrison and Barbara Binder walked out the door. They neither embraced passionately nor kissed affectionately nor looked in a guilty way to right and left. Each one said something to the other, and their hands touched as they parted. Then each one went to a separate car. Alex saw Jay check his watch.

Barbara started her car first, made a U-turn, and headed down the hill toward Comm Ave. Jay went the other way, over the crest. Alex stayed well back and lost him, but he guessed Jay ought to be headed intown. Sure enough, he spotted the Celica a block ahead of him on Beacon.

From there he felt safer staying close, because now he'd picked Jay up at an anonymous point. He followed the Celica through a logical if zigzag route over to Brookline Avenue and then across the thin strip of green, the so-called Emerald Necklace, that separated Brookline from Boston. Jay was headed right into the Medical Area. Only he kept going, past the glass tower in which his office waited on the fourth floor, in which his patient lay on the seventh in drugged or agitated suspension, Alex didn't know which.

Maybe he was going to some other hospital, Alex thought,

maybe Children's or Beth Israel, but instead the Celica drifted along with the intown traffic past all the hospitals to the red light at Park Drive. Alex waited four cars back, wondering which way Jay would turn. He could go toward Cambridge or toward Roxbury or straight ahead alongside the mammoth brick castle that wasn't Sears anymore. Jay went straight, toward Kenmore Square, then forked right onto Boylston. That would take him into the Back Bay or downtown. Where the hell was he going? That look at his watch had meant an appointment. Alex didn't like it. He followed his client down Boylston past all the lights of Fenway Park over to his left. He remembered the Sox were at home playing Milwaukee. Suddenly Jay signaled for a left and turned into the lot of the Howard Johnson motel, a low-slung two-story building that stretched back a block to the ballpark's right-field stands. What the hell was he doing there? Did he have another date in somebody else's bed? Alex double-parked. Jay parked in the lot and hurried inside.

Jay didn't have to be going to anybody's room, Alex told himself, because the place also had a cocktail lounge. He'd never been there, but he recalled that Meredith once had a student who tended bar there and knew some of the Sox lesser lights who'd go drinking after the night games. She'd gotten friendly with the now-departed Eddie Romero, if Alex remembered right. Alex parked in the lot too, away from Jay's car, and walked to the motel door with his head down. Jay might still spot him, and then there would be a confrontation, and maybe that would be just as well. On the other hand, the small lobby was brightly lit, so the windows ought to act as mirrors on the inside.

Jay wasn't in the lobby. He might have disappeared down a corridor. Alex stuck his head around the corner into the lounge. It was much darker than the lobby, though spotlights illuminated acrylic poster paintings of old ballplayers on the wall—Ted Williams, Joe Cronin, Tris Speaker, Yaz, Smoky Joe Wood. This being Boston, the baseball heroes were all white. So was the man sitting opposite Jay Harrison, a white man with longish brown hair, neatly parted, and a trim mustache.

The man was wearing a sports jacket and a tie. Compared to Jay, he seemed trim, athletic. He was a conventionally nice-looking man, with almost fashion-model looks, though an executive-attire model, not particularly young. What made him important enough to drag Jay away from Barbara? And from his patient? Alex was tempted to walk in, sit down, say, "Oh, how are you Jay, what's up and who's your friend?" But he decided he might learn more if he waited. Not here, though. He went back out to his car and turned on the game. The Sox had been hitting this week, and tonight they were leading 8–3 in the eighth. He listened till the game ended, 8–5. It didn't mean anything. It was only late April, that was all.

If he'd ever met Meredith's student who worked in there, he thought, he'd know whether she was the young, curly-haired blond woman he'd just seen behind the bar. But Meredith had merely told him about her, repeating the names of the ballplayers the student mentioned even though they meant nothing to her. Meredith had been fresh off the plane from London in those days, though even now she insisted baseball was a bore, too slow. Maria, on the other hand, was happy to go to games. She liked the hidden green field, the whole hidden fantasy world of territories inhabited by personages with litanies of achievements and quirks. She liked being with him in this world they shared. Taking Maria to Fenway had led Alex to conclude that baseball parks and ballplayers allowed boys to find a substitute for doll-houses and dolls. None of which helped Alex to guess what Jay Harrison's appointment here in very foul right could be about.

No ballplayers showed up, none that Alex could recognize anyway, but sometime after midnight Jay and his friend finally wandered out. The friend didn't seem too steady. When they shook hands Jay put his left hand around the other man's fore-arm as if either to help hold him up physically or to reassure him that things were going to be okay. Then the friend went off to a red BMW, in which he sat while Jay went to his own car and drove away. Jay turned right, back down Boylston, toward either the hospital or home. Alex waited so he could follow the man Jay had been drinking with. He didn't plan to follow very far.

The BMW turned left on Boylston, and so did Alex, following to where the street merged into the curve of Park Drive on the edge of the Fens. The BMW went left again, and then bore right to stay off the entrance to Storrow. The driver signaled for the left fork that would get him onto the next stretch of Boylston, into the Back Bay. Alex floored the gas pedal, and the old Saab lurched ahead as if to cut the BMW off. The other driver slowed down, mindful of his shiny fenders, and leaned on his horn. Alex braked hard, linings screeching in response, just before he would have come alongside the other car. He twisted the steering wheel to the right. As planned, his front bumper banged into the left rear fender of the BMW. He hit the horn and jumped out screaming.

"Where the hell did you learn to drive, asshole?" Alex yelled.

Other late night motorists edged around the accident, honking loudly to join the fun. The man who had been drinking with Jay, now minus his tie, climbed warily out of his car. He didn't yell or scream, just complained that Alex had cut him off and then driven out of lane. He made it sound as if everybody had it in for him tonight.

"Yeah, and how would you know?" demanded Alex. "You stink like a distillery, Mac. Either you give me your name and insurance like you're supposed to, or else I take your plate number and go right now and get a cop."

The driver agreed to exchange licenses and policy numbers. He ducked his head, the lank brown hair falling in front of his eyes, as he hurried to get his license out. He was drunker than Alex had expected. He read out loud from his license, as if speaking the facts aloud would make them more true. The license testified that he was Dr. Thomas Dumars of Topsfield, Mass.

"Listen," Alex said, pulling his own wallet out. "I got mad the way you were weaving, but you know, on second thought, it's just a little dent." On Alex's car, it was just one more deformity of the bumper. On Dumars's it was a couple hundred body-shop bucks. "Let's keep the insurance and the cops out of it. What do you say?"

Dr. Thomas Dumars squinted at Alex, looked around at the headlights that flicked past, and nodded quickly, a small, sharp nod, caught in a headlight beam, a nod as if a secret deal had just been made in a few words that meant more than they said.

Alex said, "All right. Get home safe now." He felt vaguely guilty not waiting for a cop, since Dumars could in fact be a danger on the road, especially if he was headed all the way home, not just as far as Joy Street on Beacon Hill. But Alex had found out what he wanted to know. On balance it seemed better to stay anonymous and unpoliced. He thought it wouldn't hurt to go back to the bar, because the place was close to the Medical Area and open late. It could be that either Jay or Dumars was a regular there. It could be that the bartender or a customer could tell him something he didn't know.

First, though, he'd call Jay from the phone in there. He'd demand Jay's version of the night's events. Then he'd see whether or not he could shoot it full of holes.

The phone was in the coatroom, not really a room but just a little alcove painted to look like a locker room, with a rack and hangars for coats. The lockers had been painted in muted colors on the white plaster wall. The one closest to Alex was depicted with an open door; inside hung a pair of cleats, a baseball glove, a towel, and an indistinct pinup with exaggeratedly female curves. Alex listened to Jay's office phone ringing. He watched the bartender handing draft beers to the waitress. There were only three tables occupied, plus one man sitting at the bar. Jay picked up the phone on the fifth ring.

"Dr. Harrison," he said. He sounded edgy. He was calling himself Doctor.

"Jay," Alex said.

"Alex? I've been trying to find you. Your girlfriend said she didn't have any idea where you were. When the phone rang I thought it might be the kidnapper. No word yet. It's past midnight, but I'm still waiting. I'm glad you called. I wanted to say I was sorry about this morning."

This morning. Alex could barely remember what Jay had done to be sorry about. Blown up at Alex's suggestion he might not be sharing all the data? And now?

"Uh-huh. Since then I've been running around following up some leads," Alex said.

"Well, I am sorry, sorry I got so pissed off. It was having Fridley take over that way and then treat me like a suspect. That got to me, and I took it out on you. What have you found out? What do you mean, leads?"

"I found out that Tom Dumars has been having an affair with the mother of one of his patients, a woman named Claudia Stevens. I found out that word about Linda's marrow being taken has apparently spread on the medical grapevine, because the doctor at MGH who I talked to about Tom already knew. I found out that you seem to be in touch with Barbara Binder, close touch, the kind that makes people gasp and ooh and ahh. I know you and Tom Dumars had a long talk tonight outside the hospital, at a place you might have chosen because you thought you could meet there unobserved." Alex counted these discoveries on the fingers of the hand that wasn't holding the phone. He knew he was letting his mouth run away with him. He wanted explanations. He was tired of trusting the doctor, and tired of suspecting him too.

Jay said, "How did you find out those last few things?" He sounded tired. He ought to be tired, he'd been busy. Alex turned away from the bar and stood facing the painted locker, tapping the toe of his sneaker against the bottom of the sheetmetal doorframe that wasn't really there.

"Following you." Alex counted taps, one through ten, waiting for Jay to respond to that. When Jay didn't, he added. "First I broke into your house, before you and Barbara showed up. Then I followed you to your get-together with Tom. You told me you wanted to hire somebody who'd identify with the patient above everybody else, remember? That's what I've done. I hope you can explain to me how nothing I saw tonight has any bearing on where Linda's marrow is."

"I didn't hire you to follow me." Jay sounded disappointed, like somebody whose real or metaphorical bubble has burst. "I meant I wanted somebody that wouldn't take any show-offy chances, you know that. To be blunt, I hired you to deliver something and to do certain research, to bring me certain facts. You told me about Barbara, you told me about Tom. I thought I ought to talk to them both. I don't owe you explanations. When you get back to your desk, your shop, wherever you do your paperwork, you can send me a bill."

Blew it, blew it, blew it! Alex was shouting at himself inside. Too much pressure, not enough patience, stripped the goddamn threads off the motherfucking bolt. His toe tapped harder, insistently, against the brown paint.

"What about Linda?" he demanded. "What about getting her marrow back?"

"She's my patient," Jay said, and now he sounded mad too. "She's my patient, and I'm taking care of her the way my judgment tells me to. You've never even met the woman. Your judgment doesn't seem very good right now. And maybe your doctor never explained something else to you, Mr. Glauberman. When you have a cancer, it's a strong sign that you're mortal. Like the rest of us. You seem to think it makes you into some kind of a god."

The phone clicked dead. Alex held his toe still. Then he set to kicking the wall as hard as possible, like a pitcher knocked out of the box, trying to demolish his locker on the way to the shower, trying to take his failure out on whatever was closest to him. His shoe bounced off the wall but he kept kicking. A dent appeared in the plasterboard. Brown paint chipped off too.

"Hey, you!" the bartender said. "Hey! You!" Alex looked over his shoulder to see her shaking a finger at him as if it were a magic wand that could command better than words. Alex stared at her and stopped kicking, embarrassed. She was good at this. She had to be, because she had to deal with a lot of stupid, angry drunks. The guy drinking at the bar had turned to stare, too, a man with a bandage over one eyebrow, a man maybe the bartender's age. Look at the weird old guy kicking in the painting, they would both be thinking. Alex started to mumble an apology about being sorry, but the bartender suddenly broke her eyes away from his. Something seemed familiar about her expression. Then it was gone. She wasn't paying him any more attention. Had there been something in his own eyes, he wondered. Something in them that she didn't want to see?

"Sorry," he said. He walked quickly out of the bar, into the motel lobby, and out into the night. Tomorrow, unless the marrow turned up, he'd have to chase after Barbara and Tom and see whether he could drive any wedges between their versions of tonight and Jay's. Or turn what he'd seen over to Fridley. Right now it was time to give it all a rest and go home.

TWENTY-EIGHT
Chaff of the Harvest

"Jesus, Bobby," Sandra said. She stared with wide eyes, while her dimpled chin dropped. "That was him. That was the guy that delivered the money. I swear it was. What was he doing here? Was it an accident? If it wasn't an accident, what's he trying to prove? Making sure I see him like that? What's going on?"

She was whispering, but sharply. Her *s*'s came out in a hiss every time. When he didn't answer, her face firmed up. Now she didn't look charmed or pliant or even scared. Now she was giving him that hard-bitten don't-bullshit-me look. He couldn't find anything to say. Her expression confirmed what he'd feared. She was about to bail out now for sure.

"All this time I kept going over it," she said. "Thinking what would've happened if they caught me this morning. So even if he wasn't—even if that wasn't him, I made up my mind already. No deeper, Bobby. No deeper for me."

She was waiting for him to say something, and while she waited she was turning her head back and forth between him and whoever might be watching.

"How can that be the guy?" he started to say. But she interrupted him.

"I think we have to—you have to . . . I think it's time for you to give up."

Yes, he'd expected this. He'd expected it since he'd found out she screwed up in the sperm bank. He'd managed to talk her into not rushing into anything, into waiting till he could get here in person. He'd longed to stay away, but she was too dangerous to leave alone. So he'd rushed back, even had a car waiting where he was going to need it. Still he shrank from taking the next step. "What do you mean, give up?"

"Let them have the stuff, Bobby. Before she dies. Even if you are a doctor, you don't know what's too long." Her look now conveyed not only determination but skepticism. She still wasn't sure she believed the doctor part. Maybe because he

187

didn't match her image of what a doctor was like, maybe because people took orders from doctors, and she didn't want to take any more orders from him. She said, "You don't know how long is too long."

"I know," he said. "I know how long. Don't worry. And I can't believe that was the same guy. That looked like a guy with his own problems. Probably he's staying here. Can't you ask them that, at the desk?"

"Only if I want to attract attention. Probably, the thing is, probably in that situation, on the beach, they'd want to use an undercover cop. Not that you warned me about any of that. If he's a cop, then they're just waiting for—"

"They wouldn't wait, would they?" Here at least he had logic on his side.

She shot him another dagger, but then she relented. They wouldn't wait, that was true. They'd pounce. She took another of those obvious glances around and then she patted his hand on the bar. "Okay, it wasn't him. And okay, you had a good idea. A great idea. And you didn't tell me what was going on, with good luck I never knew. Better for both of us, okay. But it didn't work, Bobby. Now you've got to face that."

And if I don't, he thought, you'll face it for me. You figure they'll let you off on a lesser charge if you turn me in, especially if you can save her life. If you can keep it from being murder. So fine. Let's play it that way.

"Okay," he said. He made himself smile, which wasn't hard. This was something he was good at, charm. Charm and good looks, he should have found a better way to capitalize on those. What if, what if. He was getting really tired of himself, almost as tired as he was getting of her.

"Okay, I know it. But there's a lot I still haven't told you, for both our safety, both our sakes. Now listen. There's one more batch of the marrow that's buried back on the beach. I wasn't going to use it because it has some—some technical deficiencies. It's the—how can I put this? It's the chaff of the harvest, so to speak. But there ought to be enough of the nucleated cells. Pick me up when you get off work, we'll drive down and catch the dawn again. We'll dig it up as soon as it gets light."

"And you'll give it back?"

"I'll give it back, and then I'll disappear. You won't have to take any more chances. Nobody will get hurt. I'm sorry I put you through that scare this morning. It seemed like the best thing."

"Yeah, but you didn't tell me—Hi, what can I get you?" she said to a fat man in a madras jacket who sat down on the next stool. He sat down on the next stool even though there were lots of empty ones. Was she right? Could they be under observation? They better the hell not be. Probably the fat guy was just jealous. If the barmaid was going to be friendly, she ought to be friendly with everybody at once. "Jack and ginger," the man said. She went and mixed the drink and brought it back.

The man who called himself Bobby Lynch didn't look at the man in the plaid jacket. He just put two quarters on the bar as if he were leaving a tip. "Thanks for the directions," he said. It was a poor exit line, but it would have to do. He crossed the street to McDonald's and called from there, dialing the number she'd given him, which rang the house phone behind the bar.

He said, "I'm getting so jumpy. You're right, we've got to get this over with. I'll be across the street when you get off work. Like last time, in front of the Star Market?" He wanted to add, *and don't tell anybody you're meeting me,* but that would be pushing her credulity too far. Anyway, she wouldn't. She was scared. So far she was still most scared of getting in too deep, even if she might be starting to be scared of him.

When she said okay, she'd pick him up, he was surprised at the will to believe that was unmistakable in her voice. Too bad it wasn't so simple. That would be nice, to just dig it up and give it back, leave it on the doorstep like a baby. But he couldn't do that. He wasn't in the driver's seat anymore.

DAY THREE

TWENTY-NINE
A Dead Girl

This time Alex rode up the beach, in a pale green four-by-four with a U.S. Department of the Interior seal on the side. A Cape Cod National Seashore employee was driving. His Smokey the Bear hat went pretty well with his ruddy face and bristly red mustache. The ranger's name was Frank Corcoran, and he'd taken charge of Alex when Alex stepped out of the helicopter onto the beach parking lot.

The helicopter had been piloted by a wiry guy who'd introduced himself only as "Slim." Slim, as near as Alex had been able to figure out, was a civilian pilot under contract to the state police, whose copter in turn had been commandeered by the FBI. Like any helicopter pilot Alex's age, he had presumably acquired his skills over the jungles of Vietnam. Slim claimed to know nothing about why Fridley needed Alex ferried across Massachusetts Bay like this, beyond what Alex already knew. Fridley wanted him to look at "something" on the beach. Alex didn't know whether "something" meant a footprint or an identifying object or something else. He could imagine that Fridley had put a lot of people to work sifting through the sand. On Frank Corcoran, now, he tried the same question he'd put to Slim: what was worth bringing him all the way here in such a hurry to see?

"A dead girl that a jogger found," Corcoran said with a shake of his head and hat. "I wasn't supposed to tell you anything, but I wouldn't want anybody to spring that on me."

It was ten o'clock now, a lot later than it had been the last time Alex had been here on this beach. The sun had risen way up toward its zenith, casting only a short shadow of the truck on pale yellow sand. The whitish cliffs and deep blue waves were breathtaking, but they lacked the dawn's sense of magic, of things transforming and coming alive. There were no fishermen, but more beachcombers. There were a lot of tire tracks in the sand.

A dead girl, Alex thought. Meaning somebody fully grown, or else the ranger would have said "a dead little girl" instead. Could it be Barbara? He was starting to wish he'd never located her.

"I appreciate that," he answered. "And the special agent wants to know whether I recognize her?"

But Corcoran only shrugged. "What do I know about it? Did anybody tell me they were going to be paying over any ransom money on my beach?"

The distance that had taken Alex half an hour to walk took less than five minutes to drive. As they approached the place where he'd left the mailbag, he cursed silently because he still saw two posts before the two merged into one. When the Jeep got closer he saw new, smaller posts, red ones, surrounding the area. The red posts had plastic ropes strung between them. There were figures standing about, looking out to sea or turning toward the truck. Corcoran stopped about fifty feet away.

These other men, all of them men, were in suit pants and shirt sleeves. One of them came forward, turning into Jim Fridley. He offered Alex a hand down out of the high-slung truck, but Alex didn't take it. A steady south wind blew a fine mist of sand up the beach from the direction Alex and Frank Corcoran had come.

Fridley led Alex along a path formed by two rows of the short red posts and plastic streamers. Alex expected to be warned not to disturb anything, but Fridley just said, "Come take a look." No doubt all the forensic wizardry, the measurements and photos and gathering of samples, was all done by now. Alex took a breath to get ready. Then he was standing over her. Fridley was saying, "Is she the one? Is somebody trying to send us a message here?"

The woman lay curled halfway into a fetal position on her left side. Her face looked pale. Her fringed suede jacket was zipped up almost to where her throat had been cut. Blood stained some of the long leather fringes. The sand below her neck was brown with sun-baked blood. From the neck down, though, she might have been sleeping. She might have been asleep when this happened to her. She could have been curled like this for protection from the wind.

The last time Alex had seen her, this woman had been staring at a guy trying to kick in a wall. Now she was like a dead deer stiffening, no longer moving through her element, but inert and dried up and surrounded by men whose business this was. She was like a deer tied to a rack on top of a hunter's car. Alex looked away, toward the ocean, then back. He didn't feel queasy or disoriented, the way he'd felt when he'd watched Jay lift somebody's encased marrow into the nitrogen mist. That had made him feel how fragile life was. This sight was different. It wasn't about fragility but about pain and suffering and death. It was awful, but he found himself more steeled to face it. Perhaps because this wasn't his first corpse.

Still, it took a while for Alex to understand what the FBI agent was asking: not whether he knew the woman, period, but whether she was the one he'd encountered last time he was on this beach. That's why Fridley had rushed him down here. He wanted to know right away, and perhaps he wanted Alex to see her in this context, not on a slab in the morgue. Alex thought about the shock of recognition in the darkened bar. That had been, if anything, her recognizing him. His mind had been on Jay, Barbarella, Tom Dumars. He hadn't noticed the resemblance, if there was one. Could he see it now?

If she were standing up, maybe. If she were in a wetsuit instead of the fringed leather and the jeans. If she were wearing a long blond wig. If she were waving her arm enthusiastically. He discovered he was holding his breath.

He let himself breathe. "I don't know. Probably she's about the right build. Mostly I remember the way she looked against the dune, the way she moved. I never got this close to her. It might be, it might not." He looked at Fridley, who was watching him closely, coldly, without anger or expectation that Alex could see. "I'm not trying to give you a hard time," he said. "I just don't know whether it's the same woman or not."

"Take your time," the agent said. "Point out to me where she was when you first saw her, up on the steps. Go through that again. And tell me what she looked like then."

Alex went through it all again—who did what, and where the bottle landed, and how she dragged the money up the cliff, and where he dug. Only when he pointed out where he'd dug did he realize there was a new hole, maybe a yard or a yard and a half away. He looked down at the corpse again. "Was she digging? Was there a shovel? Did she have any sand under her nails?"

Fridley didn't answer.

"Did they—do you think whoever was digging, or whoever killed her—do you think they took something out?"

"Like another one of those coolers? I can tell you this, I wish I knew. We're going to dig the whole area soon." A walkie-talkie on his belt crackled, interrupting him. He backed out the designated path and spoke into the radio while he looked high up on the dune. Alex saw a figure at the top of the steps. There must be more men up there, searching the bushes and paths. Fridley wiped away the sand the wind had blown against the back of his neck and jerked his head to signal that Alex should approach.

"I don't get many corpses," Fridley said. "Kidnappers have a different profile than killers, generally speaking. They might both act out of vengeance, but kidnappers aren't out for blood. Excepting terrorists who take hostages. She's no hostage. If that's her purse in the car, her name was Sandra Stewart. Her roommate says Stewart never came in last night, though that's not so uncommon. The roommate says she called Tuesday night to say she was on a junket with a rich new boyfriend. In Las Vegas. Then she came back and wouldn't talk about it at all. Stewart worked a night shift in a cocktail lounge not far from the Dennison Center. I'm not telling you all this for your curiosity. I want to know, does any of that connect with anything Harrison might have told you, anything you learned about this Foster, anything at all?"

Alex said, "Was it the Howard Johnson lounge? I know Jay Harrison went drinking there last night, with Linda Dumars's husband. I followed him there. Ask Tom Dumars if somebody sideswiped him on Park Drive afterward. That was me."

"I thought I told you," Fridley began, but then he waved off the rest of his speech with a gesture that meant either impatience or disgust. Instead he said, "And?"

"And that's all, except I called Harrison to ask for some explanations and he told me I wasn't investigating this for him anymore."

"So the doctor and I agree about something. Is it out of line, the doc commiserating with the patient's husband over a drink? Might be, might not. You don't know." He turned his head to look at the corpse, or pretend to. "It might have saved a life if you'd told me this last night."

"Yeah," Alex said. But he didn't see how it could have. "Well, I didn't tell you then, but I told you now." His words sounded stupid. They reminded him of the words of a certain Oakland cop to Huey Newton, in a story he'd read about the early days of the Black Panther Party's street-corner monitoring of the police. "Are you a Communist?" the cop had demanded of the Panther, and Huey had retorted, "Are you a Fascist?" The cop had taken refuge in, "I asked you first," and Huey had parodied, "Well I asked you second," and given the cop a look that asked what kind of moron playground shit was this. For that reason if no other, Huey Newton had been slated for everything that happened to him next.

"You told me now," Fridley repeated sarcastically. "And one more time now, do you think it's the same woman that you say you handed over the mailbag full of money to?"

"I did hand it over, though I don't know whether it was full of money because I never thought to look. I don't know, honestly, whether she's the same person or not. I think she might be. That's the best I can do."

"Then I'm through with you for now," Fridley said. "Frank, get him the hell off the beach."

Fridley pulled the ranger aside for a few words, and then the ranger drove Alex back down the beach. The south wind blew the fine sand against the windshield. If Corcoran wanted to know any more about ransoms or murders or stolen bone marrow, he didn't ask his passenger. When they got to the lot, there was no more chopper. Instead a tow truck operator was hoisting up the front end of a pink Chevy Nova. Corcoran said it was the car they thought the dead girl had come down in. She must have parked it there and then walked along the beach. She'd left her purse locked in the car.

Yes, Alex thought, and depending on when she got off work she could have made it here by, say, three thirty this morning. Had she come alone and been followed or surprised? Or had she come with somebody who killed her and disappeared up the steps? The jogger must have found her body shortly after dawn.

"This is as far as I can take you," the ranger said. "You're going to have to get back off Cape your own." He shrugged, but just with his shoulders. His mustache didn't twist into either a smile or a grimace. "He says he wants you out of his way."

"So you've got orders to maroon me?"

"I wouldn't exactly call it that. It's about a mile down the road to Route 6 there. You can thumb your way home, or else flag down the bus from P-town when it goes by a little before noon. Look, it's a nice day. It's spring. It'll be a nice walk." He turned to survey the back of the Jeep, littered with coffee cups and newspapers and boxes that had held several dozen doughnuts once. He said, "There's no food left, but if you want you can grab yourself something to read."

Alex took him up on the offer. He found the morning's *Herald* and the *Globe* sports section, reporting on the Red Sox victory whose last three innings he already knew all about. He also found a Dennison Center house organ, the *Weekly Wrap-Up*. The *Wrap-Up*'s logo included a man with a stethoscope and a woman bent over a microscope. Both figures were contained within the outline of a gift-wrapped package shaped like the Dennison's glass tower. Presumably all this was stuff Fridley and his minions had left behind.

THIRTY
Stuck Out His Thumb

The government vehicle dipped onto the beach, out of sight. The tow truck pulled Sandra Stewart's car the other way down the narrow blacktop road. Soon it disappeared among the trees. That left Alex alone in the lot, alone except for a fisherman messing with his gear. The fisherman, who was somewhere between forty and fifty with white-speckled kinky hair, straightened and then turned around. He eyed Alex with the kind of curiosity that people who belong someplace reserve for people who don't. This struck Alex as slightly strange, since the fisherman was a burly dark-brown man. African-Americans were about as common out here as they were in Fenway Park.

"Catch anything?" Alex asked. He hoped that any conversation, however trifling, might lead to a ride. The man only scowled into his bucket through the wire-rimmed glasses he wore.

"I was going to offer you these papers to wrap them in," Alex went on. His mouth had gotten ahead of his brain, which was noticing that the car was a beat-up white Peugeot, a 505 from the early '80s, the model with which the French carmaker had gone beyond mechanical ignition and carburetors, and Alex had stopped working on the relatively rare breed. In Alex's experience, the only Americans who hung on to Peugeots did so out of some nostalgic or romantic notion about France. Once they would have smoked Gauloises. Even back when everybody smoked cigarettes, the people who smoked Gauloises had been surrounded by an aura of unhealthy decadence, of being just that much closer to the edge. Alex didn't know what symbols people now in their twenties used for this purpose, but he suspected Sandra Stewart had done it somehow.

And Foster, had he once smoked the pungent, musky French cigarettes in the deep blue pack? Could this possibly be him now, disassembling that fishing rod and getting ready to stow it in his Peugeot 505?

The fisherman shook his head disgustedly, as if at Alex's silent question. Dropping everything but the *Weekly Wrap-Up* in the trash can, Alex kept going. He could always stick out his thumb once the man got his gear packed and was ready to deal with the rest of the world again. Alex walked away from the ocean and from the blood soaked into the sand.

Could Jay have killed her? Could Jay have sliced neatly with a scalpel and left the woman there to drain and grow cold? He'd had time. So had Tom Dumars, if he could have steered straight and stayed awake. Or wasn't it that simple? Was there some more indirect connection, some more complex system of levers and hydraulics that accounted for the fact that this dead woman had been in the same room as those two doctors late last night?

The undulating road offered just what the ranger, Frank Corcoran, had promised: slow passage through a rare, fragrant, gentle spring day. Alex's feet landed on top of the dancing shadows of new green leaves. But he kept seeing Jay and Tom in the bar, Jay and Barbara on the couch, Jay and Dee and Foster in the van rolling west. And Linda Dumars, just a shape on a hospital bed.

That hole in the beach, which could have cost one woman her life, might hold some hope for the other woman still. If anything had been buried there, what else but Linda's bone marrow could it be? Yet the fact that somebody had died at that spot made it seem ever less likely that the marrow could be in careful and businesslike hands. A week ago Linda Dumars had taken her chance, had done the brave and medically indicated thing. Now the part of herself she needed most was quite probably dried up and gone. Alex Glauberman, would-be savior, could only put one foot in front of the other down a seaside lane.

The fact was, Jay Harrison's parting shot last night had been well-aimed and true. Alex had assumed he must possess a special aptitude, a special calling for this mission. Maybe he didn't. More to avoid these thoughts than in hopes of learning anything, he opened the *Weekly Wrap-Up* to read as he walked. His own shadow darkened the glossy, half-tabloid-size pages. He scanned headlines about fund-raising drives and testimonial dinners, then turned the page.

The next two pages were about research projects. Upbeat headlines accompanied head-and-shoulder file shots of the investigators. The pictures were crisp and clear, the boldface words proudly announcing advances in the use of monoclonal antibodies and interferon, strides in the attempt to isolate elusive oncogenes. In other circumstances Alex might have read these pieces, but not now. Turning to the center spread, he found a special feature entitled "Marrow Transplant Unit Success Rate High." That explained why Fridley brought this fluff along.

Alex stopped for a minute to scan the article. He stood on the side of the road by a vine-covered trellis that formed the gateway to the yard of a shingled cottage. Nothing was blooming yet, but the vines, actually branches, were thorny. Alex supposed there might be roses here in a month.

Jay's boss Daniel Weinstein led off the article, citing statistics about remissions, length of stay, and rates of complications of various sorts. He also talked about the increasing willingness of insurers to pay for marrow transplants, though Alex was sure Jay or Carol Wagner had told him insurers were getting balkier about uses for which there wasn't documented high rate of success. Alex's eyes skipped to the half-page photograph, a group shot of the unit personnel. His eyes held fast to a man on the left side of the front row, a man with a big smile for the photographer, a toothy smile on a boyishly appealing face. Alex knew this face. In his mind it was linked with the face of the bartender, the woman dead on the beach. Why?

He thought back to the day he'd delivered the money. He tried to picture the men he'd seen go by in the Cherokee, that morning and the fisherman who'd come over the dune. That wasn't it, none of those had been this man. He checked the caption, which identified everybody, first row, second row, left to right. The caption said this was Gordon Kramer, the senior resident. That meant the one who'd gone to med school with Dr. Steinkuhler, the one she said was Jay's research assistant and protégé, though Deborah McCarthy had suggested maybe not. The man Steinkuhler said would be Jay's next fellow, but Deborah said was off interviewing for a job someplace else. Alex shut his eyes, remembering that he'd talked to Kramer on Monday. He recalled that the resident had been clad in scrubs and a gown and cap. His face had been pale. The pallor plus the getup had made Alex think of a nun.

Alex opened his eyes and looked back at the photograph.

Yes, this was the same guy, though he looked different in civilian dress. That didn't account for the feeling that he was somehow connected to the woman on the beach.

Then he had it. This was the man who last night had been wearing a bandage over his eye. The one who had been sitting at the bar, Sandra Stewart's bar, and had turned around to see what the commotion was all about. Alex took two quick steps through the vine-covered trellis and down a flagstone path. But he saw the cottage was just a summer place; no phone service would be connected now, and anyway the door would be locked and the shutters nailed up tight. His best bet was to run back to the lot and press the fisherman into service, however reclusive the fisherman might be. He started running, fast, with his head down.

A motor sound stopped him, a sound to which he was attuned. He knew even before he looked up that the dirty white Peugeot would be rolling providentially along the road. Alex stuck out his right thumb and waved his left hand rapidly to try and indicate distress. He was about to jump out and block the road when the driver pulled over and pushed open the passenger door.

"You need a lift?" the fisherman asked. "I thought you might need a lift, but you didn't say so. You need a lift, you got to speak up."

"What I need, please, is a ride to a phone at least. And toward Boston, too, if you're going that way." Alex tried to ignore the man's gruff, slightly bullying tone. He found it harder to ignore the deep and raspy voice. He had to say, "My name's Alex Glauberman. And you?"

"Glauberman. I thought so. Somebody named Meredith, with a British accent, told me I should try to grab you down here. Only I didn't want to grab you in public. I told her my name's Paul Foster. She said if I hauled ass I could catch you down here with the Feebies and police."

"You told her your name's Paul Foster?"

"I did. It once was. I used to operate under that name, though not since a long while ago."

THIRTY-ONE
The Chicken or the Egg

Mary Forziati bent over her binocular microscope, watching the sperm cells swim like tadpoles. Really they were much less complex than tadpoles. It was just a figure of speech to refer to the bobbing, rounded part as a head and the long blindly whipping part as a tail. These weren't organisms, just specialized human cells. Yet they did look like animals, animals that lived all crowded together like the alligators she'd once seen crawling all over each other in the pen of a Florida alligator farm. Cells or tadpoles or alligators, it was hard to believe that every guy on the street had millions of these critters bumping into each other between his legs.

A lot of this batch were swimming helplessly in circles. They were never going to fertilize anything that way. Some of them looked kinked and crooked, and some had deformed heads too. She noted the quantities of each type and compared them with the notes describing a sample taken from this same specimen before freezing. All in all, most studies showed that previously frozen sperm were about fifty percent as effective as the ones contained in fresh semen were. Still, even fifty percent was fifty percent of millions and millions per vial. It was a number like the federal budget, hard to comprehend.

Mary found it a lot easier to comprehend producing one egg a month, like some kind of very fussy chicken, though she knew this comparison to be unscientific too. Did chickens have periods if their ova went unfertilized? She knew a lot of human physiology, from study and from picking it up around the hospital. She didn't know much about other species, though.

When she thought about it, she figured out an answer that made sense to her. Chickens had no wombs, that was why they had to lay their eggs as eggs and then sit on them all that time. Without a womb you didn't have any menstrual blood. Satisfied with solving that puzzle, she went back to the one that had been bothering her for twenty-four hours now.

If you wanted to make off with some frozen semen, why come when the bank was open for deposits, the way the pretend nurse, the would-be thief had? Why come when Donna was here and all those nervous, jumpy guys were waiting their turns out front? Why not come on one of the quiet days when the bank was closed, and Donna was up in Dr. Taylor's office, and she was alone here in the lab? Half the time she didn't even lock the door when she went out for coffee or to the bathroom, because that was always when Taylor decided he needed something, and as chief urologist and sperm bank director, he felt it beneath his dignity to carry around keys. As if only janitors did that, or maybe he was just forgetful, but anyway he didn't like being confronted by a locked door. Now everything was different. But until now, nobody used to lock up anything except meds.

So that nurse, or whoever she was, hadn't planned very well. She hadn't planned very well, or she'd been in a hurry, so she couldn't wait until this morning, say. Why would somebody need to steal sperm in a hurry, that's what Mary was trying to figure out. By now she knew what was missing from the blood bank, of course. Her own blood froze, thinking about the woman whose chances of recovery had plummeted as a result. She'd gotten the secret out of Edie. Edie had felt responsible, so of course she'd been eager to talk.

Why in a hurry? She'd been over lots of reasons, but now she thought of a new one. Maybe the thief hadn't been for real. Maybe this had been a diversion. Maybe she'd wanted to fail, wanted to attract attention, to divert attention from something else. But from what?

Mary let that idea rest while she finished up her notes on this sample. Then she chucked the rest of the vial. This semen had been donated for research purposes. No swimming up anybody's vaginal canal for those guys. Whoever they had belonged to could manufacture umpteen million others to do the job. There was a wastefulness about the whole thing that was very much like a man. It was like the way the FBI agent had to unload all that stuff about the history of kidnapping—to prove he was an expert, to prove it did make sense to hold semen for ransom, the same as holding the vice president of a bank.

Maybe she was judging him harshly, but then she'd never had too much respect for the FBI. They were what Thomas

Jefferson had in mind, as somebody had once said to her, when he decided the people needed to be protected from their government by a bill of rights.

The next sample had fared a lot better. More of the little critters swam straight, and fewer had cockeyed "heads" or "tails." She noted the numbers, along with the necessary data about freezing technique, duration of storage, and donor age. When the computer eventually crunched all this data, the findings were supposed to allow better prediction or improvement of fertilization rates. In the back of her mind she was still thinking about the FBI agent, about dragnets and dissidents. What if the maybe-nurse had been running *away* from somebody? Making a fuss to attract attention and thus protection, like Cary Grant at that auction in *North by Northwest*? No, these wild theories were only getting her further and further from the mark.

Hiding, though, there might be something to that. Not trying to hide herself, but trying to hide *something*. Like . . . no movie came to mind. Suppose that woman had come in here not to take something out of the tank but to put something in? This didn't explain anything, Mary thought with some disappointment. It didn't explain the timing, certainly, which was where she'd started. Yet it was an intriguing idea, that somebody would try to hide something here in her long-term storage tank. Unlikely, but simple to test. You didn't have to feed a year's worth of data into any computer. You just had to look in the tank.

But she'd looked in the tank. Yesterday she'd checked the whole rack, thoroughly, painstakingly. So the only place anything could be hidden was underneath, in the very bottom, under the rack. That was possible. You couldn't see down there, not with the rack in the way, not with all the vapor rising up. To check this she'd need a long pair of tongs, longer than the regular ones for getting vials out. Someplace there was a pair of extra-long tongs. Oh, under the sterilizer. She was just picking them up, ready to test her unlikely hypothesis, when somebody knocked at the hallway door.

That was how she happened to have the tongs in hand when she opened the door to find a white-jacketed man in the act of pulling a stocking cap down over his head. He barged in, shoving her backward with a hand against the base of her throat. By reflex she jabbed at his face with the tongs. It was a ski mask, the kind with eye holes but nothing else. She saw a rip appear beneath the right eye, and inside the rip a patch of white skin and a red scratch. She knew she ought to jab the pincers into the man's eye, but she couldn't. What was happening? While she hesitated, he got a hand on the tongs and forced her arm down. He kicked the door shut behind him. For a moment they stood frozen that way. Blood welled out of the scratch under his eye and soaked into the knitted stretch fabric around the rip. He twisted the tongs out of her grip and flung them behind her. There was the sound of shattering glass.

That sound got her moving again. She tried to bring her knee up into the man's crotch. He grunted and whacked her face hard with the back of his hand. She stumbled. Before she could straighten up he was reaching out both hands for her throat. Her mind kept working as his hands came closer. If he'd bothered to hide his face he must not have planned on killing her. So what? She reached behind her, found something solid, and tried to swing it. It was the microscope—too heavy, too awkward, badly balanced. He was on her again before she got her arm halfway up.

"Just stay goddamn still, woman," he said, and now his hands did close on her throat. Her fingers reached for his eyes. Still squeezing her windpipe, he lowered his head between his arms, so all she could scratch was the back of his neck. Then he butted her collarbone, hard, and through the fog and pain she tried to say, "Okay, I'll stay still." Her only hopeful thought was that he'd said "woman" and not "bitch." He butted once more, and when she went limp he let go of her throat. She landed painfully on the floor, the man standing over her, breathing hard, his head wagging from side to side.

"The closet, get in the closet." His voice was muffled and unfamiliar. Rumor had it that security had been on the lookout not only for a white woman, the pretend nurse, but also for a black man. This man was white. Should she do what he said or keep fighting? She slid back on the floor, toward the open closet. He stood over her, touching his wound, looking at his fingers, gauging how much blood. She slid back into the closet, scanning the lower shelves for some kind of weapon in case he came in too. The door slammed against her toes.

Everything was dark now. It was too late to find anything.

Everything was dark except a slit of light where the door hadn't closed because of her toes. She pulled her toes back, expecting him to shut her in totally. Nothing happened. She got up on her knees, turned her head sideways, cautiously brought her ear as close as she dared to the slit. She listened. She heard his heavy breathing. That was all.

"Stay in there," he commanded. "I've got your scissors now. I don't want to have to cut your throat." Did he really say that? She shrank back, but then put her ear to the crack to listen again. A hiss. A sound she'd know anywhere. He was opening one of the tanks. Then a different kind of hiss, an intake of breath as the cold hit him, as it probably burned his wounded face. So he was leaning over the tank. He'd come to make good on the theft. He wanted specimens, wanted them violently. She felt herself shaking, shivering. He wanted them enough to strangle her or cut her throat. This had to go beyond money, beyond ransoms. It was like men coming after their ex-girlfriends. *If I can't have her, nobody can.* Could a man feel that way about semen? About his ex-woman's new man? *If I can't knock her up, nobody can?*

She made herself stop shivering, and then she put her eye to the slit. She needed to know what her attacker was doing, to try and figure out what he was going to do next. She pushed ever so gently, and then she could see his back as he reached into the tank. With his gloved left hand he held the rack up high. His right shoulder dipped. She couldn't see what he was doing. Then, as he twisted, she could see his right arm bent at the elbow, the forearm resting against the rim of the tank. His elbow was jiggling. What on earth was he doing, rolling imaginary dice? She started to shiver again.

What was he doing? He wasn't hurrying. Except for the way he was using his left arm to hold up the big rack, he looked like a man leaning against the rail of a dock, fishing with a hand line, jigging for crabs. He began to raise his right forearm, slowly, as if pulling something up. He turned his head in her direction. She shrank back, slid to the far end of the closet. After a moment, his footsteps came her way. His breathing wasn't as heavy. He didn't say anything. With relief, she watched the slit of light disappear. He was done with her. She was safe. Slumping onto the floor, she heard scraping sounds. He was pushing something, the desk, against the closet door. After that she didn't hear anything.

She was safe, but she'd also been just a few minutes too late in her thinking. He'd fished something out from the bottom of her tank, with a hook on some kind of shaft, or maybe with a magnet on a line. It had to be. What else could it be? The stolen bone marrow must have been sitting at the bottom of the long-term semen storage tank all this time. Only now it wasn't. Now he had it. She waited a minute, till she was sure he must be gone, and then crawled forward and tried to force her way out with this news.

She turned the knob and put her shoulder to the door and pushed. Pushing didn't seem to do any good. She turned around and put her back to the door, pushing that way, getting more strength out of her legs. It wasn't any better. She remembered the scraping sound, how long it had taken him to push the desk against the door. There'd been scraping, and then quiet, and then scraping again. He'd needed to push first one side, then the other. The desk had been too heavy for him to push all at once. Still she shoved, with no effect, and then she stopped shoving and began just plain pounding her fists against the door. Maybe someone would hear.

After a while her fists hurt from pounding. She'd have to try pushing again. It was so infuriating that she'd come to the right conclusion just a few minutes—maybe seconds—too late. The specimen must have been there since, when was it, Monday, according to what Edie said. Who could have put it in there? And then she remembered something else.

On Monday a repair technician had come—to check the automatic draw devices; they did that from time to time, reasonably enough. She remembered his uniform, a blue uniform, and an ID tag which of course she hadn't thought to check. She remembered his mustache, his heavy dark-rimmed glasses. She thought now that he'd also worn a cap, some kind of logo cap. Had he been carrying anything, a container? He'd had a toolbox. She hadn't paid much attention to any of this at the time.

She'd gone to the front room after a while, and she'd still been in the front room when the repairman had left. Now that she thought of it, now that she *had* to think about it, something mildly strange had happened then. He'd come out that way, through the front, and he'd said everything was set, no problem, or some such parting words. She'd looked up to acknowledge them and noticed one of the guys in the waiting room giving the repairman a very funny look. The patient had stuck his head back in his magazine as soon as he felt her eyes on him. But now she thought about that funny look. It was as if the patient had recognized the repairman but didn't recognize him, as if he hadn't been sure whether it was the person he thought or not.

Did that explain anything? It didn't matter now. Mary Forziati pushed, without result, and then went back to pounding on the closet door.

THIRTY-TWO
Traveling Clothes

Motels and restaurants and woods and ponds and closed-up T-shirt shops flashed by. The 505's valves sounded worn. Alex went on telling Linda Dumars's story and the stories that seemed to be linked with hers. Foster's sudden appearance was like a magic show where the magician promises a rabbit but only produces handkerchiefs and snakes and flowers from his hat. Just when you've almost forgotten to watch for it, the bunny comes hopping out of the magician's mouth. He told Foster what he knew and what he suspected. Foster had promised that he'd give a story in return.

Alex had changed his mind about the phone booth. Gordon Kramer could wait a little while. The thing to do was to go methodically and carefully, as Hans Heidenfelter would advise, not jumble up the small parts or strip the threads from any more bolts he might need. The thing to do was to feel out what surrounded him. Now that it had come down to murder, the wrong move could panic the kidnapper. The wrong move would be even more likely to panic the kidnapper than before.

Or wasn't that it, Alex asked himself as he talked. Meredith had once claimed that he approached his investigations like a squirrel with a nut, or a boy with a new treasure. He'd pull out some nugget and stare at it from several angles, then hide it away in his pocket again. He knew he had his reasons for this, the same reasons that had him running a one-man repair shop.

"Yeah, I do remember that trip," Foster said when Alex was finished. "I remembered a lot about it after Dee called me, and more after you and me got through wolf-talking each other on the telephone." In *telephone* he put the accent on the last syllable. The cadence reminded Alex of somebody else, but he didn't know whom. "I was remembering the scheme to kidnap Henry Kissinger. Was that in that diary? Kind of a party game—what would we want for ransom, what were we making for demands. Get us out of Vietnam. Free the Panthers in jail. Let the Indians have Wyoming. Change the national anthem to 'Dancin' in the Street.'"

As he talked, Foster watched the road. He gripped the black plastic steering wheel in his big hands. He flexed his fingers, raising all four from the wheel and closing them one at a time, in sequence, like a musician playing a scale. He'd had nice hands, Dee had said in her journal. Bald and bearded in Dee's picture, he'd stood out more, like a wrestler. Now his pepper-and-salt hair, medium length, went with his wire-rimmed glasses to give him a milder, almost bookish look. He had a day's stubble on the puckery pores of his cheeks and chin. He had wide cheekbones that rounded out his face, like the Foster in the photograph, though below them now there was slack skin around saggy jowls.

"Not so militaristic, you know? Swinging and swaying and records playing, instead of rockets and bombs and all of that?" He shot Alex a quick glance, so Alex nodded vigorously. Foster had sought him out and picked him up for some reason, he was sure. Now Foster was painting the picture of himself that would go with that reason. Everybody did this, by force of habit, because you couldn't just expect to be seen all at once and convincingly for the whole person you were. Black men, Alex thought, needed to develop that picture-painting habit more than most.

"Sure," Alex said. "An invitation across the nation, a chance for folks to meet." With Jay, this recitation would have gotten him points. With Foster, it might or might not. But Foster had a point. "The Star-Spangled Banner" celebrated a fort, people holed up inside it, siege mentality, is somebody going to take

210

away what we've got. The other song was about stepping out and reaching out—and feeling safe among your fellow citizens on the streets.

"Dee helped me get a lawyer after we rattled around coast-to-coast," Foster said, eyes again on the road or the scenery or the past. "A lawyer to see about my, uh, fugitive status. I don't know if she told you that."

"She did. Eventually you sent her a postcard, saying dishonorable but free."

"Yeah, well, that was just me being careful to give that impression, you know. I never did get discharged, because I never did go back and trust my body to the justice of a military court. Civilian court either, since I had a suspended sentence for an old bullshit charge still hanging over me. I thought it'd be better to get to be somebody else."

"You got a new identity?" Alex said. He remembered that the new-identity business had held a fascination for both Foster and Jay.

"That's it. It wasn't too hard. Nobody was looking for Paul Foster the way they were going after Eldridge Cleaver, and they didn't even manage to find Eldridge at that time. You might know somebody yourself that went through some of that, that operates under a different name than the one when the teacher called the roll in first grade."

As a matter of fact, Alex did know somebody like that. "Did you have to start a lot of things over?" he asked Foster. "I tried to find you through the alumni office at Morgan State, but I didn't have any luck."

"They wiped me off their list, is that what you ran up against there? Some things I had to do over. When I got around to it I went back and got a new high school diploma, a GED. Sometimes I dabble with college courses, mostly art courses, on the side. For a while I had to be real careful about contact with my folks, because you don't know who might decide to take an interest. Then too I was into some other shit that, you know, made me want to stay close to the ground. But lately I'm a solid working citizen. And I've got a family of my own."

Foster glanced in the rearview mirror and fell silent. Alex remembered the moody conversationalist of Dee's journal, alternately reaching out and barring the door. To keep the conversa-

211

tion going he asked a hitchhiker kind of question. He said, "What kind of work do you do?"

"Used to be printing and copying, now I'm into graphics and desktop publishing." But Foster didn't seem to want to talk about his work, either, because he lapsed into silence again. "It's a long way from making revolution," he said suddenly. "But I tell myself it does something for the community, gives a few young people some training, some employment, you know."

"Dee said your brother had a printing shop."

"J.T.'s shop went bust a long time ago. Then he went to work for the government. The way they say about kids, small business is just a phase you pass through. But you see what I'm saying. I've got this shop right now. I've got my family. None of it's under Paul Foster, you know what I'm saying? As years went on by, I stopped being careful. Now, say somebody started taking a big interest in Paul Foster all over again. Say some white men in dark suits started in banging on my mama's door. Say they threatened to come down hard on her neighbors, say they called on everybody that might have a relative on probation or what have you. Sooner or later they'd find out where to find me. I didn't want any part of this, I told you that right off, but when the FBI came looking, I thought it was time to get out the old traveling clothes. I drove up to Boston, I know some folks here. I came knocking on your door bright and early this morning. If I can help you clear this up, it's good for you, and good for me, and my mama's neighbors, and that woman laying in the hospital bed."

Not bad, Alex thought. Not a bad story. A few parts underside and a few parts upside of the American dream. Was it the truth?

"What about the fishing rod?" Alex asked. "When you drove to Boston from wherever, why did you bring a deep-sea fishing rod along?"

"Oh, the fishing rod? When your—is that your wife, the one that told me where to find you?"

"My girlfriend. Woman friend."

"When she told me the police took you to look at something on that beach, I thought I ought to have some way to look a little bit like I belong. And my friend that I'm staying with, he's a fishing fiend. Otherwise I would've had to run up and down the beach, be a jogger you know, and I don't know if I'm in shape for that."

"Uh-huh," Alex said. "How come Dee knew where to find you, by the way?"

Foster signaled with his right blinker and slowly, not hurrying, pulled the car off onto the shoulder and stopped. He twisted to face Alex, his torso barely fitting between the seat back and the steering wheel when he turned. He said, "I didn't come to get interrogated. It's damn stupid for me to come here at all. That's what my wife told me, that's what I told myself all the way up. Now here I am. We can try to figure out who's been using my old name, or I can go back home and wait for trouble to come to me. The answer to your question is one day I found myself in Oakland and I got an itch to see if I could go locate Dee Sturdevant across the Bay."

When Alex didn't say anything, Foster faced forward again and put the car into first. He shifted into second too soon, dropping the r.p.m.s more than he ought to, then did the same thing when he shifted into third.

"I think we ought to stop long enough to call Jay's secretary," Alex said, "and ask her a few questions about this Kramer so we can decide what to do next."

"Yeah, okay." Foster rubbed his stomach. "I'll dial and get her on the phone. You talk and I'll listen. And we'll get something to eat."

They stopped before the bridge at a doughnut shop, where Foster bought two for himself, chocolate, and two for Alex, the powdered sugar kind. Alex didn't know whether this was some new commentary on their partnership or whether Foster just liked chocolate best. He was still thinking about what Foster had said about getting an itch. He thought that maybe one reason they were together now was that, under pressure, Foster had gotten another one—an itch to take a break from his family and his shop and run around and do crazy shit like this again. Alex understood that kind of itch. He also understood why Foster wanted to place the call: to make sure Alex wasn't going to call anybody else and announce who had picked him up. Even when you ran around doing crazy dangerous shit, you ought to do it in a cautious way.

"Is this Ms. McCarthy?" Foster asked. "Mr. Glauberman would like to speak to you, hold on."

"Alex?" Deborah sounded confused. "Who was that? Was that the police? Things are crazy here. Some woman got murdered, on the same beach you took the money to. The police say Jay knows her, or he might know her. They want to know was he at such-and-such a barroom last night? Was he 'in the habit' of drinking there?"

"Was he?"

"Huh? Well, not a habit, but I know it's a convenient place he goes once in a while. I don't know where he was last night. Except he was here from about one o'clock on. He stayed here all night. Linda had some trouble, something in her lungs, she had to get a transfusion to stop her from bleeding inside. So Jay was here later, everybody testified to that. What about before? Were you—did you go to his house?"

"Yes. And then I followed him to the HoJo's they're asking about. He didn't tell you that? Where is he now?"

"Up on the unit. He wants to stay close to Ms. Dumars, he says."

"Deborah, listen. I'll be there in a few hours, I'll sit down with Jay then, but I need to know something now. About Gordon Kramer."

"Gordon Kramer?"

"Yeah. Is he there, is he back from wherever he was?"

"No, I don't think so. He had an interview in Florida about a job, some HMO. He arranged time off so he could stay down through the weekend. The FBI asked about him already. I guess they talked to him. Anyway, I know they said he did make his interview yesterday."

"When you said it was high-risk, being Jay's protégé, did you mean anything specific about him?"

"About Gordon? Well, only that a lot of people thought Jay would take him on as a fellow next year, but Jay didn't. He's getting a guy from Stanford. He decided, just between you and I, that Gordon wasn't serious enough about patient care. That's what I meant. Why? I mean, how come you're asking this?"

"Because I think Kramer knew the woman that was killed." He still didn't want to reveal that he'd seen Kramer in the bar, that he knew Kramer wasn't in Florida late last night. "How did he take the rejection, would you say, when Jay decided not to take him on?"

"Not too bad. The writing was already on the wall, though, by that time. After Jay didn't take him to Las Vegas. He was mad then. From then on he seemed to take it in good grace. Some of them act like it's the end of the world if they don't get the residency or the fellowship they want. Like they'll never get to play with the big boys now. Gordon didn't seem that way, from what I saw."

"Las Vegas?" Alex asked.

"That's where the national heme-onc meetings were. Hematology-oncology. If a resident is part of an important research team that's presenting a paper—oh, you know, it's like a sophomore getting invited to go party with juniors or seniors, it's a sign you're considered mature, or sexy, or something like that. What are you getting at, Alex? You think Gordon Kramer stole bone marrow to get back at Jay, sour grapes?"

"I don't know. I'm not ready to rule Jay out, or that they could be involved in this together. I want to talk with Kramer. Do you know where he is in Florida? Can you give me his home address and phone too?"

THIRTY-THREE
I Invented You

Alex remembered a conversation between himself and Maria, when she must have been two or three or four, those years that all blurred together now. They'd been at a fast-food place in a mall, the Meadow Glen in Medford, he thought. They must have been on an expedition to buy her clothes. Mostly as an experiment Alex had made a comment about the black woman at a table across the room. He'd said, "Do you like the boots she's wearing, that black woman sitting over there?"

It wasn't that he'd wanted to call Maria's attention to the divides and oppressions of race, if she didn't know about them

215

yet. Rather, he'd wanted to know how much if anything she'd picked up on her own. A while later Maria had screwed up her nose in a signal of thought and said, "Kim is a black woman?" Alex had just said no and let it drop. Kim was white-skinned with dark, nearly black hair, which meant that Maria hadn't yet understood that these distinctions were made on the basis of skin. Kim did have a minority status, but it was invisible, and anyway, Alex had been sure Maria didn't yet know what a lesbian was.

By mutual consent, Alex and Foster had let the matter of their different races hang unmentioned—except for the doughnuts, perhaps. They'd operated on the tacit assumption that the kidnapper had thought the most effective red herring would be one with dark skin. They'd operated on another tacit assumption, which was that they'd do their work together here and then go back to their largely separate worlds. They'd speculated and made plans as if, between them, there weren't any special fears or suspicions at work. By and large this was how European-Americans and African-Americans got along, to the very limited extent that they did.

As a piece of their partnership, Alex navigated while Foster drove. If Foster knew Boston, he wasn't letting on. The car had Massachusetts plates, license number 897DFH, which Alex had committed to memory. But the plates might have been borrowed. So, despite Alex's Gauloise intuition, might the car. His speculations about the location of Foster's new life had wandered from Brooklyn to Harlem to Bridgeport to New Haven to Buffalo and points west. From the Southeast Expressway, Alex navigated them in via Morton Street and the Jamaica Way, a route that took them through the southern reaches of Boston's black community and then retraced parts of the way he'd come as a squatter in Deborah's car and also the way he'd followed Jay. The route led to Coolidge Corner in Brookline. That was where Deborah had said Gordon Kramer lived. The address turned out to be an apartment building on a residential block off Harvard Street, about midway between the bagel bakery and the birthplace of JFK.

Outside the entrance, at the end of a short sidewalk, stood a cluster of retirees, short men in bright colored polyester slacks and zippered jackets and cloth caps with brims that snapped. The old white men looked at Foster coming down the path, looked away, and seemed to shrink backward and downward. Alex pressed the bell marked Kramer, which had no companion name. They'd thought of calling in advance but turned down the idea. If he was home, they wanted surprise.

The speaker grille crackled unintelligibly. Alex hovered between "Gordon" and "Dr. Kramer."

"Yo, Doc," Foster said.

The speaker crackled again, something that might have been "who is it?"

"Yo, Doc. My name is Foster."

". . . don't know who you are," the box said. The words came slower and louder, though still nearly lost in static.

"Foster. I want to talk to you about Jay Harrison. I can't explain all that through this goddamn machine."

Yeah, Alex thought, but Kramer could quickly decide to run out the back door, or worse. Kramer might be only a cog in all this. On the other hand he might be sitting up there with a plastic pouch and a hungry cat. Foster, Alex thought, was being a little reckless with Linda Dumars's life.

No more scratchy words came out of the box, only a long, loud buzz. Alex pushed the door open. Foster gave him a big shrug. They climbed to the fourth floor. The building had no elevator. Foster knocked.

"It's unlocked," somebody called from inside.

As the door opened, Alex heard a sound that was a mix of two sounds: a low, dull roaring and a higher-pitched hiss. He knew that sound, because he used it to bend brake lines and free up tight parts. He pushed in beside Foster, which wasn't easy, given the man's bulk. The two of them stood there staring at Gordon Kramer, who sat in a formless stuffed bean-bag chair. In one hand he held a lit propane torch. With the other he lifted a white box—Styrofoam—and turned the sharp cone of blue fire to it.

"Good afternoon, gentlemen," he said, raising his voice slightly so it would carry over the sound of the torch.

When the blue flame hit the white surface, it bounced back in a circle of bright dancing orange petals. But only for an instant, because then the whole circle melted inward. It left a gaping black hole and a smell like ashes and epoxy in the air. Everything had happened faster than Alex could move.

"Just a demonstration, gentlemen," Kramer said. He tossed the box toward them, where it fell into two pieces on the floor. "Just packing material. But this isn't." He reached behind him to come up with a shiny, fat, silvery thermos. He set down the torch long enough to unscrew the cap. A swirl of genie smoke rose from within. Then he held the torch in one hand and the smoking uncapped bottle in the other.

"Please sit down, over there on the couch," Kramer said in that same lordly tone. His words conveyed the attitude of pompous villains in old British spy movies, but his voice trembled and his eyes darted up and down. The man was strung tight. If you nicked a high tension wire, it would snap and then whip all over the place.

Foster and Alex both sat down as directed, on the couch about eight feet away from the senior resident, the thermos, and the flame. Kramer placed the cap on top of the bottle but didn't screw it in. The cloud turned into a wispy plume.

"In the bottle," Kramer said, "is cryopreserved material protected only by liquid nitrogen and a plastic pouch. The torch will boil the N-two, melt the plastic, and thaw the marrow in no time flat. Believe me, I know what I'm talking about. I assume you gentlemen are from the police, and I wouldn't be surprised if you had some brethren keeping watch outside."

"No, we're not cops," Alex said. "My name is Alex Glauberman. You and I met on the unit, on Monday. I don't know whether Jay explained who I am. He hired me to look into a blackmail note, and then into the missing marrow. This is Paul Foster, an old friend of Jay's."

"And I'm Donald Duck," Kramer said. "I remember you from last night. You tried to kick down a wall. You might be what you say, but he's not. I invented Foster. So don't try to jerk me around."

"You invented me?" Foster leaned back and spread his arms over the back of the couch. His right arm lay against Alex's shoulders. He was trying to sound amused, but Alex could tell how tense his muscles were. Alex felt mesmerized by the steady blue flame of the torch—steady, yet with a flicker along its edges, the flicker that always reminded him of a snake's tongue. To preserve the specimen, Jay had said, the thawing process had to be done as delicately as the freezing. First the marrow had to sit in the upper part of the tank, in the vapor area, and then it had to be placed, double-bagged, in a controlled-temperature water bath. Alex made himself look Kramer in the face.

A Band-Aid had replaced the previous night's white bandage above his left eye, but there was a new bandage beneath the eye, a hospital-type dressing of gauze and paper tape. Kramer was pale, with dark straight hair, a square chin, and rather hollow cheeks. He'd look intelligent and sensitive when he wasn't strung so tight.

Foster said, "Inventing me. I always gave my mama and my papa credit for that."

"Uh-huh," Kramer said. "I mean, Foster is somebody Jay knew twenty years ago, whose name I happened to run into, that's all. If you want to prove that's who you are, maybe you'd like to toss me some ID."

"No. No, I wouldn't like to do that. I don't carry ID in that name anymore."

"Well, then, I'll just have to go on the assumption you're police."

"That's funny," Foster said. "You don't know how funny that is."

"Nothing's funny. Everything is very serious. I never meant for the patient to be hurt, but some things have gone wrong. Whatever brought you here is one of them. There's no time to screw around now. All that's left for me to do is try and run for it, and you are going to have to help. Otherwise, I'll have to break the bone and suck of the substantific marrow, as a French poet said."

His chin wobbled and his tongue stumbled over the strange and awkward phrase. He was showing off, but not enjoying it. If they could keep him talking, there might be a slim chance of the propane running out.

"You're interested in poetry?" Alex said.

"Like Emily Dickinson?" Kramer rested the torch in the crook of his elbow and turned down the flame. The roar and the hiss got quieter. He was careful. The torch itself indicated that. Somewhere along the line he'd guessed he might have to use the marrow as a kind of hostage, so he'd gone out and bought a weapon with which he could threaten it.

"No, not really," he went on. "I just know how to ask a librarian for help. I had a quote from James Baldwin, too, something about the rope and rape, fear and hatred deep as the marrow. I thought of using it to tie Mr. Foster in tighter, Mr. Foster and Jay."

Kramer's eyes flicked over the black man's, as if testing for a reaction, as if he were worried this might really be Foster though he couldn't understand how.

"You ever read Baldwin?" Foster asked in an easy, conversational tone.

"No, I just had all these marrow quotes, all dressed up with no place to go. Not for any nefarious purpose, originally. I'd been planning to work some of them into a little talk at a conference I never went to, that's all." Kramer flushed and pressed his lips together to keep the words in. Something was bubbling inside him, trying to escape as speech.

"You mean the one in Las Vegas," Alex said quickly. "The heme-onc?"

"That's right, yeah. I thought I was in the club. But it's who you know, not what you know, and all of a sudden Jay Harrison didn't know me at all. I guess you figured that out, didn't you? And what else? Did she recognize my voice, was that it? Just like that guy waiting to bank his juices for posterity. You don't forget the voice that gives you the bad news."

Kramer jerked his head and shut his lips again, then raised the torch and the bottle. "Believe me when I tell *you* now to be careful. This one here is the only specimen left. I want you to know I've been careful as Hippocrates with the patient's marrow. This batch never left the hospital, till now. I was going to give it back for payment already received, but now I have to offer a new exchange, my life for the patient's, in effect."

"All we want is to get the marrow back safely," Alex answered him. He didn't have any idea what the man was talking about. Was "she" the bartender, Sandra Stewart? He still didn't see that connection. He was aware again of the tension in Foster's arm, and of the fact that Foster, more than Kramer, could be placed in the vicinity of the beach where she'd died. But that didn't make any sense. And who was the guy waiting to bank his juices, that got the bad news?

"So let's get down with it," Foster said. "What's the proposition. How do we get this thing resolved?"

"The proposition is that one of you will drive me where I want to go. We walk to my car, one of you and me. The one who doesn't go will have to stay here. I'd take care of him with an injection, except then I'd have to set my hostage down. So I guess we'll have to tie him up." Kramer jiggled the torch nervously. He hadn't had much time to figure this part out, Alex thought. He'd be making it up as he went along.

"In the car, I'll ride in back with the window open. If anybody follows us, if there are any roadblocks or wrong turns or accidents, the marrow goes crackle-splat all over the road. And you won't feel the liquid N-2 when it hits you from behind, because you'll be numb. The effect on your skin will be the same as if I threw acid. We leave within five minutes, or the offer doesn't stand."

"Okay," Alex said. It was better than okay. It meant he didn't have to let Kramer or the marrow out of his sight. He just hoped Kramer didn't change his mind. He turned to Foster. "Okay?"

"Okay," Foster said, "as long as I'm not the one that stays here hogtied. I'm not going to be the sacrificed lamb."

Alex didn't like that. That meant Foster had to be the one to handle Kramer—to avoid panicking him but also to decide whether and when to try and jump him if things looked about to go wrong. Alex wanted to be that one. Kramer said, "That's between the two of you. Make up your minds now."

"It's my ass that Feebie has on his brain," Foster said. "He finds me here, and the stuff gone, you know who he's going to blame."

"Okay," Alex said. What he'd admitted this morning remained true: his tamed malignancy didn't give him any superpowers. Maybe the best bet was to look for a chance to overpower Kramer now, while it was still two against one.

"Lie down, on your stomach," Kramer ordered him. "And you, Mr. 'Foster,' unplug the phone over there and tie him up with the cord. Glauberman, cross your legs, at the knees. You, tie his ankles and then tie his hands behind his back. Tight. I'll take your performance here as a test of your good faith."

Alex lay with his cheek against the dusty living room rug and felt the cord cut into his ankles. He couldn't see Kramer now. All he could see was the doorway leading into a kitchen, an old-fashioned kitchen with a dirty linoleum floor. The whole apartment had the air of a place where the inhabitant was only camping out. There was a second phone in there, however, sitting on the table. If he could get to it, he could call for help as soon as they left. But not if he was thoroughly tied up.

Alex tried pulling his wrists apart against the pressure of the next cord, the handset cord, but Foster wasn't giving him much slack. Did Foster too want him stuck here, securely, unable to call for reinforcements? Maybe Foster had visions of Kramer's car running into a fusillade of machine gun fire like Bonnie and Clyde. The marrow might survive that, and the occupants not.

"Good," Kramer said. "Now let's go." There was no "gentlemen" anymore, no pretense, nothing but fear and threat. Yet Foster didn't get up right away.

"Let me roll him over on his back," Foster said. "Like a turtle. I know you don't believe me, but I could be in almost as deep shit as you." When he bent further to roll Alex over, he whispered, *"You got to trip him if you get the chance."* Then he stood up and said, "Okay, now what?"

"Go out the door ahead of me. Stay ten feet ahead. When we get downstairs I'll tell you which way to go."

On his back, Alex watched Foster walk out the door onto the landing. He craned his neck to watch Kramer turn off the torch and then tighten the silver cap a half turn. The plume of vapor slimmed down into a thread.

"I don't want to attract attention," Kramer said, as if his audience would appreciate an explanation. "But it only takes one hand to open it and the other to dump. The plastic will crack when it hits the ground. The marrow will seep out as soon as it starts to thaw. It needs to thaw just right—not that way—or it dies."

This was the truth, Alex knew, and he thought he should tell Foster not to try anything. But he kept quiet. He couldn't stand the prospect of lying there like a trussed turkey while the kidnapper strolled away from him with the prize.

222

When Kramer had almost reached the door, Foster moved. He turned around and charged back into the apartment. Kramer twisted the cap loose and dropped it, but he didn't dump the contents. As Foster must have hoped, he backed up toward the kitchen to make another stand. Alex went with the program. When Kramer tried to step over his bound feet, he kicked upward. Kramer jumped and tried to regain his balance, the container now clutched in both hands.

Alex watched it happen in slow motion, in the helpless way you watch your favorite coffee cup crash to the floor. The steaming thermos tilted back toward Kramer, who stiffened his arms by instinct, trying to get the thing away from him before the supercooled liquid started pouring out. Then he let go, right over Alex's head. Foster leaped from the other side and grabbed. A splash of liquid nitrogen shot upward, a fizzy frothing streak. Alex rolled away, shutting his eyes. He felt his hair stiffen and turn to icicles against his head. When he looked back, the thermos sat on the floor, steaming. Foster's big hands came down to screw on the cap. Then Foster left the marrow behind as he plowed ahead into the kitchen, where Kramer must have gone.

Between Foster's legs Alex could see Gordon Kramer, crouched, a small serrated steak knife in his hand. Kramer lunged forward, but Foster dodged and got him by the wrist. Foster twisted the doctor's arm behind his back, then took one hand off long enough to rip the kitchen phone cord out of the wall. He pushed Kramer back into the living room, kicked his feet out from under him, straddled him, and started tying him up.

"Oh yeah, I'm the real Paul Foster," he said between heavy breaths, whipping the plastic cord around Gordon Kramer's wrists. "You better believe it. Now it's my turn with that stuff."

Kramer wasn't fighting. He started to shake and moan, then convulsed with loud, racking sobs. Alex struggled to free his own hands, but couldn't. Kramer was out of the picture but something wasn't right. Alex started wriggling toward the squat, silvery thermos. Foster finished with the wrists and turned around to work on Kramer's feet.

"You think you fucking invented me," Foster pronounced. He tightened his last knot with a hard, jerking motion and stood up, brushing his palms together in a satisfied way. "You think you invented me," he repeated more calmly, "but I was always out there. You think you're the only one Jay Harrison ever did wrong?"

Alex had managed to get to the thermos, and now he flipped on his side and curled up, wrapping his thighs and belly around the vessel that held Linda Dumars's suspended cells. Foster laughed and tugged Alex's head back by the hair, just above where the fierce cold had been. His scalp felt raw. Foster tugged backward, his knee behind Alex's spine. Alex wouldn't let go.

Foster said, "You want I should turn that torch on you, or break your neck, which?" He yanked at Alex's bound feet. Alex let his thighs be pulled away.

"Now I've got what I've been after," Foster said. He lifted the container carefully, smoothing his thumbs along the shiny sides. "Now the both of you just stay here and keep out of trouble. From here on it's all between me and Dr. Jay."

THIRTY-FOUR
For You, Doctor

From weakness and drugs, Linda Dumars had slept most of Day Number Two away. Then there'd been last night, coughing till she didn't care what happened to her as long as she could rest. But she'd insisted on being awakened in time to call the kids before they left for school.

Tom hadn't been there, only Juanita. She hadn't asked about Tom, and nobody had said. Probably Tom hadn't been home all night. Juanita had put Claire on one phone and Nicky on the other. Claire had talked about something—jam on her cereal. Linda had said that sounded awful, though she hadn't possessed the energy to care whether it had been jam or glue or Nicky's salamander.

Afterward, that not-caring had made her unreasonably sad. Thousands of times before she'd listened to Claire's energetic rambling with half an ear, but now there might be so few times left. It had taken every ounce of her energy to tell the kids that soon Daddy would bring them in to see her, just through the plastic curtain, because she wouldn't be well enough yet for them to come into the room. It had taken all her energy to keep from telling some part of the truth. After that effort she'd slept again, for the remainder of the morning it seemed.

Now it was Day Three, a sunny afternoon. Nobody had kept any promises. Now Harrison was lecturing her. She'd asked him for a straightforward presentation of her chances. He'd said her condition was stable for now, and he'd started talking about the long run. It was hard to believe in the long run. She fought to keep her mind from wandering.

"We've activated a match search, of course. We did that right away. We might get you a match within about five weeks. If we have to wait that long, your debilitated state could mean it'll be a tough fight getting past the graft versus host disease. If we recover your own marrow, on the other hand, you won't be myelosupressed as long, and we won't need to worry about the GVH because we'll be dealing with autologous cells."

Even when she concentrated, there wasn't anything in his words. She knew all this. She knew Caesar conquered Gaul. She knew there wasn't any real-number square root of negative one.

Yvonne had come in with the doctor, but she wasn't standing by the bed. She was pretending to fuss with the oxygen tank and whatever all those other emergency devices were. The doctor looked around uncomfortably, as if he wished the nurse weren't there or he wished she'd do his talking for him, Linda couldn't tell which. He started to say something more but seemed to be tongue-tied for once. He took a step closer and gulped a breath of the supersterile air. His cheeks and eyes puffed out, like a toy Claire had, a rubber head whose features you could move around that way.

I'm drifting off into a very weird place, Linda thought. She had never done any psychedelics or downers, but she wondered whether this was what they were like. Or was this what it was like to drift into death? *No, I won't.* She ought to be thinking positive thoughts about her future—about getting divorced and where she and Nicky and Claire would live. "That's why I've overstepped my medical role," Harrison was saying. "I need to tell you about a conversation I had when I went out drinking with your husband late last night."

Linda pressed a button to raise up her back. "Well, tell me," she said irritably. It felt good to be irritable. "Don't stand there beating around the bush." The top half of the bed rose. She felt like a building block being raised into position by a crane. She wanted to be upright when she found out it was Tom who was killing her, just as she'd thought.

"He told me some of what I've been hearing already: that you two were about to break up when you first got diagnosed. He said he was having a serious affair then, he was feeling estranged from you, he was feeling as if he didn't really know his kids at all. He knew all about babies and toddlers and preschoolers, but he didn't know anything about his own children, he felt. He said the first diagnosis brought you two back together, more or less closing ranks against the disease, but that was just temporary. This recurrence had, if anything, had the opposite effect. He basically told me he didn't want to have to take care of the sick and the dying at home as well as at work. He feels you don't much like him, either. He thinks you're always fantasizing about other men."

"Does he?" Linda said. The doctor was presenting Tom's version of their marriage with clinical detachment. If Tom had her cells, still had them, alive, what did her doctor or her husband expect her to do? Plead?

Tom liked her to plead. There was the time years back when he'd sat on her car keys, when he'd claimed she was about to sneak out someplace and leave the kids alone in their cribs. It was really him who'd done that—snuck off with the fawning intern, the one who'd later written her the letter of apology about how "we women all learn from our mistakes." Well, she'd refused to plead for the car keys. But she'd plead now, oh yes she would.

"Alex—that's the private detective I hired—tells me lately Tom's been having a relationship with the mother of a former patient of his. Yet I have to say that despite everything, Tom seemed to be worried sick about your condition. During our conversation he drank like a fish. He was on the edge of tears. I'm being as frank as I can. The opinion I came to was that he might conceivably have arranged for you to die if he'd stumbled on a simple and safe way and convinced himself it was for everybody's good. But I didn't believe he would have planned anything as complicated as this. That was last night. Then something happened that I don't understand. Someone who witnessed our conversation—your husband's and mine—was killed. I thought you ought to know all this. Maybe you can tell me something that will help."

Someone was killed? The three words seared her. They cut a path of pain, but also they sealed her juices in. Someone else had died over this, over her stolen blood-making cells. She felt this unknown person's company and loss at one and the same time. "Oh my God," she heard her shadow of a voice say. "You think that Tom—"

The phone rang, interrupting her. By habit she reached out her hand.

"Hello?" she said faintly. With her other hand she rubbed the green plastic thing around her gums. "Hello?" she said again.

"I want to speak to Dr. Harrison." It was a deep male voice she didn't know. She thought it had some South in it. "To Dr. Harrison in person. It's urgent. They told me he was with you."

She said, "It's for you, Doctor. But can't it wait?"

"Hello, Jay Harrison," the doctor said. He listened without speaking. It couldn't wait, apparently. Some other emergency. And somebody who witnessed his conversation with Tom had been killed. Linda started to cough again. Yvonne looked up and took a step toward her bed. Harrison moved his lips, but Linda couldn't hear over the barking going on in her lungs and throat. Now the doctor was bouncing on the balls of his feet. He put down the phone and stared at her. She tried to breathe normally.

"That was a man claiming to know where your marrow is," Harrison told her. "I'm going to meet him right now."

"What?" Linda felt ready to jump up and go with him. Blood hammered in her temples, and adrenaline surged through her heart. But everything was dreamlike. "A man? What man?"

"His name is Paul Foster. I think . . . I'm afraid all along this has had to do with me, not with you at all. Yvonne, get somebody else to check the other charts. I'll call in as soon as I can."

"Do you want me to notify the police?" Yvonne asked.

"No. He wants me by myself. Just go on as if it didn't happen. But I think, Linda, we'll have you back together soon."

He rushed out through the portal, leaving the two women staring at each other, leaving those words trailing behind.

Downstairs, though nobody knew it, Mary Forziati tried again, pounding her fists against the closet door.

THIRTY-FIVE
Hold the Knife

For a while Kramer kept shaking, convulsed by his spasms of shame and defeat. Alex felt like doing the same, but instead he rolled onto his side, drew up his knees, and tried to stand. He knew his bonds were only telephone cord—just plastic with tiny copper filaments inside. He could find something to cut them on, if he could get upright and hop around. If he could rock himself over onto his knees, then he should be able to stand.

He threw his weight that way but kept falling back onto his side. Not enough momentum. Make yourself insubstantial, he thought. He felt too fucking insubstantial already, insubstantial and stupid. But each time he rocked, he got a little further. It was like rocking a tire out of a rut. Finally he got up far enough to wedge his right elbow under his side for support. His arm felt wrenched half out of its socket. The cord sliced hard into the back of his wrist. He rested with that pain while Kramer's sobs subsided into gasps, the way a baby's would. With a big push Alex managed to get to his knees. He saw Kramer blinking at him. Now the only thing that kept him from standing was that his legs were crossed above the ankles. Foster had trussed his turkey well.

"That was really him, really Jay's Foster?" Kramer asked in an unsteady, used-up way.

Alex pointed his left foot and flexed his right, trying to slide his left ankle over his right heel. It wouldn't go. He stopped and tried to stretch the cord by pulling his legs apart. Direct the energy just where you need it, he thought. Leave the rest empty. Breathe out the pain. Finally he got the one foot around the other. He took time to steady himself. If he fell and landed sideways, he'd have to struggle onto his knees all over again. When Kramer repeated the question, he said, "Yes, Jay's Foster, that was him."

"I don't . . . this isn't making any sense. I can't—up until I drove off the road, I thought I had it all under control."

"Under control," Alex said. Hogtied on the floor, the doctor still couldn't understand how come he wasn't in charge. Shifting his weight forward, Alex got the tips of his toes under him. He straightened his legs, shifted his weight back, and came down easily on his heels. He was standing up, no problem. The kitchen would be the best place to find something sharp. He bunny-hopped to the doorway and leaned against it. "Did you kill Sandra Stewart?" he demanded. "Was that part of keeping it under control?"

"I didn't mean to do that. She wasn't going to get hurt either. But then it got down to her or me. I couldn't let her go to the police. If it came down to me or you—or me or the patient— you'd kill me, right?"

Alex hopped through the kitchen doorway, not answering Kramer's question.

"Did I do it for nothing?" Kramer called after him. "She was right? You were the one on the beach? You came to the bar to spy on us? You were playing with me? Why?"

"I'm going to find a knife," Alex said, "and then you're going to help cut me loose, so we can try to make it one murder on your conscience and not two. Linda Dumars deserves her marrow back, not to have it be the prize in some kind of grudge match going on between Foster and Jay." He didn't know why that should make any difference to Kramer. But what could he give the man? He could answer his question. He said, "I was in the bar because I followed Jay and Tom Dumars there earlier. I wanted to ask the bartender about them. I didn't recognize her or you, not then."

Gordon Kramer jerked his knees up, folding into a ball, so that Alex thought he was about to start sobbing again. Instead he started to laugh, though the laughter was on the edge of wailing.

"Ohmygod," Kramer said finally, straightening again with a jerk. "That's tragic. I mean, that's really high tragic. That bar.

I met Sandy because I got in the habit of going there. I should say Bobby got in the habit of going there. He went there because that pathetic place was the site of my big defeat. Where things came apart. It seemed like a good place to start over, take a different fork of the road. You followed Jay there? I didn't know he made a habit of the dump."

Who was Bobby, Alex wanted to know. He had a Jay, a Tom, Deborah's husband Richard, there wasn't any Bob. It didn't matter. Foster was who mattered, and the only way to get after Foster was to get loose. He hopped into the kitchen, looking for the knife Kramer had tried to use. He didn't see it. He saw two wooden drawers under a counter. He hopped to the first and turned his back to it, closing his fingers around the knob so he could pull. Inside, his fingers recognized the blade of a knife.

Kramer was talking again, not as loud. Alex strained to make out the words as he slowly closed his fingers around the handle of the knife. Kramer was still going on about that bar.

"HoJo's," Kramer muttered. "That's where Jay took me. His idea of kindness—give me the bad news in some anonymous dump, neutral turf, where I didn't have to walk out past anybody that knew he just turned me down. He took me there to tell me I didn't have his high seriousness of purpose about getting people well. All that shit. So Bobby went back there to drink. Bobby went back there the way you can't keep your tongue off the tooth that hurts."

"Bobby?" Alex said this time. He started bouncing back toward the living room, the knife behind him in his right fist.

"Yeah, Bobby. My alter ego. Maybe I can plead insanity, dime-store schizophrenia, multiple personalities. My Bobby side, it was only my Bobby side that did all this. Would you back me up on that, if I do what you want me to do?"

"Yes," Alex said, knowing it was a lie. He stood over Kramer, who looked up at him out of wet, shiny eyes.

"Sure you would. Tell me another. But maybe I am crazy. I'm a gambler. I bet six years, more, on the wrong horse. All gamblers are crazy—when they lose."

Kramer started to giggle. The giggles went back toward sobs. Alex just wanted him to hold the knife. He had to sound sympathetic. He said, "You felt that Jay led you on, told you he had a future for you? And then he kicked you in the teeth?"

Kramer sniffled, and then from some hidden reserve he got some of that old sarcasm back. "Crazy when they lose," he said. "Brilliant when they win. My late, great father was a doctor, the old-fashioned kind. Let's put that in my plea. He doled out prescriptions and aspirin, and told people what was going to kill them and what specialist to go see. I was going to be on the next step up, the frontiers of science. All my eggs were in that basket. Six years of postgrad and five big figures in loans. When the eggs break, make an omelet. That's what my father used to say. Snatch victory from the jaws of defeat." Lying on his back, Kramer closed his eyes. Sarcasm had faded into self-pity. Alex wanted to throttle him, but didn't. Kramer didn't sound finished yet. Alex gave him one more minute to get it all off his chest.

"So I was going to start over, in a big way, three hundred grand in cash and all my bridges burned. Find myself. Oh yes, and leave a cloud over Jay. Nothing that could be proved, but he'd be suspected, him and this Foster. Do you know how I learned to put Bobby together? From Jay. He told me how to make false identities. He liked to be asked about his wild-oats days. He made it sound so full of that high moral purpose and fun too. I never, I just never really thought I could get caught."

"Gordon," Alex said. "I can't change that. But I want you to cut through this cord with the knife I've got behind my back."

"You cut mine first," Kramer said.

"No thanks. You did get caught. Now it's about getting yourself the best deal."

"Oh, what the hell," Kramer said. "You don't know what it's like, to watch yourself keep doing stupider and stupider things. Driving drunk. Choosing that beach to cut her artery on. Tie it in a ribbon, I thought, give them Bobby if they can trace him, Bobby the killer and Bobby the kidnapper too. That leaves Gordon okay, once the marrow turns up, once I get it back, not screwing up like Sandra, and I leave it some convenient place. Only I screwed up and let the other one cut me, mark me like a pile of bad bills. Couldn't show up at work on Monday like that. And then I went to get stitched—good medicine—that slowed me down disappearing, I thought I had time. And then Foster. Foster, Jesus. But that bastard made a fool out of you too."

The parts made sense to Alex, most of them, but not the

whole. Time was passing, time he knew he didn't have because the silvery jug kept getting farther and farther away. "Hold the knife, please, Gordon," he said as gently as he could. "Hold the knife steady, that's all you have left to do."

THIRTY-SIX
Science

Kramer did it. He held the little kitchen knife tightly enough in his bound hands. When the blade finally cut through the phone cord, Alex whirled around and grabbed it and sawed feverishly to free his legs. He left Gordon Kramer there on the living room floor. He had no more use for Jay's former protégé.

Downstairs the men in the snap-brimmed caps were still talking, and Foster's Peugeot was gone. Alex ran the two blocks to Harvard Street and dropped a dime into a pay phone. He called Jay's number, because Foster had said that everything was between him and Jay now. Deborah answered. She said Jay had left.

"He was up on the unit, but now I don't know where he went. Usually he tells me. He must have been in a hurry. I don't know."

"It's important," Alex said. "Don't bullshit me. I know who has the marrow."

"You *know* who has it? Who?"

"Foster. Now tell me the truth. Where's Jay?"

"I don't know. But I'm *sure* he'll want to hear about this. Did you tell the police?"

"Not yet. But if I don't find Jay, I'll have to. They'll put out an all-points for Jay, Foster, Jay's Celica, Foster's Peugeot. So tell me. Where's Jay?"

"I wish I knew, Alex. I'll have him beeped, right away. Can you give me the number where you are?"

"I call you back in about ten minutes, instead."

"Good. I'll find him. Soon."

By the time this conversation was over, Alex was nearly sure that through the past several days Deborah McCarthy had been telling him the truth. Because she was an awful liar. When she lied, she sounded like a recording. She didn't sound like her.

Luckily Coolidge Corner was still the kind of shopping district where old men and old women got out of cabs. Alex jumped in the one unloading down the block. The Dennison Center, he told the driver, and fast, please. When they got there he told the driver to go on into the parking garage and to cruise slowly up the ramp, because he was looking for somebody's car. The driver didn't comment. He negotiated the spiral, the spaces radiating in and out from the spiral like a model of a chromosome, or the way Alex imagined a chromosome to be. At the sixth-floor level, some empty spaces started to show up. Medical science could tell a great deal by looking at chromosomes. Foster's white Peugeot told Alex what he needed to know.

Deborah sat at her desk, staring at her computer screen, waiting. When she saw Alex her fingers started flying on the keys. She stopped and shook her head.

"I couldn't find him," she said. "He won't answer the page."

"He went to meet Foster."

"Did he? Then you know more than I do. Can I have the key to his house back, please? Did you find anything there?"

"Just him and Barbarella. When he agreed to meet Foster, he must have suspected he was taking a chance. You're the person he would have told where he was going, just in case."

"Well . . . that's true. He said downtown, on the Common. Where there would be a lot of people around. In front of the information booth."

"No," Alex said. "And you're a bad liar. Foster's here in the building, somewhere. I think he's trying to cut some kind of deal with Jay."

"Then let him." Deborah stuck her chin out. Her brows knitted. She looked like herself again. She stood up and put a hand against his chest. She was more comfortable challenging him with the truth. "What do you care what kind of deal? All that matters is Linda's cells."

Alex shook his head again. She was right, but the words didn't signify anything about what he ought to do. He rubbed his wrist where the indentations from the phone cord lingered on his skin.

Deborah took her eyes from his, shot them to the open hallway door behind him, then back. She let her hand drop but didn't move from where she stood. Behind her the door to the examining room, which had always been open before, was closed. It would be a safe place, and she could see to it that Jay and Foster weren't discovered or disturbed. Alex took a small step closer.

"No." This time she put both hands on his shoulders and tried to push him back. Her touch was springy, elastic. It had a power his t'ai chi teacher would like. "Not unless you're sure Jay's involved in it," she said.

Jay was involved, everybody's motives seemed to swirl around him, but he didn't seem to be involved in the way she meant. "They're in back?" Alex asked.

"No, in there." She jerked her head toward the wall that separated them from Jay's office next door.

"Then I won't disturb them. I'll just listen, that's all."

Deborah thought that over. Close up like this, her eyes were catlike in a way Alex hadn't noticed; green like Meredith's, but with black lashes, quick, furred.

"From the beginning, it was Foster?" she demanded. "Did Jay know that?"

"No, it wasn't Foster. It was Gordon Kramer. But Foster wanted it too. He says he has his own grievance against Jay."

"That's no reason for you not to let Jay handle it."

"Just trust the doctor?" Alex said. "No. I can either listen in or call the police."

Deborah didn't argue. She took her hands off his shoulders. She even tried a smile as she got out of the way. "You don't trust anybody," she said.

Alex opened the door softly and closed it as softly behind him. Jay's examining room was like any other: black Naugahyde table, small efficiency sink, antiseptic yellow baked enamel drawers and shelves. His diplomas hung in here, on the otherwise unadorned walls. Alex tiptoed to the black door that connected this room to Jay's office, Jay's burrow with the Japanese patterns and the blown-up cells and the baseball stars. He pressed his ear against the door. He could hear Foster's voice.

"So when Dee read me the letter, I said, 'Goddamn. Jay wrote it.' Because how many people would know, and remember, where and when I picked you up? Only you, and me, and Dee. So you wrote the letter, and why? To set me up. You took the stuff and used me as a decoy. That's what the facts said to me."

"No," Jay said. "Barbara knew too. I guess I told her, and she remembered. Funny the things you remember. Baltimore Beltway, sunny day."

Foster's voice came across edgy, accusing, while Jay's had that forced medical calm. How long had they been talking, and about what else? Alex felt he had come in on the middle of the movie, and he had only the soundtrack, not the screen. He knelt down, pressed his ear tighter, and shut his eyes. He tried to see Foster flexing his fingers, Jay's hands resting on the desk. In this silence they'd be staring. Foster wouldn't have the marrow with him, not here. He'd have it stashed someplace only he knew.

"Barbarella," Foster said at last. "Tell me where does she fit in."

"*She* wrote *me* a letter, no blackmail, just an invitation to get together, after she saw me in *People* and knew where I was. It was kind of mushy, she says. How fate had thrown us together. How I happened to be standing on that particular road I'd told her about, on that particular sunny day. How you and Dee and I happened to stop a thousand miles later for a swim. Only I didn't get her letter. Somebody must have lifted it from the mail room or the mail cart. They must have used what they learned to make up that other letter, the threatening one, supposedly from you."

"And you just fell for it." Foster's voice rose, incredulous and disgusted. "You started waving my old name all around?"

Alex opened his eyes, stared at the phone, yellow like the shelving, mounted on the wall next to the door. He could pick up the phone, call security, leave it to the SWAT team. But he waited. He wanted to hear Foster out. Something wasn't clear. Alex felt he had the whole mechanism disassembled, but the parts were out of order because somebody had purposely kicked them across the floor.

"I didn't start waving it. Not with your name in it. I took some risks to protect you."

"Protect me? You hired a detective to find me, man. And

then you gave my name to the FBI. You didn't think, what could Foster be into now, or what old trouble could be still hanging over his head."

"I did think. I rewrote the blackmail letter to keep you out of it. When they found out I'd messed with it, I was trapped, so I had to tell them why. Anyway I knew *I* didn't steal the marrow. I didn't know for sure about you. I still don't, dammit. What do you mean you know where it is?"

"I mean I know where it is," Foster added, slowly and flatly, as if speaking to someone who refused to understand a simple fact. "We're chasing each other round and round the tree, Jay," he went on more mildly. The mildness allowed Alex to take an easier breath.

"All right, I read the facts wrong," said Foster. "You didn't put my name to that note to set me up. But you still took it into your head I wrote it, you see what I'm saying? Twenty years go by, and somebody that once picked you up thumbing—and doesn't have any dirt on you to peddle—takes it into his head to hit you up for ten thousand bucks? And then he steals something off you, after he warned you he was looking your way? What kind of sense does that make? Or is it because black males are drawn to blackmail, drawn to be doing stupid-ass angry things? And you supposed to be a scientist, Dr. Jay."

It was as if Foster had caught himself about to start yelling and willed his volume back down. Or as if he'd caught himself on the verge of confessing to too much faith in Jay's good sense, and then needed to retreat into disdain. Alex felt the limitations of blindness. He couldn't tell what Foster wanted. He didn't know what Foster would do if he didn't get what he wanted from Jay.

"I didn't de*cide* you wrote it," Jay maintained doggedly. "I just didn't rule that possibility out. Not till last night, when Barbara explained the way I just said. Till then I was thinking maybe you, maybe somebody you told . . . See, the extortion letter sounded like it was prompted by me being in the magazine. I thought that was a sensible hypothesis. Somebody saw me there and said hey, now Jay Harrison is big and important and he's got bucks."

"Yeah," Foster said. "Now you're talking, because way back in some corner of your mind you kind of thought you deserved to get held up. And see, there's something else. You

236

were sure it all got started because you got your face in a magazine."

Jay didn't answer that. Alex pressed his ear tighter against the black-painted surface. Would Jay's answer matter? Alex still felt Foster's hand yanking his hair, Foster's knee in his back, prying him loose from Linda Dumars's marrow. He could still picture the way Foster had rubbed his own two hands together, a man celebrating a long task completed well. If Foster was determined to act out Jay's nightmare, Jay had better have something very convincing to say. Alex closed his fingers around the doorknob and twisted gently. Locked. There wasn't anything he could do either, except to join the conversation by yelling or banging on the door.

"Uh-huh," Foster said. "You got brains, Jay, you got some decency, but all the time you think the world turns around you. You were like that then, you're like that now. Somebody used you that way, Jaybo, somebody that had your number. Nobody long lost that saw your picture. Somebody working here in your hospital that's got a burr up their ass about you."

That was right on target. It explained Jay's mistakes, mistakes Alex himself had swallowed.

"Yeah," Foster said into Jay's silence, and Alex thought he heard a soft sound, twice, the sound that brushing hands together might make. "Uh-huh. Glauberman figured this out, figured who that was, your man Gordon Kramer, more than I did. It was Kramer set me up, it wasn't you. Then he got a shock when the real Paul Foster took him down. But time's passing, and I need to go. As soon as I can, I'll call you and tell you where that missing bone marrow is."

Jay found his voice at last. "Gordon—you confronted him, confronted Gordon? But he's in—you saw the marrow? Does he have it now?"

"Now? No, not now. I got it from him. I don't want it, the woman you're taking care of needs it, but it's got to be done my way. The way I say. Because the minute her stuff shows up, there's going to be Feebies coming out of the walls, and you ain't gonna be the one in charge. It's going to take a lot of time and a lot of talk. You have to go through that. I don't. The safest thing for me is to make my ass as hard to find as it was before."

"You've got the marrow?" Jay said. Alex wasn't sure he'd

heard any of the rest. Alex had heard it. He wasn't sure what to believe. Either Foster was lying, or it was Foster who'd kicked the parts all over the floor.

"It's where I put it," said Foster, with an irritated edge. "Somebody's got to trust somebody. From where I'm standing, the best way is that you've got to trust me."

Alex banged on the door at last.

"Deborah?" Jay said.

"No, it's Houdini."

The door opened. Alex held up his wrists like an escape artist. Foster was standing halfway between the desk and the door, betraying surprise for the first time since Alex had met him. He was swallowing hard, blinking behind his glasses as if Alex were an apparition he wanted to deny.

"It's all right," Alex told him. "I'm a step ahead of you, but back there you were a step ahead of me. Kramer told me a lot more after you left. Seeing you go off with the marrow broke whatever defenses he had. You planned it like that?" Alex heard the hopefulness in his own voice. "I mean, what you said about how you'd been after the marrow all along, about using the torch on me. That was for Kramer's benefit?"

"Mess with his mind, you mean?" Alex thought he saw faint amusement pass through Foster's eyes, but then they were steady again. Mess with Kramer's mind and yours too, partner, that amusement would say. "I thought it might do that. I sure as hell wasn't about to cut you loose, not then. I thought I might as well get to make the rules for a change." He looked at Jay, who was still holding onto the doorknob, twisting it back and forth. "I think we're done talking. Now I need an hour to get out of the way, then I call you and say where it is."

"Do it," Alex said. "Give him an hour, Jay."

"I don't know," Jay said.

"Do it," Alex told him. He turned back to Foster. "You're sure it's someplace safe?"

"Safer than it's been," Foster said.

"Okay," Jay agreed. Graciousness flowered on his rounded face. "Thanks for your help," he said. "It's—well, it's nice to see you again."

"Yeah. Just like old times." Foster turned around and walked quickly out the door.

Alex watched him go. There was still time to call security, before the Peugeot was out of the garage. But Alex's marrow told him to take the man at his word. For Linda's sake, he hoped his marrow knew best.

THIRTY-SEVEN
Post Mortem

Six weeks later, Alex walked into the family room of the Bone Marrow Transplant Unit at the Dennison Center for Cancer Treatment and Research. The family room, intended for small conferences between staff and relatives, was full to overflowing. Nobody wanted to sit down on the couch or the few upholstered chairs. Everybody insisted on standing up. Barbara Binder was there already, as were Mary Forziati and Kevin Royce—now discharged—and Deborah McCarthy and the hospital security chief and five or six unit staff whom Alex didn't know.

Gordon Kramer wasn't there and wasn't coming. His death had made only a small item in the newspaper, even smaller than the sparse story about his arrest. Together they added up to this: a Dennison Center resident, on bail after confessing he'd murdered his girlfriend, had mixed himself a suicide potion that worked. His colleagues said the whole thing came as a complete shock, but they described the murderer-suicide as a troubled young man. His hopes for his medical career had perhaps been beyond his abilities. Perhaps, an unnamed colleague speculated, the same had been true of his hopes in love.

Those words prettied Kramer up, Alex thought. They cheaply diverted attention from the heart of the matter to matters of the heart. Kramer was somebody who couldn't handle failure, and who hadn't ever had an open-ended chance to learn what, for himself, might constitute success. He took that problem out on people who were vulnerable. He'd come of age in the eighties. What else could you expect?

If the power of the high gods prevented Kramer's death

from being more of a story, it prevented Linda Dumars from making the news pages at all. The Dennison was everybody's favorite charity. The advancement of treatment techniques depended on fundraising, on public confidence, on insurers being convinced the new techniques were effective and safe. The medical grapevine knew part of the true story, but the medical grapevine had its own reasons for hanging tough in a situation like this. The rumors would keep Jay Harrison from ever being chief of service or medical director anywhere. But he'd claimed he didn't want any of that.

One of the staff latched onto Alex, a heavy-set, thin-voiced woman who turned out to be Edie, the cryopreservation specialist from whose tank Linda's bone marrow had disappeared. Edie told him there was a combination lock now, and the number got changed every week. She said anyone who went in there had to show ID. She said, "I know this must sound like locking the barn door after the horse is gone."

When Jay Harrison entered, everybody quieted down. Jay took off gown, cap, and gloves and dropped them onto an empty chair. Alex watched him work his way through the crowd to Barbara, standing alone in a corner. He took her hand and said something, a few words, his expression unreadable from where Alex stood. The crowd figured out there was going to be more waiting. A hesitant babble re-emerged.

Then the door opened, and Yvonne Price stood there with Linda Dumars at her side. Linda was wearing faded green hospital scrubs and a hospital cap. She looked like the hostess at a pajama party, smiling broadly, choosing from some eccentricity to appear in her shower cap. In a few days she could go home to her kids, though for a while she wouldn't go out, and she'd be held to a limited diet and visitor list. It was unusual to permit this many visitors even here in the hospital, but she'd been kept in isolation for an extra week after her counts had returned to acceptable levels. Her recovery was no ordinary recovery. Some collective sigh of relief and absolution had to be arranged.

Jay started to clap, and Alex found himself joining in. "Happy Breakout Day," Kevin called. Linda smiled even more broadly, showing a lot of straight white teeth. She looked pale but otherwise strong and excited. She looked ready to face the world outside her sterile room.

"I just want to thank everybody awfully much," Linda said. "You know I can't kiss you or shake your hands yet. In spite of everything, I consider myself very lucky. Without this treatment I probably would have been in and out of the hospital for the rest of my life. Now I hope I'll be able to relax and get on with it. Each one of you has been a big part of making that possible. I really just want to say thank you. I'd also like to thank someone I've heard about who isn't here, whom I suppose I'll never get to meet."

Sounds like a canned testimonial, Alex thought as the crowd applauded again. Carefully worded not to refer out loud to anything real. In truth, the hospital was lucky she wasn't suing. But her smile came back, and it lingered especially on him. He felt a quiet glow of satisfaction in spite of the things he'd done wrong. He'd done a lot of things wrong, but he'd done some things right. He remembered the very nervous hour in Jay's office—him and Jay and Deborah—waiting for a telephone that didn't ring. And then a messenger had showed up with a package for Dr. Harrison, COD.

There was too much Lone Ranger, Alex felt, about the person Linda would never get to meet. Foster took a lot of chances, even if he did turn out to wear a white hat, or a black hat, or whatever the hell color hat the good guys ought to be distinguished by. Though maybe it was just that Alex would never forget being tied on Kramer's dirty rug, watching Foster's broad back go out the door. Meredith claimed the Foster who left Alex tied was, paradoxically, very much the same character who'd once tossed a pair of wire cutters over a chain-link fence. He might have good and practical reasons for his actions, but he was also somebody who liked to put people in a situation and see how they'd react. If that was true, Alex thought, it could be a dangerous trait. In the moment Foster was scooting out with the marrow, Alex would have been happy to see Special Agent Fridley fly through the window, turned-up nose leading, cape streaming behind, machine pistol gripped in both hands.

But Linda didn't have to worry about any of that. For her, today was simply a great day. Alex knew that in her place he'd be smiling too. He was smiling himself, because about a week ago his double vision had disappeared. He hadn't even been able to say exactly when. He'd just been grateful. That was how Linda

241

would be feeling. Grateful. Even when she woke with nightmares about empty bones, still she'd be grateful that trying to live without marrow was over except as a dream.

The ceremony was short, just the applause, and Linda's thanks, and some cake served by the dietary aides. Kevin, now bushy-haired and bearded, circled around Linda like a mother bear around a cub, anxious to come between her and any threat. Linda seemed flattered yet uncertain how to respond. There were advantages on both sides to a mandatory no-touch period, Alex thought. In the meantime Alex made small talk with Jay and Barbara, though he couldn't say he felt comfortable with either one of them.

It didn't really help that he'd apologized to Jay for his suspicions, and Jay had apologized for firing him. They'd pretended to find it amusing that Alex had spied on him, and that Alex had read guilt into Jay's box of old papers and poetry books, when all Jay had been doing with those was trying to play detective himself. The truth was, however, that spying on Jay and Barbara had left Alex embarrassed. Not from what he'd seen, but from what he'd sensed.

Alex liked the idea of old lovers' reunions, he even cherished a few such fantasies himself. These two, though, had seemed in too much of a hurry, needing each other too much. They'd needed each other not out of love or chemistry, but to answer some question or questions that had troubled them for a long time. At least that's what Alex read into it. He didn't know whether they were still seeing each other, and he didn't want to ask. He left them to having and eating their cake, if that's what they were doing, and drifted over to Deborah McCarthy. He would have preferred her to Barbara Binder, hands down, if he'd had such a choice. Deborah was very reserved and businesslike with him now.

When Linda Dumars went back to her isolation room, the gathering rapidly broke up. Alex rode down in the elevator with Mary Forziati, the sperm bank tech. She also deserved credit, he thought, and by stretching a point he might be able to share some of his satisfied glow with her. She could use it, because her nightmares would feature a masked man who wasn't the Lone Ranger at all. She'd relive those hours pounding on the door of the dark closet with life-or-death news whose value seemed to plummet with every minute that ticked by.

"I hear you would have found the marrow by process of logical deduction," Alex told her, "if Kramer hadn't barged in right then."

"Well," she said, "I wish I'd logically deduced a lot sooner. All of a sudden a man had his hand around my windpipe. As far as I knew I was fighting for my own life, not anybody else's." She folded her white-coated arms as if to ward off a shiver. "And I didn't know he'd already murdered a woman early that day."

"I think he barely knew what he was doing any more," said Alex. "He couldn't handle that things hadn't gone according to his original plan. The other thing that's scary is how close he came to making that one work."

That original plan had been simple, and it had seemed safe. The exchange on the beach would have gone very much the way it actually happened, except the note in the cooler would have said something short and cute like *Look for the marrow in the sperm bank tank*. The transplant would have gone forward, everyone would have breathed a sigh of relief, and in due course an investigation would have revealed that a phony technician had hidden the one specimen in Mary's tank shortly after a phony delivery man had stolen the two specimens from Edie's. Both men would have been remembered only as uniforms, caps, glasses. At most, somebody might remember the false hair color or the equally false mustache.

It was only because of an ex-patient, a lawyer whom Kramer had informed of the sad results of a biopsy seven months back, that Kramer was forced to deviate from his plan. The lawyer, getting his counts checked post-treatment, had happened to be sitting in the sperm bank waiting room on Kramer's all-important day. And as Alex knew from experience, you didn't forget the voice that laid a cancer diagnosis on you. The patient had looked up and dismissed this as an oddity, but when investigators got around to interviewing everybody who'd been in there that day, the lawyer would have mentioned (in fact, had mentioned, now) how the phony repairman sounded just like Dr. Kramer to him. Knowing this, Kramer hadn't been able to earn his $300,000 with a short cute note. He'd stalled, substituting the Emily Dickinson poem plus his own hungry cat verse, until he could mail the second batch from out West. He'd figured he could find a way to retrieve the first specimen some other day, some other month, after all the excitement had died down.

From there everything had come apart fast. He'd driven off the road where Nevada met California. He'd sent Sandra to clean up after him, to retrieve the first specimen under cover of a semen-napping, while he established an alibi by keeping his Florida interview date. When she didn't succeed, he'd flown back to Boston without checking out of his hotel. He'd lured Sandra to the Cape and killed her, then hurried to get hold of the marrow as best he could.

"He did things that were dumber and dumber, as he put it," Alex summed up. "But to start with, the idea wasn't so dumb. It could have worked. It almost did."

"Almost, uh-huh," Mary said. A tired grin flickered across her freckled face. "That's how it is here, I can say that for sure. If you worked in a hospital, you'd know how many things that almost went right go wrong. And how many things happen the other way around. But it's better than working for Mega-Toxic Chemical, you know what I mean? I mean, some lab where they invent new ways to give people cancer. At least the idea here is to help people get well."

"Uh-huh," Alex agreed, but none of that was what he wanted to talk about. This conversation wasn't sharing any glow. Instead it was taking a distinctly depressing turn. Suddenly he just wanted to get out of there. It wasn't Mary Forziati's fault. Maybe it was Gordon Kramer's ghost, still wishing to be Bobby Lynch, now trapped forever in this institution where so many people's dreams didn't come true. Anyway Alex felt tired of the whole industry: cancer, and cancer patients, and all the people who took care of them too.

When the elevator reached the lobby level, Alex said a quick good-bye and headed for the street. Outdoors it was a gorgeous June day, one of the rare, really spring ones. Alex looked forward to two small things and wished for one big one. He looked forward to a Chinese dinner out with Maria and Meredith, and to filling the two seats he'd bought for himself and Maria at Fenway Park. He fervently wished never to see the inside of the Dennison Center for Cancer Treatment and Research, ever again.